DUEL OF WITS

The chess game began in silence. Nicholas, Livia soon saw, was a thoughtful but decisive player. His opening was bold and well calculated to lead the inexperienced into trouble. It was a clever move, but her father had taught her a gambit that might serve. It did. Nicholas looked at her with some respect, but she kept her head demurely down.

"Mrs. Royce, you are a devious player." Nicholas studied the board with renewed concentration.

"So was the woman I was named for. She had to be. All that power behind the throne is really hard on women."

"I daresay. And who, may I ask, were you named for?"

"Livia. Augustus' wife. If she'd been a man, she would have gone down in history as one of the abler rulers."

"But she was a woman," Nicholas pointed out, a strange gleam in his eye. "And able or not, a most unwomanly one."

"You believe in womanliness, Mr. Warwick?" she parried as she disposed briskly of one of his bishops.

"I do indeed, Mrs. Royce. It's a rare quality."

"That it is, Mr. Warwick," she answered, smiling. "Checkmate."

The Widow's Gambit

ANTHEA MALCOLM

ZEBRA BOOKS
KENSINGTON PUBLISHING CORP.

ZEBRA BOOKS

are published by

Kensington Publishing Corp.
475 Park Avenue South
New York, NY 10016

First printing: May, 1988

Printed in the United States of America

For Doug, who believes in approximations.

For shame! deny that thou bear'st love to any,
Who for thyself are so unprovident.
Grant if thou wilt thou are belov'd of many,
But that thou none lov'st is most evident . . .

Shakespeare (Sonnet X)

surviving brother, but Justin had been his hero.

Chapter 1

"I don't know why you want to be a widow, Livia. You don't even want to get married." Claudia Neville sat back and eyed her younger sister. "Besides, you won't be able to dance. You'll have to sit among the dowagers and you'll be bored to tears."

"Fustian! Old women are just as interesting as young men. Probably more. And I'm much too inquisitive to be bored." Livia was on a chair, dusting the moulding. "I hate Thursdays! Why do we always clean on Thursdays?"

"Because Mama did, I suppose." Claudia resumed polishing the legs of the old beechwood table. "You've missed a spot above the door."

Livia grimaced, climbed down and moved her chair. "Let's be daring," she said as she climbed up again. "Let's clean on Friday next week. Better yet, let's go to London and find you a husband."

"So I'm to have a husband, but you're much too nice to want one for yourself. Thank you very much." Claudia rose, covered the tin of beeswax, and folded the polishing cloth.

"Oh, no, Claudia, I didn't mean it that way. It's just that you and I are—different. As you very well know," Livia added, seeing the laughter in her sister's eyes. "You're such a forgiving sort of person, and you always seem to bring out the best in people." Livia climbed down once more and placed the chair against the wall. "It's not that I don't like men. I do. But it's so hard to take them seriously. For an hour or so, perhaps, but for a lifetime? Never!"

"All the more reason we should look for a husband for you. There must be at least one sensible man in London."

"A sensible man? Oh, you don't understand me at all!"

"You want a foolish one? There are plenty of those here in Oxford."

Livia refused to be baited. "Exactly. That's why we're going to London."

"But not only for me. It's not fair."

"It's not a question of fairness. It's a question of what we're able to do. We can only afford to bring one of us out, and you're the eldest, and the one—"

"And the one most likely to catch a man's fancy," Claudia finished in a mocking tone. "That's arrant nonsense, Livia. You're just as handsome as—oh, you know what I mean. And you're much more intelligent."

Livia grinned. "Only bookish. And that's very off-putting. Don't be a goose, Claudia, you have to have someone to take you about and we don't have the money to hire a chaperone. It's out of the question for unmarried young women to live alone in London, but it's quite another matter if one of them is a widow."

Claudia voiced the obvious objection. "But you aren't a widow."

"And you'd let a little thing like that stand in our way? For shame, Claudia!"

They had reached an impasse. In the end, of course, Livia would win. She was not domineering, but she could nearly always bring Claudia about when she was determined to do so. And she was determined about this. Claudia's warmth and beauty should not be confined to Oxford for another year.

It was not that Claudia lacked suitors. From her late teens she had drawn attention. The eldest Winslow boy who lived across the road had haunted the house for nearly a year, and there had been several others. But most of these were too young for Claudia, who had been mature at seventeen, and the Winslow boy had gone to London and married his cousin. Mr. Bartley, the curate, who had made Claudia an offer two years before, was not what Livia had in mind for her sister.

Had their mother still been alive, things might have been different. Anna Neville had been nearly as forceful a woman as her daughter Livia. She would have contrived for her children to break from their setting. But Mrs. Neville had died six years before and her husband, a gentle, vague, scholarly man, had given no thought to such things as come outs and husbands. Even if he had, there had been no money.

After his wife's death, Dr. Neville's health had deteriorated. He had still managed to do enough tutoring to support his family, but he had relied heavily on Livia to help him with his work, while Claudia had run the house and nursed him through his chronic illnesses. Neither girl had had time to think beyond the next day and the next meal.

Then, last summer, Dr. Neville had quietly died. The money he left, his solicitor assured the distraught Misses Neville, was enough for them to continue to live quietly in Oxford for the rest of their days. Livia had other ideas. Livia calculated that the same money, spent in one daring gamble, was enough to give Claudia a season in London and a chance to find the husband she deserved.

The only obstacle she could foresee was that they did not have a suitable female relation to serve as their chaperone. There was Mrs. Henderson, their housekeeper—dear Henny, who had looked after them since their mother died—but it was impossible to imagine her making her way in fashionable London. Livia had mulled over the difficulty for several days. The obvious solution, indeed the only one, she decided, was for her to become a widow. The fact that she had never been married was of very little moment. Claudia's objection was trivial.

11

"To make it even more respectable," Livia said, quite as if Claudia was in perfect agreement with her plan, "we can say I'm the eldest. And think of all the black clothes we have among us." She smoothed her black bombazine skirt—they were still in mourning for their father. "If I don't become a widow, what do you suggest we do for a chaperone?"

"Perhaps we don't go to London at all."

"Claudia!" Livia looked at her sister in real alarm.

"No, listen, Livy. As it is now, we have enough to live here in some comfort. If our London plan fails—"

"If our London plan fails, we still have this house. But it won't fail."

"You can't possibly know that for a certainty."

That was true, Livia was forced to concede. It was what made the plan a gamble. But a gamble well worth taking. "And what do we do if we stay here?" she asked. "Wait for Mr. Bartley to make you another offer?"

Claudia smiled in spite of herself.

"It's not funny," Livia said, though her lips twitched. "I know you want to marry and I can't believe Mr. Bartley is what you have in mind."

"No," Claudia admitted. She had never been able to lie to Livia, and deception was not in her nature. "But I'm not going to let you sacrifice your future for my sake."

"Sacrifice!" exclaimed Livia. "Good God, Claudia, do you imagine I want to stay in Oxford for the rest of my life? Do you think Diana does?"

That silenced Claudia. At sixteen, their youngest sister, Diana, had no interest in beaux or dancing or any of those pursuits common to girls her age. It was not that she was a hoyden—when she put her mind to it she could be quite well-mannered. But most of the time her mind and all her energies were absorbed by her pencils and sketchbooks. Livia and Claudia could recognize talent. Diana's drawing was exceptional, particularly her protraits, and she had a wicked gift for capturing the person behind the face. If continued residence in

Oxford would be stifling for Livia and Claudia, for Diana it would be insupportable.

Seeing she had lost on this point, Claudia decided to change tactics. "All right," she said. "Diana deserves to go to London. I deserve to go to London. What about you?"

"Well, I may not deserve to go, but I would certainly like to."

"Of course you deserve to go, Livia. But not as my widowed elder sister-chaperone." Claudia looked at her sister, her lovely dark eyes full of concern. "What if the plan is a success? What if I do marry? What about afterwards? As far as everyone is concerned, you'll still be a widow."

"The best of both worlds. The status of a married woman and none of the encumbrances."

"Do be serious. You might change your mind. You might marry. What would you say to your husband?"

Livia suppressed a sigh. This debate was far older than their quarrel over the London venture. It was impossible to explain to anyone with Claudia's love of home and family: men were perfectly agreeable to talk to, but the idea of spending the rest of one's life married to one of them promised nothing but boredom. Livia balanced the feather duster in her hands and considered for several seconds. "That my first marriage was an elopement and my husband was killed in a duel before it could be consummated?"

Claudia tried to look severe and failed miserably. She collapsed, laughing, onto the sopha. Livia joined her, and the matter was temporarily dropped.

It was Claudia who raised it again. That evening at dinner she appealed to Diana for support. It was a mistake. Diana said she wanted to go to London as much as her sisters did. If Livia had to acquire a dead husband to get them there, she had no fault to find with the scheme.

"But people in London society are fussy about family and pedigree and that sort of thing," Diana added, reaching for another piece of bread. "You can't just be a made up

13

person's widow."

"She isn't going to be anyone's widow at all," Claudia insisted.

"Be quiet," Livia said amiably. "You're right, Diana, it will have to be a real person. It's going to make things much more complicated. I wonder who we can use?"

"Livia." Claudia set down her fork and looked at her sister in alarm. "You wouldn't really marry someone?"

"On his death bed? No, of course not. It would take far too long to arrange. What we need is someone who has died within the last year or so and doesn't have any close friends or relations." She fell into a frowning silence. So did Diana. Claudia looked helplessly from one to the other, aware from past experience that there was very little she could do to stop them.

"John Royce," Diana said suddenly.

Livia looked up. "I thought his name was James."

"It was John, and he answers perfectly. You remember him, don't you? His family had thrown him out, he was single, and he'd been years on the Peninsula."

Livia remembered Captain Royce very well indeed. It was last spring, just a year ago, that he had spent a very pleasant afternoon with the Nevilles, bringing messages from their soldier half-brother. Less than two months later the sisters had been saddened to learn of his death at Waterloo.

"But he does have relatives," Claudia said quickly. "Suppose one of them turns up in London?"

"For all they know," Diana pointed out, "he could very easily have married Livia. For that matter, for all we know, they might really have slipped off and gotten married." She turned to Livia. "You didn't, did you?"

"Do you imagine I'd tell you if I had?"

"You could tell Claudia you had," Diana suggested. "Then maybe she'd stop worrying. Livia Royce. It has rather a nice ring to it, don't you think?"

Claudia continued to object throughout dinner. Her sisters

14

refused to answer her. After dinner, Diana took out her sketchpad and Livia picked up a book. Claudia mended a tear in one of Diana's dresses with vicious industry. At breakfast the next morning, Livia and Diana took Claudia's silence for tacit consent. At luncheon, Claudia said that if they were determined on this idiotish scheme, they might at least discuss it sensibly. They discussed it sensibly for a good part of the afternoon. By teatime they were still at an impasse, and they were expecting guests.

"I'm going to put it to Harry and Jack," Claudia said at last as she laid the cloth. "If they don't think it's a totally shatterbrained thing to do, Livia can become a widow and I won't say a word more against it."

Diana was indignant. "You're going to put our future in the hands of two undergraduates? Why, they're mere boys!"

"They're three years older than you, puss," Livia said, adding another log to the fire, "though I have to admit not always as sensible. Boys must take longer to ripen."

"But—"

"But their families belong to the *ton*, and they know London ways," Claudia said. "Which is more than we do, no matter how many books we've read."

Livia poked up the fire. "Claudia's right, Diana, we should talk to them. Harry's actually very clever, though he takes queer starts sometimes. Jack's Latin is deplorable, of course—"

"But he has very nice manners," her elder sister added, "and he always seems to know just what is the proper thing to do. I trust his judgment. Now do be a help, Diana, and go ask Henny if there's any more jam. Jack's very partial to jam."

Harry Warwick and Jack Newfield were cousins by marriage. Acquainted from birth, they had been inseparable since the day their families first sent them off to Eton. They had come up to Oxford together and, searching for the private coaching needed to pass their examinations, discovered Dr. Neville.

In general, the Neville girls had had little contact with the undergraduates their father tutored. But Harry and Jack had been genuinely fond of Dr. Neville and, on learning of his death, they paid his daughters an awkward call of condolence. They were charmed and came again. Claudia was the initial magnet, but Livia gave them a reason to return. She was quite prepared, she told them, to serve as their private tutor as her father had. Her Cicero was good, and she had read Seutonius and Seneca and Horace and Livy. It was an unconventional arrangement, she knew, but she would be glad of the money.

They accepted at once and became frequent visitors to the cramped stone house on the outskirts of Oxford. More, they became friends. They admired Claudia, and they had the greatest respect for Livia's intelligence. They treated Diana with the friendly tolerance they would have accorded a younger sister.

Last week Livia had told Harry and Jack of her hopes for Claudia's future. They were enthusiastic. Of course Claudia must go to London. Of course she should make a splendid marriage. They would be in London between terms. They would help. After all, there were things a man could do.

They had been disarmingly vague about the nature of their help. But today the Nevilles wanted their advice. Claudia put the matter of a chaperone before them. Was it wrong for Livia to play at widowhood?

"I don't think it's wrong," Harry said, looking thoughtfully into his teacup. He was a tall, gangly, fair-haired youth, prone to sudden swings of mood. He looked up with an engaging grin. "Unless you get caught. Then it's awkward, but no more than that. And it will be great sport."

"Shouldn't have to play the widow, though," muttered Jack, a darker, slighter version of Harry with perhaps half his wit but something more of unflappable good humour. He wrinkled his forehead in concentration, absently scraping the jampot with a spoon. "Is this really the last of it? I hope Mrs. H. will make more this summer. Can't face swotting Cicero without

16

strawberry jam."

"Don't be an ass, Jack," Harry admonished him.

"Jack ass." Diana, lying sprawled on the floor, giggled, then relapsed into contemplation of the fire.

"We're not talking about jam," Harry said. "This is serious."

"Jam's serious, isn't it? Fellows have to have strawberry jam, don't they? Someone's got to make it. Why not Mrs. H.? Ought to incorporate her. Henderson, Ltd. Make pots of money . . . pots of jam . . . pots of money for pots of jam . . ." His voice trailed off. "I say," he said suddenly, "maybe that's the answer. No need for Livia to trail widow's weeds. Bring you all out at once."

Diana surfaced again. "I don't want to come out."

Jack ignored her. "Sell shares, that sort of thing. I could ask Uncle Walter." Jack considered. "No, not enough time. Livia's right. Has to be a widow."

Diana looked up. "Then we're going to do it?"

Claudia gave her a wry smile and nodded.

"It has to be soon, though," Harry said. "You have to be seen. Well, Claudia has to be seen. Give her every chance there is, though there's no question that she'll take." He looked at her admiringly. "She'll have her pick of husbands before the Season's half out."

"But, I say," Jack broke in, "it's not all that easy. Right places, you know. Introductions. Almack's. That sort of thing."

"We're going to introduce them," Harry said, his head filled with visions of Claudia entering brilliantly lit rooms on his arm.

"Can't," Jack told him. "Has to be a woman. Lend her countenance. Else might think Claudia's a—" His delicacy prevented him from going on.

Harry, who had never aspired to the muslin company, did not at first take his meaning. Then he blushed and subsided.

Livia had the sense not to laugh. "It's kind of you, and of

course we want to see you in London, but we never expected to rely on you to make our way." Jack had raised a new problem, but it was one to which Livia had given much anxious thought. Provincial they might be, but she was not naive enough to believe that invitations, those passports to respectable alliances, were showered on young women who had not been properly introduced into society. Her assumption of widowhood would ensure their respectability. It would not open the doors which must be opened if Claudia was to make the match she deserved to make.

"We have a cousin in London," Livia went on, "that is, she's our father's cousin. I'm afraid she's the only one of his relations who would have anything to do with him after he married."

The young men nodded. They had already heard the story of Dr. Neville's imprudent marriage—a beautiful young widow, half Italian, and carrying her first husband's child into the bargain.

"Cousin Sophronia visited us once," Diana said. "I liked her. She wasn't at all put out because we weren't proper young girls."

Claudia rose and refilled their cups. "She sent us a very kind note after Papa died. I'm sure she'll be happy to introduce us to her friends."

Harry was dubious, but Jack was frankly incredulous. "Sophronia Neville? Oh, no! She writes letters to the *Times!*"

A dispirited silence followed this outburst. Harry scowled at Jack. Claudia had to go to London and Jack had no business putting paltry obstacles in her path.

Jack tried to make amends. "Thing is, someone's got to take you about. Show you how to get on. Get you invited to the right houses, see you meet the right people."

Diana sat up. "But what's wrong with Cousin Sophronia? Doesn't she know the right people? Isn't she respectable?"

"Oh, she's quite respectable," Harry said. "And she knows everyone in the *monde*. The problem is, I don't think they take her very seriously."

"Worse," said Jack. "She doesn't take the *monde* seriously. Earnest old lady. Good works. Not the thing for Claudia."

"Nonetheless, we'll make do with what we have," Livia said. "She was kind to us, and she thought Papa had been shamefully treated by his family. Surely she'll make some effort to help."

"No, wait." Harry put down his cup and leaned forward. "What about your mother, Jack? Couldn't you persuade her to take Claudia about?"

"Might, ordinarily. But my sister's going to be confined. Mother's got her hands full." He thought a bit. "What about Lady Francesca?" He turned to the Nevilles. "Lord Lyndale's daughter, Harry's sister-in-law. She's a widow, a real one."

Harry frowned and shook his head.

Diana turned their attention. "I think," she said, gazing at the ceiling, "we should simply put an advertisement in the *Morning Post*. Claudia, beautiful daughter of the late Dr. Neville of Oxford, arriving in town the tenth of April. Suitors accepted from two to four."

"Don't be a wretch, Diana," Livia said. "You make it sound like an auction."

"But it is, Livia." Claudia's face quivered with laughter. "I'm going on the Marriage Mart. What else is a young woman to do? I do want to marry. And have a houseful of children," she added firmly.

Livia allowed herself to be pacified. "Well, the quality of men in London is sure to be at least as good as it is in Oxford. And the quantity will be greater. But you won't marry anyone you don't like."

"Oh, she's bound to like scores of fellows," Harry broke in. "Lots of good fellows about."

Jack ignored this byplay, his face intent with concentration. Suddenly his brow cleared. "I say. Aunt Isabel. Great old girl. Full of fun. Up to the rig, all the thing, you know."

"She's my aunt, too," said Harry, aggrieved. It was the

obvious solution, but he wanted at least some of the credit. "Other side," he explained, noting the girls' puzzled looks. "She's my real aunt," he continued, his confidence returning. "My father's sister. Her husband was Jack's uncle. Not his blood relation," he concluded, delivering the *coup de grace*.

Jack ignored these aspersions on his family claims. "Time on her hands. Love to take you about."

"But she doesn't know us," Claudia protested.

"That's no problem," Harry said. "She's up in Northhampton now but she always goes back to London for the Season, and she usually stops to see us on the way. We'll write to her tonight."

Claudia was not sure they should impose on their friends' aunt. Livia, who had had doubts about Cousin Sophronia from the beginning, had no such scruples. "We'll be happy to meet her," she said.

Jack leaned back in his chair. "Solves all your problems. Are you sure there isn't any more jam?"

Isabel Crawford was not an idle woman. Her correspondence alone took a full two hours every morning and included most of the diplomatic circles in Europe. She read all the latest novels. She visited widely. She was indefatigable in attendance at shops, theatres, and social events. Since her husband's death, she had divided her time between the homes of her three married children and the Warwick family home in London where Harry lived with Nicholas, his elder brother and guardian. Lady Crawford had always nourished a soft spot for Harry and for her husband's nephew, Jack.

She responded promptly to their letter, as they had known she would. She would visit Oxford on the following Tuesday, if that was convenient, and would be glad to meet Miss Neville and Mrs. Royce.

Lady Crawford arrived on Tuesday as she had promised. Harry and Jack—more nervous than they would let on—

escorted their aunt to the Neville house and left her to become acquainted with their very great friends.

Harry had described Claudia Neville as lovely. For once, Lady Crawford thought, her nephew had understated the matter. Miss Neville was an undeniable beauty. Tall and full-figured, she had a creamy, almost translucent complexion set off by large dark eyes and an abundance of dark, almost black hair. The widowed Mrs. Royce—Livia, Jack had called her—was less striking but possessed her own share of good looks. Shorter and of a slighter build than her sister, her eyes and hair were merely brown, but the eyes were large under delicately arched brows and the hair was glossy and tinged with red. The youngest sister, she was told, was out.

Harry and Jack had said very little about the reason for the visit, but Lady Crawford had had no difficulty in understanding what her nephews expected of her. There was very little money, and Miss Neville needed a husband. Would their aunt please put her in the way of finding one?

It was not a promising situation. But Miss Neville's appearance was exceptional and the family, if impoverished, was good. "We are very minor Nevilles," Mrs. Royce told her, "but we are Nevilles, and no one need be ashamed of us. Many men can afford to marry women without fortunes. Why shouldn't Claudia have her chance?"

Lady Crawford agreed. "Of course she should have a chance. Lack of fortune makes it difficult, but not impossible." A pity, she thought, that marriage should be a woman's only path to comfort and respectability. "Then if Miss Neville marries she will be able to bring your youngest sister out." She studied Mrs. Royce. Despite the severity of her hair style and her high-necked black dress, the girl appeared not much older than Miss Neville. How long had her husband been dead? Jack had mentioned Waterloo. Less than a year ago. But she spoke of Captain Royce in a matter-of-fact manner, without the least trace of grief or sentimentality.

"Of course, we should all be in black gloves," Mrs. Royce

went on. "Our father died just before I had word of my husband's death. But it seems dreadfully unfair that Claudia should have to wait another year. Is it so very bad for her to throw off mourning?"

Lady Crawford considered a moment. "The high sticklers might have cause to object, but I have never thought it necessary to be overly nice in these matters, especially when there are other claims to be considered. In matters of one's past, I have always found it helpful to preserve a decent obscurity."

Lady Crawford had been willing to meet her nephews' friends, but she had made no promises. After half an hour in their company she realized, with surprise, that she had every intention of helping launch Claudia Neville into society. The girl was certainly wasted in Oxford. It would be diverting to watch the effect of her serene and unconventional beauty on the *ton*. She was bound to cause mischief to the schemes of a score of matchmaking mothers. To one mother in particular, Lady Crawford thought with satisfaction. She resolutely turned her thoughts from that direction. It would be unfair to use the girl only for her own amusement.

They discussed ways and means. The sisters, Lady Crawford found, were determined to live within the monies they had decided they could spare from their small capital and were not above all kinds of cheeseparing expedients. They would rent a small house, but they would not keep a carriage. They would have to hire servants—their housekeeper, Mrs. Henderson, was remaining in Oxford—but as few as was decently possible. "I shall make a fashion of simplicity," Miss Neville announced. "And I shall not have a lady's maid. I'm perfectly capable of putting on my own dresses. Nor will I crop my hair. I can't afford it, and it wouldn't suit."

Lady Crawford sighed. They were refreshingly direct about money, but there were great gaps in their store of knowledge. They knew the price of a joint of meat, but were woefully ignorant of the cost of the extravagant but necessary trifles found in the London shops.

"I'll see what I can do about a house," Lady Crawford said, "and you'd best leave the servants to me as well." She raised her hand to silence their protests. "You don't know London, and you're sure to be cheated. I will write when it's arranged, and then you should come as soon as you can. London will be thin of company till Easter, but you'll need some time to settle in."

It was early evening before Lady Crawford returned to Oxford proper and was able to reassure her anxious nephews. She and their great friends had indeed gotten on famously and they had been quite right in thinking that Claudia would take.

"Not," she cautioned them over dinner at her inn, "that she's likely to make a brilliant marriage, but I think she may be settled quite comfortably. And then of course she can see to her sisters."

"Oh, Livia can look after herself," Harry said carelessly. He was fond of Livia, but his mind was elsewhere. He had one more request to make of his aunt, and he had just the slightest doubt about making it. In fact, it was not until the next morning, when they were settling Lady Crawford into her carriage, that Harry asked quite casually if he and Jack might hire the butler for the Nevilles' London house.

It was an odd request, to say the least, and Lady Crawford was inclined to deny them outright, but there were a thousand things to do and finding servants at short notice was a distinct bore. "When do you come down?"

"Four days. End of Hilary Term."

"We have six weeks before we have to come back," Jack assured her, "so we'll be able to take the Nevilles about. Round the town, you know. You won't find them a bother."

Lady Crawford surveyed her nephews. "I have always understood," she said, "that the purpose of the period between terms is to allow the extensive reading that is prevented by the pleasures of university life. Still, there is undoubtedly much to be learned from the pleasures of town." She signalled her coachman. "You may hire the butler," she called back as the coach got under way, "but I will discharge him if he is not thoroughly satisfactory."

Harry left the inn yard in high spirits. Jack did not share his confidence. "My dear fellow," he protested, running quickly in order to keep up with his friend's lengthy stride, "we don't know anything about hiring butlers. Least," he added, for Harry was sometimes surprising, "I don't. Always left that sort of thing to Mother."

"Oh, well," said Harry, with his usual optimism, "it can't be that difficult."

Jack was not at all sure this was true. He said so.

"It doesn't signify," Harry continued, "because we don't have to look for a butler."

Jack paused, frowning. "But you said—"

"I know. Don't you see, this is a chance to do something for Jonathon."

Jack continued to frown. "But the girls don't need an actor," he said logically, wondering what he had missed.

"Of course not. They need a butler."

Jack puzzled this over for a few minutes, then ran to catch up with Harry again. "But Jonathon isn't a butler."

"Not yet," Harry said. "I don't see why he couldn't be one. You know he needs work."

"Yes, but dash it, Harry, actors can't be butlers. It just isn't done." The idea offended Jack's delicate social sense.

"How do you know?" Harry demanded with bravado, for he had some doubts on this score himself. "Besides," he added, "if Jonathon can play Touchstone and Tyrrel, he ought to be able to manage a butler."

There was something, Jack felt, vaguely wrong with this logic. He examined it carefully. It sounded all right on the surface, so after a little more haggling he gave his tacit consent. After all, Harry was quite capable of acting without it.

They adjourned to a tavern much frequented by students and carefully composed a letter to Jonathon Sandringham which artfully blended appeals to his humanitarian instincts, the challenge of a new and difficult role, and his need for ready cash.

"He's getting on in years," Harry pointed out, "and I'm sure he's not working at the moment. Still, we have to be careful how we put it. He's a proud fellow, and going into servitude—"

"Service, Harry, service!"

"May seem a cut beneath him. Still, he's a great sport and will be no end of help."

Jack was forced to agree with this, but before Harry had finished the letter he thought of another difficulty.

"I say, what about Nicholas?"

"What about Nicholas?" Harry knew very well what his cousin meant, but he did not want to deal with the problem of his elder brother just yet. He blotted the paper carefully. "Nicholas doesn't have anything to do with Jonathon."

"Not Jonathon. The Nevilles. Has to have something to do with them."

"I don't see why. We're going to be there when they need an escort. They'll know all kinds of people before a month's out."

"But, dash it, Harry, Aunt Isabel's going to be bringing Claudia out. Aunt Isabel lives in Nicholas' house. Bound to notice they're around."

Harry dismissed the objection. "Oh, Nicholas is sure to find the girls charming." He folded the letter and prepared to leave the tavern.

Jack was not so sanguine. Of course Nicholas would find Claudia charming. But Livia, Jack suspected, was something outside of Nicholas Warwick's experience. Jack wondered how Nicholas would describe her. He didn't think the word was charming.

Chapter 2

Three weeks later, a hired carriage delivered the Neville sisters to their new home in Charles Street, just off Berkley Square. "A jewel of a house," Lady Crawford had written to Livia, "completely furnished. Lady Hartlebury was to be here in April, but broke her leg, poor soul, and will be laid up at her daughter's home in Sussex for the entire Season. I was able to obtain it on excellent terms." Lady Crawford omitted her own contribution to these terms and her promise of future favours to Lady Hartelbury's younger daughter who would be coming out in two years' time. "You will find it quite small, but in view of your bereavement you will not be expected to entertain. I have engaged a parlourmaid and a chambermaid and a scullery girl as well. They're inexperienced and young, but should do well with a firm hand. The cook has been something of a problem—it is so difficult to find a really good French chef and I had several disappointments—but I trust Mrs. Fraser will do, she has excellent references. You should probably have a footman, but that can wait for another day. Harry and Jack have engaged a butler. His name is Sandringham. They are somewhat vague about his last position—some trouble there, I think—but they vouch for his complete honesty and I have taken him on their recommendation. His manner is quite correct, and he is an imposing figure of a man, but if you ever have the slightest doubt, do not hesitate to let me know. I will call on you the morning of the fourth, I trust you will be quite recovered from the fatigues of your journey, and there is a great deal to be done."

A great deal had already been done, Livia reflected, as their carriage pulled into Charles Street. It was close on five o'clock, and the girls were tired, disheveled, and just a trifle cross. "Oh, I *do* want tea!" Diana exclaimed, "and a hot fire and a good stretch." She jumped from the carriage before the coachman had let down the steps and ran halfway down the street and back before her sisters had alighted. Secretly wishing she could do the same, Livia called Diana to order, led her sisters sedately to the door, and rang for admittance.

The butler was indeed imposing—well over six feet, with massive shoulders, admirable legs, a fine aquiline profile, and hair of a rich, auburn hue. Dyes it, Livia concluded. Must be well into middle age, but he doesn't show it. I do hope it isn't drink. She resisted an impulse to offer him her hand and, with all the gravity she could muster, informed him of their names and their immediate desire for tea. She sought his eyes for evidence of condescension, but found only a hint of sympathetic interest. If he was a friend of Harry and Jack's, heaven knew what story they'd told him.

The staff was lined up in the hall—Mrs. Fraser, the cook, a solidly built woman who clearly knew her own worth, Mary Beth and Sarah, the upstairs maids, and Jeanie who helped in the kitchen. Sandringham informed Livia that tea was laid in the drawing room. Mary Beth led them upstairs while the butler vanished with a discreet murmur about seeing to their luggage.

The evening passed in happy exploration of the house. Despite Lady Crawford's description, it seemed to have an immense number of rooms and to be immensely overfurnished. Livia determined to make a clean sweep in the morning, relegating all the unnecessary little tables and cabinets and chairs to the attic, along with a quantity of porcelain and glass *objet d'arts* of obvious value but dubious beauty. The rooms were exquisitely proportioned and would do better without them.

When Lady Crawford arrived at ten the next morning, Livia and Claudia were well into their transformation of the Charles Street house. They were both early risers and energetic by disposition as well as necessity. "Everything Chinese goes," Livia told Sandringham. "Everything Egyptian as well," Claudia added, looking with distaste at a side table of streaked zebra-wood supported by heavily gilded legs in the shape of obscure deities with stiff wings and long, curving tails. Mary Beth and Sarah were packing innumerable dust-catching ornaments in cotton wool, while Livia made a careful inventory of everything consigned to the attic, "for when we leave we shall have to return everything to just where we found it."

"The house looks quite bare," Lady Crawford said as she walked through the denuded drawing room, "and it's a vast improvement. Add flowers. They'll do wonders, and they're flattering to the complexion."

She gave a final nod of approval and took Claudia upstairs to review her wardrobe and plan an attack on the London shops. "I have procured cards for the Waterford ball," she told her protegée. "It's on the sixteenth, just after Easter, and the first really important event of the Season. Lavinia Howland, the Dowager Duchess of Waterford—her son has the title—is an old friend of mine. All her entertainments are famous, but this one will be special; she's bringing out her daughter and everybody of importance will be there. It will be a splendid introduction."

Livia, meanwhile, gave further directions to the two maids and descended to the kitchen to compliment Mrs. Fraser on the previous night's dinner, in particular the subtle flavour of the fish sauce. Livia hoped she sounded knowledgeable—she was a self-confessed disaster in culinary matters and had always left them to Claudia.

Mrs. Fraser, who was inclined to be frosty, thawed under Livia's treatment and allowed as to how young ladies didn't need such a great quantity of food when they were dining *en famille*. Though that young one, of course, she did have an appetite, down in the kitchen at dawn to beg a roll or two and a bit of cheese, gone sketching she said, such a mite of a girl, she didn't think she should have gone out on her own, but then it wasn't her place to say anything when her sister had told her it was all right, but then perhaps she wasn't used to London ways. Oh dear, thought Livia, so that's where Diana's got to. I'll have to have a talk with her. She reassured Mrs. Fraser and smiled at Jeanie, the scullery girl, who was standing shyly in a corner. Just a baby, she thought, why, she must be younger than Diana.

Livia returned to the drawing room and sat down to review her notes. Lady Hartlebury's establishment was far larger than her own home, larger than any she had visited, but she did not find it daunting. Since her mother's death, Livia had managed the household accounts and balanced the family's small budget, which often required considerable ingenuity. But—even when added to the translations she did with her father—this had not been enough to keep her occupied. She welcomed the increased scope for her talents.

She pocketed her lists and ran upstairs to see how Claudia was faring with Lady Crawford. She found the latter surveying the room with a thoughtful frown. Every stitch of Claudia's wardrobe was laid out on bed, dressing table, chairs, and even lamps. For the past three weeks Claudia and Livia had cut and stitched and trimmed and altered. They had engaged a local seamstress and even Diana, who was clever with her fingers, had been pressed into service. The result, which had seemed bounteous in Claudia's bedroom at home, looked meagre indeed in Lady Hartlebury's London chamber. There was Claudia's one real evening dress of primrose crêpe, over a year old but not worn above half a dozen times and fortunately cut on classic lines. There was the sprig muslin trimmed with blue ribbon that Claudia had made just before their father's death and two or three other dresses deemed suitable for afternoon wear. Livia's best muslin had been let out to fit Claudia's more ample form and trimmed at sleeves and neck with dark green velvet ribbons that matched those on a bonnet Claudia had remodelled herself. After anxious consultation with back copies of *La Belle Assemblée,* they had constructed a walking dress of a fine dove grey and an evening gown of the palest blue with an overdress of turquoise crêpe, both made from old gowns of their mother's. There was also a pelisse of dark blue velvet and a fur muff that their father had given Claudia on her eighteenth birthday.

In pride of place lay Claudia's own creation. The purchase of the length of heavy cream-coloured satin had been their greatest extravagance, and from it Claudia had fashioned a gown of the greatest simplicity, cut low to reveal her creamy shoulders, artfully tucked to give shape to her bosom, and containing not a jot of ruching, beading, tucking, or other trim to distract the eye from the form of its wearer. Lady Crawford paused in her perambulation, running the thick satin through her fingers. She looked at Claudia who was watching her with anxious eyes.

"For the Waterford ball?"

Claudia nodded.

Lady Crawford had intended to present Claudia with a dress for this occasion, but Claudia had totally disarmed her. The girl would be stunning.

Lady Crawford smiled. "Yes, I see, a virtue of simplicity. You have excellent taste, my dear. An eye for line and colour. Perhaps a bit understated, but better to err on that side, and when we have added a few trifles you will make a most creditable appearance. Now," she said briskly, "to the shops."

Diana reappeared as they were about to leave the house. It was Lady Crawford's first glimpse of the youngest Neville and Livia wanted her sister to make a creditable appearance. She looked critically at Diana. Her hair was sadly disordered, but at least her dress was neat and her hands clean.

Diana curtsied politely to Lady Crawford, but her gaze had a directness that would have been rude in an older person. Lady Crawford, Livia saw with relief, returned the look with equal directness and a friendly smile. Good. Diana had passed inspection.

Livia would have been less sanguine had she known that her youngest sister left the house again later that afternoon, using the tradesmen's entrance. She wore a dark cloak and a scarf covered her vivid titian hair. A sketchbook was tucked under her arm and there were sharpened pencils in the pocket of her old grey dress. Avoiding the more fashionable streets where her sisters and Lady Crawford might be found, Diana wandered where she pleased, stopping to sketch whatever caught her eye—children playing in a fenced garden, a dandy ill-at-ease in his surroundings, a cress-seller calling her wares. Diana lost her direction several times and at dusk found herself in Mount Street, not far from her new home but in an area frequented more by the Charles Street servants than by their masters.

It was a heavy, musky night. Rain had fallen earlier and threatened again. Diana's dress was splashed by mud, as were her serviceable walking boots. Her scarf had fallen and her hair cascaded down her back. She might have been mistaken for a shop girl hurrying home to a frugal supper, but her luxuriant hair, her trim figure, and her bold curiosity suggested something more.

She stood on a corner, debating which way to turn. She was about to cross the street when her way was momentarily blocked by two carriages which had locked wheels. The drivers, a tall grizzled man in a battered top hat—an ex-sailor by the sound of his language—and a shrill, over-dressed fop in a coat with absurdly padded shoulders, were exchanging insults.

Street scenes delighted Diana. She forgot her hurry and drew back into a doorway where she could climb a step to better see the argument. She was smiling with amusement, oblivious of the other watchers, when her view of the altercation was suddenly blocked by a large expanse of shirt, none too clean, partly covered by a greasy fawn waistcoat. Diana was tiny and had to look up to find its owner's face. He was a youngish man, not unhandsome, but with a face flushed with the drink that was all too apparent on his breath. He had apparently just come from the tavern next door.

Diana, made uncomfortable by the look in his eyes, turned her head away. His eyes traveled down her body and his hands, braced against the door by which she stood, moved down to take her lightly about the hips and draw her toward him. Diana, like her sisters, was well-versed in what happens between men and women and knew that it was not always pretty. "A guinea," he was saying heavily. "A guinea for one like you. A golden guinea for a golden girl."

Diana was shocked into awareness of her vulnerability. Generally unconscious of how she appeared to others, she had thought her role of spectator rendered her invisible. She was not missish and she did not scream. She twisted expertly to one side, pushed hard with both arms against his chest, darted under an upraised arm and ran down the street, only to be sent sprawling by an older, coarser man who tripped her up, kicked her with his boot, then yelled to her admirer, "Here's your fish, Luke. She's slippery. Grab her while you can!"

Luke stumbled after her and had her by the arm while she was still struggling to her feet. Diana was now seriously alarmed. She screamed, kicked, and hit blindly at her tormentor. A crowd gathered and watched the new entertainment, the carriages with the locked wheels having disengaged and gone their way. Diana sank her teeth into Luke's wrist. He howled, then howled again in astonishment as an expert fist smashed his jaw and he landed in a heap in the middle of the street, blood mingling with the grease on his clothes. The impartial crowd cheered. Diana, breathing heavily, stood still for a moment, then found herself pulled unceremoniously into a curricle and driven off as the crowd, divided on the merits of the outcome, loudly debated her future.

The owner of the expert fist drove his horses down Mount Street with practiced ease and pulled up by a lamp post in the relative quiet of Berkley Square.

"Now, let's have a look at you." He laid a hand on her arm. Diana, fearing she had escaped a crude tormentor only to find a more subtle one, made to leap from the curricle. "Don't be afraid, I won't harm you. You seemed in need of rescue," he added with a reassuring smile.

Diana looked at him for the first time. He has a nice face, she thought. Good eyes. Strong line to the jaw. She suddenly recollected herself, lowered her eyes, and said softly, "I am much indebted to you for your services, sir." Her voice was low, musical, and clearly educated.

He frowned. "Good God, girl, what were you doing in Mount Street?" He reached out, took her chin in his hand, and turned her head to the light. "How old are you?"

Diana face him squarely. "Eighteen," she lied. "And a half," she added, throwing caution to the winds.

"I don't believe a word of it. Where do you live?"

"If you tell me where I am," Diana replied with great dignity, "I can find my own way home. There is no need to trouble you further."

"I am not in the habit of abandoning infants," he retorted. "Tell me where you live and I'll drive you home. Or," he added darkly, "I'll call the Watch and give you in charge as an abandoned female."

"You wouldn't dare!"

"No?" He seized her arm again. "I've had a hard day. I long for my dinner, and I have no desire to prolong this conversation. I am eminently respectable. If you won't give me your name, tell me who has charge of you and where you live."

Diana gave him the number in Charles Street. "Please take me there at once," she added coldly. She tied her scarf round her head, hiding her hair, and sat erect, eyes straight ahead, thinking furiously.

When they arrived, Diana jumped down from the curricle,

but was detained by its owner who made fast his horses and announced that he would see her in himself. She led him to the area door. With any luck, Mrs. Fraser would be too busy to pay attention and Jeanie would vouch for her as a fellow servant.

The owner of the curricle rapped sharply on the door. It was opened by Sandringham. Beyond him stood Mrs. Fraser and Jeanie and, beyond them, Livia, a worried frown creasing her forehead. Diana did the only thing possible. She burst into tears.

Her rescuer looked about the assembled group with mounting fury, then addressed Livia as the person with the most apparent authority. "Does this child belong here?"

Diana, still hoping to retrieve something from the debacle, shut off her tears and turned piteous eyes to Livia. "Oh, please don't be angry, ma'am. I didn't mean to be late, but I got lost and this gentleman very kindly brought me home."

Livia had had a bad hour or two when she returned home and found that Diana was not in the house. Visions of disaster had filled her head, but she had tried to keep her fears from Claudia and the servants. She had long since learned that—especially in a crisis—hysterics were a waste of time. At Diana's entrance, relief came in a flood, but when she spoke her voice was crisp and composed. "It's all right. Come inside and get warm." She turned to Diana's rescuer, words of thanks on her lips, but he forestalled her, speaking through clenched teeth.

"This child, ma'am, was lost in a disreputable part of Mount Street. She was being subjected to the grossest of insults, and threatened with something far worse. She appears gently brought up—at least her speech tells me she is so, though her behaviour belies it—but believe me, I would not send the meanest serving wench out after dark in that part of town. I do not know what position she occupies in this house, but she is clearly not being given proper supervision. I trust you will consider your obligations and not let it happen again."

His voice cut like a whip. No one had ever spoken to Livia in that tone. Her face went white and her hands trembled. She had been worried by Diana's absence, but the stranger's story and his accusations shocked her more than she cared to admit. Raised by indulgent, affectionate parents, Livia was used to gentler treatment. The fact that the stranger's words cut close to the truth did nothing to make them more palatable.

She clasped her hands tightly to regain her composure. "I am indebted to you, sir, but I need no lessons on how to manage this household. I am quite capable of handling the incident. I regret that you have been needlessly troubled." Then she made her mistake. "Pray take some refreshment before you leave." She nodded to Sandringham, took Diana by the hand, and turned to leave the room. Speechless, the gentleman clapped his hat on his head and stormed out the door.

Keeping Diana firmly by the hand, Livia sought out her elder sister. She did not trust herself to speak and she needed Claudia's calm good sense.

Diana took up a stand before the fireplace, feet apart, hands behind her back, and faced her sisters. "I thought it was a very good performance," she said, addressing Livia. "He must expect all girls to be missish. He is an odious, high-handed man."

Livia closed the door to the hall as if she wished she could slam it. "That's true at any rate."

"You were splendid," Diana added, not entirely for ulterior purposes. "The Empress Livia putting Augustus in his place."

Livia paused, halfway across the drawing room. "Why Augustus?"

"Well, how should I know all the people she put in their place? I'm sure she put Augustus in his place, lots of times. After all, he was her husband. Don't you think she did?"

"I don't expect she had to do it very often, once was probably enough. In fact—"

"Livia," Claudia interrupted, laying aside a novel Lady Crawford had lent her, "whom have you been putting in his place?"

35

Remembering that she was—technically at least—the family chaperone, that she was angry with Diana, and that this was no time for debating the finer points of classical history, Livia told Claudia of the events in the kitchen, omitting only her offer of a drink. Perhaps that had been a mistake—though a very satisfying one.

Diana, applied to, was forced to give some account of the event, including an explanation for her torn and dirty skirt. Being an honest, forthright girl, she did so, laying rather more stress on her own pugilistic abilities than on the near success of her attacker. Of course, she admitted, she should never have stayed out so late, nor should she have strayed into unfamiliar streets. She was certainly well served for having done so, for she had lost her sketchbook which had had a particularly good rendering of two little girls rolling hoops near the Serpentine in Hyde Park.

Livia said that that was not the point. Why had she gone out at all without some female companionship? Claudia suggested mildly that perhaps Diana should spend her time with them. Diana looked rebellious, and the tears which now flooded her eyes were genuine. "It's not fair! It's not at all fair! Girls go about alone all the time and no one bothers them. It was no worse than walking down Bond Street in the afternoon and being ogled by those stupid macaronis Harry talks about, all straining for a glimpse of leg when a lady gets into a carriage. He was drunk, that's all."

Livia, still smarting from the tongue-lashing she had received below stairs, threatened to send Diana back to Oxford. Claudia pointed out that shop girls and servants might walk alone with propriety, but girls like Diana did not. Diana insisted that such distinctions were odious.

Claudia agreed that they were indeed odious but reminded her that they existed. Diana returned to the unfairness of her lot. She hated shopping, she could not go into society, and she was not a school girl to be let out on a leash with a governess in tow. This was her only time in London in her whole life and her one chance to see something of the world and they were not to deprive her of it. If Livia tried to make her stay sedately at home, she was no better than that odious Augustus person. This last cut deeply. Livia, her anger spent, at last hit on the cogent argument.

"The thing is, love," she said, pushing Diana's hair back from her hot forehead, "we can't afford a hint of scandal. Our position is precarious enough, and we mustn't do anything to spoil Claudia's chances."

Diana was immediately penitent. Claudia negotiated the compromise. Jeanie would accompany Diana when she left the house, but on no account was Diana ever to remain out beyond five o'clock. Livia would make it all right with Mrs. Fraser and, if necessary, they would hire another girl for the kitchen.

Livia sighed. That would have to do. But considering all that had happened, they had come out very well indeed.

Chapter 3

"Neville?" Letitia Amesbury said at breakfast at Warwick House the following day. "I don't remember any Oxford Nevilles. There were the Nevilles down in Shropshire but the line died out, I think, when George—or was it Samuel? No, I think it was George, he was the third baronet—had that very messy accident with the hunting rifle. We didn't talk about it, of course, but everyone knew what had happened. His wife went quite mad with grief, she was a Pemberley, you know, and her brother had been cashiered out of his regiment for killing his commanding officer, a Colonel Mannering whose sister ran off to Gretna Green with William Reid, the youngest son of Lord Bridlington, who promptly disinherited him and the poor girl was quite ruined and devoted her life to horses and was said to have married her groom, though I never believed it of her. We met her older sister up in York—she had married one of the Pelhams—when Papa took us up for the shooting, horrid journey, I was just thirteen and I haven't been able to abide the sound of guns since. Do they shoot?"

"No, Letty, I'm sure they don't shoot," Isabel Crawford assured her sister-in-law. She smiled across the table at Harry. "Not at any rate in London. They're quite presentable. Their father was something of a scholar and they're very well educated."

"Oh, dear," Mrs. Amesbury murmured. "Not blue-stockings. So unsuitable for young girls, and how will they ever get husbands? Men don't at all like that sort of thing, why there was poor Eliza Carstairs and as pretty a thing as could please and with a tidy sum of money and Lord Forsythe nearly brought up to scratch and the wretched girl would not keep still. I think it was the *écossaise* at Lady Belnap's ball in the spring of 1808 that did the damage." Mrs. Amesbury looked at the fourth occupant of the breakfast parlour. "I don't know how often I've told Francesca to mind her tongue, not that it matters so much when one is a widow . . ."

The gentle monologue went on and on. Harry reached for his coffee cup to conceal a grin. Like his father's sister Lady Crawford, his mother's sister Letitia Amesbury was a widow, but there the resemblance ended. Aunt Letty, who made her home with the Warwicks year round, was a dear, but a trifle—well more than a trifle—wearing. When he could get a word in edgewise, Harry returned to the original point of the conversation: would Aunt Isabel please give up her monopoly of the Nevilles, if only for a day? He and Jack wanted to see them.

Lady Crawford, who had been neglecting her own duties and was positively promised at a reception at the Belgian Embassy, gave her assent to a Sunday excursion, stipulating only that they go somewhere quiet and out of the way and on no account go driving in Rotten Row.

Harry understood that his aunt had some reason for not exposing Claudia to fashionable London until the night of the Waterford ball. He nodded agreeably.

"Hampton Court," he said. "Sure to be nothing but cits on a Sunday. I know you need the carriage, Aunt Letty," he added hastily before Mrs. Amesbury could break into speech. "We'll go by water. Diana wants a boat ride. Seems funny, though. I haven't been to Hampton Court since I was ten and Justin took me for a treat." His voice softened, as it did whenever he spoke of his dead brother. He was a little in awe of Nicholas, his

39

surviving brother, but Justin had been his hero.

Flipping idly through the *Morning Chronicle*, Justin's widow did not appear moved by similar memories. In fact, as far as Harry could remember, Francesca had found widowhood irksome from the beginning. Even when Justin was alive, she had not treated him with the respect Harry thought his brother deserved.

Mrs. Amesbury suggested that Francesca might like to go to Hampton Court with Harry and Jack. To Harry's relief, Francesca pronounced the notion "inexpressibly dreary," the gardens over-rated, and no pleasure to be had in being herded like sheep from one room to another. Besides, she had another appointment.

Mrs. Amesbury then said brightly that Isabel must bring her friends to the house soon. "I do think we should meet them—after all, they will be making their come out from Warwick House, as it were—which people might find odd as they aren't any relation, though I know Lady Barton-West brought out all three Sudbury girls, and they weren't related to her at all—that is, they may have been slightly, because Maria Sudbury married one of the Barton-West boys, but that was years before—I do hope Nicholas will like them."

"The Nevilles?" said Harry, helping himself to kippered herring. "Oh, he's bound to." Nicholas had been surprised on learning that Lady Crawford had agreed to sponsor two young women from Oxford, but he had not, as Jack had feared, kicked up a fuss. "Anyway," Harry said, "Nicholas has charming manners—at least that's what everyone says."

Francesca looked up from the paper and smiled drily. "Naturally. He's a politician."

"Yes, dear," said Mrs. Amesbury, "but you know I can't help but think that his heart isn't in it much of the time, being charming I mean. I've despaired of his ever taking a serious interest in a young woman."

Harry grinned. "Oh, well, that's different. I can't imagine Nicholas taking a serious interest in anything as trivial as a young woman."

This drew smiles from Lady Crawford and Francesca, but Mrs. Amesbury for once had found a subject worth sticking to. "It's no laughing matter, Harry. I was saying to Isabel just the other day that it was high time Nicholas married again. It's been three years since poor Lillie died, and Gwendolen ought to have a mother, she's already ten, and very advanced for her age. Besides, Nicholas has been sitting in the House for years and I guess he's gotten used to it, though I've never understood why he likes it, it seems to make him angry so much of the time, but I do feel politicians need wives more than most men. Fortescue got dreadfully seedy when his wife died and he lost the next election, and Ratisbon stayed a bachelor and never did amount to much, he always fell asleep on the back benches, whatever they are, it must have been the appalling amount of brandy he put away, though where he got it during the war I don't care to say, though he did go abroad a great deal, and we can't expect Francesca to be with us forever you know."

"Why not?" Harry asked, polishing off the last of the herring.

"I think," said Francesca, who had been running Warwick House and serving as Nicholas' hostess for the past three years, "that Aunt Letty means I may marry again."

"Oh." Despite Francesca's formidable court of admirers, Harry had not given much thought to this possibility. "Are you planning on it?"

"Not in the immediate future."

Observing this byplay, Lady Crawford wondered once again if Francesca and Nicholas would make a match of it. Nicholas should certainly marry again, and his brother's widow was the obvious choice. Francesca had beauty and wit and at twenty-four was not designed for a celibate life. She had a knack for organizing large entertainments which, Lady Crawford admitted, rivalled her own. She could converse intelligently on most of the political questions of the day, and if her wit was

41

sometimes touched with acid, she was undeniably clever. It did not seem likely that Nicholas would fall in love again—in fact, Lady Crawford was not sure that it would be a good thing if he did—and Francesca was sophisticated enough not to mind. She would have to see how the wind blew in that quarter.

Francesca folded the paper and pushed back her chair. "I hope your friends like Hampton Court. I should warn you, though, we're all going to be out on Sunday. Nicholas is quite likely to ask you to take Gwendolen with you."

Harry's face fell. He was fond of his motherless niece, but he had looked forward to being seen with Claudia, even among the cits, and he did not want his time taken up by a brat. Still, when Nicholas asked him later with that rueful smile that always undermined Harry's resolve, Harry said of course, he would be glad to take her with them. Privately he cursed his troublesome niece. Gwendolen was known for demanding all kinds of information and a fellow did not always have it at his fingertips. Hampton Court was sure to be a trial.

For Gwendolen, the day promised unusual pleasures, chief among them being out of doors and away from the continual cautions of her governess. She promised Harry faithfully that she would not chatter if he would only not be difficult if she chose to run about and if he would please, please let her go through the maze. Harry, who at heart was a kind person and felt sorry for the child cooped up all day like a trussed chicken, promised that she could run about the maze as much as she liked, but she must on no account get lost or Nicholas would have his head. Oh, and she must be sure to be polite to the Nevilles.

This last was unnecessary. Gwendolen knew well enough when she should be on her manners. She was rude only to bores and to those pompous adults who patronized her, and she was always willing to give newcomers the benefit of the doubt.

Harry and Jack, with Gwendolen in tow, called for the Nevilles at nine on Sunday morning. Claudia fully justified Harry's pride in being her escort. The day was fair and she was wearing a green pelisse, the colour of new grass, over Livia's muslin. Instead of the matching bonnet, she had chosen a straw gipsy hat, tied under her chin with a pale green scarf. The hat was no longer fashionable, but the effect was decidedly dashing.

They embarked at the Westminster stairs which were crowded with watermen crying, "Sculls, sculls! Oars, oars!" Harry skillfully made his way through the throng and selected one somewhat less rough-looking than the rest. Their boat pulled out and turned upriver amid a score of others bound on similar errands of pleasure. Harry pointed to the Parliament buildings on their right—"that's where Nicholas spends all his time," he said with pride—and the larger bulk of Lambeth Palace, home of the Archbishop of Canterbury, on their left. Soon they were in open country.

Jack, who was quite as appreciative of Claudia's charms as his friend, attached himself to Livia. He was aware of the price she paid for her masquerade, and he was anxious that she not be neglected. He realized that he was in danger of being put off by her outer garb and went out of his way to make amends. "Thing of it is," he explained, "doesn't seem quite proper to talk to Mrs. Royce the way we used to talk to Livia. Your bereavement and all." Livia assured him that the last year had inured her to the loss of Mr. Royce and she was quite longing to be amused, so would he please put off that long face, at least for today. Thus agreed, they settled themselves happily in the expectation of what Jack predicted would be a fine voyage.

Diana and Gwendolen were left to make the best of each other's company. Diana was quite willing to be pleasant. She had been left much to herself in the last few days and was looking forward to conversation. A child was quite as likely to be entertaining as an adult. But Gwendolen was not cooperative. She preferred to observe a new acquaintance from a distance until positively assured that it would be worthwhile to commit herself to interaction. At this stage, she was likely to be seen as dour and withdrawn. Some concluded she was shy, but not anyone who had met her alert and judgmental eyes. After a few attempts at conversation, Diana shrugged and turned her attention to the river.

This suited Gwendolen very well. Diana, she decided, was a sensible sort. She was less sure of Mrs. Royce, but Miss Neville was absolute perfection. She had the sweetest smile and made you feel warm and comforted, the way you felt when you were very young and your mother came into the nursery, dressed for the evening in something soft and filmy, with diamonds gleaming at her throat, and put her arms around you and kissed you goodnight. To her chagrin, Gwendolen felt a sudden upwelling of tears and turned her head resolutely away from the others. It had been many months since she had allowed herself such thoughts.

They pulled up at the water stairs, pausing to let a boatload of assorted adults and children mount before them. Harry dismissed their own boat, Nicholas having promised to send the carriage for the return journey. As they made their way toward the buildings, they looked up at the dark, almost purplish brick of the Palace against the blue of a cloudless sky, the charm of the old Tudor buildings blending with Wren's formal additions. Jack admired the regularity and sweep of the latter, but Livia said she infinitely preferred the older parts. Diana, who had a good eye and fine judgment in such matters, was applied to, but she had wandered off. Livia turned to Gwendolen and asked for her opinion. This so startled the child that she was betrayed into spontaneity. She pronounced strongly in favour of everything that was unplanned and irregular, for she hated always having to walk in straight lines. Jack raised his eyebrows, but Livia nodded and said that expressed her own feelings to perfection. She made no further effort to converse with Gwendolen, but turned to follow Claudia and Harry who had gone on ahead. Gwendolen ran to catch up with her.

They walked through the Great Gatehouse and across the Base Court to Anne Boleyn's Gateway at the foot of the stairs leading to the Great Hall. Diana was already there, sitting on the bottom step.

They moved as a group into the Clock Court, pausing in the archway of the Clock Tower so that Harry, remembering something that had struck him when he was ten, could point out the "A & H" entwined in a true lover's knot in the groined ceiling. "Henry had them all over, badges and all, when he fell in love with Anne and took Hampton Court away from Wolsey. Then when he married Jane Seymour he ordered them all removed, but somehow this one got overlooked. At least, I think that's the way it happened. Justin told me about it."

"Do you think it was fair?" Gwendolen asked suddenly. She and Livia were standing a little apart from the others.

"Fair?"

"I mean his killing her, just so he could marry someone else."

"Hardly fair. He wanted a son, of course."

"But she could have had more children." Gwendolen thought a moment. "They say she went with other men. I know what that means, you know," she added, as Livia looked at her sharply. "But maybe she was lonely or just liked to dance and laugh and he was too busy for her. Divorce would have been better."

"I think Henry was in a hurry. He was well served, too, for it was Anne's daughter who finally came to the throne."

"She was better, wasn't she? I mean, she was a better queen than he was a king?"

"She certainly was a wiser and more capable ruler," Livia said judiciously. She took Gwendolen's hand and led her after the others.

Harry had arranged to have them taken around the public parts of the buildings, for some rooms were still occupied by the "Grace and Favour" residents given quarters by permission of the king. Their guide was the deputy housekeeper, a stately, imposing woman who pocketed a sizeable fee and took them through the Great Hall and the old Tudor Galleries and then on through the State apartments in Wren's addition. They came out into the open air at last, stupefied by the number and splendour of the reception rooms, bed-chambers, dressing-rooms, and closets they had seen.

"I should like to have lived then," Harry announced, with visions of striding about in doublet and hose while men with pikes flung open doors and shouted, "Ho, the King!"

"When's then?" Jack asked.

"Oh, Henry I guess. Though Charles would be all right too." Harry also fancied himself in a plumed hat and cape.

"Well, I wouldn't, not at any time," Diana said. "All those petticoats, however could you get about?"

"Not half as well as now," Gwendolen cried, lifting up her skirt and running off down one of the long avenues of lime trees extending eastward from the Palace. "Catch me if you can, Uncle Harry!"

Torn between his self-image as a gentleman and his longing for physical activity, Harry hesitated a moment, muttered, "Brat!" and raced after her.

They came back happy and subdued and joined the others in wandering about the gardens. Diana soon left them, sketchbook in hand, declaring they could find her in the Fountain Court when they tired of their rambles. The sounds of a regimental band which played in the grounds on Sundays attracted Harry and he begged Claudia to go with him, for he had heard there was dancing.

"But the maze, you promised!" Gwendolen was hot, disheveled, and seething with indignation.

"But that's just the thing, I adore puzzles!" Livia intervened before Harry could recall his obligations. "Off you go, children. You too, Jack." She waved an imperious hand. Claudia giggled and went off, a man on each arm.

Gwendolen was torn between pleasure and doubt. "Do you really want to go?"

"But of course. I've never been through a maze. It must be much like chess, and I'm very fond of chess. Besides, what can an old woman like me want with dancing?"

"Old? You're bamming me! Why you don't look much older than Miss Neville."

"Yes, but you see, I've been married. That makes a difference, you know."

Gwendolen thought a moment. "You mean, when you're married you're not allowed to do anything that's fun?"

"Not exactly." Livia's voice trailed off. She had been talking nonsense and was trapped.

Fortunately, Gwendolen ignored her. "I'm sure that's not true. My Aunt Francesca lost her husband too, and she's very fond of dancing and she's not old at all. Of course, she's not in black now, but even when she was I think she missed it, going to parties and all. I don't think she's very happy when she's by herself. Do you miss him a great deal?"

"Him?"

"Your husband."

"Oh, no. That is, yes, of course. I mean, it's been some time now and I've become used to it." Livia was not sure she sounded convincing and contemplated a diversion, but at that point the maze came into view. Gwendolen ran forward happily and they spent the next hour scrambling about, calling to each other across blind alleys, and steadfastly refusing help from the man perched on a stand high above the maze to succour the hopelessly lost.

Sated, they wandered further among limes and horse chestnuts to the Diana Fountain. Gwendolen's reserve had gone. She told Livia she might call her Genny and then pronounced the day perfect. "Imagine, a whole day without old Calabash. Miss Calisher, my governess," she explained. "She means well, but she's always afraid that something terrible is going to happen, and that takes the fun out of things. She's been with us for ages, and of course Daddy had to give her something to do, so that seemed to be me. She was with Mummy when she married Daddy and then Mummy died and then Nurse went away and Miss Calisher was the only one.

47

Aunt Letitia—she's really Daddy's aunt, she's my great-aunt—could have looked after me, but she's a scatterbrain and has nervous spasms, so that wasn't any good. Then there was Aunt Francesca, she came to us when my Uncle Justin died, but she was in a fragile condition, Daddy said, and I wasn't to bother her too much, though I think she's really bored by children. There's been a lot of death, hasn't there? But I guess you're used to that."

"Yes," said Livia gravely, explaining that she had lost her father a few months since and her own mother when she was much younger.

"Mothers are hard," Gwendolen agreed. "That's why Eddy and I get along, I think. He lost his mother when he was a really little boy. I'm not sure he remembers her very well, but you do notice it, you know."

"Yes, you do notice it." Livia looked at Gwendolen in some wonder, then changed the subject. "Is Eddy a close friend?"

"Well, yes, though he's years younger—only seven. Well, almost eight. He's Lord Melbrooke's son. Lord Melbrooke and Daddy have been friends forever, but Eddy lives in the country most of the time, so he doesn't see his father much. Sometimes he comes to stay with us. Daddy wanted me to stay at Melbrooke with Eddy, he said I wouldn't be so bored if I could run about more and have horses and dogs to play with, but I couldn't let him sacrifice himself for me that way. He needs to have someone sensible to talk to and Aunt Francesca is out a great deal and Aunt Isabel isn't always with us, so I screamed and carried on until they were all afraid I'd be sick, so of course they had to let me stay in town." She paused a moment. "It's all right to be devious, isn't it? I mean, sometimes that's the only way you can get things done."

Livia choked. "It puts one on a distinctly lower moral plane," she said when she had recovered, "but I'm afraid you are quite right. Sometimes it is the only way."

The sky had turned cloudy and, recollecting the time, they turned back toward the Palace and the Fountain Court.

Gwendolen continued to chatter happily, principally about her father whom she clearly adored. In fact, Livia thought, she seemed to hold Nicholas Warwick in a good deal less awe than Harry did.

"Of course," Gwendolen acknowledged fair-mindedly, "some people think he's difficult. Once I heard Uncle Justin call him an autocrat, but it's just because he's used to being in charge of things. He's very good at it, and he likes being in charge."

Livia smiled. "I can understand that. I like to be in charge of things myself."

"Do you?" Gwendolen looked up at her, evidently impressed. "So do I. That is, I expect I shall like it, when I have anything to be in charge of."

Diana was not there when they reached the Fountain Court, but they found Claudia in laughing conversation with Harry, Jack, and a third young man. He was made known to them as Mr. Jeremy Warkworth who had been up with them, Jack said, during their first year at University, at the end of which he had obtained a First, a tremendous feat. Mr. Warkworth demurred politely. He had exquisite manners, but his eyes kept straying to Claudia with all the yearning of a young puppy who longs to be noticed. Familiar with the symptoms, Livia charitably turned him back to her sister. Harry was standing by protectively, torn between pleasure at being noticed by the older man and jealousy at Jeremy's intrusion on their party.

It was only later that Harry gave vent to his temper. He had ushered the party, including the errant Diana, into the Warwick carriage, then driven to a small but respectable riverside inn where he bespoke a private parlour for their dinner. The ladies had retired for a moment and he was alone with Jack.

"Damned impudence! Not only does he follow us about all afternoon, he has the infernal cheek to ask her to dance."

"Not today, old boy. You danced with Claudia. I danced with Claudia. Warkworth didn't."

"I mean for the ball, the Waterford ball. Didn't you hear? He asked her for the first quadrille."

"What's wrong with that? Got to dance with someone. Can't dance with you. You don't like the quadrille. Frankly you can't even dance the quadrille. Why not Warkworth? Good family, good *ton*. Got a First, too."

Harry glowered. Well into his second year, his academic performance still left much to be desired. "That's not the point. Claudia can't waste time on young sprigs like Warkworth. She's got to make a match, someone substantial, someone who deserves her."

"She's not going to marry a man just because she dances with him," Jack pointed out reasonably. "Girl's got to start somewhere. Besides, they like to fill up their programs, looks good. More popular a girl looks, more popular she is. Claudia'll be all right."

Harry still had his grievance. "He presented her to his grandmother, too. Didn't you see? Don't you know what that means?"

"He couldn't help it. Old Lady Greville swept right down on top of us. Couldn't pretend we weren't there. Besides, Lady Greville liked her. I could tell. Called her a 'sweet girl,' pounded her parasol on the pavement. Shows she meant it. Important, that, having the old ladies like her."

"But Claudia can't marry Warkworth!"

"Of course she can't. He's too young and he hasn't a groat. Don't know why you're in such a stew." An awful suspicion crossed Jack's mind. He looked at his friend.

"Don't be a fool," Harry said.

Claudia's return brought Harry out of his sulks. The dinner was highly successful and they were all rather silly in the carriage going home. Gwendolen declared it had been the best day she had ever spent—well, at least the best in a long, long time—but she was strangely reticent when her father inquired about the excursion.

"You see, Dido," she confided to her black cat when she was

50

safely in her own room, "it would never do to put it to him straight away. When people get a certain age, they don't like other people making plans for them. Mrs. Royce is funny and sensible, but she's not really the mother type. She'll make a good aunt. Miss Neville is just what we need, she's so lovely and sweet, and he'll have to have someone to look after him, truly he will, because I'm past ten and someday I'll come out and get married or run away to America and then where will he be?" She shook the cat in her earnestness and it gave a protesting cry, then curled up in her lap under her soothing hand. "So I'll have to lead him very, very carefully until he gets the idea all by himself."

At breakfast the following morning, Francesca, piqued by Harry's constant references to "Claudia—I mean Miss Neville," insisted that he bring her and her sisters to tea. Harry rolled an agonized eye in Lady Crawford's direction and she skillfully pleaded Miss Neville's appointment with the mantua maker, a trip to a new milliner's, and some vague but time-consuming family business. It was decided instead to invite the Nevilles to dinner before the Waterford Ball.

By this time each family was growing curious about the other. Nicholas remarked to Francesca that anyone who could draw such sustained interest and effort from Harry must be worthy of notice. Francesca smiled. Gwendolen had said little about the Nevilles other than that they were very agreeable ladies and yes, thank you, she had enjoyed the outing very much. These comments were so unlike her usually outspoken views on persons and places that Francesca's attention was definitely caught.

Claudia, receiving Francesca's prettily penned invitation to dinner, remarked that it would be nice to meet Harry's family. Livia nodded. Harry had said very little about his sister-in-law, Lady Francesca, but he had an endless fund of stories about his Aunt Letty and Livia was eager to meet her. She also had considerable curiosity about Mr. Warwick. Though Harry's description of his brilliant, powerful elder brother did not

51

wholly accord with Gwendolen's glowing and affectionate account of her father, they were agreed that Nicholas Warwick combined charm, intellect, and wit. He would provide a welcome contrast to the arrogant and ill-bred gentleman who had been Diana's rescuer.

It was not until she entered Warwick House on the evening of the Waterford ball that Livia learned that the eminent Nicholas Warwick and the high-handed gentleman who had brought Diana home were one and the same person.

Chapter 4

He was now formally dressed in cassimere knee breeches and an impeccably cut black coat, his light brown hair brushed immaculately back from his forehead, but there was no mistaking the direct gaze or the air of authority. He had risen when the butler threw open the drawing room doors. Livia noted a puzzled look in his eyes and prayed he would not recognize her. She was still wearing black, of course, but her dress was of a softer material, the sleeves full and gathered with tiny jet buttons at the wrists, and the neckline—though scarcely décolleté—was at least lower than that of the prim, high-necked dress she had worn on their encounter in the kitchen.

She met his eyes as Lady Crawford performed the introductions and knew that her prayers were in vain. Though his manners were perfectly correct and his face continued pleasant, she knew beyond a doubt that he recalled every moment of their last encounter, down to her final contemptuous dismissal. She knew also that he was Nicholas Warwick—Harry's brother, Lady Crawford's nephew, and her host—and that she was in a dreadful coil.

Then Livia realized that Mr. Warwick was moving on to greet Claudia and that there were other people in the room. She had been too preoccupied to follow Lady Crawford's introductions, but she had little difficulty in recognizing the rest of the Warwick household. The slender, fair-haired young woman with the aristocratic features and coolly elegant manner must be Lady Francesca, Harry's widowed sister-in-law, and the plump, pleasant-featured woman must be his aunt, Mrs. Amesbury. The only stranger was a quiet man about Mr. Warwick's age. Mercifully, Mrs. Amesbury informed Livia that he was Edward, Lord Melbrooke, a long term friend of the family and a close colleague of Nicholas', though he sat in the other Chamber. Livia also learned that he worked much too hard, as of course Nicholas did too, and that he had a dear little boy who resided in the country, his wife, poor soul, having died two years before. On approaching, Lord Melbrooke was informed that Mrs. Royce had lost her husband in France—such a nasty, dangerous country—well, it was actually Belgium, but that was a nasty dangerous country too—and they would have such a lot in common and if they would just excuse her, she must speak to Parkhurst. Lord Melbrooke sat beside Livia, his friendly smile allaying any embarrassment.

"A somewhat daunting introduction," he said. "I'm sorry about your husband. It was at Waterloo, I believe."

Livia nodded. She was now able to converse about John with tolerable ease. She thanked Melbrooke, said something similar about his wife, and suddenly remembered where she had heard about him before. "Don't you have a little boy called Eddy who plays with Gwendolen Warwick?"

Melbrooke nodded. "When he's in town. I'm afraid my work leaves me little time for being a father, and unlike Nicholas I haven't got a houseful of female relations to look after him."

Though clearly a fond parent, Melbrooke did not dwell long on his son but moved skillfully onto topics he thought would be of more interest. One of his greatest charms, Livia was to learn, was that he was able to discourse knowledgeably on almost any subject, discerning his companion's interest with a few simple questions. She toyed with the idea of telling him about her earlier encounter with Mr. Warwick—surely he would know what to do—then reluctantly put it aside. It was a problem she would have to solve for herself.

To her surprise, she enjoyed the dinner. There were only eight of them and conversation was general. Harry was unusually quiet, but Lady Francesca proved to be quite as amusing as Lady Crawford and both Mr. Warwick and Lord Melbrooke were entertaining *raconteurs*. Livia was much relieved, for she was seated on Warwick's right and did not know how she was ever to go on with him.

Claudia, she was pleased to note, conversed with ease. She was seated on Mr. Warwick's left and drew his attention through most of the dinner. Livia said little until Mrs. Amesbury asked if she had seen Miss Linwood's exhibition of needlework at Saville House. Livia admitted that she had not. "But you must, my dear, you must, they are the most extraordinary things you ever saw, and so life-like, she has copied some of the Italian masters, at least they're always called masters, though I've never understood why they should be thought any more masterful than our good English painters and I'm sure our dear Mr. Reynolds is much more wholesome than those heathenish popish pictures which she has copied so that I swear they cannot be told from the oils themselves."

Francesca hastened to turn the conversation and asked if Mrs. Royce and Miss Neville had seen the marble antiquities that were to be purchased for the British Museum. They had. Livia dropped her studied manner and spoke with real enthusiasm. "We went to Burlington House three days after we arrived, we wanted to see them above everything. Our father—he was in Greece when he was young—said the Parthenon made him believe that the gods could truly exist." She stopped in some confusion. Religion, she suspected, was never discussed in polite society.

But this company, at least, took the comment in stride. Lord Melbrooke asked where she stood on the propriety of Lord Elgin's appropriation of the marble fragments. Livia said that she would always be grateful she had seen them, but she had to side with Lord Byron for it seemed both shameful to bring them to an alien country and unconscionable for the government to spend such an enormous sum when other needs were so pressing.

Claudia said that, for her part, she stood firmly on the side of Keats and Haydon and that the marbles were a treasure for which the country would be eternally grateful. Mr. Warwick confessed that his public and private selves warred on the issue. Lady Crawford was of the opinion that Lord Elgin was now heartily sick of the matter for he would not get above half of what the treasure had cost him. Mrs. Amesbury said that, treasures though they undoubtedly were, and much better off in England than in some nasty foreign country with Turks and other heathens, they should never have been put on public exhibition. "Those undraped men, not what one would like a young girl exposed to." Livia started to speak, then resolutely checked herself, but Claudia raised clear dark eyes and said calmly, "I honour your feelings, ma'am, but don't you think that what is known is far less upsetting to a young girl than what can be only imagined?"

Mrs. Amesbury was not certain what she thought, so there was a slight pause. Francesca looked at Claudia in some surprise and even Nicholas Warwick, Livia noted, was smiling.

"Of course, ma'am," Claudia continued, her eyes sparkling, "having a brother may make all the difference."

Mrs. Amesbury was not sure how it would, but she had had a brother so she confessed that this must be true. She recalled him sadly, dead these fifteen years, then she thought of Justin, and then of George Howland, the Duke of Waterford.

"It's sure to be a sad crush," she said, referring to the Waterford ball. "I wouldn't miss it for the world, and then it is Marianne's debut—George's sister," she explained to Livia and Claudia—"not that I haven't seen her time and time again these years, quite handsome she has turned out, though not just to my taste. Francesca," she added loyally, "was a much greater beauty."

Francesca laughed. "Oh, come, ma'am, I am not an ape leader yet."

Nicholas covered his aunt's confusion with a remark about the innumerable faces of beauty. He was a kind of nephew, Livia was forced to admit, though when they rose from the table, she was still uncertain of how to approach him.

The ladies retired upstairs to repair their toilettes before starting for the ball and were just gathering on the landing when a hiss from the floor above caught their attention. "Please, please, may I come down for a moment?" came a loud whisper. "She said I mustn't, but I do so want to see you in your dresses." Without waiting for permission, Gwendolen ran down the stairs in her nightgown, her hair tousled. "Oh, you're all so beautiful!" she cried. "Are those real diamonds, Aunt Isabel?"

"Yes, child, they are real diamonds, and you've seen them many times before, so don't bam me."

"And you look very nice too," Gwendolen went on, turning to Mrs. Amesbury and then to Francesca and to Livia. "But you," she said to Claudia, the object of her foray, "look like a fairy princess!"

Claudia laughed, leaned down and kissed her on the cheek, then told her to be good and run upstairs. Her governess, Miss Calisher, could be seen above, wringing her hands.

Lady Crawford had reason to be pleased. They did indeed look well. She herself was in lavender, a favourite colour since her youth, with some really lovely Mechlin lace on the bodice and sleeves and a matching velvet ribbon round her throat. Her hair was dressed in the antique Roman style and she wore a delicate tiara set with diamonds. Francesca was wearing aquamarines, hardly a fine jewel, but a perfect foil for her dress, a filmy blue-green gauze which brought out the green in her eyes, worn over an underdress of turquoise satin. Even Mrs. Amesbury was fine in chestnut-coloured satin trimmed with dark brown braid and a turban of the same material which sported a long brown plume fastened with a diamond clip. Lady

Crawford regretted the plume, but had not been able to dissuade her from it. Mrs. Amesbury declared that she had always worn a plume in the evening. She felt it lent her distinction.

But it was Claudia, wearing the unadorned ivory satin, who stood out from the rest. Her hair was swept back from her forehead and caught up in a simple twist which only someone with Claudia's bone structure could have carried off. Her arms were encased in long kidskin gloves, a gift from Lady Crawford, and on her feet were satin slippers which matched her gown, with ribbons that crossed the instep and tied round her trim ankles. A shawl of ivory silk, brought by her brother on his last leave, was draped over her arms. She had steadfastly refused Lady Crawford's offer to loan her jewels suitable to the occasion and wore only a single strand of pearls which had belonged to her mother, but she had placed a single ivory rose in her hair.

Lady Crawford timed their arrival nicely. There was, of course, a vast crush in the streets before Waterford House, rendered worse by the onlookers who came to gape at the gentry, but most of the guests had arrived and they did not have to wait much above twenty minutes to disembark from their carriages. Harry was conscious of a good deal of nervousness—Claudia was sure to be a hit, of course, but he did want her first entry into society to come off perfectly. He wondered if Lady Crawford shared his concern. He suspected that it was not simple benevolence that had led his aunt to agree to present Claudia to the *ton*, but—despite a good deal of careful probing—he had not been able to discover what her motives were.

Waterford House was the largest private home Livia and Claudia had ever seen. It was brilliantly lit both in house and gardens and staffed by footmen wearing haughty expressions, powdered wigs, and livery of red ochre and gold. Not one of them was under six feet tall. They must order them by the gross, Livia thought.

She found herself in a large circular entrance hall paved with white Italian marble and decorated with statues of a vaguely classical cast. At the back of the hall rose a broad marble staircase and at its head stood the Dowager Duchess with her son and daughter.

It was Livia's first duchess and she was curious. Lavinia Howland, a tall, handsome woman with a regal carriage, wore a dress of rose madder satin, the sleeves long to hide the flabby arms of middle-age, the bodice low to show off her still impressive bosom, and the hem thickly encrusted with small brilliants. Livia thought these could not possibly be diamonds, but Lady Crawford, who should know, later assured her that they were. The duchess' fingers were liberally covered with jewels, and her neck and ears were hung with the famous Waterford diamonds, which would some day belong to her son's wife.

George Howland, Duke of Waterford, had inherited his mother's good looks and something of her bearing, tempered by the more easy going nature of his deceased father. His sister Marianne, just eighteen, was a perfect replica of their mother. Already she had formidable presence. She was reputed to be the catch of the Season, and well she might, for in addition to 60,000 pounds, she possessed considerable personal attractions. She had pale skin, good teeth, and eyes of a deep blue set under carefully arched brows. Her hair was pale yellow and mostly her own. It was done up in scores of tiny ringlets that framed her face, a long curl falling over her left shoulder. She was dressed in a fine French silk of the palest pink with scalloped flounces halfway up the skirt. Silk roses of a darker hue trimmed the neck and sleeves and a coronet of small pink roses from the famed Waterford hothouses adorned her hair.

The duchess acknowledged Mrs. Royce with a brief nod, but paused somewhat longer over Miss Neville, an odd look on her face. Harry looked from Marianne's pale prettiness to Claudia's vibrant beauty, then met Francesca's eyes. Francesca was too well bred to display surprise, but Harry controlled himself with effort. He knew now what Lady Crawford had intended.

Marianne greeted the Neville sisters with a fixed smile. It was her brother, the duke, who really seemed to see them, and though his manners were rigidly correct, Livia fancied his eyes lingered on Claudia for a moment before he turned to greet Lady Francesca.

Jeremy Warkworth emerged from a knot of people at the entrance to the ballroom. "My dear Miss Neville, I had about given you up. The quadrille will be forming this quarter hour. You have not forgotten, have you?" he continued anxiously. "Pray do let me help you to enter, it's already a sad crush." He offered Claudia his arm, but it was Nicholas who effectively parted the crowd and led them to seats at the far side of the ballroom. Jeremy hovered near Claudia's chair, fearful lest she be snatched from him.

The Neville sisters looked about with unabashed interest. The ballroom was draped with pink silk, the exact shade, Livia guessed, of Marianne's dress. It lined the walls and hung in great swags from the ceiling where it was caught up by large rosettes of a deeper tone. Crystal chandeliers shed their brilliance over the room. White pillars were ranged against the walls and on each stood a crystal vase filled with the Waterford pink Chinas, an exquisite rose, though lacking in scent. At the end, under the musicians' gallery, a trellised bower had been erected enclosing gilt chairs for the favoured few and a somewhat larger armchair intended, no doubt, to enthrone the duchess.

Francesca and Lady Crawford had both been stopped by acquaintances. Harry had gone in search of Jack, Nicholas was speaking to Melbrooke, and Jeremy Warkworth was monopolizing Claudia, so Livia found herself endeavouring to satisfy Letitia Amesbury's genealogical curiosity.

"Royce? One of the Devonshire Royces? I knew old Sir John when I was a girl—he was much addicted to hunting, unfortunately—and of course he liked his port, but I think the line died out, there was a second or third cousin who inherited, but on the female side, so the name was changed. Odd that your husband was still called Royce, but perhaps I don't know all the collateral branches." She paused to open her fan, while Livia searched her memory for what little she knew about her husband.

"It was a different family, I think, ma'am. He was from the north. My father's family was also from Yorkshire." Here she was on safer ground.

"But of course, and the two families knew each other. So much more suitable, I think, that way there are no unpleasant surprises. One of my oldest friends, Jane Chester, her father arranged a most brilliant match, not at all to her liking since she had formed quite a *tendre* for a young man on the neighboring estate, and then there was madness in the family and she quite retired from the world, but fortunately there were no children and when he died she went abroad and married a Frenchman, and you can see what all that led to."

"Waterloo?" Livia was tempted to say, but instead she rose and politely excused herself. The quadrille was forming and she wanted a better view. Jeremy must stand higher in society than she had supposed, for he led Claudia to the group which included Marianne and her brother.

Waterford and Marianne were an unusually handsome pair and Marianne, the fixed smile still on her face, moved with considerable grace. The night was to be her triumph and she had a right to see herself as the prize jewel in a setting created expressly for her. Claudia and Warkworth, both dark and of a height, offered a sharp contrast to the blond ducal pair.

Afterwards Livia found she could not recall the other dancers who made up the set. What stayed in her mind was the image of the two couples as they moved through *Le Pantalon* and *L'Été* and the other figures of the dance. Marianne was a lovely girl but was surrounded, Livia decided, by entirely too much pink. The jewel was lost in its setting. Claudia stood out in sharp relief, whether moving with the enchanted Warkworth or, more strongly, when the dance brought her into contact with the handsome Waterford. The duke's eyes, Livia noted, strayed to Claudia frequently and Marianne's smile grew even more fixed. Livia heard someone murmur, "Quite charming," but could not tell whether the speaker referred to Marianne, Claudia, or the scene at large.

Lord Melbrooke joined Livia and pointed out some of the political figures in the room. Livia's eyes returned to the Foreign Minister, Lord Castlereagh, who was standing in conversation with several other middle-aged men of serious mien. "He's handsome," she said, "but I do not like his eyes—he must be a very unhappy man."

"He's a dangerous one. That's Lord Sidmouth on his right, the Home Secretary."

"And the younger man, the dark one with the Mephistophelian air?"

"Oliver Merriman. Very intelligent and quite as formidable as Mephisto. I will present him to you, if you like, you might find him amusing." He paused, apparently feeling some further explanation was necessary. "Castlereagh and Sidmouth are in the Opposition. Merriman is a Whig, a member of my own party, though not one of our set. I should perhaps warn you that he's something of a rival of Nicholas Warwick's."

Livia regarded Oliver Merriman with increased interest. "I see."

Lord Melbrooke, who disliked discussing a colleague behind his back and was loath in any case to talk about the fragmented state of his own party, turned the conversation. "I am sorry your situation does not allow you to dance. You are surely too young to spend the evening watching others enjoy themselves."

"Oh, but I am quite amused," Livia assured him. "I love watching people and making up extravagant stories about their lives. You must not feel I want entertainment. I would like to see you dance yourself."

"I would gladly dance with your sister. She is quite lovely."

"Then you must engage her. Claudia," Livia said as the quadrille ended and Jeremy restored her sister to her, "here is Lord Melbrooke who would like to dance with you and has been too diffident to ask."

"It would give me great pleasure," Melbrooke murmured.

"It would give me great pleasure as well. Mr. Warkworth, I have enjoyed our dance so very much, but I must not dance with you again, I am told it is not at all proper." She dismissed him with an enchanting smile and Jeremy retired, his head full of bad poetry. "Lord Melbrooke, I am promised to the younger Mr. Warwick for the two next and then to his friend Jack Newfield." She studied her card, which as yet had few entries. "Then the elder Mr. Warwick has asked me for the first waltz, but I would be most happy to give you the second."

Harry arrived to claim her for the country dance just then forming and Livia lost sight of her sister for a while. She returned to Mrs. Amesbury whom, she feared, she had been neglecting, but found her happily occupied with several acquaintances. Livia breathed a sigh of relief and was borne off by Lady Crawford who wished to greet some of her own friends. These included several of the patronesses of Almack's, that holy of holies for a young woman who wished to meet eligible men. Nothing was said at this point about procuring admission for Mrs. Royce and her sister, but Lady Crawford assured Livia that the matter would be taken care of later. "I'm sure we can rely on Emily Cowper—Emily Lamb that was—she's a good friend of Francesca's and a thoroughly nice woman, though I'm not sure she's happy in her marriage. Lord Palmerston, the gentleman standing by the pillar over there, is one of her most ardent admirers. He sits in the Commons, but it's an Irish title, so it's all right."

Livia caught occasional glimpses of Claudia dancing with Harry and then Jack and then with several strange men who appeared to have managed introductions. "She will do very well," Lady Crawford told Livia. "Her card is already filled, and I have had no end of questions about her." Lady Crawford's eyes went from Marianne to Claudia and then to the duchess, ensconced in her floral bower. Only someone who knew the dowager duchess well would have recognized the signs, but her grace was definitely disturbed. Lady Crawford permitted herself a small smile. She had known the duchess for over thirty years. Lavinia Shaftesbury she had been then, a tall, striking girl with a large fortune and an overdeveloped sense of her own importance. The families had been acquainted for years and the two girls, much together, were supposed on that score to be friends. They had been mock rivals for the attentions of a score of young men until Lavinia, with an eye to the future, made a dead set at Arthur Howland, eldest son of the Duke of Waterford.

Lady Crawford had behaved beautifully throughout— Arthur was a trifle slow for her taste, though quite sharp enough for Lavinia—and left an amusing houseparty a week early to give Lavinia a clear field. And had Lavinia been grateful? No. She had excluded her friend Isabel from the bridal party in favour of one of Arthur's homely cousins, patronized her insufferably through the years and—the cut that really rankled—destroyed an elaborate ball, a month in the planning, by making off with the minor Hungarian royalty that was the reason for its existence. Lady Crawford retaliated by flirting shamelessly with Arthur whenever they met, but since Lavinia didn't seem to notice and Arthur bored her, this was far from satisfactory.

Then at last, in Oxford of all places, she had found the chance to pierce that self-satisfied armour. The plan had come to her five minutes after she entered the Nevilles' house and saw Claudia's blazing beauty, undimmed by her somber black dress. Returning to London, Lady Crawford had called on her "dear Lavinia" and begged—yes, actually begged—for cards of invitation to be sent to her friends Miss Neville and Mrs. Royce. Lavinia had of course obliged her "dear Isabel," never dreaming until that satisfying moment on the stairs what potential explosives she was allowing into her house.

Isabel Crawford was a very happy woman.

After his dance with Claudia, Jack would have cheerfully remained in the ballroom. He liked the company of women and, as he told Harry, there were "lots of devilish pretty girls about." His friend was made of sterner stuff. Considering he had done more than his duty in partnering Claudia and fetching her a glass of lemonade, he dragged Jack off to an adjoining room in which refreshments were laid out.

"I say," Jack confided to Harry, "Claudia's making a hit. Always said she'd make a hit. Know what Warkworth said?"

"What?"

"Said she had eyes like the winter sky after a storm."

Harry stared at his friend in disbelief. "Must have been foxed," he declared. "Besides, her eyes aren't grey, they're brown. Brown can't be stormy."

"Well, can't say they look like a muddy road. Mustn't be literal. Use license, that's what poets do."

"I still say he was foxed."

"No time. Mean to say, been hanging around watching Claudia since he danced with her. No time to get foxed."

Harry sighed. Jeremy Warkworth had been a ripping upper classman only a year ago. Sad to see such a downfall.

Guessing his friend's thoughts, Jack nodded. "I know. Pity. Still, if he had to go, he couldn't do better than Claudia. Fine girl. Have some champagne." He retrieved two glasses from a passing footman's tray and handed one to Harry. The Waterford cellars were famous and they did not stint their guests.

Jack drained his glass. "Thing is, there's Lady Francesca."

"Oh, Francesca's all right." Despite his reservations about his sister-in-law—Francesca was a clever woman, but lacked the warmth and gentleness he so admired in Claudia—Harry was loyal to his family. He looked suddenly at Jack. "Why are you worrying about Francesca?"

"Not her. Claudia. The duke likes her."

"Francesca? Of course he does. He's been hanging around her these last five months. He danced with her tonight. The waltz. That proves it."

Jack was distracted. "Lady Francesca is a good dancer. Anyone would like to waltz with her." He took another glass of champagne and recalled his previous point. "Claudia. The duke likes Claudia."

"How do you know?"

"Asked her to dance and she turned him down."

"Turned him down?" Claudia was too agreeable to turn anyone down, least of all a duke.

"Well, had to. Card all filled up. Waited too long—lots of other fellows before him. So he asked to take her down to supper and she said yes."

Even Harry was alive to the favour conferred by this invitation. He considered it while he drained his glass and reached for another.

Jack went on. "Should have asked Lady Francesca. Cut like that, she's sure to mind. Public and all, you know. Not good form."

"Oh, that's all right," Harry reassured him. "Waterford asked Francesca first. She'd already promised to go down with that fellow with the eyebrows—what's his name? Merriman."

Jack was relieved that the proprieties had been observed, but he was curious about Lady Francesca's behaviour. "Why didn't she wait for the duke? Must have known he'd ask her."

"She likes new people. Gets bored a lot otherwise. Besides," Harry added with a rare flash of insight, "I think she doesn't want the duke to be too sure of her. She's a clever woman."

Jack nodded and they solemnly toasted Lady Francesca with fresh glasses of champagne.

"All the same," Jack said, "one thing for Waterford to not be too sure of her. Another for her to not be too sure of him. Still don't think she'll like it."

Before Harry could reply, young Ralph Jefferson put his head round the door. "I say, splendid creature, Harry. How'd you come to meet her?"

"Oxford," Jack answered for him.

"Oh. Family from around there?"

"That's it," Harry said, contriving to kick Jack in the ankle. There was no point in concealing that the Nevilles were daughters of an Oxford scholar, but there was equally no point in advertising the fact.

"Lucky dog," said Geoffrey Middleton, following Ralph into the room. "I never met girls like that when I was up at Oxford. Everyone's talking about her."

"Never met any of that branch of the family before," Jefferson said.

"They travelled a lot," Harry explained. "Rome mostly."

"Oh, that accounts for it. The sister's a widow, isn't she?"

"That's right. Married to a soldier."

"Whirlwind romance," Jack supplied. "Friend of her brother's."

"She met him when he was on leave," Harry said, his imagination beginning to soar. "They were married after two weeks. Then he went back to the continent and was killed."

Jefferson and Middleton looked sympathetic. Middleton asked if he had died in action.

"Waterloo," Jack said. "Splendid hero."

"Decorated for bravery," Harry elaborated.

"Saved the general's life," Jack added.

"Wellington?" asked Jefferson in awe.

"No, no," said Harry hastily.

"Some other general," explained Jack, taking more champagne.

Harry was not to be outdone. "Did you hear about the time he was sent behind the enemy lines to rescue some of our men?"

Their companions, the number of which had grown in the last few minutes, shook their heads. Harry took another glass of champagne and began the story.

The Duchess of Waterford surveyed the supper room with satisfaction. The tables were covered with fine linen damask, set with pre-Revolution Sèvres porcelain, and lit by perfumed wax tapers in girandole-candlesticks of cut flint-glass. Footmen in the Waterford livery passed deftly between the tables, carrying platters of lobster patties, aspic of chicken, thinly sliced ham, and a variety of whips and jellies. The duchess loathed the undignified spectacle of her guests scrabbling for food laid out on serving tables.

As was her right, Marianne sat at a table somewhat larger than the rest, surrounded by a dozen or so young men of impeccable lineage though some, the duchess feared, had pockets to let. Still, it was not money Marianne would need and her mother's heart rejoiced to see her daughter beautiful, confident, and the centre of attention.

Well, one of the centres. The duchess turned with a frown to the table where her son was playing the gallant with that dark girl in the plain dress. There was a constant coming and going around them that distracted the eye from Marianne's table. A pretty girl and all very well in her place, but that place was not at Marianne's ball. Really, men failed to understand these things. For her son to distinguish the little nobody by taking her in to supper was beyond belief. The duchess had forgotten the girl's name, but she remembered how she came to be invited. Her lips tightened. Isabel Crawford could not be faulted for having a pretty young friend, heaven knew there seemed to be an unusually large number of them around, but this particular friend, with her dark, almost foreign look, stood out in a way that Lavinia Howland found most undesirable. There had been a sister, too, she recalled. She sought her out among the throng that crowded the room and made movement hazardous. There, at a table in a far corner with Letitia Amesbury and Mrs. Amesbury's friend, Lady Augusta

Harleigh, and Warwick and Melbrooke. She looked unremark-
able enough and seemed to have little to say for herself. Hardly
worth Isabel's attention, the duchess would have thought,
though her quondam friend was known for her freakish whims.

A footman appeared unobtrusively at the duchess' side. The
Regent and a group of his friends had arrived, and she hastily
left the room to greet them.

Livia was indeed having little to say for herself. She had
watched Claudia's progress with great pleasure, from the early
dances with their few acquaintances, to the growing crowd
begging for introductions, to her distinction by Waterford.
Claudia was smiling happily at the duke, but she had smiled
equally happily when dancing with Harry and Jack and Jeremy
Warkworth. The evening was, Livia supposed, a triumph, but
she wished she did not have this small feeling of discontent. An
unwelcome thought crossed her mind. Could she be jealous?
She gave it some thought and decided in the affirmative. Of
course she was jealous. Whatever she had said to Claudia back
in Oxford, it was dreadful to sit soberly on the sidelines when
her whole body longed to be dancing. It was the price she had
agreed to pay when she had insisted that only one of them
would be brought out. So jealousy was normal and expected
and not the real reason for her unease.

She turned back to the conversation. On one side, Mrs.
Amesbury and her friend were gossiping of past entertainments. On the other, Warwick and Melbrooke were engaged in
heated conversation about Lord Sidmouth's latest outrage. It
was Warwick, of course. Livia had been uncomfortable ever
since their meeting at dinner, and his tacit decision to ignore
their former meeting, while the act of a gentleman, did not
reassure her. For Claudia's sake, she did not want him to think
badly of her and, for Claudia's sake, she resolved to confront
him this evening.

Her chance came as their party returned to the ballroom

after supper. Melbrooke stopped to speak to an acquaintance, and Nicholas was left to shepherd the ladies back to their seats. "Mr. Warwick," Livia said in a low voice, "could you walk with me a little. I have a few words I would like to say to you."

"I am at your service." Nicholas' eyes were veiled. He saw his aunt comfortably situated and walked down the ballroom with Livia, drawing her into a window embrasure at the other end of the room. He waited for her to begin.

"Mr. Warwick, I must apologize for my behaviour the other night. You will understand that I was greatly overset and perhaps did not express myself as I ought.'

"On the contrary. I am sorry if my words gave you pain. Your young charge had been difficult. I confess," he added, with a rueful smile, "I would have liked her to show just a little more gratitude. She did not seem to understand the danger she was in."

"You certainly had my gratitude, at least." Livia's eyes held a note of mischief. "Though it may have been difficult to comprehend."

"I am sure my own words contributed to the misunderstanding. I would not have spoken to you so, if—" He paused, suddenly embarrassed.

"If you had not taken me for the housekeeper?"

"Precisely." He smiled again. "Though that is hardly an excuse. I pride myself on never speaking unjustly to anyone, but I fear it is false pride. Of late my temper appears quite uncertain." He paused. "I take it the girl is none the worse for her experience?"

"My sister is quite well, sir."

"Good God!" The exclamation was unintended, but Nicholas was clearly shaken. He recalled the child's torn dress, muddy boots, and unkempt hair. He suspected the Nevilles had little money, but Mrs. Royce dressed with some propriety and Miss Neville with real elegance.

Livia had no trouble reading his thoughts. She had been feeling far more charitable toward him these last few minutes, but his expression put her once again on the defensive. She tried to pass it off. "Diana is used to walking. At home she went regularly for long walks in the country, and she is unused to city ways. We have spoken to her, of course, and she will be more careful in the future."

"Surely you will not allow her to roam about unattended?"

"No, she understands it is different here. But does it not seem unfair? She is a healthy girl and detests being shut up indoors. Doesn't Harry? Don't you?"

Nicholas stiffened. "That is not at all the same thing."

"But that is what is so unfair! Diana is wild to see London. She has an immense curiosity and an eye for the novel. She draws quite beautifully and loves to sketch from life. She has twice the energy of the rest of us. To doom her to trailing after us would only make her rebellious. Indeed, I think young girls would be far less troublesome to their elders if they were given more freedom, not less."

If Nicholas thought of his own daughter and her timid governess he could not be blamed, but the thought did not improve his temper. "I believe, ma'am, our first obligation is to see that those entrusted to our care are not exposed to harm."

"Even at the risk of their being stifled?"

"I hardly think learning the rules for good behaviour can be described as stifling."

"Indeed. Do you not sometimes feel stifled yourself by all this?" She gestured at the silk-hung ballroom behind them.

Nicholas was startled by her intensity. Livia coloured, then said quickly, "I beg your pardon, that was unforgiveable. I did not intend to speak slightingly of your friends, and I have certainly enjoyed myself immensely tonight."

Nicholas doubted this last was true. He spoke gently. "Perhaps you are chafing under the requirements of your mourning. I have always thought it a heavy burden when one is young. I know it was so for Francesca."

Livia was silent for a moment. His sympathy had nearly undone her, but she felt he did not yet understand. "True, I do

71

find the rules irksome, and often nonsensical, but I know what they are and I have no difficulty in living by them. Diana is different. By and large she behaves sensibly, but it is her own sense that she follows. I am not sure but that, for her, she is right."

"Then I think, Mrs. Royce," Nicholas said with a touch of his earlier austerity, "that you had better keep a close watch upon her. If she does not have the control within herself, it will have to be supplied from without."

Not by me, Livia thought. At least, not in that way. Diana was sensible enough to handle herself with care, and Warwick should know that Livia would never willfully neglect her. She resented his assumption of superior wisdom, and she found it hard to reconcile his seeming arrogance with his moments of genuine kindness. They said little more, and parted with some dissatisfaction on both sides.

Nicholas' dissatisfaction was soon pushed to the back of his mind. He had not seen Harry since early in the evening and thought it prudent to seek him out. He found him in a small closet, being very sick into a silver basin.

"Rather made a cake of yourself, haven't you," Nicholas said as Harry emerged from the basin with a damp forehead and cravat askew.

"Yes, rather. I say, I'm sorry, sir, I didn't mean—that is, it was just the fellows and we got to talking and my glass always seemed to be full. I didn't want to make a scene . . ." His voice trailed off. He was clearly miserable.

"Don't refine too much upon it. I daresay you aren't the only one so afflicted. I think it might be a good idea if you put in an appearance by Aunt Letty, just to see how she's doing. When you're quite recovered and fit to be seen. And if I were you, I wouldn't take anything more to drink."

"Yes, sir. I mean, no sir. I mean, thanks awfully, Nicholas."

Nicholas smiled, and returned to the ballroom. Young scamp. He'd have to learn. Still, he was a good lad. He stopped suddenly, recalling his conversation with Mrs. Royce. What would he have done if it had been Genny? Damned woman, of course it was different with girls. He strode on, looking for Mrs. Amesbury. He'd have to warn her about Harry.

At two-o'clock the ballroom was still crowded. Faces were flushed, laughter was louder, and the dancers seemed less decorous. At two-thirty the crowd was beginning to thin and guests were lining up to take their leave of the duchess. Her daughter, an indefatigable dancer, was still on the floor. At three Lady Crawford sought out Nicholas and told him it was time to round up their party. "It doesn't do, you know, to stay too late. Much better to have people wondering where you have gone than when you are going to leave."

Claudia informed a crestfallen young Dunstable that she would be unable to dance with him, but to console him said he could escort her to her carriage and yes, he could call, but not tomorrow, that is, not today, but the day after. Jeremy Warkworth, who had been hovering nearby, looked so downcast that Claudia assured him that he would also be welcome. This seemed to offend Dunstable, but Claudia reconciled him with a brilliant smile. She was in charity with all the world and, as she took her leave of the duchess, failed to notice the distinctly unfriendly glint in that lady's eye. The Regent had complimented her grace on the evening's entertainment and informed her that her daughter was a "damned handsome young woman," then spoiled the effect by asking about the dark girl in white and actually getting himself presented to her.

Lord Melbrooke said his goodbyes in the great driveway before the house, claiming that he needed a walk in the cold early morning air to recover from the heat of the ballroom. With an imperious hand, Lady Crawford waved away Dunstable, Warkworth, and several other young men who had collected about Claudia and bundled the Nevilles into her carriage. She was longing for private conversation.

In the Warwick carriage, things were quieter. Mrs. Amesbury had fallen asleep in a corner of the carriage as soon

73

as the horses were underway. Nicholas was tired and disturbed by the Home Secretary's behaviour; Mrs. Royce had upset him and Harry had been something of an ass. Francesca seemed to be having her own private joke, and though Nicholas was in no mood to ask to share it, Harry appeared to understand what it was about.

"York and Lancaster." Francesca went off into a peal of laughter. Harry joined in. They laughed all the way to South Audley Street. As the carriage pulled up in front of Warwick House, Nicholas' curiosity got the better of him.

"All right," he said repressively, "I've endured this mummery for the past quarter-hour. Either stop it at once or tell me what it's about. What about York and Lancaster?"

"The white rose and the red," Francesca explained. "Miss Neville and Marianne."

Though Marianne's roses had been pink and Claudia had worn one of ivory, Nicholas saw the analogy. He didn't think it was particularly funny. He said so.

Harry choked. "The duchess. Her face—"

"I am not aware that her face is particularly amusing. Not to my taste perhaps, but I believe she is accounted quite handsome."

"But don't you see," Harry tried to explain, "she cut her out. Everyone should have been looking at Marianne, and everyone was looking at Claudia."

Nicholas, who had noted the sharp contrast between Marianne and Harry's friend, caught Harry's drift. "I see. York supplants Lancaster. That's one of the vagaries of social life. No young lady can have everything her own way."

"But she planned it. You know," Harry was suddenly sober, "she must have known from the beginning that this is what would happen."

"Who? Miss Neville?"

"No. Aunt Isabel."

Nicholas was brought up short by this imputation of duplicity. His lips relaxed into the ghost of a smile. He looked at his sister-in-law for confirmation. Francesca nodded.

"Well," said Livia, in the privacy of Claudia's bedchamber, "whom have you fixed upon?"

"Fixed upon?" Claudia met her sister's eyes in her dressing-table mirror, her brows rising. "My word, you are previous. Who may have fixed upon me? I shall certainly wait until I am asked."

"Nonsense. You could have any of them you choose. It needs only a trifle of demonstrated partiality. You are much too nice to everyone."

"If I am, it is because I like everyone. Well," she added, noting her sister's skeptical look, "not at all in that way."

"Did you like the duke?"

"Well, of course. He was most kind. Perhaps a little formal after all the boys, but that was something of a relief."

"Kind!" Livia exploded. "Kindness has very little to do with it. You are a beautiful woman."

"Yes," Claudia acknowledged. "And being with a beautiful woman increases a man's consequence. It makes him feel so much better about himself. And when they are attentive to me, I feel beautiful in return. Consequently, I have had a wholly delightful evening." She stretched her arms over her head. "The Warwicks are charming, don't you think?"

"Would you have expected Harry's family to be anything else?" Livia returned lightly.

"Seriously," said Claudia. "The little girl is adorable. Mrs. Amesbury's a bit of a babbler, but she's good-hearted and she means well. And didn't you like Lady Francesca?"

There was the slightest of pauses. "I liked the fact that she liked you," Livia said.

Claudia turned her head, her hair, half unpinned, streaming over one shoulder, and looked curiously at her sister. Normally they found themselves in complete agreement about people. "But she was so obliging. Of course, she's a good deal more modish than we are, but don't you think—"

"I think," said Livia, "that she's an intelligent woman who's easily bored and is looking for anything that will amuse her."

"Well," Claudia said, with one of her surprising descents into the prosaic, "if I amuse her, so much the better. Lady Crawford says it's the mothers and sisters who really count."

Livia smiled and let the matter drop. She picked up her reticule and gloves, which she had set down on Claudia's bed, and moved toward the door. "I've told them not to wake us in the morning. Sleep well. It was a wonderful success."

But Claudia, who took success less seriously, was still preoccupied with the Warwicks. "You liked Mr. Warwick, didn't you?" Her tone implied that Livia could hardly have failed to do so.

Livia looked at her sister for a moment, then turned the door handle. "Goodnight," she said firmly.

Chapter 5

The following day Livia and Claudia breakfasted at noon. Diana had left a note asking them particularly to be in for tea since she hadn't talked with them for an age. Her sisters, who had given little thought to Diana in the past few days, silently acknowledged their guilt. Sandringham poured coffee and inquired what he should do about the flowers. There were quite a number of them, he said, laying down a tray with several cards and notes.

Most of the flowers were roses in varying shades of white, though a bunch of violets had been left by someone named Skeffington—Claudia said she could not recall him, but she supposed they had been introduced. Jeremy had sent a single ivory rose along with three very bad stanzas comparing it unfavourably to Claudia's appearance the evening before. Dunstable's modest offering was accompanied by an impassioned letter, while Waterford's more opulent bouquet included a few lines reminding Claudia of her promise to drive with him the next day. A bunch of early jonquils proved to be from Lord Melbrooke who, with rare tact, had sent them to Livia as well as to her sister. There was also a note sent round an hour before by Lady Crawford informing them that she would call for them at two. "For now is the time to be seen," she wrote, "and if the day is fine we will drive in the park.

Depend upon it, you will find many beaux eager to resume their acquaintance with you."

As Lady Crawford predicted, the day saw a renewal of interest by a number of Claudia's admirers of the previous evening. In addition, she was introduced to the Dowager Marchioness of Langdon, who had noted her with approval in the Waterford ballroom, and to Lady Myerson who, owing to a recent falling out with the duchess, had not been invited but who boasted a large acquaintance. The marchioness was driving with her granddaughters, two shy but pretty girls who were quite taken by the dark beauty of whom everyone was speaking. "Fortunately they're both fair," Lady Crawford noted, for she encouraged the connection.

The following days saw an increasing number of invitations arriving with the morning post. Claudia, and of course her elder sister, were asked to routs, soirées, evenings of cards, evenings of music, evenings of dancing, and even to a masquerade which Lady Crawford told them on no account to attend. "You will have plenty of time to amuse yourself after you are married," she counseled. "Only the very rich can afford to flout convention without loss of face." Soon the Nevilles were caught in the happy dilemma of refusing invitations or of attending several entertainments in one evening.

On their rare afternoons at home, Claudia's growing court of admirers haunted the house. Warkworth was faithful, as was Dunstable, and even shy Skeffington made himself known. Sir Everard Huntley, who had estates in Derbyshire and was on the prowl for a wife, was a frequent caller, as was Lord Seaton. Seaton, though handsome and amusing, was unfortunately impecunious and Lady Crawford warned Claudia against him.

Harry and Jack dropped by several mornings a week and the sisters dined frequently with the Warwicks. Diana, despite Nicholas' specific request, steadfastly refused to go into society and told Livia to plead her youth and inexperience if she was unwilling to tell the truth and plead her bad manners.

Claudia had clearly edged out Marianne at the ball and appeared likely to do so for the remainder of the Season. A wag dubbed the ball the "War of the Roses" and it caught on. A clever mind with too little to occupy it pointed out that the man who had put the white rose of York on the English throne was Richard Neville, Earl of Warwick, sometimes called the Kingmaker. Nicholas Warwick sadly refused to behave like a Kingmaker, at least where Claudia was concerned—the title really should have gone to Lady Crawford. Someone else, remarking that George (Duke of Waterford) appeared to be torn between his attraction to Miss Neville and his loyalty to his sister Marianne, said that he was reminded of the way the fifteenth century George (Duke of Clarence) had shuttled between York and Lancaster. Bets were laid on how long it would take Waterford's mother to reclaim him.

All of this put Claudia more in demand than ever and, as Diana put it, elevated their rank, for Claudia now added two earls and a marquis to her entourage. Claudia advised Diana to dampen her hopes. "I don't doubt that I shall settle tolerably well in the end, but these attentions signify nothing. I am a novelty and shall be replaced the moment another fresh face makes an appearance." Diana snorted, but held her tongue. Claudia treated her beauty as a useful commodity, much like having twenty thousand pounds in the funds, but realized that its cash equivalent was likely to weigh heavier in the balance.

Vouchers for Almack's finally arrived, Emily Cowper having persuaded her fellow patronesses to support the Nevilles' application. Before their first venture into the Wednesday night balls, Livia and Claudia dined at Warwick House. Lady Crawford, Lady Francesca, and Lord Melbrooke were going to Almack's as well. As they were about to leave, Francesca urged Nicholas to come with them. He declined, pleading the press of business. On Francesca's insistence he said he would be hanged if he'd spend the evening stifled by propriety just to please her. Something about his choice of words seemed to disturb him. Avoiding Livia's eyes, he turned quickly and

79

apologized to Claudia, saying that on any other occasion he would be more than happy to partner her.

He was almost tempted to do so on this occasion, for Claudia looked unusually lovely. She was wearing a dress of green sarcenet (cut, as any woman could have told him, on the same lines as the ivory gown she had worn the night of the ball) with an overdress of a pale green spider gauze. Francesca, who had ascertained Claudia's choice of garment the previous day, was in a pale blue French silk shot with silver that emphasized her fair colouring without making her look insipid. Nicholas wondered briefly if Waterford would attend tonight and how he would conduct himself toward the two women to whom he was paying court.

Nicholas was aware of Waterford's interest in the beautiful Miss Neville and thought that Francesca might have reason to be annoyed. In any case, he would have expected her to avoid Miss Neville, for Francesca had little taste for her own sex, finding their preoccupations trivial and their conversation tedious. But to Nicholas' surprise, Francesca had sought out Miss Neville's company. Perhaps, he thought, she found it prudent to keep her competitor under observation.

When he had chaffed her about her new friend, Francesca said it would be amusing to observe the lovely Claudia's fate on the Marriage Mart. Could her beauty really overcome her lack of fortune and family connections? Nicholas accused her of want of feeling. "Not at all," Francesca told him. "The Nevilles know what they are about, and they're quite able to take care of themselves."

Nicholas thought this certainly applied to Mrs. Royce, but her sister seemed made of softer stuff. Miss Neville was everything he thought a woman ought to be. He was thinking of her warm interest in other people, though he was not indifferent to her beauty. Nonetheless, his aversion to Almack's kept him at home. He much preferred to talk to Miss Neville in his own drawing room.

*   *   *

Waterford did not find Almack's stifling and was already present when Lady Crawford's party arrived. It was the first time the duke had addressed Claudia and Francesca together, and Livia was laying silent odds on the one to whom he would give first preference. She turned to Lord Melbrooke and saw a speculative gleam in his eye. "I will lay you a shilling," she said in a low voice, "that the honour goes to Lady Francesca. She has the prior claim and I am sure his grace is perfectly correct in such matters."

"Done," said Melbrooke who rated Claudia's attractions as superior. "Besides," he said with an engaging smile, "Waterford is a great catch and has learned to be cautious. He's careful to not be too particular in his attentions to any one woman."

Livia, however, was right as Melbrooke acknowledged later by slipping a shilling into her black-gloved hand. Waterford danced the correct two dances with Lady Francesca with all the appearance of being thoroughly content with himself and his partner. Melbrooke was forced to admit that they made an unusually handsome pair—Francesca managed to endow Waterford with greater dash than he usually exhibited—but when the duke later danced with Miss Neville, Melbrooke judged this pairing to be equally attractive.

Though limited to sitting on the fringe of the dance floor or strolling about the room, Livia did not find the evening at all tedious for by now she had a number of acquaintances. On one of her perambulations she came across Lady Sefton, to whom she had been introduced at Waterford House, and made her a courteous bow. Lady Sefton reached out and laid a hand on her arm. "I had not realized, my dear. Such a sad loss. But I know how proud you must be of him."

Livia stared at her blankly for an instant, remembered she was a widow, and murmured a disjointed reply. She thought that Lady Sefton was only being kind and meant that poor John—it was John, wasn't it?—had died for his country. But when Lord Desmond, a very high stickler, informed Livia that he would have considered it an honour to call such a man his friend, and young Julia Claremont said in awed tones that she

81

hoped her own marriage would be as romantic as Mrs. Royce's, Livia was convinced that someone had been talking. Being no fool, she had a fairly good idea of who this might be and resolved to confront them at the earliest opportunity.

Opportunity came the next day when the culprits paid an early morning call in Charles Street. They were going back to Oxford, but would be down again in June after Trinity Term.

Claudia was genuinely sorry to see them go, and even Diana allowed that she would miss them. Livia admitted to no such feelings. "For I am not at all sure we won't pay a price for your friendship," she declared with mock severity. Harry and Jack were outraged and demanded an explanation. Livia gave them one. "It has come to my attention that my late husband has acquired a decidedly heroic character. I am sure I never gave him credit for it. I have been ignoring the sympathetic glances and the whispers—after all, I am young to be a widow—but Lord Desmond was really the end of enough." She retailed her encounters of the previous evening.

Harry and Jack made no attempt to deny the accusation, but exchanged guilty glances.

"We were going to tell you," Harry said sheepishly. "I'd no idea it had gone this far."

"At the ball, you see," Jack explained. "Accident. Sort of."

"I see." Livia drew a deep breath. "Well, if it isn't too much trouble, you might tell me exactly what my past history has been. Just to avoid any future embarrassment." She looked from Jack to Harry.

"He was decorated for bravery," Harry said. "He charged up a hill to save his men's lives. Got wounded."

"But saved his men?" Livia was interested.

"No, lost them all. Still, it was a splendid try."

"More," Jack admitted. "Saved a general's life."

"Oh, no," Livia moaned.

"Not Wellington," Jack hastened to reassure her.

"I should hope not," Claudia declared. "Really, it is too bad of you. Whatever possessed you to embroider so? Livia might

82

have been caught giving you the lie."

"It can't be helped now," Livia said. "I seem to remember Miss Claremont telling me something about my—what did she call it?—my romantic courtship. Surely that has very little to do with saving a general."

The culprits exchanged glances again. "Not quite myself at the time," Harry said.

"Hasty affair," Jack explained. "Met on leave. Off to the battlefield and all that. Married after two weeks."

"And widowed right after," Harry added. "At least you weren't married very long."

"I can't tell you how much you relieve my mind. Is there anything else? I think Lord Desmond mentioned a severe head wound. When exactly was that?"

The young men looked alarmed. "I never said that," Harry protested. "Did you?"

"Not me, old boy. 'Pon my honour. Must have been someone else."

"Do you mean," Livia demanded, "that the whole of London is now convinced that poor John or James or whatever his name is was a hero and there may be any number of stories of his bravery floating about?"

Jack was suddenly struck by a thought. "Ought to have been a hero, Livia. Stands to reason. Shouldn't marry just an ordinary soldier, not good enough for you."

"I'm sorry, Livia." Harry was now becoming alarmed at the ramifications of their story-telling. "We wouldn't have done it if it wasn't for—"

"We didn't mean—"

"We only told Middleton and Jefferson—"

"Never dreamed that—devilish queer business—"

Livia finally ushered them out to their waiting carriage, a grave look on her face, but when she came back into the breakfast parlour she looked at her sisters and burst into laughter. "I suppose," she said between gasps, "that all the preposterous plots in romances are thought up by undergraduates. Oh, dear!"

Claudia giggled. "It really is quite wretched of them."

"Quite wretched," Livia agreed, "but with luck we shan't meet anyone who really knew James."

"John," Diana reminded her. "Anyway, there's nothing we can do about it."

This was true, so Livia dismissed the matter. "I daresay they exaggerated. Poor John will be forgotten within the week."

Diana got up suddenly. "I'm off," she said. Then catching Livia's eye, "It's all right, Jeanie's waiting for me belowstairs." She kissed her sisters and ran out.

Since the night of her rescue by Nicholas Warwick, Diana had settled into a subdued but happy routine. She rose early and, if her sisters were sleeping late, breakfasted in the kitchen and helped Jeanie prepare trays for Livia and Claudia. Jeanie was then free to accompany Diana on her forays into the world beyond Charles Street.

Some days they were entrusted with shopping for Mrs. Fraser. Sometimes Sandringham went with them, bent on an early morning errand for the house. Without his formal attire, Sandringham took on a slightly raffish air. He showed them the markets at Covent Garden, where they browsed among the stalls of the vegetable and flower sellers; he introduced them to his friends, a motley collection of actors, stagehands, printers, pamphleteers, and illustrators, though he was careful to keep them from the more disreputable women of his acquaintance.

Other days they explored on their own. Hyde Park was a favourite, particularly the banks of the Serpentine where they could watch the waterfowl, or the paths where early riders cantered and children ran ahead of their nursemaids. Diana was never without her sketchbook, but—to Jeanie's disappointment—she spent as much time in looking as in drawing. When she did take up a pencil, however, her movements were quick and precise and the scene rendered came wonderfully alive.

Diana was surprised to find that Jeanie had a family not two miles from Charles Street. Of course, she thought, girls in service don't spring full-blown from nowhere. Contrite, she suggested they pay them a visit. Jeanie hesitated, Diana insisted, and an hour later found the two girls in a shabby street off St. Martin's Lane. Jeanie's home was two attic rooms where her mother looked after four younger children and a mother-in-law bedridden with dropsy and did the sewing that supplemented Jeanie's earnings. There did not appear to be a father and Diana did not care to ask.

The visit depressed Diana, but it gave her the opportunity she had been seeking. Jeanie had gone good-naturedly wherever Diana led, but she was inclined to chatter and Diana sometimes found her companionship a burden. Besides, the girl was clearly needed at home. They soon arranged things to their mutual satisfaction. Diana insisted only that they meet each day at four so they could return to Charles Street together. Whatever she did, Diana was never late for tea. It was the one time she could be sure of seeing her sisters.

Diana did not limit herself to street life but also haunted the print-shops—Colnaghi's in Bond Street and Mrs. Humphrey's in St. James', each pane of its bow windows covered by a plain or coloured print. She became acquainted with the work of the great Gillray who had died of drink and madness the year before, though she preferred the witty Cruikshank brothers and especially Rowlandson, whose delicacy of execution was at such odds with the scurrilous nature of his subjects. Later she moved further afield and discovered Ackermann's Library of Fine Arts in The Strand where she could purchase pencils and drawing paper, browse among books, and check out prints and drawings to study at home.

One memorable day she approached Rudolph Ackermann himself and showed him her work. He looked at it without surprise, offered one or two criticisms, then paid her eight shillings for a study of Sandringham's head. It seemed a fortune. Diana knew that she could now make her own way, but was unwilling to share this knowledge with her sisters. It seemed only fair though to tell Sandringham. "It's because you're well-known, that's why he was interested. He didn't want to look at anything else." Sandringham doubted this, but his vanity was touched and he agreed to keep her secret.

She went to Ackermann's two or three afternoons a week, generally arriving about one. On the day of Harry and Jack's departure, she had made a detour to fetch some blue worsted for Mrs. Fraser and was later than she liked. She was hurrying up The Strand when she found herself sprawling just outside the Library entrance.

"You clumsy idiot!" she roared, scrambling for the ball of worsted, her pencils and her sketchbook.

"Oh, I say, are you hurt?" A young man with long brown hair and a long anxious face helped her to her feet. "I'm most frightfully sorry. Is there anything I can do?"

"No," Diana said ungraciously. "Nothing at all." She took the worsted which he was holding out and stalked into the Library, her hair, unloosed from its pins, flying behind her.

The young man ran to join his companion who had gone on ahead. "You might have waited," he said aggrieved.

"Her fault entirely," the other returned in a sulky tone. "She wasn't looking and she's made us late and we'll never get a table now. Stupid little girl."

The young man looked at him in astonishment. "Are you blind?" he exclaimed. "That girl is not a girl. I mean, she's not a little girl. I mean, well, yes, she is little, but, but Paul, did you ever see such splendid hair? She's a veritable Diana!" Henry Ashton had a romantic turn of mind but a good classical education. And that, of course, was how the trouble started.

Henry and Paul had been friends for the past year, Henry's romantic ardours and unrelenting good humour serving as a foil for Paul's moody streaks and periods of intense absorption in his craft. Henry wrote, sometimes seriously. Paul was a painter. His world was narrow and his interests parochial.

Henry considered Paul's talent greater than his own and was generous enough not to resent it.

He took Paul's arm. "Come on, we'll get in at the Old Shepherd. They do a very decent pigeon pie."

In the end, it was Henry who brought Paul and Diana together. His infatuation was rekindled a few days later when he spied the red-haired girl coming out of Ackermann's. He ran after her, tipped his hat, and held out the stub of a well-chewed pencil. "Pardon me, may I return this? I think you dropped it the other day."

Diana stared at him blankly. Then recognition stirred. She looked at the pencil. "No." She shook her head. "Not possibly. I chew mine horizontally." She turned away.

"Oh, I say, don't go. Not yet. I haven't really apologized. We should never have left you without making sure you were all right, but we had an appointment, you see, and the tables were going to be taken and I could tell Paul was going all sulky, but we went to the Old Shepherd instead and the food was ever so much better, so it turned out all right. I wish you had come with us, only it's not quite the place for ladies, and I say, can't we give you tea?"

Diana was not amused by Henry's impetuous explanation, but neither was she offended by his casual invitation. She considered him thoughtfully. "It's early."

"For what?"

"It's early for tea."

"That doesn't matter. I'm always hungry. Aren't you?"

"Yes, but—"

"Well then." He took her arm as though it were all settled. "We'll have to fetch Paul first. He was supposed to meet me here half-an-hour since, but he's probably in old Crock's bookshop round the corner." He paused and stared at her. "It's your hair, you see. Extraordinary colour. Catches the light. He's absolutely got to paint you!"

They found Paul deep in a folio of Holbein drawings at the end of a dark aisle in Crocker's Bookshop. "Oh good," he said, looking up as Henry came toward him. "I'm ravenous." Then, catching sight of Diana, standing a few steps behind. "Oh, you."

"Yes, wasn't it a coincidence?" Henry interrupted tactfully. "I ran into her again just outside Ackermann's."

Paul grinned unexpectedly and looked almost boyish. "Been haunting it, you mean. He's been on your trail for the better part of a week. Well, come on child, you may as well eat with us." He led the way out of the shop, nodding carelessly to old Mr. Crocker who grunted in reply, not raising his eyes from his book. Henry, more polite, gave Diana his arm and they followed Paul up the street.

Most spirited girls would have bitterly resented Paul's cavalier treatment and the epithet of "child," but Diana did not regard it. She took in Paul at a glance and recognized his behaviour as a grosser echo of her own—the brooding concentration, the preoccupation with one's own perceptions that looked like, and often was, pure selfishness.

There was a brief argument about their destination, Henry insisting that they could not take the girl to a tavern or coffeehouse, while Paul pointed out that they could not afford anything else. They settled at last on an obscure tea-shop cum pastry-cook which, except for two elderly women in unfashionable bonnets, they had to themselves. There were faded prints of pre-fire London on the walls, brown gingham curtains, and a tortoiseshell cat on the windowsill. Diana stroked the cat absently. Henry ordered tea and buns, then felt in his pockets for a packet containing the remains of the piece of Stilton that had been his breakfast. Diana contributed an apple. Paul stared out the window. Diana found a fresh page in her book and made a quick sketch of the cat which she tore out and offered to Henry. "That's to thank you for the tea. I know your friend's name is Paul, but I don't know your name. Mine is Diana."

Henry gasped, remembered his manners, and introduced himself. Paul came out of his silence and looked at Diana, then exchanged glances with Henry. He nodded. His eye fell on

Diana's sketch and he took it from Henry's hand and studied it for a few minutes. He looked at Diana again and this time really seemed to see her. "Where did you learn to do this?"

"By using my eyes." She stared at him without affront. Paul laughed. She passed her sketchbook to him and he began turning the pages, pausing now and then when something took his eye. At a drawing of a rearing horse he reached absently in his pocket for a pencil, then raised an interrogative brow. Diana gave her assent and Paul quickly changed the angle of the back legs. "See? Much better." She nodded. The horse had bothered her, though the sketch was one of her favourites. She remembered the morning clearly: the young man on the dappled grey he could not quite control and the young woman—she was certainly not a lady—who had caught his eye. The woman had picked up the skirt of her red dress to avoid being splashed by mud and perhaps to show off shapely legs encased in jean half-boots—Jeanie! Diana gave an anguished cry, seized her sketchbook, and fled.

Henry looked after her in astonishment. Paul was offended. "Damn!" he said.

Diana's forgetfulness had reduced Jeanie to tears. "For whatever should I do, miss, if'n you was to not come back, and me being responsible like and your sisters being so kind to me and all?" She had been waiting for Diana above an hour and was terrified that she should be abandoned and lose her place. Diana was contrite and promised never to be late again. Fortunately Claudia and Livia were still out on her return and she had only to endure a black look from Mrs. Fraser who needed Jeanie's help with dinner.

In fact, far from being angry with Diana, Livia was concerned about the lack of time she and Claudia were spending with their younger sister. Though she lacked Claudia's strong maternal feelings, Livia had long felt responsible for holding their family together and she understood, perhaps better than Claudia, Diana's difficulty in fitting into a conventional mold. Sometimes, in the privacy of her bedchamber, Livia wondered what would happen to Diana and to her even if Claudia was comfortably settled. Livia hadn't changed her own views on marriage, but she had always thought that Diana would want to marry when she was older. That was the beauty of their London plan. Once Claudia had made a good marriage, she would be able to find a husband for Diana. With both her sisters settled, Livia could live as she pleased. But since their arrival in London, Livia found it harder and harder to imagine Diana ever becoming a respectable wife and mother.

Livia was not one to brood. She pushed these thoughts firmly aside and told herself that it was Claudia's future that mattered now. There would be time enough to worry about Diana later. But she did make a point of asking Diana to accompany her on a visit to Sophronia Neville. "Claudia is engaged with the Langdon girls, but I promised Cousin Sophronia most faithfully I would be there. It is a meeting of some kind, and I have the direst feeling I shall need moral support."

The three sisters had called on Cousin Sophronia shortly after their arrival in London. She was much as they remembered her, a tall, vigourous woman of some sixty years with wiry grey hair, sharp blue eyes, an aquiline nose, and a formidable chin. She had seen a good deal of the world, she told them, it was not to her liking and she had devoted her life to changing it. Though she was happy to see the girls, she did not expect them to be interested in her work, that was for those who had the calling, not that they wouldn't be welcome, but she could see they had other fish to fry. Quite right, too, since they were young and pretty. She gave them tea, bread-and-butter sandwiches, and a large number of statistics on infant mortality and girls sold into prostitution. During tea, Diana made a quite wicked portrait of their cousin which, to Livia's horror, she insisted on presenting to their hostess. Sophronia was delighted and had it framed and hung in her drawing room.

She had steadfastly refused to visit the house in Charles Street but now and then sent pamphlets or extracts from the papers. Then, despite her resolve to leave them be, she had asked them to attend a public meeting, her invitation couched in offhand terms that almost concealed her palpable eagerness to improve their education. For the sake of the family—and out of curiosity—Livia had promised to come.

She was grateful now for Diana's company and noted with approval that her sister was looking quite presentable, her dress neatly pressed and her hair pinned in some semblance of order. Livia had long since forgiven Nicholas Warwick for the accusations he had hurled at her when he brought Diana home, but she had not been able to forget Diana's shabbiness on that night and the story of apparent neglect that it suggested. Warwick's "Good God!" on learning that the girl was her sister still made Livia's face hot with shame.

The hackney let them off in a quiet street off Manchester Square before a small, neat house with a freshly painted door and a well-polished knocker. Sophronia met her young cousins with evident pleasure, then passed them on to a table where her companion, a Miss Melmott, was handing out printed bills and soliciting donations. They were there, the bill informed them, in the service of The Society for the Prevention of Cruelty to Climbing Boys.

Livia and Diana found seats near the back of the room and surveyed the crowd with interest. As Livia had expected, it was unfashionable and consister mostly of women, not all of them middle-aged. There were a number in their twenties and even a sprinkling of children. The men were a varied lot, a retired military officer or two, she guessed, three or four clergymen, and some young men who looked as if they might be journalists.

One man caught her eye by his bearing. He was not tall and he was soberly dressed, but he carried himself with great assurance. He turned to reveal finely cut features and really beautiful grey eyes, both familiar to Livia though she could not at first place him. When recollection came, she smiled in amusement, for she had last seen him in the Waterford ballroom dancing with Lady Francesca. Oliver Merriman, Melbrooke had told her. A rival of Nicholas Warwick's.

Merriman caught her glance and her smile and bowed slightly, a puzzled look on his face. There was no help for it. Livia bowed in return. He would think her very forward.

Livia's embarrassment was overtaken by the speakers, for they described in dispassionate detail the horrors faced by the small boys, some as young as five, who were forced into the painful and dangerous task of scrambling up chimneys to sweep them free of soot. At the conclusion of the meeting she was sitting in appalled silence when Cousin Sophronia swept up with the grey-eyed man in tow. "My dears, allow me to present Mr. Oliver Merriman. M.P.," she added, beaching him as though he were a boat and retreating in the swell of the crowd around them.

He bowed, then said in an amused voice, "I am afraid you now have the advantage of me. Miss Neville is an estimable woman, but she is likely to be careless about details."

Livia remedied the omission. "Mrs. Royce. Miss Diana Neville."

"Ah. I thought perhaps we had met before, but I am wrong. My memory for names is usually quite good."

Livia hastened to explain her earlier behaviour. "Yes, I too thought we had met. My memory for faces generally stands me in good stead. We have not met, but I have seen you. At the Waterford ball."

He made the connection. "Of course, Neville. The enchanting young woman who took everyone's attention."

"Our sister. Miss Neville"—she indicated Sophronia—"is a cousin of our father's." Livia paused a moment. "I would not have expected to find you at such a gathering."

"It is an interest of mine. How did you find the afternoon?"

Livia chose her words with care. "One knows, of course,

that such things go on. But one does not really know them, if you see what I mean."

He nodded. "Exactly. Life would be insupportable otherwise. We do what we can, but change must be slow."

At this point one of the journalists claimed his attention. Livia and Diana sought out Cousin Sophronia to take their leave and Livia promised to send a greater contribution than they could comfortably afford. "A sop to my conscience," she explained to Diana as they looked for a hackney.

Diana grimaced. "I could not give my life to it."

"Nor could I. But we must not be forgetful." Livia hailed an approaching carriage and gave the driver their direction. As she settled back against the shabby, none too clean squabs, she thought of the other interest the afternoon had brought. "What did you think of Mr. Merriman?"

Diana considered. "He has a striking face."

"That's not what I meant."

"If you like, I think he's handsome."

"And?"

"And I don't think I would trust him."

Chapter 6

"Nicholas," Mrs. Amesbury said a few days later, "may I have the barouche on Tuesday next? I want to drive down to the cottage at Windmere to speak to Cartman about the roses. He's planning to extend them all along the south front and that won't do at all for it's just there that we play croquet and you know what havoc a loose ball can play when the plants are tender, and besides he's besotted with those new yellow teas he had from Lady Bishop's garden and it's positively bilious on the complexion which is what I told Mrs. Wilton when she was about to buy a length in that shade for that sallow-faced daughter of hers, and I've written to Cartman ten times at least but I don't trust the man unless I see him myself. If you don't mind, that is."

Nicholas rightly interpreted this last as an inquiry about his need for the carriage and assured her it would be at her disposal. There was no real need for the journey, but his aunt wanted occupation and he was happy to oblige her. The residence she persisted in calling a cottage was in fact a house of ten or more rooms with a number of outbuildings located in a small but pleasant park on the banks of the Thames near Richmond. The property had come to her from her mother, and it was a favourite excursion for the Warwicks during the spring and summer months.

"I propose to take Gwendolen," Mrs. Amesbury continued, "the child has been very quiet lately and Miss Calisher has developed a cough and is not feeling quite the thing. I've asked Isabel, but she tells me she's engaged. They're such horrid things, coughs, I had one last winter and it would not leave me until I tried dear old Lady Burleigh's infusion which she had from her daughter-in-law who had just come back from Baden and it had completely cured her little boy who they feared was taken with an inflammation of the lungs. And speaking of little boys, Nicholas, I spoke to Melbrooke and he is agreed to have Eddy come to us, he misses the child terribly and it's so convenient, for Gwendolen likes to play with him and he can see his father at any time. Why don't you come with us, you've been looking fagged to death and I'm sure it would do you so much good."

"Thank you, Aunt Letty, but I'm much too busy." Nicholas kissed her cheek and left the room, for he was already late for an appointment.

Mrs. Amesbury then applied to Francesca who declared that she was engaged to go shopping with Miss Neville on Tuesday but would be glad to come if she could bring her along. Francesca was not so engaged, but the unbuffered company of her late husband's aunt was not to be endured for an entire day. She was certain she could persuade Claudia to come and had long been wanting an opportunity for more intimate conversation than was possible at the entertainments where they usually met. Francesca was still piqued at Waterford's desertion—she had seen little of him since the evening at Almack's—and had not yet decided if she should make an effort to bring him back. She would not interfere unless she were in truth determined to become a duchess herself. And of that she was still not sure.

Mrs. Amesbury then bethought herself of Mrs. Royce. "Such a sensible young woman, and she is sure to be a help about the roses. I suppose," she added, "we should ask the younger sister too, it will be company for Gwendolen. We shall be crowded, but I daresay the children will not take up much room and it's much cosier with a large party. I'll write to Cartman today and tell him his wife should lay on a luncheon."

But the party was destined to become even larger. Lord Melbrooke was driving into Surrey to pick up his son and a stop at Richmond on the way back would be most welcome, he told Mrs. Amesbury when she extended an invitation, but in that case it would also have to include his nephew who would be driving with him. "A young man who spends all his time in his rooms and scarcely seems to know a soul. I promised my sister I'd look in on him now and then, take him out of himself."

Mrs. Amesbury assured Melbrooke that they would be delighted to have them; "for you know we are all females going together and it is such a comfort to have a man or two around." They were destined to have still another man. As the party gathered on the Tuesday, Nicholas appeared mounted on a beautiful dark chestnut and informed his aunt that he intended to ride along with them.

"But your work," Mrs. Amesbury protested.

"Surely I may be allowed a day of dalliance, Aunt Letty. Besides, Cassius is resty and needs the exercise." He bowed to the Nevilles, but his eyes were on Claudia. She was wearing a lavender sprigged muslin with a spencer of violet silk and a high-poked straw bonnet tied with violet ribbons. She is an enchanting girl, he thought. Francesca agreed. Her own dress, of a pale green, fitted her beautifully and her hat was quite as charming as Claudia's, but the honours clearly went to the other girl. Francesca was a realist and did not begrudge Claudia her looks. She had more than her own share of beauty, and fortunately Waterford was notoriously susceptible to flattery. Francesca rarely stooped to it, but then she rarely had to make an effort to attach a man.

Nicholas looked with some curiosity at Diana. He had not seen her since the night he had so unceremoniously brought her home. The child's looks were much improved. She wore a simple white muslin dress sashed in dark green and looked younger than ever. Her behaviour, however, had not altered. He would have expected her to have the grace to look confused, but she eyed him steadily and, he could swear, with a trace of amusement. Too much by half! Mrs. Royce had yet to teach her manners.

Genny, he noted with approval, was quite animated. She contrived to seat herself between Francesca and Miss Neville. His aunt appropriated Mrs. Royce who carefully placed Diana on her other side, thus allowing her sister to escape in contemplation of the passing scene. For someone so lax in discipline, Mrs. Royce seemed curiously protective of her youngest sister.

Nicholas quickly gave up these reflections in favour of unfettered enjoyment of the day. They had had an unexpected streak of good weather and today was no exception. Once past the outskirts of London, Nicholas gave Cassius his head and had an exhilarating gallop, ending in much satisfaction for man and beast. He drew in the reins, waiting for the barouche to catch up, then fell sedately behind for the rest of the journey.

Windmere was charming. Built in the last century, the house sat on a small knoll that sloped gently down to a border of willows standing guard over a small backwater of the river. Sweetbriars were just coming into bloom. The teas, Cartman lugubriously informed his mistress, had fallen victim to blackspot, tidings which afforded her no small satisfaction. The party had not proceeded beyond the terrace running the length of the south front when the sound of carriage wheels called their attention to new arrivals. A small, sturdy boy with a crop of unruly light brown hair came hurtling around the corner of the house and with a shout of "Uncle Nicholas!" hurled himself upon that gentleman who swung him up in the air, then put him down with a muttered "Rascal! Mind your manners." His father joined them more conventionally, followed by a slight, intense young man who did not appear to be looking forward to the day with any real pleasure.

Melbrooke introduced him as his sister's son, Paul Redmond, but long before the introduction Diana had recognized her acquaintance of the tea shop.

Paul was clearly unsettled by his recognition of the girl he thought he had lost forever. He was observed by Livia, who put it down to shyness, and by Nicholas, who diagnosed *gaucherie*. The moment passed quickly, however, for Mrs. Cartman called them into the house where a simple collation, Mrs. Amesbury assured them, was laid out in the white-panelled dining room. The meal was delightfully informal and of an abundance to satisfy even the appetites of children and grown men. Conversation was general and spirits high. Francesca told a number of amusing stories of her travels with her father on the continent. That reminded Mrs. Amesbury of her dear friends the de Veres who had been trapped in Brussels the year before, the younger de Veres, that is, not the older brother who was in some position with the Admiralty. Nicholas countered quickly with a mild scandal involving the sale of Naval commissions, which led Melbrooke to recount the most recent additions to the betting book at White's. Claudia described the dreadful consequences of an undergraduate wager—three boys sent down and one laid up with an inflammation of the lungs from falling in the river and being obliged to walk all the way back to his rooms without his breeches after midnight. Livia said that was the night one of the Fellows of Christ Church was found in bed with a woman who insisted she was his wife, a scandal that led to his expulsion when it was found to be true. It had, Livia said, given their father great satisfaction for he had been obliged to resign his own fellowship when he married their mother. Paul and Diana were quiet, but Gwendolen and Eddy, at the table through Nicholas' intercession, giggled a good deal.

After the meal, Mrs. Amesbury retired to rest. The others drifted outdoors, the children running across the lawn to a point where steps descended to a narrow strip of shingle by the river. Livia made for the grove of willows nearby. She loved the water and she treasured moments of solitude, a rare commodity in these past weeks. From the distance she heard the voices of the men, punctuated by Francesca's silvery laughter and Claudia's lower-pitched tones.

The park was larger than she had at first supposed. She wandered along the bank for a half-mile or so, feeling easier with herself than at any moment since their absurd masquerade had begun. She reached a large ditch which marked the end of the property and turned back reluctantly. Claudia was much on her mind. The day would end and they would be back in London, gambling on Claudia's marriage and Claudia's happiness. Livia hoped the one did not preclude the other. She gave herself a quick scold. Happiness was relative and one could hope only that one would be happy sometimes. As for marriage, that was a gamble in any case.

She began to walk more briskly and had reached the willow grove when she heard a sharp cry from ahead and to her right. That would be near the river. She remembered the children, picked up her skirt and ran toward the sound. Gwendolen, her face intent with purpose and desperation, was making for the river bank, but Livia headed her off. Trembling, the girl pointed. Eddy was in the water. It barely reached his chest, but he could not stand against the current and was being pulled downstream. Livia pulled off her shoes, tied her skirt around her hips, slithered down the bank, and let the river take her.

She was nearly overbalanced by the shock of the cold water. Clinging to the bank for support, she cautiously made her way to a backwater where Eddy had caught hold of an overhanging branch which had saved him from being carried out into the swifter portion of the river. Livia scooped him up and his arms went tightly about her neck. He began to tremble and not, Livia suspected, just from cold. Gwendolen reached them, flung herself on the ground, and stretched her arms down to help Eddy up over the bank. It was too high for Livia to climb, so she fought her way upstream till she reached the shingle and the steps leading back to the lawn.

The three of them looked at each other. They had shared an

adventure. The children had shown some presence of mind and did not deserve to have hysterical adults deprive them of it. She spoke briskly. "Genny, do you think you could find a large towel or some other covering? Be quick and quiet." Gwendolen nodded and ran off. Livia stripped off Eddy's shirt and trousers and dried him as best she could with the dry portions of her skirt. "It was very sensible of you to take off your shoes and stockings before wading," she told him. "And it was sensible to go with the current and try to keep to shore. Currents can be dangerous things if you don't watch for them. Do you swim?"

"A little," Eddy said in a small voice. He was still shivering.

"Good. You must get your father to give you lots of practice. You can see how important it is." She looked up, searching for Gwendolen and saw Nicholas Warwick striding rapidly across the lawn.

"My dear Mrs. Royce, has there been an accident? What have you been up to, you young scamp?" This last was addressed to Eddy who raised miserable eyes to Livia.

"Yes, the stupidest thing," she said. "We'd been down at the shore collecting pebbles and I saw such a pretty one a few feet out, so I waded in to get it and stumbled and Eddy came to my rescue, but then I'm afraid he stumbled too and got rather wet, and I do hope it won't keep him from going to the rescue of ladies in the future. It was a very gallant thing to do."

Nicholas looked at Eddy's discarded clothes lying sodden on the grass, then at Livia's feet. "Wading in your stockings? A queer freak."

"Oh, but I did remove my shoes."

"You'd best remove your stockings as well, you'll catch your death. And you too, young man," he went on as Gwendolen came flying across the lawn with a large white towel. He took it from her, wrapped it round the shivering boy, and picked him up. "I don't think there's any need to disturb the others about this incident—particularly Aunt Letty. Let's get you to the kitchen to get warm. Genny, do you think you could find some dry clothes for Eddy? There should be some in

100

his portmanteau in Uncle Edward's carriage." Gwendolen nodded and ran off on her second errand. Nicholas gave Eddy a reassuring look. "After all, old chap, all's well that end's well."

"A trite observation, but a welcome one."

Nicholas turned to Livia in astonishment. "Trite, madam?"

"Yes, though certainly true." She grinned.

Nicholas was torn between amusement and pique. "You should come and get dry yourself," he said, starting back to the house. "Your skirt will hardly pass inspection."

"In a moment," she called after him. "I must retrieve the shoes."

A few moments later Livia found her way into the kitchen. She was clutching her shoes and the children's shoes and stockings in one hand and her own wet stockings and Eddy's dripping clothes in the other. Mrs. Cartman helped her hang these in front of the stove to dry, then urged her to stand near herself. Gwendolen and Eddy, now in dry clothes, were seated close together near the fire drinking hot spiced milk.

Nicholas looked at Livia in some concern. "Can I get you a glass of sherry? You will be cold."

"I am not such a poor creature, to be overset by a little damp. It was a great adventure, was it not?" she said, turning to the children who smiled at her happily. The afternoon was turning out far better than they had any right to expect.

"Indeed. Even though the ending was a trite one." Nicholas' face was grave, but his eyes held the hint of a smile.

"I should have the grace to blush, but sadly it's not one of my accomplishments. Forgive my forward tongue."

Gwendolen looked puzzled by this exchange. Eddy nudged her and whispered, "I'll explain it to you later."

Nicholas ignored Eddy's comment. "I believe there's a fire laid in the library. I'll be glad to keep you company there if you like. You'd do best to keep out of sight till you are dry. And you two," he added, turning to the children, "do you think you could contrive some very quiet occupation, something that has absolutely nothing to do with water?" He smiled and left the room.

Livia, clad in a pair of coarse dry socks Mrs. Cartman had pressed upon her, but with skirt and petticoat still damp, made her way to the library. Nicholas, a book in his hand, was standing near one of the long windows which overlooked a vista of well-tended fields. A fire was blazing on the hearth and Livia moved toward it thankfully.

"I am most grateful to you for your help," she said in a natural tone. "I did not mean to tease. I had hoped the whole matter could pass without observation."

He turned and looked at her. "In other words, you would have done quite as well without my interference. No doubt. Still, you should at least be grateful for my connivance at this ridiculous story. I'm hardly likely to believe that a woman of your years and sense goes wading with children. And in her stockings."

Livia, who might certainly have done just that without a thought, was in no position to plead her youth. She was not at all sure she appreciated his description and for a moment regretted both the severity of her dress and the odious cap that covered her hair. Her reply was more tart than she had intended. "I had not expected you to give me the lie. A gentleman is expected to accept any story told by a lady, no matter how outrageous."

"So. I am both trite and not a gentleman. Perhaps not, but I have some experience of ladies' stories."

Livia looked stricken, and he went on more kindly. "Come, let us not quarrel. I am persuaded it was your presence of mind that prevented what might have been a tragic occurrence. I am most grateful to you and so is Melbrooke, though I agree he is not to know of it."

"Thank you," she said simply, but could not then resist adding, "And thank you also for preserving my reputation as a woman of sense. I do appreciate the fire, and I shall soon be quite dry. But don't let me keep you indoors, you will be missed."

"Not at all. I am escaping an expedition to look for early berries. I am notoriously poor at berry-picking. As a matter of fact, I had hoped to find young Redmond here to propose a game of chess. He's a tolerably good player, but he appears to be nowhere in sight. Probably off sketching. He's always had a hand and eye for it, and he paints very well indeed. He spent two years studying in Germany and people who know say he has a lot of promise. But his mother worries about his dislike for company. That's why Melbrooke brought him along, though it doesn't seem to have done much good. The boy should be left alone."

Livia privately agreed, but since she thought it probable that Paul was not alone, said nothing. She turned to give the back of her skirt the benefit of the fire. "If you would care to, I would be glad to give you a game of chess. I may not be tolerably good, but it will serve to pass the time."

Nicholas looked at her in some surprise.

"My father liked to play," she explained. "He taught me. My brother was always much too impatient for the game."

Nicholas pulled a small table up to the fire and brought out a set of well-polished rosewood chess pieces, not expensive but carefully crafted and much handled. They had, he said, belonged to Mrs. Amesbury's late husband. Livia sat, choosing a chair that would not be injured by her still damp dress, and they began the game in silence. Nicholas, she soon saw, was a thoughtful but decisive player. His opening was bold and well calculated to lead the inexperienced into trouble. It was a clever move, but her father had taught her a gambit that might serve. It did. Nicholas looked at her with some respect, but she kept her head demurely down.

They went on with the game. After a time Livia ventured a remark. One of her knights was threatened and she needed time to think. "Your horse. A beautiful animal, but he hardly lives up to his name."

"Cassius? I got him off a man who neglected him abominably and at that time he did indeed have a lean and hungry look. If the association is not trite."

"The bard is only trite with overuse. Though he didn't always have his facts straight." She lifted a pawn, hesitated, then put it back. "Neither did Plutarch, which perhaps was Shakespeare's problem. I've sometimes wondered if he hadn't confused Caius Cassius with Quintus Cassius. Quintus was known to be horribly greedy and corrupt into the bargain. They were contemporaries, you know." She tried a feint with her remaining rook.

"I know," Nicholas remarked drily. He moved and took the rook. "That wasn't wise."

"Perhaps not. But my knight is safe. More important, so is my queen."

"Mrs. Royce, you are more than a tolerable player. You are a devious one." Nicholas studied the board with renewed concentration.

"So was the woman I was named for. She had to be. All that power behind the throne activity is really hard on women."

"I daresay. And who, may I ask, were you named for?"

"Livia. Augustus' wife, you know."

"I consider myself tolerably well educated, Mrs. Royce. The name in itself has a pleasant ring, but the associations do not. Whatever was your mother about, naming you for such a dreadful woman?"

"Oh, but she wasn't all that dreadful. And it wasn't my mother, it was my father. It was his period, you see, and he was very attached to Claudius. He thought he was much maligned and wrote endless polemics on the matter. He was hoping for a son, hence Claudia."

Nicholas moved a piece at random and muttered, "I see. Did your mother mind?"

"Our names? Only when it came to Diana. My father wanted to call her Agrippina."

"I was thinking rather of the history. Not exactly for the ears of infants."

"But certainly no worse than fairy tales. Think of Livia as a cruel stepmother." She toyed with her queen. "Of course, she could be considered a rather dreadful woman, I do see your point. She poisoned people when they were inconvenient and she was most unkind to Julia, and she was certainly cruel to Tiberius when she forced him to divorce Vipsania. But none of it was out of meanness or spite. She had goals beyond herself, and a kind of severe integrity." She caught his eye and went on defensively. "Given the times. If she'd been a man, she would have gone down in history as one of the abler rulers."

"But she was a woman," Nicholas pointed out. "And able or not, a most unwomanly one."

"You believe in womanliness, Mr. Warwick?"

"I do indeed, Mrs. Royce. It's a rare quality. Your sister has it, I believe."

Livia's face softened. "Yes, that's just the word for it. Most men fail to see beyond her beauty."

"Then most men are fools." He studied the board for a moment, but his mind was not on the game. "Do you not sometimes feel," he said tentatively, "that there is something heartless in throwing your sister on the Marriage Mart as you have? She surely deserves better than that."

Livia looked at him in astonishment. "But how else is she to meet eligible men? I assure you, Claudia has every intention in the world of marrying."

"Forgive me," he said with a gentleness he had not hitherto shown. "I am intruding insufferably. But I understand she not only intends to marry, but to marry well. That does not bode well for her future happiness."

These remarks were uncomfortably like those Livia had addressed to herself earlier in the day. She did not relish hearing them from Warwick and felt compelled to contradict him. "It bodes well for her future comfort. Happiness is quite a matter of chance."

"Chance? One might think so, viewing the marriages of one's friends and acquaintances."

Livia looked at him in surprise. She knew that Warwick had

lost his wife, but she had supposed the marriage had been a happy one. She lowered her eyes and studied the chess board.

"But that's hardly a view I would have expected from you," Nicholas went on. "I had taken you for a romantic."

"I? Nonsense." She disposed briskly of one of his bishops.

Nicholas studied her in surprise. "Surely your own marriage—"

Livia had forgotten her marriage. She stared at him a moment, then returned to the board. "I do not care to discuss my own marriage. Checkmate."

After lunch, Diana and Paul met, by prearrangement, at a gate leading into a neighboring field and thence to a small rise from which they could see the river. Diana was carrying a large worn reticule of her own design and Paul had a sketchbook under his arm. They climbed in companionable silence till they reached the crest, then settled with one accord near a fallen tree.

"Why did you run away?" Paul asked. "Henry was very upset about it. Was it something he said?"

"No." Diana pulled out her sketchbook and fumbled in her reticule for a pencil. "It's complicated. I was supposed to meet someone, and I forgot. I wasn't really supposed to be out alone at all, and I didn't want to get Jeanie in trouble. I'm sorry about Henry. Tell him from me."

"Funny thing, meeting like this. I don't go out often with Uncle Edward, though he's a good sort and we have dinner now and then. Being in company can get tiresome."

"I know."

"Not today, though," he hastened to add. "Your family is easy to be with. Have you been in London long?"

"A few weeks. We came so Claudia could find a husband, but husband hunting is a lot of bother. There's no end of shopping and fittings and calling on people and being called on and none of it making much sense. They seem to like it though."

106

"Your sister has an unusual face."

"Claudia? Yes, most people think so."

"No, the other one. Miss Neville is lovely, of course, but—Mrs. Royce, isn't it?—her face has the more interesting lines."

Diana looked up from her drawing for the first time. "You're right, of course. I don't think most people notice that."

"Most people can't see what's in front of them." Paul found a fresh page in his sketchbook and quickly laid out a view of the fields below, a clump of oak in the foreground and Windmere and the river beyond. Diana went on working, finished her drawing with a large flourish, tore it off the block and laid it beside Paul. Then, arms around her knees, she stared off toward the river. A boat was being pulled past the willows and she could hear the sound of distant voices.

Paul looked at his work, grunted in dissatisfaction, and put it aside. His mind was clearly elsewhere. As he did so, he saw Diana's offering and picked it up. A young man with tousled hair and cravat askew lay on the ground, propped on one elbow. As a likeness it was not quite accurate, but it caught its subject's air of moody discontent precisely. "May I keep it?" he asked. Diana nodded. "Who taught you?"

"A friend of my father's, when I was young. Then no one. Mostly by drawing every day. They thought I had a gift, so they didn't bother me about learning other things." She looked at him with a mischievous smile. "It was very useful."

"Yet you come to a spot like this and you choose to do a figure you might see anywhere. Isn't that a waste?"

She knew he was teasing, but she replied seriously. "No, I like to be outdoors. I like looking at landscapes, but not rendering them. People are more interesting. To me, that is," she added, lest he think her critical of his own efforts. "It's how I understand them."

"So now you understand me?"

"In a way. I think we're much the same. Not in our work, of course. I don't paint, not even watercolours, and I don't do things on a large scale, but in what work means to us."

She did not comment, he noted, on the disparity in their training or talent. Not, he thought ruefully, that there was necessarily much difference in the latter. Paul knew he was good, whether or not others yet recognized him. Diana knew she was good and made no apology for the smaller scale of her work. Paul had long since had his fill of simpering females who wanted his comments on their bits and daubs. Here was a girl who might be worth knowing.

"I was working on a picture for the Academy. They turned it down. Did Henry tell you?"

She shook her head. "I'm sorry."

"It wasn't quite right." Paul had no false modesty, but he was honest with himself. "I had to scrub out a lot of it and then it wouldn't go right and then of course it was too late, the Summer Exhibition's already opened. It was Diana in the woods, but a very English woods and I didn't want her at all goddessy, just a young girl who likes to run free. I had a model and she wasn't bad, but she was too old and too knowing, if you know what I mean, so I had to let her go. That's when Henry got the idea. It was your hair, and then your name, of course, made it seem right, and that's what I was going to ask you when you ran off. Do you think you could? It's hard work, but you seem able to sit still and that's the main thing. It won't take very long to finish. There's a place in Charles Street, not your street, the one off St. James' Square, that might take it on commission if I can get it to them by June."

Diana looked at him, considering. "I could, of course. That is, I'd have to arrange about times, and I think I ought to see it first."

"To be sure I'm worth your trouble?"

"Yes. And to be sure I'm right for it."

"Oh, you will be," Paul assured her. "You certainly will be."

They walked down the hill not long after and found their hostess on the terrace in agitated conference with Cartman about the south front. The others had returned and Mrs.

Amesbury, who was not at all sure of the effect she wanted to achieve, was calling on them severally for advice and opinion. They debated the merits of a rock garden, an artificial stream with a small waterfall, and more roses.

"I thought you were concerned about stray croquet balls, Aunt Letty." Nicholas came out on the terrace, followed by Livia and the children.

"Oh, Nicholas, I'm sure none of us plays croquet any more. Francesca says the game fatigues her, and I can never persuade Gwendolen that it's a healthy activity for a young girl."

"I loathe croquet," Gwendolen said under her breath.

"And you're much too grand to play with us, Nicholas," his aunt continued.

"Not that, I hope, though it's hardly my favourite form of relaxation. What do you say, Miss Neville? Does croquet fatigue you?"

Claudia smiled at him. "If I'm out of doors, I confess I much prefer a brisk walk. It's a confining game."

"There, you see? We'll extend the roses. They'll improve the view from the dining room, I never liked that flat expanse of lawn." So saying, Mrs. Amesbury swept happily indoors where tea was being laid. She had acquiesced in Cartman's plan and adopted it as her own. Would that the opposition were always so easily persuaded. Nicholas winked at Francesca, but she was talking to Melbrooke and didn't see him. Instead, he met Livia's eyes and smiled, then gave Claudia his arm and led her into the house.

Chapter 7

' The day at Richmond left Francesca curiously dissatisfied. She had, in fact, enjoyed herself, though family parties were generally not to her liking. Claudia Neville was an agreeable girl, but not insipid as agreeable girls so often are. Claudia had little taste for gossip and was not at all malicious—qualities which, one had to confess, did lend spice to social intercourse —but she had intelligence and a sense of humour and Francesca was not bored in her company. Though Nicholas and Melbrooke had both paid her a good deal of attention, Claudia had not monopolized them and had taken care that the others should not be slighted. Francesca laughed. What an odious paragon!

Francesca was no nearer untangling her own feelings toward Waterford. Claudia professed to enjoy his company, but she also liked that young sprig Warkworth, to say nothing of the dozen or so other men who hovered around her. Claudia's affections were certainly not engaged, neither by Waterford himself nor by his ducal crest. Francesca could retrieve him with a clear conscience.

But there was the rub. Did she want him? She was not, of course, in the throes of passion, but neither had she been when she had married Justin. Theirs had been a companionable and amusing marriage and she had missed him very much in the months after he was killed. She expected no more from a second husband. George unfortunately was not amusing, but he was considerate and kind and manageable. His mother was impossible and would have to be dealt with firmly, and George would have to be steered from his prosy habits and speech lest he become insufferably dull like his father. Still, it would be very pleasant managing his house and fortune.

Francesca was quite content running Warwick House, but she knew she could not continue to do so forever. She did not want to marry Nicholas—she would never be able to control him—but until recently she had been sure he would never marry again. Yet his behaviour toward Miss Neville, while restrained, differed noticeably from his manner toward other women. And if Nicholas married, Francesca had no intention of remaining a tolerated relation in someone else's household. Claudia, she thought, would suit Nicholas very well. And if they made a match of it, Francesca would have a clear field with Waterford.

She rang for her maid. She was engaged at a soirée given by the Comte de Lisles, an old friend of her father's. Waterford would be there but Claudia would not, for she did not move in the émigré community. Tonight was the time for decision and Francesca was still undecided. When in this state she took longer than usual over her toilette, and this evening she drove Phillips to distraction as she demanded one after another of her gowns. She settled finally on a violet silk, a harsh colour that accorded with her mood. With Phillips' help she piled her hair high on her head, fastened long falls of diamonds in her ears, and clasped an exquisitely cut necklace of the same stones round her neck, gifts from Justin on their marriage. Surveying herself in the glass, she decided that the effect could not have been better designed—the dress was cut daringly low, but the overall effect was regal. As she came downstairs, Lady Crawford nodded appreciatively and even Nicholas, who seldom gave Francesca his full attention, looked at her with admiration.

111

In the de Lisles' drawing room, Francesca moved easily from group to group—she had a large acquaintance—until her attention was claimed by Waterford who crossed directly to her on his arrival.

"I came solely in the hope of seeing you tonight," he said with practiced ease, raising her hand to his lips.

Francesca knew better than to allude to his recent inattention. She gave him a ravishing smile. "Will you walk with me a little? There's a fearful crush, but I fancy the next room may let us breathe. And I have a delicious story to tell you."

She took his arm and they passed down the room, their progress slowed by the mass of guests. She was unaware of the sudden stir behind them, but she could not ignore the accompanying shout. "By all that's wonderful. Francie!"

Francesca turned. A tall, broad-shouldered man in the uniform of a Hussar regiment was making his way toward her, only momentarily impeded by the Ladies Pembroke and Swinnerton who were standing in his path. Francesca broke off her conversation and stared at him in astonishment. She could feel Waterford stiffen beside her. Pity, since he was unbending nicely. The meeting would be awkward, and there was the matter of her regrettably childish nickname. Torn between anger and amusement, she awaited the encounter with outward composure.

"That's a fine way to greet an old friend," the newcomer said cheerfully as he came up to them. "It must be five years. You're looking very grand." He had taken Francesca's hand in both his own before he became aware of the man standing beside her. He released her hand and bowed.

Francesca, put momentarily off balance by this onslaught, recovered her poise. "Waterford, may I present—" she stared briefly at his insignia of rank—"Colonel Scott. A friend of my late husband. We knew him in Lisbon. Colonel Scott, his grace the Duke of Waterford."

Waterford bowed correctly, then excused himself. They

must, he said, have a great deal to talk about.

Colonel Scott steered Francesca neatly into an adjoining room and found a quiet corner. He had gone suddenly serious. "I'm sorry about Justin. I'd seen him in Vittoria shortly before his death, but then we moved on to Sorauren and it was months before I heard what happened. I wrote, but perhaps my letter went astray. Mail packets were unreliable in those days."

"I got your letter, thank you." She looked at him a moment, then turned away. "Have you just arrived in England, Colonel Scott?"

"Two days since. And dash it, Francie, this Colonel Scott business is a bit much."

"Not at all, I'm impressed. The last time I saw you, you were a mere lieutenant."

"Battlefield promotions. And it's only Lt. Colonel. Francie—"

"Don't use that ridiculous name. I'm no longer a child."

"You're certainly not. But don't play the grande dame with me. If you'd rather not know me, I'll take my leave." He swept her an ironic bow. "Lady Francesca."

"Don't be an idiot, Gerry. Of course I know you. But this is hardly the place to talk. Come to me tomorrow morning. South Audley Street, I'm still with Justin's family."

"I have been something of a boor, haven't I? And I've taken you away from your duke. Is he your latest conquest?"

Francesca shut her fan with a snap. "The duke," she said repressively, "is a very old friend of Father's."

"He can't be too old," Gerry protested, "he doesn't look a day over thirty."

"That isn't precisely what I meant."

"No, I daresay it isn't. Still, you could do far worse. You make a handsome pair."

"I've been married once, Colonel Scott. I'm not sure I want to essay it again. Besides," she added with a rueful smile, "he's been paying court to the latest beauty. I have to wait my turn."

"That's a hum. You've never had to wait on anyone."

"Perhaps I'll introduce you. To the beauty, that is. You can provide a distraction."

"Anything to serve you." He raised her hand to his lips, but there was laughter in his eyes. "Come, I can play propriety as well as anyone. I'll return you to your duke."

A few moments later Gerry found his way to the card room with unerring instinct. The meeting with Francesca had disturbed him more than he cared to admit, and he was in need of male company. As he suspected, Lionel Sedgwick was at the hazard table. He had met Sedgwick by chance that afternoon. An old friend who had sold out the year before and returned to London, Sedgwick had greeted Gerry enthusiastically and brought him along to the de Lisles'. Gerry watched the play for a bit, but declined to join them—he had little money and had learned early to avoid the tables. His friend left the game soon thereafter.

"Don't stop on my account," Gerry protested.

"Not a bit. Don't want to get in over my head." Sedgwick stopped a passing servant and asked for brandy. "Saw you talking to Lady Francesca. Knew her before, did you?"

"Yes, in Portugal."

"Daresay she's changed a good deal."

"In some ways." Gerry considered the changing Francesca. "Wasn't at all high-toned when I knew her. But we were younger then." He paused. "Anything between her and Waterford?"

"Can't say. Been seen a lot with Lady Francesca, but he's not the only string to her bow. Waterford's been seen with others too."

"Including the latest beauty?"

"You've heard? Glorious girl, have you seen her?"

"Hardly. I just got back. I don't think much of beauties, as a rule. They're usually a dead bore."

"Not this one. Miss Neville's an enchanting creature."

"Neville?" Gerry had some interest in the ramifications of the Neville family. "Where's she from?"

"Oxfordshire, I think. Up that way anyway. They're new to London. Old family, of course, the Nevilles go back practically to the Conquest. There must be Nevilles scattered all over England."

Gerry nodded. They couldn't be related. His thoughts drifted back to Oxford and he lost the thread of his friend's conversation.

". . . and there's even a bet down at White's that Waterford will make the beauteous Claudia an offer before the Season's out."

Gerry was startled out of his revery. "Who?"

"Miss Neville."

Gerry choked on his brandy. Claudia? There couldn't be two Claudia Nevilles in the county and both of them beauties. He felt his way cautiously. "I take it the family is here, Miss Neville's parents?"

"Oh, I don't think she has any parents, at least none that I've heard of. She lives with an older sister. Lady Crawford's been taking them about."

Stranger and stranger. Gerry's Claudia had no parents, but neither did she have an older sister. Moreover, she had no business being in London. The last time he had seen her, almost a year ago, she had been in mourning for her father and worried about her family's reduced income. She was certainly unacquainted with a Lady Crawford.

Gerry was not good at concealment. His friend looked at him in some concern, then said, "I say, Scott, are you all right?"

"All right?" Gerry looked at him in surprise. "Of course I'm all right. The thing of it is, Sedgwick, don't know what she's doing in London, but I think Miss Neville may be my sister."

Sedgwick gave a whoop of laughter, then called to some nearby friends. "Linton, Harris, come over here. You've got to meet an old friend. Germanicus Scott. He thinks he's the brother of the peerless Miss Neville!"

This caused no little stir and broke up several games. Introductions became general and Gerry was bombarded with questions. How did Miss Neville happen to have a brother named Scott? They had had different fathers. Was she really his sister? He wasn't sure. Well, then, didn't he know his sister's whereabouts, whoever she might be? No, he'd been traveling and had not had a letter for the past two or three months.

There was a general move to escort him therewith to Charles Street, but cooler heads prevailed, one faction pleading the lateness of the hour, another that Miss Neville was undoubtedly out, a third that if they were in fact unrelated, the eruption of a gaggle of bosky young bucks into her home might set Miss Neville's back up. The drinking continued. The war had dispersed the English about the face of Europe, and gatherings like this allowed catching up on the whereabouts of friends and acquaintances.

"I say," said a young man later in the evening, "did you know a Captain Royce? Died at Waterloo."

"John?" asked Gerry. The other nodded. "Lord, yes. Met him first in the passes when we were coming down into Spain." He smiled reminiscently. "My horse was shot from under me and he came to my rescue. Good man to be with under fire. The wild ones usually are."

"Wild?" This was Jeremy Warkworth, looking concerned.

"I didn't know him earlier, of course," Gerry went on, "but he said his family bought him a commission so he'd stop embarrassing them. Drank hard. Fought hard. Loved hard. It was a good thing his father packed him off."

"Why did he exactly?" someone asked.

"Debt. And a girl, I think. Probably several—he liked women. I remember him damning Wellington up and down for allowing officers only forty-eight hours' leave. The general insisted that was time enough to spend with any woman, but Royce always had two or three at once and that wasn't enough time for him. Left a string of bastards all across the Peninsula."

This last met with no response. Gerry looked up in surprise. The silence was broken by Jeremy Warkworth who was

116

quivering with indignation. "I trust he settled down after he married your sister."

Gerry stared at him in consternation. "Oh. Well, of course marriage always has a—a—chastening effect." Sister? Dear God, which one? Wait a minute—he rapidly turned over possibilities—not Claudia, he'd heard her spoken of as Miss Neville at least twice this evening. Certainly not Diana, she couldn't have grown that much. Livia then. But why put such a story about? Had Livia actually married John? When Royce was going home on leave the year before, Gerry had asked him to stop in Oxford to leave some messages for his sisters, but surely he would not have—Livia was scarcely his type—no, it was absurd.

Sedgwick came to his rescue. "I daresay there's a good deal we don't tell our wives. In any event, Royce was a brave man. By the way, Scott, what general was it whose life he saved?"

By this time Gerry was ready for anything. He swallowed the last of his brandy. "Must have been before my time."

The following morning Colonel Scott, bathed, shaved, and fortified with three cups of strong coffee, walked briskly down Charles Street. His doubts that the *ton*'s Miss Neville and his sister were one and the same had vanished. The descriptions he had elicited matched Claudia all too closely, while those of Mrs. Royce, at least in height and colouring, suggested Livia. Moreover, Linton had asserted that he had once caught sight of the youngest sister, a child with a mop of flaming hair. That had to be Diana.

It was not yet nine o'clock, but the hour did not disturb Gerry. His sisters had always been early risers. The door opened to his knock and Sandringham, his coat not yet settled on his shoulders, looked at the visitor with what he hoped was the requisite hauteur. None of Miss Neville's suitors had the temerity to call before noon.

"Good morning," Gerry said heartily, stripping off hat and

gloves and handing them to Sandringham. He strode into the elegant little hall and looked about him approvingly. "Well, man, where are they? Miss Neville and her sisters," he added, noting the butler's surprise.

"Miss Neville has not yet risen, sir." Sandringham's tone was frosty. "She never receives in the morning. If you would care to leave a card—"

"Don't bother, I'll go up. Which is her room?"

Gerry was halfway up the stairs before Sandringham—who was, after all, well known for his MacDuff—bounded after him, turned him around, and blocked the way. He was, Gerry realized in surprise, perfectly capable of throwing him out, and moreover had every reason to do so. He pulled back, prepared to offer an explanation, when there was a scream from above and Diana came hurtling down two flights of stairs to fling her arms around her brother's neck.

An hour later it was sorted out. Gerry had wrung Sandringham by the hand, assuring him of his everlasting goodwill for protecting his sisters, and the family was gathered about the dining room table. Gerry surveyed them happily. Diana was unchanged. Livia, in a black dress and with her hair wound plainly around her head, looked older and rather tired. Claudia, in a morning dress of blue muslin ornamented with knots of pink ribbon, seemed younger and more beautiful than ever. "I'd scarce have recognized you," he told her frankly. "So you've become the toast of London?"

"Hardly that." Claudia laughed.

"How did you know?" Diana asked at the same time.

"I went to a reception last night and was—er—informed of it. By an old friend. There were a score of fellows talking about you. Seems there's a bet on at White's—" He broke off. That was better left unsaid. "Sorry. Anyway, there was mention of a Miss Neville, and then I heard she came from Oxfordshire, and then that her given name was Claudia, and I thought what a coincidence. But when they told me she had an elder sister who—tell me one thing, Livia."

"Of course, Gerry. What is it?"

"Were you at any time in any way married to John Royce?"

Livia and Claudia exchanged glances and burst into laughter. "I thought his name was James," Diana said calmly, buttering another piece of toast.

"See here—" Gerry began.

Livia stopped laughing. "Gerry, I had to do something to turn myself into a respectable chaperone."

"You didn't have to marry him! You didn't marry him, did you? Or anything?"

"Gerry, don't be wicked, of course she didn't." Claudia poured him another cup of coffee. "She became his widow after he was dead."

"That's the way women usually become widows," her brother retorted. "I knew it was high time I came home." He settled back and waited to hear their story.

Livia took it up. "Your friend Royce came to see us in April of last year. He said he was on leave and had letters from you and you'd asked him to call. We had a long talk and we walked by the river and he stayed to tea. We pelted him with questions all afternoon and he told us about Salamanca and Vittoria and Orthez. He said you'd been very brave and had been wounded more than once but we weren't to worry. I'm afraid we didn't ask him much about himself, it was you we wanted to know about. But he was perfectly agreeable and polite and fun to be with, wasn't he?" She turned to her sisters for confirmation and they nodded. "So we were very upset when we read the casualty lists—we read them all the time because of you—and found that he'd been listed as killed in action at Waterloo. But he seemed safe enough, I mean when I needed a husband. That is, a dead husband. We knew at least that he didn't have any close family—his parents had both died, he'd told us, and he didn't have any brothers or sisters—so that wouldn't be a problem."

"No, that's not the problem," Gerry admitted. "But what the devil possessed you to set it about that he was a hero—"

119

"She didn't." Claudia leapt instantly to Livia's defense. "Jack and Harry got a little carried away, I'm afraid. Undergraduates," she added, forestalling his question, "students of Papa's. They helped us plan this, so they're in the know."

Gerry groaned. "I knew this smacked of an undergraduate trick."

"Not at all," Livia said crisply. "It's been going very well. We couldn't have foreseen that Harry and Jack would talk, though I suppose," she added ruefully, "we should have foreseen that the champagne would go to their heads. Actually, we were as surprised as you by the stories they put about."

"You couldn't have been that surprised," her brother told her drily. "The trouble is, he wasn't a hero at all."

"We know that," Livia said, "but no one else does."

Gerry shifted in his chair. "They do now," he said gloomily.

"You mean you told them?" Claudia demanded.

"I had no way of knowing—"

"Of course you didn't," Livia said. "Anyway, it can't be helped. We'll simply say his reputation was exaggerated or something."

Gerry shook his head regretfully. "Won't do. John had a reputation all right, but it wasn't the right sort."

"Do you mean he was a rake?" Diana asked with great interest.

"A most notorious one," her brother assured her.

"Oh, dear!" Claudia exclaimed, but Livia's lips were twitching.

"It really is very funny," she pointed out. "Poor John, whose given name I can never quite remember, is going to earn himself a place in history."

"You wouldn't think it was funny if you'd heard some of my stories. Lord, I don't know what got into me."

"Brandy probably," Diana said.

Gerry aimed a blow at her. "No wonder I got some peculiar looks. I'd traduced a lady. By the way," he said, echoing his friend's words, "what general was it whose life John saved?"

"That was Jack's contribution," Claudia said.

"But he assures us most earnestly it wasn't Wellington," Livia added.

"So I should hope," Gerry said fervently. His expression changed and he sat back and looked at his sisters. "It's a queer freak, your being here. Why didn't you let me know?"

"But we did," Claudia insisted. "There wasn't much time, and we couldn't tell you at once because we couldn't give you our direction, but we wrote as soon as we arrived. Not," she added with some asperity, "that you were very helpful in that regard, Germanicus Scott. It had been three months since we'd heard from you. We thought you were still in Cracow."

Gerry grinned, unrepentant. "London agrees with you at any rate. You're all looking splendid. All except you, young scamp," he said to Diana who was wearing her old grey dress, "you could do with some proper clothes. And you too," he addressed Livia, "that's an appalling get-up, and I wish you'd let your hair down. It's money, I suppose. And propriety, you told me. Still, you can't tell me that this house and everything don't cost the earth." He sat up suddenly. "You haven't sold the Oxford house?"

"Gerry, you can't think we'd do that without consulting you," Claudia protested.

"Then what have you done?"

"Papa left us some money."

"I know, but—all of it?"

"Not quite all."

"Good God, Claudia! Why didn't you tell me? I could have helped."

"That," Livia said with some asperity, "is precisely why we didn't tell you. No, Gerry, we've been over this before and it's no use arguing. Some day you'll have a family of your own to support. We're quite determined to do this ourselves."

"We can always go back home," Claudia insisted. "But we won't have to. I'm going to see to that."

"Claudia, I don't want to see you go wrong over this."

Claudia smiled warmly at her brother. "Don't you know I'm a reigning beauty and can have my pick? I can't possibly go wrong."

Claudia's future was also under discussion in the Warwick schoolroom. Gwendolen and Eddy were curled up with lesson books, Miss Calisher having retired to take a salt gargle for her throat. Gwendolen, in need of a confidant, had disclosed her plans to her younger friend.

"So you see," she was saying, "she's really the wife Daddy needs. I think he likes having a pretty woman around because you know Mummy was pretty, but Claudia's dark so she won't remind him of her too much, and she's very kind, and I know he likes her. I like her too. So the thing is that I have to find a way to put it into Daddy's head and make him think it was his idea."

Eddy was glum. "I don't see why she has to marry your father. I'd rather she married mine. He needs a wife too, and your father has Lady Francesca and Mrs. Amesbury to look after him and mine doesn't have anyone except Lane, and he doesn't count."

Gwendolen was horrified. She had not expected treachery in her own ranks. "But that's just it. Daddy's used to having women around to take care of him, so he needs a wife more."

"But my father can make her a Lady," Eddy insisted. He had fallen in love with Claudia the moment he saw her on the terrace at Windmere. "That's important to women."

Gwendolen was afraid this might be true, so she played her trump cards. "But I'm a girl, so I need a mother more. And I'm older. And I saw her first."

Defeated, Eddy lapsed into silence. Gwendolen took pity on him. "Maybe your father can marry Mrs. Royce. She's a sensible lady."

"But she's married," Eddy protested.

"Not any more. I mean, she's married, but she doesn't have a husband. So that's all right."

"I don't think so," Eddy said dubiously. The remarriage of widows had not yet come within his experience. He had another thought. "Well, if he can marry a widow, why can't your father marry Lady Francesca? He's known her for ages and she already lives here. Anyway, I thought if men and women lived together they had to get married."

"Oh, that's all right. Aunt Letty lives here too. But Daddy can't marry Aunt Francesca. She's his brother's widow, and that isn't good at all. You remember what happened to Henry the Eighth, he got into all that trouble with the Pope and then he started killing all his wives. I wouldn't want that to happen. Besides, I don't think Aunt Francesca would like to be a mother. And I'd rather have Claudia. I don't know why you can't take Mrs. Royce."

"I wouldn't want a mother who wore black all the time."

"She only has to for a few years."

"But then I'll be grown up and it won't matter any more."

"It will matter to your father."

"Yes, but by then he'll be too old to care."

Gwendolen wasn't sure this was true, but she didn't press the point. "Anyway, you can come visit us."

The door opened, but it was not Miss Calisher. Francesca stepped in to tell them that that lady was feeling poorly and had been persuaded back to bed by Mrs. Amesbury. Nicholas said it was much too fine a day for lessons and proposed a walk by the Serpentine. She was going. Were they interested?

Of course they were. While they made ready, Francesca descended to her own room to put on pelisse and bonnet and fetch her reticule. As she tied the bonnet, a ridiculous but charming high-poked confection ornamented with rose-coloured ribbons, she surveyed her reflection gloomily. She had been sadly unsettled by her meeting with Gerry. It took her back to her first summer in Lisbon. 1809. The war had been going badly, but Lisbon had a gay, frenetic quality. Or so it had seemed to her. She was just seventeen when she arrived with her diplomat father, an indulgent parent who had little time to spend with his daughter. There was much movement of troops in and out of Lisbon in those years but there were always men around, Riverton and Tillman and the handsome Portuguese captain with the dark mustaches—Vilheira his name was—and an assortment of blond Hanoverians. But it was mostly the three of them, Justin and Gerry and Francesca, who were together. They rode and danced and got into scrapes and laughed a lot. In the end, of course, she had married Justin and outgrown that sort of larking about.

Gerry had not really changed at all. She gave the ribbons a vicious twist. She missed her youth. She certainly had not counted on the aging effects of an early widowhood. She looked once more at her reflection, liked what she saw, and laughed. She would not be such a fool as to live in the past, and at twenty-four she was far from her last prayers. She opened the door and went downstairs.

The walk restored her good humour. She was fond of her brother-in-law, and when he chose to relax he could be a charming companion. The children ran till they were exhausted, then came panting back to them and demanded refreshment. "If you're very good," Nicholas told them, "I'll buy you an ice at Gunter's." They gave a whoop and tore off, then stopped and slowed to a sedate walk that mimicked their elders. Nicholas bundled them into his curricle, placed Eddy firmly between his legs, gave the office to his bays and not long after pulled up in Berkley Square, under plane trees just coming into leaf.

It was one of those warm cloudless days that come sometimes in the spring. The square was thronged with strollers. Waiters ran back and forth carrying trays of sorbets and ices to ladies waiting in their barouches and phaetons while their male companions lounged against the railings. Nicholas and Francesca stopped to greet an acquaintance and the children made for the tables that had been placed out of doors.

When they were halfway across the square, Eddy pulled at Gwendolen's sleeve. "There, you see," he said smugly. He pointed to a table where a tall officer sat with his arm around a lovely woman who looked very much like Claudia.

Gwendolen shook her head. "It can't be, she'd never let a man do that, not in public." But a few steps more convinced her that the unthinkable had happened. Not only was her prospective stepmother resting comfortably in the officer's embrace, she was looking up at him with an absolutely disgusting expression. Her sisters seemed to approve, for they were laughing. Gwendolen's faith momentarily wavered, then she squared her shoulders and pushed forward. She would just have to save Claudia from herself.

Francesca and Nicholas were soon aware of the same scene and, like the children, pulled up abruptly. Nicholas felt as though a cold wind had suddenly blown across the square. He had not thought to find Miss Neville a vulgar flirt.

Francesca reminded herself sharply that Gerry had a life of his own which she knew nothing about, though it did seem hard that Claudia should have snatched him away just when they had met again. "He comes from Oxford, I believe," she told Nicholas. "They probably knew each other there. Come, I'll introduce you. It's Colonel Scott. He was a friend of Justin's."

They put on smiling faces and continued across the square. Eddy was standing near Gerry, fingering his buttons with awe. Gwendolen looked at them triumphantly. "He's her brother!"

Chapter 8

When the Warwick party returned home they were met by a distracted Letitia Amesbury. "Oh, Nicholas, what are we to do, things are in such a coil, I don't know when I've been so worried since Pug had his last attack, but Dr. Burton says he is in no doubt of the outcome, only she mustn't be disturbed. Well, of course I told him I think we know how to care for our dependents, but he will huff and puff as though one is an idiot and go on about salt gargles and hot bricks and a darkened room. I'm so upset and I don't know how I shall finish my Berlin pattern, for we were enlarging it to fit the Grecian chair in my dressing room and I always come such a muddle about proportions but she's good at that kind of thing, of course she should be since she has the teaching of Gwendolen and she seems to understand proportions all right so I suppose Miss Calisher is a good instructress after all, no matter what some people say and always so willing to be of service, that is, when she isn't with the children, and so helpful about sorting wools, and whatever we are to do with them I don't know."

By these tidings Nicholas ascertained that Miss Calisher had taken a turn for the worse. Without being told, Gwendolen took Eddy by the hand and led him quietly upstairs. Illness, of course, was not a cause for amusement, so they maintained sober expressions until they reached the safety of the nursery where they were overcome with laughter. A wonderful holiday was in view.

Downstairs, Nicholas led his aunt into the drawing room and Francesca rang for tea. Between them they gradually soothed Mrs. Amesbury, and by teatime she was able to make light of her earlier anxieties.

Unfortunately this state did not last. Dr. Burton called in again that evening and Nicholas, who had purposely delayed attendance at the House, was able to get a more straightforward report on the patient's progress. Dr. Burton did indeed huff and puff, as Mrs. Amesbury had described, but his message was clear. Miss Calisher was no better, and she might become worse if the infection settled on her lungs. Skilled nursing was required. The issue would be decided shortly, but in any event there would be a prolonged convalescence.

Nicholas returned thoughtfully to the drawing room where the ladies were waiting for news. "She is certainly ill," he told them, "though Burton is persuaded she will recover. But the business will take some time. I've arranged for day and night nurses, Aunt Letty, so you won't fag yourself to death running up and down stairs. There'll be someone here within the hour." He sank into a chair. The others were silent. Except for Mrs. Amesbury, who depended on her for companionship, no one attended much to little Miss Calisher, though she had been with the family for years. She filled a very necessary place, however, and they were all aware of the coming readjustments in their lives.

"I shall see Edward this evening," Nicholas said. "There is no positive danger, but it would be best if the children were out of the way."

"Perhaps one of your sisters," Francesca suggested.

"I'm afraid not. Elinor's children have the measles and Jane's out of the question. She's near her confinement and that always makes her nervous. It will have to be Waverley," he said, referring to his county seat. "We'll be going there later

127

in the summer and in the meantime Mrs. Brennan can look after them and the country air should do them good."

Lady Crawford nodded approvingly. "Sensible, Nicholas. Though I daresay Gwendolen won't like it."

Nicholas smiled and prepared to leave the room. "Then I count on you to persuade her."

As his aunt had foretold, Gwendolen didn't like it. "I almost threw a tantrum," she confessed to Eddy, "but then I saw it wouldn't do. Daddy is set on it, and so is your father."

"We can ride at Waverley," Eddy reminded her. "And there won't be lessons." Though he would miss his father, Eddy was not at all sure that Waverley was such a bad thing. There was a black pony that he longed to see again.

Gwendolen regarded him with exasperation. "But we can't *do* anything at Waverley. Not anything about Daddy and Claudia. And I don't know how they'll manage if we aren't here to give them a push at the right time."

Eddy still nursed a grievance. "It's all right for you, but I don't see why I should care who your father marries. It would be different if it were my father, I wouldn't mind giving up ponies or anything."

"That's the most selfish thing I ever heard! We're friends aren't we?" Eddy nodded reluctantly, though he wasn't sure it was quite right to be friends with a girl. "And you spend all your time with us when you're in London. So if Daddy marries Claudia, you'll see her whenever you come to London."

"But she won't be my mother."

"That won't matter, she's the nicest person imaginable and she won't make any difference between us. Except of course for you being a boy and me being a girl, I guess that makes some kind of difference to a mother. Besides," she went on kindly, "we'll probably spend a lot more time down in Waverley after they're married because Claudia told me she likes the country, and I can see to it that you come to stay with us down there too."

Eddy was silent. As usual, Gwendolen had overcome him by

the sheer force of her argument. He did not want to be a selfish boy, and he supposed if Claudia were to marry anybody but his own father it should be Uncle Nicholas. "But I don't see what we're going to do about it," he pointed out. "They're sending us down to Waverley tomorrow." He thought for a moment. "Do you think it would help if I got sick?"

Gwendolen was touched—Eddy hated to lie abed. She gave his offer serious consideration. "It's a very good idea," she admitted, "but I don't think it would work. I've tried it before, and they always find me out and then things are worse than ever. No, I think the only thing we can do is run away."

"Run away?" Eddy admired the audacity of the plan, but he doubted that it was practical. "Where would we run away to? We haven't any money."

Gwendolen admitted the problem and they considered alternatives. They quickly realized that there were few adults who could be trusted not to give them away. "In fact," Eddy said, "the only person I can think of is Mrs. Royce. She's a good sort."

"She is that." Gwendolen considered rapidly. She was adept at foreseeing future permutations and would one day be very good at chess. "But when we're found, Daddy would be angry with her and that might lead to a Breach Between the Families. That wouldn't do at all."

Eddy seized on the new idea she had introduced. "But what's the point of running away if we're going to be found?"

"Don't you see? If we aren't found, we won't be able to do anything about Claudia because we'll be In Hiding. So we have to be found, but not too soon. If they find us right away they'll be worried and then they'll get angry and then they're sure to pack us off. But if they don't find us for a long time, they'll worry and worry until they're so relieved to have us back they won't want to let us out of their sight. Besides, if they won't promise to let us stay, we won't let ourselves be found."

Eddy followed this with some difficulty, then returned to the earlier problem. "We still haven't anyone to run away to.

We've thought of everyone we know." He was seated at the schoolroom table, moodily drawing pictures of running horses. In the middle of his third he stopped and looked up. "What about Cousin Paul?"

"Eddy, that's a simply brilliant idea!" In her exuberance, Gwendolen threw her arms around him.

Eddy disentangled himself with dignity. "But I don't want to get Paul into trouble. Won't they be angry with him?"

"Probably. But people are always getting angry with Paul, so it won't make much difference to him. And he's part of the family, so they can't make a Breach. Now let's make a list of what we need to take. We'll have to walk, so it can't be more than a small bundle each. We don't dare leave now or they'll miss us at teatime, but if we get up very early tomorrow they won't look for us before nine."

In the event, it was long past eleven before anyone thought to inquire about the children. Nicholas had left the house early, expecting to be back by noon to drive them to Waverley. Francesca and Lady Crawford, who had returned from Lady Blakemore's rout at four, were still abed. Mrs. Amesbury was in the sickroom, wringing her hands over a new crisis and driving the maids to distraction with orders for hot water, poultices, aromatic spirits, and clean sheets. The kitchen staff thought the children were in the dining room, Parkhurst assumed they were in the nursery, and the upstairs maid believed them to have gone down to the kitchen.

A passing comment by Rose, the parlour maid, to the effect that someone really ought to see that the children were properly outfitted for their journey led Susan, the upstairs maid, to make a trip to the nursery. She returned with a puzzled look on her face and a letter in her hand. The beds, she said, contrary to what was usually to be found, were neatly made.

Parkhurst was applied to. He judged that the letter, which

was addressed to "whosoever may find this" printed in large capitals, should be given in hand to someone of responsibility. This clearly was not the distracted Mrs. Amesbury, so he ventured to send Susan upstairs again to Lady Francesca's room, begging her pardon, but this might be an emergency.

Francesca opened the letter which was unsealed but fastened with a pin, read it through quickly, rang for her maid, then dispatched Susan to Lady Crawford's room with a message that Lady Francesca desired her attendance as quickly as possible.

Twenty minutes later the two ladies intercepted Nicholas as he re-entered the house and requested him to step into the library. "We have," his aunt informed him, "a problem." She handed him the letter.

Nicholas took the letter over to the window. Gwendolen wrote an atrocious hand, though her spelling was impeccable. "Good God!" he breathed. "What have you done?"

"Questioned all the servants. There is a reported disappearance from the kitchen of a large number of gooseberry tarts. Eddy's lead soldiers are not on the shelf where he usually keeps them. Dido is still here which suggests that Gwendolen does not intend to stay away long, for she's very attached to her cat. All the menservants have been sent out to make inquiries in the neighborhood. I know you want to do something, Nicholas, but don't make a cake of yourself. We need to think."

Nicholas threw himself into a chair and groaned. "We'll have to let Edward know."

"I sent round a note asking him to come immediately," Francesca said.

"Where in God's name could they have gone? And why did they go?"

Lady Crawford looked at her nephew with pity. "It's quite clear why they left, Nicholas. They had no intention of being packed off to Waverley. Where is more difficult. Gwendolen is a sensible girl and will have some sort of plan in mind. If they aren't with Edward—whom, I could add, they might see as a

131

more sympathetic parent—then they might have tried to find Mrs. Hobbes. You remember, Eddy's old nurse who retired somewhere in Holburn."

"Or they might have gone to the Nevilles," Francesca said, remembering the scene at Gunter's. "Eddy quite admired Colonel Scott. Shall I go round?"

Nicholas nodded his thanks and got to his feet. "Let me go with you, then we'll try to find Mrs. Hobbes. I must be doing something. Aunt Isabel, could you stay and talk to Edward when he comes? We won't be long."

The culprits meanwhile had set out with high spirits and an unaccustomed sense of freedom. The morning was grey and cold. They had never been out at that hour and were surprised that so many people should already be abroad. Or not yet come home. As they made their way up South Audley Street, Gwendolen saw at least three men of her father's acquaintance making their unsteady way down the street. "Too foxed by half," she told Eddy, parroting her Uncle Harry's speech. "I'm certain they didn't notice us."

The children turned east at Grosvenor Square and made by degrees toward Oxford Street from where, they knew, they could find Paul somewhere in the vicinity of Bloomsbury Square. He had lodgings, he had told them, in Little Russell Street in sight of St. George's, not the fashionable Mayfair church but the one near the British Museum.

They stopped in Hanover Square to eat some of the tarts Eddy had pilfered the night before, attracting curious stares that led Gwendolen to hurry Eddy abruptly along. Though they had worn their plainest clothes, she knew their fabric and cut marked them as children who should not be abroad unattended.

By the time they reached Oxford Street their euphoria had abated and Gwendolen's feet had begun to hurt. They had left fashionable London behind. She clasped Eddy by the hand, to which he surprisingly made no objection, and with a determined smile talked of the good times they would have with his cousin. Eddy, whose experience was that Paul seldom paid him any attention, did not answer.

She looked about for distraction. Up ahead she saw a cluster of workmen gathered around what appeared to be a small cart drawn up at the kerb. As they drew nearer she saw that the cart was actually a kitchen-table with cupboards below, fitted with wheels so it could be pushed through the streets. Steam was rising from an urn set in the table, and she was aware of the spicy fragrance of sassafras. "It's saloop," she told Eddy, "and I think I've got enough money. We can share a bowl." She pushed through the knot of men, who gave way good-naturedly, and fished in her pocket for the three halfpennies that would purchase them warmth and comfort.

Eddy drank the sweetened milk gratefully, looked in the bowl, considered, then drank again before handing it to Gwendolen, just half empty. She had not taken more than two swallows when she saw a boy watching them. He was smaller than Eddy, but his face was older and had a pinched look that she had never before seen on a child. He was dirty, from his bare scarred feet to his unkempt hair. His arms were bare too, and his thin ragged garments did not appear to keep out the cold for he was shivering.

"Is he hungry?" Eddy asked.

"Yes, I suppose he is."

"Why doesn't he get something to eat?"

"Probably because he doesn't have any money." Gwendolen felt again in her pocket. Not enough. She held out the bowl with what was left of the saloop. The boy watched her warily, came forward, then stopped. She nodded encouragement. He came forward again, grabbed the bowl and drained it greedily. Then he handed it back to her with a bobbing of the head that might have passed for a bow and melted into an alley.

"If he'd stayed, I would have given him a tart," Eddy said.

"I know. I think he was frightened."

133

Eddy was incredulous. "Of us?"

"Probably of everybody."

They walked on in silence. Near the corner of Poland Street they acquired a companion, a large yellow dog as thin and dirty as the boy. Like the boy, he played a game of cautious advance and precipitous retreat till Eddy, who was fond of all animals, offered him half a tart. The dog swallowed it in one gulp and looked for more. Eddy gave him another piece and ventured to pat his head. The dog allowed it. Eddy fed him again and soon had the animal trotting at his heels. Eddy's spirits rose.

They stopped several times to ask directions, braving curious looks. Near the Tottenham Court Road they had a scare when the driver of a cart loaded with cabbages, a coarse-looking man with blackened teeth and gin on his breath, proposed to give them a ride, whether they would or no. The dog bared his teeth and growled. The children fled back in the direction they had come and the man, unable to turn his horse quickly in the now crowded road, cursed and drove on.

The children darted down High Street and into the yard of St. Giles where they ate more tarts for comfort and courage, sharing them with the dog who had followed them. Ten minutes later an inquisitive sexton frightened them away. They plunged back into High Street, took a wrong turning, and lost their way.

They were in a rabbit warren of narrow, ill-paved streets. One of Gwendolen's boots tore on the rough stones. There was a smell of ordure and gin. Unkempt women surrounded by crying children stood in doorways, while men with vacant eyes lurched past, intent on unknown errands. Hands reached for Gwendolen's cloak, but the dog growled and she hurried by untouched. They found High Street again and got their bearings, then turned wrong on Oxford Street. A weary half-hour later brought them to Bedford Square where a toothless old woman who swept the crossing told them they had overshot their mark. Gwendolen saw tears in Eddy's eyes and said firmly, "We're almost there." They turned back to Queen

Street which led shortly to their destination.

Little Russell Street was not long but offered many possibilities for habitation. They had no further direction and were forced to begin the tedious round of inquiry at each likely lodging. The name Paul Redmond roused no hint of recognition till Eddy exclaimed in outrage as the sixth person denied them. "You have to know him! He's a very famous painter!"

This led to a round of laughter, questions, and contradictory assertions by the small group of people who by this time had gathered around them. Finally a young girl not much older than Gwendolen led them into a house across the road and up two flights of stairs and deposited them, vindicated, outside an oak door. Paul was out.

It was Henry Ashton who found them, two hours later. They had sent off the girl, assuring her they were expected, settled themselves in a corner of the landing and eaten the last of the gooseberry tarts. Gwendolen sang nonsense rhymes till Eddy fell asleep, his arm round the dog, his head in her lap. She tried not to think of what would happen if Paul failed to appear.

The landing was dark and Henry almost missed them. Hearing footsteps, Eddy stirred drowsily and murmured, "Paul." Startled, Henry dropped his key, turned, then made his way toward the huddled figures in the corner. Eddy murmured his cousin's name once more.

"No, old chap, but he'll be along in a bit. You'd better come in." As Gwendolen hesitated he added, "It's all right. I live here."

They got up, stiff and cramped, and followed him slowly into the lodgings, the dog trotting in after them. They saw a large room with two doors leading off at the other end. A high window fronted the street. There was a skylight above, a table with the remains of breakfast, some chairs, another table overflowing with books and papers, a large easel, a model's

135

stand and stool, canvases stacked against a wall, no carpet. They breathed in an air of oil paint and stale wine and decided it smelled good. Eddy spoke. "We've come to see Paul. He's my cousin."

"We walked a long way and we were tired," Gwendolen added. "That's why we fell asleep."

"I see. Does Paul expect you?"

"I don't think so," Gwendolen said.

"We wanted to surprise him," Eddy explained.

"He'll be surprised," Henry said, thinking rapidly. If this was Melbrooke's son, he had no business walking alone in London.

"This is Dog," Eddy went on. "And this is my friend Genny. Her real name is Gwendolen."

"Charmed." Henry sketched a small bow and Gwendolen returned a curtsy. "That's a very old name, you know. It's Welsh, means 'white-browed.' It suits you."

"Thank you." Gwendolen was uncertain whether or not to be pleased.

"It's a form of Guenevere, or maybe the other way around. King Arthur's wife."

"Yes, I know about her. She was unfaithful to her husband."

The girl was clearly not pleased with the reference and Henry hastened to make amends. "But the name's really older still. Gwenhwyfar. She was a fertility goddess. Oh, I say, I'm sorry." Henry was now in worse than ever.

"What's fertility?" Eddy asked.

"It's making things grow," Genny explained. "Like carrots and lettuce and babies."

"—rabbits," Henry added, fearing they were on dangerous ground. "I wrote a story about a rabbit once, but it didn't get published. I gave it to my sister instead. She liked it."

Gwendolen was interested. "What else do you write?"

"Oh, pamphlets, reviews of books. Not as interesting as rabbits, but it pays better. Actually, I'm working on a novel, but it's about people. Five volumes, and rather sad."

"Could you tell us the story?" Eddy was very fond of hearing stories.

"I'd rather not, if you don't mind. I'm not sure how it ends, and I always hate to hear stories without endings. You understand."

The children were silent.

"Have you been walking long?"

"For hours and hours," Eddy said.

"I see. Are you hungry?" They nodded. "Then why don't you rest here and I'll get some food. Won't be long. By the way," he added as he opened the door, "you can call me Henry."

When Paul arrived an hour later he found the three of them grouped comfortably around the table laughing and eating bread and cheese. A large dog padded over and looked up at him in friendly anticipation. Paul looked round the room, a puzzled expression on his face. "Where's my uncle?"

The children shrank in their seats and Henry intervened. "Not here, I'm afraid. They came alone. On a visit. They wanted to see you."

Paul strode into the room, followed by Diana who quickly went to the table and put her arms around the children. "Don't storm about, Paul. You're frightening them. Let's hear what they have to say."

Emboldened by Diana's comforting presence, Gwendolen poured forth the whole story, dwelling on the injustice of being sent off to the country when Eddy had just arrived to see his father, and omitting their concern about her own father's matrimonial future. It was an impressive performance and should, she thought, have brought Eddy's cousin round immediately. Instead he paced the room, a black scowl on his face.

"But you can't stay here. There'll be the devil of a dustup, and I'll be in the thick of it." He pointed an accusatory finger at Henry. "You will too, aiding an abduction. We'll have to take

137

them back."

"We won't go," the children said in unison, stung by the injustice of his position. "We'll keep on running away," Eddy added, for he had by now decided this was a grand adventure and he did not want to be deprived of it.

"But I have to tell your fathers where you are. They'll be frantic. It's not fair to make them worry."

"I don't want Papa to worry," Eddy said, his lip trembling. "I just don't want to be sent away."

Gwendolen turned on Paul. "I didn't think you were like that. We came to you because we were sure you'd understand. Now you turn out to be just like all the rest of them."

"Well, I am. No, I'm not really. But don't you see, I have to be. I can't take the responsibility for helping you escape from your parents. You've got to go back."

"We don't need to take them back," Diana pointed out. "We just need to let their fathers know they're all right. You can take Lord Melbrooke a letter or something. You don't even have to tell him where they are."

"Oh, no, not me. I've got work to do and I'm not going to be embroiled in this. Uncle Edward will cut off my allowance and pack me off to the country myself. He can, you know, he's my guardian."

"Then I'll do it. Someone has to go to Lord Melbrooke and Mr. Warwick, it's not fair to leave them in suspense. I'll be—" Diane thought for a moment, then had a happy inspiration— "I'll be like a courier, taking messages back and forth across the line of battle. In the meantime, they can stay with you."

"What good will that do?" Paul's anxiety was mounting. "They won't let you do it. They'll have you followed or lock you in your room or something and then you won't be able to come here and then I can't finish the picture. Your sisters will be furious."

Gwendolen did not like the way this was going. "Please, do you think you could ask Miss Neville to come here and talk to us? She won't betray us, and she can tell us what we ought to do. We can't go back anyway. It's a House of Death." She did not add that if they had to be rescued, a rescue by Claudia might do much to promote the match she desired.

It was, everyone agreed, the most sensible suggestion so far. Diana left quickly, accompanied by Paul who said nothing would induce him to stay and listen to the blandishments of his young cousin and his cousin's friend. More than Henry, more even than Diana, he was aware of what the children's disappearance would mean to their parents. He was sympathetic to their plight and did not want his determination to do the right thing weakened by prolonged exposure to their disappointed faces. Gwendolen and Eddy promised solemnly they would not leave until Miss Neville came, and Henry promised to bear them company.

But Claudia was out and thus Livia found herself the recipient of a confused story, the gist of which was that the children were safe and refused to have anything to do with their respective parents. "Short of trussing them up and flinging them into a carriage, I didn't know what to do," Paul explained. "Uncle Edward wouldn't be hard on Eddy, of course, and I daresay I could look after the little chap for a day or two, but I'm not prepared to take on a ten-year-old girl. I don't want to go to her father behind her back, because he always struck me as something of a tartar, but it can only be worse for her if she stays away."

Diana was indignant. "You promised! You gave your solemn word of honour. You can't go to her father!" She turned to Livia. "Genny wants Claudia to come and set things right, but I'm sure you'll do, Livy. Please, please come or Paul will be in the most frightful coil."

Livia privately agreed that Nicholas Warwick might be something of a tartar and that Gwendolen had indeed placed them all in a most awkward position. She would not, of course, betray the children, but the afternoon was already well advanced and something must be arranged before evening. "Of course I'll come, but Mr. Warwick and Lord Melbrooke must at least be informed that the children are safe. They must be frantic with worry. Sandringham said Mr. Warwick was here this morning with Lady Francesca and appeared quite beside himself."

She wrote a hasty note to Gwendolen's father, telling him that his daughter and Eddy were well and that she was going to visit them and begging him to do nothing further until she sent him word. Praying this would suffice, she rang for Sandringham and handed him the note with a request that it be delivered at once. "I shall be gone for some time. If Miss Neville or Colonel Scott comes in, please ask them to await my return. Diana is to stay here, too."

"That's unfair!" Diana said in outrage after Sandringham had left the room. "It was my idea!"

"It was Genny's idea," Paul muttered, secretly glad to have Diana off his hands. The day was proving complicated enough and he felt he could deal better with Mrs. Royce.

"I can't have you mixed up further in this, Diana," Livia told her sister bluntly. "You're to remain here." Livia was now on reasonable terms of amity with Nicholas Warwick and did not want him to know that Diana had been involved, however innocently, in his daughter's escapade. They were ten minutes on their way before it occurred to her to wonder how Diana had come to be involved at all and what she had been doing in Paul's rooms.

It was past four when Livia's note reached Nicholas. He was not alone and could thus not give vent to his feelings—"damn that interfering woman" would have expressed them quite nicely—but Lady Crawford read his face correctly. They're found, she concluded, but something else has happened to upset him.

Nicholas handed the letter to Melbrooke. "They're safe," he said to the room at large. "At least that woman says so." He paced the floor in his impatience. "I wouldn't have believed it of her," he continued, "she's always been able to talk to me. And taking Eddy into the bargain." He came to rest beside his friend. "Edward, I do apologize for my beastly brat of an ill-behaved daughter. Unworthy."

"What woman, Nicholas?" Lady Crawford asked, reverting to his earlier remark.

"Mrs. Royce. The letter is from Mrs. Royce. She says she's gone to see the children and she'll be in touch with us. She doesn't say where, and she doesn't say when. We're to wait. We're to wait!" he repeated, flinging himself into a chair. "Not a word more. She's probably known all along. What a ramshackle family!"

"Unjust!" cried Francesca.

"Oh, surely not," Melbrooke added. "Miss Neville would never give pain."

"Forgive my nephew, Edward," Lady Crawford said mildly. "He has a touch of the spleen. He's never at his best when other people take things in hand." She turned. "For shame, Nicholas. I'm sure Mrs. Royce is only trying to help. Gwendolen may well have sent her a message. I know she finds her sympathetic."

Melbrooke rose, crossed to Nicholas' chair and put a hand on his friend's shoulder. Nicholas looked at him gratefully. "I confess I'm relieved," he said quietly, "but I'd like to wring her neck." Melbrooke was not sure whose neck he had in mind.

Meanwhile Livia was trying, without much success, to obtain a more coherent account of the events of that afternoon. As Paul's anxiety abated, his sense of ill-usage grew and Livia found it difficult to focus his attention. It was clear that Paul knew little of how the children had actually arrived. For that, she gathered, she was to apply to Henry, a young man whose exact role in the affair had yet to be explained.

141

Gwendolen was more forthcoming. Valiantly hiding her disappointment that it was Mrs. Royce and not Miss Neville who came to their rescue—she had had visions of being carried back to the house by a radiant Claudia where her father, the scales dropping from his eyes, would recognize at once that Claudia was the Perfect Wife and Mother—she told her story with little embellishment, omitting the moments of possible danger and being purposefully vague about their motivation for leaving. Eddy added his bit. He knew enough to avoid all discussion of marriage, but he had no reticence about the details of their journey, particularly the man with the cabbages and the flight into the churchyard.

"I see," Livia said finally, though she was not sure she did. "I am sorry about Miss Calisher. Illness is a very incommoding thing in a household. But perhaps the danger has been exaggerated. Your house is large and you could surely avoid the sickroom."

"Daddy always listens to Dr. Burton," Gwendolen said blandly. "Besides, they're not sure what to do with us if Miss Calisher isn't there."

Outrageous, Livia thought. The children could find means to occupy themselves, and surely someone could be found to take them for an occasional outing. She herself might do so, and even Lady Francesca, fashionable as she was, could not begrudge an occasional hour or two. Still, it was strange that the children should take a remove to the country in such aversion. "Is your country house so distasteful, then? If I had been constrained to follow my governess about like a tame dog, I should have welcomed a chance to run about a bit on my own."

Gwendolen looked hurt. Mrs. Royce was going to turn out just like the others. "Waverley's all right," she began. "We go there every summer, and Eddy and Lord Melbrooke come too, and there are lots of people about."

"And ponies," Eddy contributed. He was still not wholly

142

convinced that following Genny's wishes had not given him the worst of the bargain.

"But if we go now, there's nobody but old Mrs. Brennan and she doesn't like children at all." This was far from true, but Gwendolen was shameless. "She shouts at us because she's angry most of the time, I think it's because her husband drinks and beats her, and she sends us to bed without supper if she thinks we've been naughty. And she won't let us keep Dog."

Eddy, to whom this was a new idea, looked alarmed. "I'm not at all sure Mrs. Amesbury will let you keep Dog if you return home," Livia pointed out, absently scratching the animal's head which was resting on her lap. She knew Gwendolen was having her on, but there was no doubting her determination to remain in London. They seemed to be at an impasse.

"I want to keep Dog!" Tears in his eyes, Eddy slipped off his chair and threw his arms around the animal who responded by licking his face.

"Well, I don't." Paul, who had been prowling restlessly about the room, pointed an accusing finger at a puddle threatening one of his canvases.

"Don't cry, Eddy." Gwendolen slipped to the floor beside him. "If no one wants us, we'll all go off together."

Livia rose abruptly, upsetting dog and children. "Eddy, if you want to keep Dog, you will have to learn to control him. Mr. Ashton, if you will find rags and water, Eddy will clean up that mess. Genny, I expect you are behaving abominably, but I have no wish to inquire into your motives. I am sure you consider them sufficient. This is clearly not the place for you. I propose to take you all back to Charles Street and then to hold a council of war with your fathers."

Gwendolen was shocked. "I wouldn't have thought you would betray us," she said bitterly.

"I have no intention of betraying you, but someone has to give ground." In Livia's mind, that someone was going to be Nicholas Warwick. "There must be something we can propose

143

that would be agreeable to all of you. I'll negotiate for you and I'll do my best to see that you stay in London, but in return you must promise to do whatever is agreed upon."

Reluctantly, Gwendolen nodded. Livia took pity on her. "Perhaps your father will allow you to remain in Charles Street until the worst of the infection is over." As she proposed this, Livia realized that it had been in her mind all along. Claudia had now made a number of friends and it was no longer necessary for her sister to accompany her to every engagement. Livia had grown quite weary of playing chaperone and welcomed the diversion the children's presence might offer. "We shall be very glad to have you," she said honestly. She looked down at Eddy's new friend, now lying on her feet. "Even Dog."

The group in South Audley Street had finished a gloomy dinner and returned to the drawing room when Livia was announced. Melbrooke, noting his friend's scowl, advanced quickly to meet her and took both her hands in his own. "My dear Mrs. Royce, we are so grateful for your help. I trust they are all right." She nodded.

Nicholas came forward. "Where are the young scamps?" he demanded.

"I have given my word not to tell."

Nicholas looked thunderstruck and Lord Melbrooke and Lady Francesca showed surprise. Lady Crawford merely smiled.

"I come as an emissary," Livia went on. "May I sit down?"

Melbrooke hastened to draw out a chair and shot a warning look at Nicholas. "Perhaps we had best hear what Mrs. Royce has to say."

"The matter seems simple enough," Livia began, "though I agree that Gwendolen's behaviour leaves something to be desired. The children—at least Gwendolen, for it seems to have been chiefly her idea—have taken strong exception to being sent off to the country. I don't pretend to know their reasons, but they include feelings of filial devotion far beyond what I have usually observed. They seem most reluctant to leave their fathers of whom, they claim, they see far too little." Nicholas made as if to speak, caught Lady Crawford's eye, and subsided. The charge was not without justification. "They appreciate the position you are in, but feel they might have been consulted about alternative arrangements."

Nicholas could no longer restrain himself. "But what in the name of heaven did they think they would do? Where did they go?"

Livia permitted herself a small, maddening smile. "I am not at liberty to say. However," she went on quickly, for Nicholas' look was murderous, "we do have a proposal to put before you."

Nicholas came and stood directly before her so that she was forced to look up at him. "Do you mean to tell me, madam, that you are holding my daughter and Melbrooke's son hostage to some harebrained scheme the three of you have concocted? I demand that you tell me at once where they are or I will have you up on charges!"

Livia stood and faced him. "Fustian. You will do nothing of the kind. To some degree I have gained their confidence and I will not betray that. You will have the courtesy to hear me out. If you do not agree to our proposal, the children will return here this evening. However, I do not vouch for their future behaviour."

They glared at one another for a moment, then Nicholas withdrew, saying with elaborate courtesy, "Pray be seated again, ma'am. We will be glad to hear you out."

"Much better," Livia said, returning to her chair. Lady Crawford smiled and even Francesca looked amused. "We— my sisters and I, and I daresay our brother too, though I have not yet spoken to him—would be very glad to have Gwendolen

145

and Eddy as our guests until Miss Calisher is well enough to allow them to return here. Sandringham—our butler—will see that they stay out of scrapes. Claudia and I will undertake to keep them up on their lessons and give them regular outings—though that is something you may prefer to do yourselves. We do not live far and you can visit as often as you like."

"That is too much to ask," Nicholas objected.

"That is too kind of you," Melbrooke exclaimed at the same time.

"How very sensible," said Lady Crawford. "Nicholas, you must clearly agree to this. The children will be well cared for and you can play the forgiving father, a role that will gain you considerable credit with your daughter. Edward, of course, understands this."

Nicholas stood irresolute for a moment, then unexpectedly smiled. "I see I must. Are you allowed to tell me now, Mrs. Royce, just where my daughter is?"

"In Charles Street, Mr. Warwick."

"She has not been there all this time?"

"I would never have connived at such a thing. I brought the children there not an hour since. When last I saw them they were drinking hot milk while Claudia told them the story of Jason and the Golden Fleece. Suitably expurgated," she assured him. "Now if you will excuse me, I think I should return. If you care to come with me, I am sure the children will be delighted to see you. They would also appreciate some nightclothes and Gwendolen would like her cat."

"I'll come with you if I may," Melbrooke said.

Nicholas rang the bell and gave directions for some clothes and necessaries to be put into a portmanteau. "The cat," he told Livia, "stays here. Genny must have some reason to return home."

Livia was about to speak, then decided he should be allowed to carry this point. She turned instead to Melbrooke. "There is one other thing. Eddy insists that he be allowed to keep Dog."

"Dog?"

"He may have a name by now. Sandringham suggested Hotspur because he has an impetuous nature, and Touchstone, for reasons I have yet to fathom. I believe Eddy inclines toward the former."

Melbrooke hesitated. Nicholas strode to his side. "Don't ask questions, Edward. Just say yes."

Chapter 9

The move to Charles Street was successful beyond Gwendolen's dreams. "It means that Daddy comes every day," she told Eddy, "and he almost always sees Claudia, and he's grateful to her which is very important."

"He's grateful to Mrs. Royce, too."

"Yes, but not so much. He doesn't seem to be quite comfortable when he's with her, but he always smiles when he sees Claudia and she smiles when she sees him."

"She smiles at everybody," Eddy reminded her. "The skinny man with the high neckcloth who always brings her flowers, and the one who patted me on the head, and even the duke who's always taking her driving."

Eddy had raised a problem that was worrying Gwendolen— the obvious number of Claudia's suitors. If her father didn't come up to scratch, as Aunt Letty would say, someone else would speak up and it would be too late. Short of confronting her father, which was unthinkable, she had not yet hit on the way to proceed. Eddy did not share Gwendolen's concern. He had formed strong attachments to Sandringham, Colonel Scott, and Dog—who by now answered to Hotspur—and was content to leave women's business to the women.

The children were getting more attention than they had been accustomed to. Below stairs, Sarah, Mary Beth and Jeanie vied for their time, while Mrs. Fraser went about happily concocting sweets. Livia and Claudia took the matter of lessons seriously, but did not insist on the parts the children found dull. Gerry and Diana were frequently from home, but when present were casually kind. Diana discovered that Gwendolen had a good eye and some skill in drawing and, like her sisters, took a delight in the mentor role. Nicholas and Melbrooke visited often, though at irregular hours, and—much to Gwendolen's surprise—Francesca often came as well.

Claudia began to turn down engagements, a circumstance that caused Lady Crawford some concern. She had come to take Claudia to the Countess of Stanhope's musicale, only to find that Claudia had forgotten the engagement and taken the children for a walk. "Not that I blame her," Lady Crawford told Livia, "the Stanhope afternoons are a monumental bore, but the girl can't afford to overlook any chances. And so much depends on the mothers. I swear I've seen more matches made around the tea table than on the ballroom floor."

Livia laughed. "Don't scold. Claudia's been so good. But she loves taking care of people and being a pampered beauty isn't quite in her style."

"Perhaps not, but it's the game she's chosen to play. I'll wait for her, if you don't mind. I'm beginning to think taking the children in was a great mistake."

"But it's I who am taking them in," Livia reminded her. "A widow. What could be more natural than a maternal gesture as balm for my wounded heart?" Her eyes twinkled.

"Gammon, my girl."

But Lady Crawford was harsher when Claudia returned. "It will not do," she said, her usually merry eyes hard and cold. "This is not a pleasure jaunt to London for the Season. A few more weeks and there will be nothing left but Oxford and penury." Claudia looked stricken and Lady Crawford pressed her advantage. "There'll be time enough for children when you're married," she reminded her. "If you marry. Remember, these are not homeless waifs you have rescued. They are exceedingly well cared for children and shockingly indulged by their fathers. You're doing more than is proper—and very kind of you, too—but you needn't take it all on your own shoulders. My nephew doesn't expect it and Melbrooke doesn't expect it. You'll only embarrass them. Leave them to servants. Or your younger sister, she doesn't have anything to do."

With a sinking heart, Claudia promised compliance and went upstairs to change her gown. Lady Crawford had a soft heart but gave it no quarter. She had seen—first with astonishment and then with dawning hope—Nicholas' frequent visits to the Neville house and his growing admiration of Claudia. Still, she placed no dependence on his interest. He had fought shy of women for years and it might all come to nothing. The girl had only the one Season and something must come of it. Lady Crawford sighed and asked for a glass of sherry.

Livia brought it to her, torn between indignation at the dressing down Lady Crawford had administered to Claudia and rueful acknowledgement that it had been deserved.

Though she was growing tired of her widowed role, Livia adored London—even the crowds, the noise, and the dirt—but above all, the sense that something new was always about to happen. In a surprisingly short time she had managed to forget the whole of Oxford. The reminder that such a world still existed was like an unexpected squall in the pleasant summer of their days. She thought with wonder of their earlier assertion that they would be content to resume their former life. Diana, she knew, would not willingly consent to leave the excitement of the city and would have to be carried by force. Claudia would face it cheerfully, but Livia would know her hurt.

"I don't like playing the martinet," Lady Crawford confessed.

"You were quite right to do so. Here it is long past Easter and nothing, so to speak, is yet fixed. I'll do my best to keep her in line."

Lady Crawford smiled. "I'm sure you will." She toyed with

the fringe on her reticule. Normally she kept her hands beautifully still. "Livia, have you given any thought to your own future after Claudia is married? Do you intend to make your home with her and her husband?"

"Of course not. We should be shockingly in the way, especially at first. I expect Diana and I will return to Oxford." She kept the regret from her voice with an effort that was admirable but not lost on Lady Crawford. "When Claudia is settled, I hope we shall be able to stay with her in London sometimes. Does that seem very bad?"

"No." Lady Crawford had released the fringe, but she looked unusually serious. "I'm certain it is what Claudia would want. But are you certain it is what you want?"

Livia was genuinely surprised. "I want to be in London," she said honestly. "So does Diana. And we both would like to be near Claudia." She frowned. "Are you trying to tell me you think we'd be in the way?"

"I am trying to tell you," Lady Crawford said, her tone at once more gentle and more exasperated than usual, "that as far as I can tell, you have spent most of your life looking after your family, and that a time will come when your family no longer needs you. I can't see you dwindling into an aunt. Haven't you thought of marrying again?"

Livia shook her head.

Lady Crawford wondered about the nature of Livia's relationship with Captain Royce. Had he been unkind? Or did Livia's reserve cover a deeper hurt at his loss? "You still mourn him?"

Livia looked up in surprise. "No, it's not that. I just don't think I want to marry. That is, to marry again."

"You don't want children of your own?"

Two months ago, Livia would have said no without hesitation. She hadn't Claudia's knack with children or Claudia's instinctive longing for them. Now—now nothing seemed as simple as it once had. "I'm not sure I'd be a very good mother," she said at last. "Or a very good wife. I haven't the patience." She paused. "Would you mind very much if I came with you this afternoon?"

Lady Crawford searched Livia's face for a moment as if about to ask more, then said in her accustomed tone, "I'd be delighted. I've long wanted to give Claudia a ball at Warwick House—nothing large, you understand, but it must be well planned. We can talk at the Stanhopes'. It's ancient music and one isn't expected to listen."

When Gerry returned a short time later he found his sisters already gone but Eddy waiting for him in the hall. The boy stared up at him with melting blue eyes.

Gerry regarded him with amusement. "Cut the line, Eddy," he said briefly. "What's the matter?"

"Nothing," said Eddy, deeply offended, "is The Matter. If something were The Matter, I'd go to Claudia or Livia."

"I stand corrected. What do you want?"

"Well, it isn't exactly something, it's—oh, hullo, Genny."

Gwendolen reached the foot of the staircase. "Eddy, you oughtn't to be plaguing Colonel Scott. You know I said I'd ask Daddy."

"Yes, and you know what he'll say. He can't this week because he's much too busy and he'll see about maybe sometime, but he'll never have that much time. My father won't either. Anyway," Eddy added with forthright seven-year-old logic, "our fathers are a lot busier than Gerry, so it would be worse to plague them. Isn't that right, sir?"

Gerry gravely agreed and suggested that, as it was a serious matter, they should adjourn to the drawing room. "Now," he said, "just what is it you want to plague me with?"

Eddy drew a deep breath. "Well, sir, it's Astley's."

"The Royal Amphitheatre?"

"Yes," Gwendolen said, "we've never been because Daddy always says we're too young to be out so late—which is nonsense, of course—"

"We aren't too young now," Eddy cut in. "I met a boy in the square who said he'd been and he's only six."

"So you're asking me to take you?"

"Oh, no, sir, I wouldn't dream of *asking* you."

"Eddy," Gwendolen said firmly.

"Well, I'm not. Only if you should happen to have time and you'd like to go—"

Gwendolen repeated her warning. Eddy looked at her with wide eyes. "Don't you want to see Astley's?"

"Of course, but—"

"That settles it," Gerry said. "Never let it be said I failed to oblige a lady. When would you like to go?"

"Oh, sir!" Eddy exclaimed.

"Will you really?" Gwendolen asked.

Before he could assure them that indeed he would, Sandringham ushered Lady Francesca into the room. She stood irresolute on the threshold as she saw Colonel Scott.

"Hullo, Francie, come in."

She gave him her hand, smiled at the children, and said under her breath, "Don't call me Francie." Then in a more normal tone, "I came to see your sisters."

"You've missed them, didn't Sandringham tell you? But come in and talk to me."

Before she could reply, Eddy interrupted to share his wonderful news. "Oh, Aunt Francesca," he exclaimed, "Gerry's taking us to Astley's to see the horses. Isn't that splendid?"

"Yes, splendid," said Francesca faintly.

Gerry cocked an eyebrow at her. "Care to come with us?"

Lady Francesca looked directly at him. She knew very well what that cocked eyebrow meant, and she had had quite enough teasing from Germanicus Scott. She smiled sweetly. "Why, yes, that would be delightful."

Eddy looked dismayed. Gwendolen said politely that it

153

would be very nice to have Aunt Francesca come with them and dragged Eddy upstairs before he could say something tactless.

Gerry surveyed his guest. "Have you ever been to Astley's?"

"I don't see how that's to the point."

He laughed. "Not quite in your style, is it?"

"You invited me," she retorted, pulling off her gloves.

"So I did. To what do we owe the honour of this visit?"

"Is it so odd for me to call on your sisters?"

"No, but they're dining with you tonight." He eyed her speculatively. "Bored, Francesca?"

"I can't imagine," she said coolly, "why I should be bored."

"Neither can I. I thought you always enjoyed being a political hostess." Francesca opened her mouth to agree, then closed it abruptly as he added, "Just like Lady Holland."

"Not at all like Lady Holland," she said crossly.

"No, I take that back. You would never elope."

Francesca dropped her reserve to give Colonel Scott the set down he deserved. "The things you can say to the widow of your best friend are quite beyond me."

Gerry thought back to distant days in Lisbon. "Was Justin my best friend?"

Francesca frowned in exasperation. "Gerry, don't be nonsensical. You were thick as thieves. When I think of the scrapes the two of you got into—"

"And you! Don't come the innocent with me, my girl, because you were quite as bad as the rest of us. Don't think I don't remember what a kick-up there was when you challenged Williamson to a barefoot race and had the poor taste to beat him by half a furlong."

"That was when I was an absurd child of seventeen."

"That was when you were eighteen shortly going on nineteen."

"You dared me."

"And then you had the gall to tell the Portuguese war minister you were glad Bonaparte was in Spain or we'd all have to go back to London and be dreary."

"That," said Francesca, deciding this was no time for dignity, "is monstrously unfair, Gerry. It was Justin and he was foxed. My father is the most forgiving person imaginable, but even he was upset."

"I remember. He said if you couldn't keep your young men in line, he'd banish the lot of you from all civilized gatherings."

"That included you, Gerry. He was already having trouble because of those appalling poems you and Justin were circulating anonymously."

"I'll allow their literary merit was slim, but their content was bang off the mark."

"They libeled everyone in sight."

"That's what I meant." He paused, then asked in a different voice, "Do you still have any of them?"

Lady Francesca was not a liar. "Somewhere with my letters," she admitted. "You couldn't expect me to burn something Justin wrote."

Gerry's face softened. "Do you miss him much?"

"Yes. At least, at first." She paused, trying to put her feelings into words. "When I remember, it's as though I were looking at another person. Justin is part of what I was then. He doesn't seem to have anything to do with what I am now."

"And what are you now, Francie?"

She forgot to take umbrage at the name. "Whatever I am, Gerry, I'm not what I was. You make a mistake if you think otherwise." She rose. "Do you still want to take me to Astley's? I go out with your sisters tonight and I'm engaged to Lady Marchfield tomorrow, but I could manage to be free on Wednesday."

He rose and opened the door for her. "Wednesday then. At your service."

He called for her in a hackney, at which Francesca wrinkled her nose. Gerry ignored her expression of distaste, saying merely that he didn't keep a carriage and could hardly have borrowed Warwick's cattle and taken the chance they would come to grief in the crowd of carriages thronging the field near the Amphitheatre. Eddy thought the hackney a lark.

They drove down Whitehall, turning onto Westminster Bridge just before the Palace and Parliament buildings. On the other side, beyond the Stangate Road, stood Astley's Royal Amphitheatre, rebuilt to greater grandeur since it had burned down—for the second time—thirteen years before.

Eddy's face fell and Gwendolen suppressed a sigh of disappointment. The Amphitheatre was a plain and unimpressive building, far from the glorious palace they had expected. Gerry, however, was unperturbed as he handed them down in front of a wooden portico that extended over the pavement to protect arrivals should the weather prove inclement. It was past five o'clock and the crowd was already growing dense. It was a mixed group—fashionables mingling with artisans and cits—and a noisy one, and there was a good deal of shoving and jostling. Eddy reached for Gerry's hand and Gerry, seeing his worried face, swung him onto his shoulders and forged a way through the doors. The crowd was streaming through the passageway leading to the pit. Gerry made for the staircase that led above.

They emerged at last into the lobby. Gwendolen gasped. It was immense, fully sixty feet across, and luxuriously appointed. There were seats against the walls and an enormous stove in the centre to take the chill off the coming evening. Eddy begged to get down so he could see it. Francesca stopped one of the women who were bringing trays from the fruitroom behind the lobby and bought oranges for the children.

They made their way slowly to the box which, Francesca was pleased to see, Gerry had taken for their exclusive use. But they were not wholly private. The back of the box was no more than five feet in height and several men had stationed themselves there, apparently searching for acquaintances in the pit below. All but one. He was perhaps forty, floridly handsome but carelessly dressed. He eyed Francesca fixedly, nodded briefly, and disappeared. It was curious, but Francesca was used to attracting stares. She dismissed the incident and turned her attention to the house.

It was magnificent, horseshoe shaped with two tiers of boxes and a gallery above, and brilliantly lit by a huge chandelier containing fifty patent lamps, a gift from the Duke of York. Blissfully unaware of the others, the children lost their manners, leaned precariously over the railing, and pointed rapturously to the arena below. They were in the first tier, not far from the orchestra which divided ring from stage. The ring, covered with sawdust and tanbark, was enormous and the stage was the largest in London, and perhaps in all of Europe. It had a vaulted proscenium and great swags of velvet curtains framing a set that was vaguely eastern.

"It's vulgar," Francesca said cheerfully, "but quite splendidly vulgar. I'm so glad I came. What are we seeing?"

Gerry studied the playbill. *"The Brave Cossack; or Perfidy Punished."*

Eddy turned round. "What's a cossack?"

"What's perfidy?" Gwendolen asked at the same time.

"Eddy was first, I think. A cossack is a Russian cavalry officer. And perfidy is deceiving someone who trusts you. Since it's punished, I think it all ends happily."

Gwendolen was suddenly serious. "Who deceives who? whom?"

"I'm not sure. There's a prince, Prince Polotinska, and then there's a woman called Balsora."

"I think Balsora may be the deceiver," Francesca said. "When John Astley wrote the play, he thought his wife would play Balsora—she played all his heroines—but Balsora wasn't the right kind of heroine, she was a temptress, and Hannah Astley refused and he gave the part to Mrs. Parker. Hannah was furious and insisted he withdraw it at the end of the season, but it was wildly popular and her husband had to keep bringing it back. A few years later she changed her mind and decided she wanted to play the temptress after all. Her husband must feel vindicated."

"Did he build all this?" Eddy asked.

"No, it was his father, Philip Astley. He died two years ago. He was said to be a splendid horseman, and his son was too. John performed in the ring when he was a little boy and danced the minuet on horseback."

Eddy's eyes were wide. "Did you see him?"

Francesca laughed. "I'm not quite as old as that, Eddy—John Astley must be approaching fifty. But my father saw him at Versailles—that was before the Revolution, of course—and the French queen called him the English Rose."

They were interrupted by a flourish of trumpets and a rolling of drums. The children returned to their position by the rail. Prince Polotinska, gorgeously arrayed, arrived on a white charger with his retinue and the stage became a mass of colour and movement and sound. Balsora, likewise gorgeously clad, teased and coquetted and, like Delilah, betrayed. Polotinska vowed vengeance on his enemies. The stage, its platforms controlled by unseen machinery, oscillated and heaved, changing shape with the changing needs of the story. Eddy recalled his lead soldiers and was delighted. Gwendolen was less pleased. It seemed dreadfully unfair to have the only significant female character behave as badly as Balsora did. Claudia, Gwendolen thought loyally, was much prettier and would never act like that. And it wasn't even as if Balsora carried out her perfidy in a particularly intelligent manner. Livia would have managed much better. Livia might not be Gwendolen's image of the Perfect Wife and Mother, but Gwendolen was developing a good deal of respect for her—not to mention affection.

The performance climaxed in a bloody battle, fought under an intense white light that mirrored the intensity of the final clash. Horses galloped full tilt across a bridge as attackers scaled walls and defenders hurled destruction down upon them. The stage was littered with men and horses, slain or in their death throes, as the prince rode, finally triumphant, to receive the applause of his people and the crowd.

The after-piece, a trifle about Columbine and Pierrot, gave the audience a chance to cool down. The effects were less spectacular, but it was funny and there were some skilled feats of horsemanship. Eddy liked the dancing horse best, while Gwendolen was entranced by Columbine who could ride balanced on one foot and leap from one running horse to another.

The crowd in the pit grew more raucous and Gerry slipped out to bespeak a hackney, returning in time to escort Francesca and the children across the lobby and down the now crowded stairs.

As they came out of the theatre, Francesca was aware of someone's eyes upon her and she turned to meet the watcher's gaze. It was the man she had seen eyeing her from behind the box earlier in the evening. He bowed now as though he were known to her. Francesca did not think he was, but she had had wide acquaintance with all types of people during her years on the Peninsula. Perhaps, she thought, an acquaintance of Justin's. She was sufficiently uncertain that she did not immediately cut him when he approached her. "Lady Francesca, may I have a word with you?"

She drew back slightly. His bow was correct and his voice was that of a gentleman, but he had been drinking and she did not like the speculative gleam in his eye. Her voice was cold. "Are we acquainted, sir?"

"Why yes, now, I believe we are. Was it Paris? or Graz? or very likely Brussels?" He lied blandly, mocking her uncertainty. "Jasper Grimson, at your service."

It was absurd, she did not know him and he knew it. She turned to Gerry and was about to withdraw when his voice arrested her. "I am cousin to Sir Peter Yardley, the late Sir Peter, that is, unfortunate fellow, carried off by consumption not four months since. Weak in the chest since he was a boy."

Francesca might not know Grimson, but she recalled Peter

Yardley very well—a tall, frail young man with an angelic face and burning eyes. He had, she suspected, been the lover of Nicholas' wife Lillie and was probably implicated in the disastrous journey that led to her death.

"Gerry," Francesca said quietly, "draw apart a little. But not too far. I must have a few minutes with Mr. Grimson." Gerry complied reluctantly, his arms around the children. Francesca turned and faced Grimson again.

He drew closer to make the conversation more private. "Much obliged, ma'am, much obliged. It was a sad loss to me, we'd been often together as boys, though we hadn't seen much of one another of late years. Still, he made me his heir. Not the title, worse luck, but his effects. Papers and things. Never threw anything away."

Dear God, thought Francesca, Lillie wrote letters and he's trying to peddle them. She tried to keep the disgust from her voice. "I can have no possible interest in Sir Peter's papers, Mr. Grimson."

"Well, no, perhaps not. But Mr. Warwick might."

"Then I suggest you speak to Mr. Warwick."

"Yes, that's what I told myself, Mr. Warwick might very well be interested. But I hear he keeps his temper on a short leash, and he might react just as you have and then where would he be? In a very awkward situation. He might not know his own best interest till it was too late."

Francesca hesitated and he pressed his advantage. "Now you can't judge that, of course, so I took the liberty of making a copy of the paper in question. Just you take it and read it, and then if you think we should talk further you can find me at the eastern end of the Serpentine the next day or two. Between nine and ten." He pressed a sheet of paper into her hand, raised his hat, and bowed again. "And take note of the date, that's the thing, the date."

He vanished into the crowd still milling in the entrance. Gerry came forward. "Are you all right?"

"All right?" Francesca looked up at him, momentarily

startled. "Yes, of course I'm all right. But it was the oddest thing."

"A spot of blackmail, Francesca?"

"I may not have always been the soul of propriety, Gerry, but I'm hardly a fit object of anything so unsavory." She folded the paper and put it in her reticule. She was not about to share Nicholas' problems with Germanicus Scott.

Chapter 10

It was not until she had dismissed her maid for the night that Francesca opened the note pressed into her hand by Jasper Grimson. It was brief, barely two lines. "Yardley," it read, "I believe you have been put to some expense on my account. Pray accept the enclosed in discharge of my debt to you." It was signed "Warwick" and dated 16 April 1813. That fitted. Lillie had died early in April of that year.

But it was clearly not Lillie's letters that Grimson was holding. If anything, the note suggested that Nicholas had paid Yardley to get them back. Nicholas had strong loyalties and would have wanted to protect Lillie, even in death. She read the note again. Nicholas was capable of irony, but he used words with precision. It did not suggest payment for goods received.

Francesca tried to recall Lillie as she had first seen her. She had been a lovely, fragile thing, five years Francesca's senior, and had paid little attention to Justin's young bride. Lillie, Francesca recalled wryly, had flirted with Justin, and she and Justin had had a brief quarrel on Lillie's account.

The following year Francesca spent some months in Warwick House while Justin was campaigning in southern Spain and she came to know Lillie better. Nicholas' wife was still lovely, but her behaviour now had a frantic quality that

162

had not been there before. She had acquired a number of admirers—Francesca remembered Sir Peter among them—and was out almost every night. She spent her days shopping—she had extravagant tastes. She loved clothes and adored jewels. Francesca overheard more than one argument between Nicholas and Lillie on that score, and Nicholas put his wife on a strict allowance. Lillie complained bitterly, yet not long after she attended a ball wearing a magnificent emerald necklace that, Francesca knew, had not been among her jewels earlier. Lillie removed it in the carriage going home, saying it was heavy and uncomfortable, but Francesca suspected she did not want Nicholas to see it.

What had happened to that necklace? It was not among her things when, to spare Nicholas pain, Francesca went through them after Lillie's death. Nor were a number of other costly trifles. Francesca suspected that Lillie had pawned them for the journey that led to her death, but could only conjecture on the circumstances surrounding that fatal carriage ride. In those days, no one dared question Nicholas.

Francesca read the note a third time. If Lillie had been accepting gifts from her admirers, Sir Peter must be counted among them. He could ill afford someone as expensive as Lillie. Francesca had heard that his estate was heavily encumbered, though he lived as though he had a secure twenty thousand a year. How like Nicholas, Francesca thought. He would not have blamed Yardley, but he would have returned the jewels or, failing that, the money spent on them. That, of course, would account for the words he had written.

Francesca put the note down, picked up a silver-backed brush, and drew it briskly through her hair. She had answered one question to her satisfaction, but not the crucial one. Why was the note a danger to Nicholas? True, it might raise questions about Lillie's relationship with Yardley, but not as letters written by Lillie would have done. It might, in fact, be read differently. Think now. Could Nicholas be connected with Yardley in some other way than through Lillie, some way that would be neither implausible nor compromising? They were not neighbours. Their estates were in different counties. They had no family connections. They had not been friends, though they both sat in the House. Yardley, in fact, sat on the opposite bench and as a matter of course would have voted against Nicholas' interests. Francesca ceased her rhythmic brushing, arrested by the thought that a far worse construction than his wife's infidelity could be placed upon the note. She needed information. It was unthinkable to apply to Nicholas, and she must be discreet. She would go to Melbrooke.

She could not find him all the next day and was considering sending a message to his lodgings when he put in a late appearance at the Bassington rout. "Edward," Francesca said, moving quickly toward him and cutting off Lady Carrington who had marked him for one of her three unmarried daughters, "I was in despair of finding an intelligent face, come talk to me, please."

Melbrooke looked with pleasure at Francesca. She was wearing a robe of the palest grey silk over an underdress of cerulean blue, with plumes of a matching blue in her hair. Not many women, he thought, could wear plumes without appearing ridiculous. She talked entertaining nonsense while she carefully steered him to an alcove at one end of the room where, screened by a pedestal supporting an Egyptian vase of hideous proportions, they could hope to have some privacy.

"Lady Bassington has collected so many bright young men," she was saying, "but except for Merriman, who is monopolizing Mrs. Royce, they all appear to be in the Opposition." Francesca's family had been staunch Whigs for several generations. "Cranford, and Winters, and Lodge. And who is the man who took Yardley's seat? He died early this year, I understand, there must have been a special election."

Melbrooke looked at her sharply, but her face was without guile. She probably didn't know the story. "His name's Denville, but he would hardly qualify. Fifty if he's a day, and suffering from gout. Not much imagination either."

"Yardley was a loss then? What was he like?"

"Very young. His father held the seat before him, and he took it easily when his father died. I believe he was honest, but I don't know that he would have had a future, he was impulsive and thoughtless."

"Not one to follow his party's lead then? They couldn't count on him?"

"I wouldn't say that. If he would have refrained from speaking, they might have found him very satisfactory. I don't recall any occasion, except the once, that he really did the unexpected."

"The once?"

"Hadn't you heard? It was an electoral reform bill. I won't bore you with the details, because like all those things it made a big stir but ultimately came to very little. But it was the first bill that Nicholas carried on his own, and he had his reputation hanging on it. Tuxford—his mentor, so to speak—wanted him to drop it, said it hadn't a chance. But Nicholas was bull-headed and pulled it off. Several of the Opposition came round, Yardley among them. That was the surprise, Yardley had never before shown any independence, and he never did again."

"Strange, I don't recall the episode," Francesca said, though by now she had a very good idea when it had occurred.

"No, not strange at all. The vote came a few days after Lillie's death. I doubt that Nicholas talked of it, and I'm sure you were much too preoccupied to attend to Parliamentary matters."

"I suppose," Francesca said after a moment, "it was his way of making amends."

"Amends?"

"Yardley, Edward. If he'd felt he had injured Nicholas. You said that he was honest."

Melbrooke looked at her in surprise. "I didn't know that you knew."

"I'm not sure that I did. Let's just say that it makes sense of much that was happening in those weeks. I'm sorry, I hadn't meant to bring it up. I don't know why I did, perhaps because I heard someone mention Yardley's name the other day." She glanced over his shoulder. "I'm afraid Lady Carrington is bearing down again. If I take her off your hands, do you think you could rescue Miss Neville? She's about to be cornered by Lord Bassington and he pinches."

Having successfully turned Melbrooke's thoughts away from her interest in Yardley, Francesca moved forward to face Lady Carrington. For a moment she had been tempted to confide the whole problem to Melbrooke. He was Nicholas' closest friend and utterly trustworthy. But the moment had passed. Francesca was a resourceful woman and did not often ask for help. She would at least wait until she had seen Grimson again.

The next morning she ordered her horse early and made for Hyde Park, followed at a discreet distance by one of the Warwick grooms. She often rode at that hour and her departure caused no comment. She had dressed in a severely cut black riding habit with a small hat innocent of ribbon from which she had removed a mourning veil. Fit dress for a blackmailer. In truth, she was rather frightened. Even a whispered allegation of vote-buying could cost Nicholas his career.

Grimson had judged wisely in approaching her. Nicholas would have thrown him out of the house, heedless of the damage, convinced his own probity would see him through. Francesca, who had grown up in the political world, was more cynical. Nicholas had to be protected. She was playing for high stakes and could not afford to fail.

The morning was overcast and there was a light drizzle. Few riders were on the trail and even fewer people on foot. She found Grimson strolling near the water, a many-caped box coat thrown over his shoulders, a cigar between his teeth. He removed the cigar, swept off his hat, and made a mocking bow.

Francesca reined in her horse.

"Well met, Lady Francesca. Will you dismount? Your groom can take your horse—splendid animal, that—and we can walk apart a bit."

"Thank you, no, I prefer to stay mounted."

"Puts me at a disadvantage, but no matter, no matter." He replaced his hat and returned the cigar to his mouth. "Makes you more secure, I wager. Women need these supports when they play their little games."

This was near enough the mark that Francesca felt it like a slap. She controlled her temper with an effort. "What have you to say to me, sir?"

"Ah, but the thing is, what have you to say to me? It was I who passed you a letter. It is for you to tell me how it struck you."

"Come, we waste time. The letter is for sale, is it not? I may be interested in buying it. Name your price." Her response lacked finesse. He would clearly have loved to draw out the bargaining, but she was longing to have done with him.

"Straight to business, is that it? Good, I like that. As you may have guessed, I am in some financial embarrassment, else I should not have been compelled to auction off this little momento of my cousin's life. So it must go to the highest bidder."

"What have you been offered?" She kept her voice level, but thought frantically of other likely buyers. If he was to be taken seriously—and she had no doubt that he was—he was prepared to approach any number of persons who would have cause to do harm to Nicholas, even perhaps some in his own sadly disarrayed party.

"That is for me to know, Lady Francesca. I do my own calculations." He removed the cigar and flicked the long ash on the ground. "I may be prepared to settle with you at once to save myself the inconvenience of a prolonged stay in London. I do not like this city, and it does not like me. Mind you, I will put up with it if I must, for I have no doubt I will get my price in

167

the end."

"Your terms, sir," Francesca exclaimed impatiently, stroking her horse which had sensed her tension and grown restive.

"Two thousand. Tonight. Tomorrow at the latest. I do not like to leave time for second thoughts. That's a bargain, it's worth twice the price."

"It may be worth nothing at all. The letter is not explicit."

"Ah, yes, but it implies, does it not, it implies. So much is in the point of view. You know that or you would not be here."

This was so palpably true that she did not bother to reply. The amount was high, but it was not impossible for her to raise. Better to have it done, and done quickly. "Very well," she said. "I can have it tonight. But I must see the letter first, the original."

"Oh, no, my lady, for that you will have to trust me. You will have to trust me in any event. I promise you I have the original and I gave you a fair copy of it. An even exchange and I will bother you no more. But the thing must be done quietly. Let's say ten o'clock in Strand Lane, the river end. You must come alone and on foot."

"In that neighbourhood I will not come alone."

He eyed her speculatively. "Yes, that's wise. But I have a better idea. Stay home, Lady Francesca, and send a man as your messenger." She hesitated. "Come now," he went on in a confiding tone, "I have been a gentleman. Remember, I must trust you as you do me. We can deal well together."

She nodded curtly, not trusting herself to speech, turned her horse's head, and cantered down the path. She was suffocated by anger and shame and a sense of helplessness. She spurred her horse to a gallop, hoping to be cleansed by its speed, and for several minutes was aware of nothing but the pounding of its hooves and the beating of her heart. As the fury of her feelings abated, she slowed to a trot and only then became aware of the horse coming up behind her. She turned her head, expecting the groom, but it was Colonel Scott, grinning broadly.

"Riding hell for leather, Francesca. Did your friend so overset you?"

She did not deign to answer but allowed him to draw up beside her. They rode for a while in silence. "Gerry," she said finally, "have you been following me? That was a private matter."

"I am well aware that it was private. You are not usually so furtive."

"Furtive?" She was stung. "At nine in the morning, in the open air?"

"With scarce a soul about and Lady Francesca holding her temper in check with obvious difficulty? I can read you well, Francesca, even at fifty paces."

She returned to her first grievance. "Gerry, you are not here at random. You have been spying upon me."

"'Pon my honour, no."

"Then you listened to our conversation at Astley's. For shame, that was not the action of a gentleman."

"Not I," he said with an innocent expression. "But I admit to information received."

"Yes?"

"Young Eddy. Asked me why the man with the mustaches wanted to meet you so early in the morning and was he one of your beaux. Is he, by the way? If so, my actions were unforgiveable. I have no wish to be party to a lovers' quarrel."

She gave a harsh laugh. "It was a matter of business, Gerry, and I do not wish you to concern yourself in it. Pray forget whatever you have heard or seen."

"As you wish." They rode for some minutes more, then by mutual consent slowed their horses to a walk. "I know the type," he said, "and it's a nasty one. I have no wish to know what you're about, but if there's the slightest possibility of danger and you're in need of a man with broad shoulders and a ready fist, fleet of foot, quick of wit—well, perhaps not the last—" His voice trailed off.

Francesca had been thinking for some time of a suitable

messenger. Her first thought had been Wilkins, the groom. She knew him to be a faithful servant but was reluctant to trust him with even so much knowledge as the purchase of the letter would require. Melbrooke was a possibility, but she disliked involving him in unpleasantness and, should anything go wrong, his own reputation might be endangered. She had nearly resolved on going herself. She was not a coward, but she did not run risks unnecessarily. Gerry would be the better choice. He could handle Grimson, and she had never known him to betray a confidence.

"Are you free tonight?" she asked. He nodded. "I am buying a letter, and the money must be carried by someone alone and on foot. It is a large sum, but that is not the problem. I must be sure I have the real letter in exchange, not a copy and not a forgery. I will tell you what the letter contains and you must verify the hand. It is Nicholas'." He looked at her in surprise. "If you come to me this afternoon, say at three, I will have the money and a specimen or two of his writing."

"I won't fail you." He pulled up his horse. "Do you ride further, or can I see you home?"

"Neither. Wilkins will accompany me." The groom was still some distance behind. She turned her horse, gave Gerry a last smile, and rode away.

By one, Francesca had returned home, changed her clothes, visited her banker, come home again, paid a clandestine visit to Nicholas' study, and abstracted two documents in his hand which she hid in an oversized folio taken from the library. She narrowly missed her brother-in-law when he came home unexpectedly. Fortunately for their relationship, he did not go immediately to his study, as was his custom, but ascended the stairs in response to an urgent summons from Mrs. Amesbury.

"Nicholas, do tell me what I should do," that lady began. "Nurse says she is doing very well but I cannot believe it, she has that dreadful pasty colour like uncooked dough and she wheezes like old Major MacMurty, though of course he was strong as a bull and liable to act very much like one, I fear, his behaviour in Bath two summers ago caused no end of comment for he chased Miss Iversen all around the pump room in his wheelchair, and I know she gave him no encouragement for she is a lady of more than strict principles which is why I think she never married though she was courted for a time by a rather stout gentleman with estates in Cumberland, but she said it would never do for it's unhealthily damp and she was subject to chills and I'm sure that's the problem with Miss Calisher no matter what Nurse says."

She paused for breath and Nicholas took her hand. "You know what I prescribe, Aunt Letty?"

"No," she said doubtfully, "though I am sure it will be very sensible because you always—"

"I think you are in great need of fresh air and a quiet ride in the park would do you a world of good and preserve your own health, which you have a solemn duty to attend to or you will be of no help at all to Miss Calisher." He pressed her hand. "No matter what Nurse says."

Mrs. Amesbury brightened. "I am sure you are right, Nicholas, though I think I may go first to Asprey's for they're holding a silver brooch that I may want to buy, though Tessier's has some lovely pieces too and he's just down the street—"

Nicholas interrupted this description of his aunt's shopping needs by escorting her to her room and calling for her maid to help make Mrs. Amesbury ready for her outing. As he came away he met Francesca on the landing, regarding him with amused eyes. "Care to go shopping, Francesca? I'm sure Aunt Letty would be glad of the company and she admires your taste."

"Not today. I've been out all morning and am going to rest." She had the sense to not hide the folio, though she was painfully aware of the purloined documents it contained.

"A pity. I have some calls to make and then I'm speaking at a meeting in support of child labour, improving its conditions that is. I was going to ask if you'd like to attend."

"Doing good, Nicholas?"

"Probably not, but one should support the people who try, else we'd never change anything. Besides, I thought this one might amuse you. It's a Miss Neville, and I understand she's a possible relation."

At another time Francesca might have been amused, but she made her excuses and escaped to her room. It suited her very well to have both Nicholas and Mrs. Amesbury out of the house that afternoon.

This was not Nicholas' first acquaintance with Sophronia Neville. In fact, few of the reform-minded members of the House had escaped her attentions. The tall, angular figure with the raspy voice and the crown of red hair was a familiar sight in the Parliamentary galleries. To most eyes she seemed ridiculous, but Nicholas admired her. It was refreshing to meet people who refused to admit of compromise or to settle for small gains.

The group assembled in Miss Neville's drawing room was much as he expected, earnest, sober, worthy, and middle-aged. Well, not entirely. There was a child—suitable, perhaps, considering the topic for the day, but hardly the place he would have brought a carefully nurtured girl. The child turned and Nicholas found himself staring into his daughter's eyes.

She was with Mrs. Royce. He might have known. Livia caught his eye and had the grace to look confused. Nicholas made his way toward them. "Is this the way you see to my daughter's lessons?"

"And a very good lesson I expect it to be. We have just heard that you are to speak. We did not know, or we might have asked your permission. I know it is dreadful to perform before people one knows, strangers are so much more charitable."

"I trust you will be charitable, ma'am, but I am not at all

sure what I have to say is material fit for my daughter's ear."

"Why not?" Gwendolen asked. "You won't say what's not true, will you? And if it's true, I'm sure I ought to know about it."

"That's not quite the point."

"But it is," Gwendolen insisted in a lowered voice, for they were attracting attention. "I can see how it might not be right for Eddy because he has trouble sitting still, but I don't understand why I'm not allowed to know about the World and Things."

"It was when they were on their way to—when they ran away," Livia explained. "She was asking about the children they saw, and I'm afraid I was hard put to answer her questions."

"I see. And what part of London were you in, miss, that raised these interesting questions?"

Gwendolen stared at him, unblinking. "I don't know."

"Oh, unfair!" Livia said.

Nicholas smiled at her. "Agreed. I should not have asked."

"Would you like us to leave?" Livia raised a hand to silence Gwendolen's protest.

"I have every right to ask you to do so, but you would take me for a tyrant."

"That is a risk you would have to run. You would also mortally offend Miss Neville who is a firm believer in women's education."

"So am I, at least in theory. I see I must bow to the force of superior argument. Unless," he asked wistfully, "you could recall a forgotten engagement? No, I suppose not. I will have to temper my remarks to fit the ears of my audience." He gave Gwendolen a quick hug and rose to meet Miss Neville who was coming to lead him to the speaker's table.

His remarks, Livia felt sure, were not in the least altered by their presence. Nicholas spoke with clarity and force and obvious conviction. His audience was with him until he reminded them of the difference between utopian dreams and political realities. Their dissatisfaction could be felt and was only partially diminished when he commended their efforts and made a number of practical suggestions for further action. Miss Neville, who was nothing if not a realist, was clearly not dissatisfied and came forward to lead the applause. Gwendolen was entranced. It was a side of her father she had never seen, and she was both pleased and surprised. Livia conceded that Gwendolen's father spoke very well, a comment that led the girl to believe Livia was deficient in understanding.

They waited for the questioners to disperse, then left the house with Nicholas, having declined Cousin Sophronia's perfunctory invitation to tea. She was a busy woman and disliked the time given to social amenities. On the sidewalk, Nicholas proposed to see them to their carriage.

"We have none," Livia told him. "We came in a hackney."

"My dear Mrs. Royce."

"It is all part of Gwendolen's education," she assured him. "It will teach her to appreciate what she has."

"And does it?" he asked his daughter.

"Well," Gwendolen said diplomatically, "I think one should learn to make do with what is available. A hackney is better than walking."

Nicholas confessed gravely that it was, but his curricle would be better still if they did not mind being crowded.

"I take it this isn't your first visit to Miss Neville's?" he asked Livia as he put the bays in motion.

"No, I went once before and took Diana." She paused, then added, "It was there that I met Oliver Merriman."

"I see," said Nicholas. It had not been lost on him that Mrs. Royce had become acquainted with his closest rival among the young Whigs.

Gwendolen listened curiously. (Livia had taken her on her lap, which was rather fun and very familyish—if only it could have been Claudia.) Oliver Merriman had called several times in Charles Street, one of the few male visitors who came to see Livia rather than Claudia, and Gwendolen was aware that while

174

he and her father were not precisely enemies, they were not on the best of terms. She wished Livia didn't like him and hoped the mention of his name wasn't going to make Daddy and Livia quarrel. For once they seemed to be getting along rather well.

But Livia, though she did indeed like Merriman and enjoyed his company, was forced to admit that when it came to questions of child labour she would far sooner trust Nicholas Warwick. It was a rather disturbing discovery and one she relegated to the back of her mind for further perusal when she had leisure.

If Nicholas was disturbed by the reference to Merriman he gave no sign of it, dropping the subject and instead asking Gwendolen if she had found the afternoon educational. Gwendolen said yes, very, and proceeded to ask her father several hard questions about child labour and about climbing boys in particular. Nicholas, Livia noted, answered in a straightforward and unpatronizing manner. When they arrived in Charles Street, Livia asked if he would stay to tea. Nicholas accepted and Gwendolen ran up the front steps ahead of them—she wanted to see if Claudia was in the house.

Nicholas handed Livia down from the curricle and to her surprise retained her hand for a moment, saying in a lowered tone, "I haven't seen Genny so—so happy for a long time. Thank you."

Livia looked at him in surprise and more than a little embarrassment. To cover both, she said lightly, "Even if the result is an unwomanly education?"

"I might have known you couldn't take a compliment," Nicholas said in the same vein. He offered her his arm and they mounted the steps together, but the intimate moment had gone.

To Gwendolen's delight, both Claudia and Lady Crawford were in for tea. Nicholas was pleased as well. After half an hour in Mrs. Royce's company, he found Claudia blessedly restful.

Gerry came in while they were talking, having spent somewhat more time than necessary in South Audley Street.

Francesca had changed her mind and now proposed driving him to a point near the rendezvous with Grimson, then waiting till he had made the exchange. Gerry did not want her to come at all, insisting that it posed an unnecessary risk. They had had a long and futile argument which Francesca won by the expedient of refusing to name the street where Grimson was to be found. Gerry was thus in a-temper. Nicholas, who rather liked the impetuous young officer, tried unsuccessfully to engage him in conversation. Gerry's sisters, from long experience, ignored him. He left early, saying he had an engagement for the evening and was dining with Sedgwick beforehand. Claudia apologized for her brother's rudeness.

"It's of no consequence," Lady Crawford assured her. "Young men are often like that in the bosom of their families. It's generally cards or a woman. Would you hazard a guess?"

"Not cards," Claudia decided. "Gerry has never taken them seriously."

Shortly before ten Francesca's hired carriage pulled up at the entrance to Strand Lane to allow Gerry to descend. Having gained her initial point, she had now agreed to return as far as Somerset Place where she would wait for his return. "It may be some time," he told her, "for though the business should not take long, Grimson may be delayed. I'll give him an hour."

"I'll give you that at most. Then I come after you. And don't think to make off with my small fortune, Colonel Scott. I'll have your hide if you do."

"Madam!" he answered in mock horror. Then, giving the office to the coachman, he walked toward the river.

Grimson was not late and seemed eager to have the transaction done. They rowed a bit over the exchange—Gerry insisted on verifying the authenticity of the letter and Grimson insisted on seeing the money—but in the end it was effected to their mutual satisfaction. Grimson pocketed the bills, bade Gerry a hasty farewell, and strode off toward The Strand.

Gerry carefully put the letter in his coat pocket, then stood and watched the river. He wanted time for Grimson to leave the area and time to savour the satisfaction of a mission successfully completed. Five minutes should do it. The light in a neighbouring building went out and the moon scarcely reached the lane, but there were lights a block away in The Strand. Gerry walked slowly toward them. Somerset Place was no more than two blocks further on. He had almost reached the entrance of the lane when he was set upon by three ruffians and left, barely conscious, in the gutter. His money, watch, and ring were gone. So was the letter.

Chapter 11

Two hours later Livia arrived home with a splitting headache. She had left Claudia and Lady Crawford at a ball given by the fashionable Lady Finch to celebrate her recent return to London. Lady Finch was a renowned hostess and her entertainment proved a great crush—or was it a squeeze? the effect seemed to be the same—but Livia had found the evening insipid. Champagne had lost its novelty, and another supper of lobster patties and aspics was more than she could face. She was tired of being unable to dance, tired of the endless gossip of the women sitting on the sidelines, tired even of the sight of Claudia dancing with the Duke of Waterford. She was in a foul temper.

As the coachman let down the steps, she gathered her shawl and reticule and tried to put her thoughts in order. She was piqued, she confessed, because Oliver Merriman had failed to appear. He was to be found at most of the houses she visited and he made a point of spending a part of each evening at her side. Livia had not realized how much she longed to be treated as an attractive woman, how much the attentions of an attractive man had meant. Melbrooke too had been absent and she had missed his quiet conversation. Even Warwick had failed to put in an appearance. Though he was sometimes irritating, at least she enjoyed their sparring.

She dismissed the coachman, mounted the steps, and was about to ring when she noticed that the front door was slightly ajar. That was unpardonable carelessness, she would have to speak to Sandringham. She pushed open the door, closed it firmly behind her, and had crossed the hall when she was arrested by the sound of raised voices from above. She looked up and saw her butler with his head against the drawing room door.

"Sandringham!" Her voice was pitched low, but its authority was unmistakable.

Sandringham quickly came down the stairs. "Mrs. Royce. I did not hear you ring."

"I did not ring. The door was open. Sandringham, why are you listening at doors?"

"It is part of my study of human nature, ma'am. Valuable in my profession. In both of my professions, I should say. And I wanted to be sure Colonel Scott was not in need of assistance."

"Gerry? What is going on in there?"

"It's not the injuries, ma'am, the brandy seems to have taken care of that. It's Lady Francesca, she's in a rare taking. Perhaps you'd best step in and see what you can do. I've always found a third person can have a calming effect."

Alarmed by the mention of injuries, Livia hastened up the stairs and without knocking opened the door. Her brother was on the sopha in his shirt sleeves, a bandage wound rakishly round his head, a decanter in one hand and a glass in the other. Lady Francesca was pacing the floor, her face convulsed with fury. Neither noticed Livia's entrance.

". . . their utter arrogance, their sublime assurance they can manage anything, their criminal reliance on their fists—"

"Not to mention their pigheaded refusal to admit to any fault." Livia assumed Francesca was talking about men. "I admit my brother is quite typical of the species, but it's no good, you know, ringing a peal over him, he will only feel sorry for himself and become quite drunk. Why don't you tell me about it and we'll see if there's anything useful to be done."

"Don't give me the spilled milk bit, Livy," her brother told her. "I deserve everything she's said."

Francesca's fury had dimmed, but she spoke with bitterness. "It's not enough that your brother gets half-killed trying to do me a service, but now that the thing has proved a rousing failure, all he can think of is to start another mill."

By this Livia understood that Francesca bore considerable guilt over whatever had happened to Gerry. She refrained from telling her that Gerry's scrapes were usually his own fault and instead removed the decanter and glass from his hands. "I do not want to interfere with what is a private affair, but if it would help to talk about it, I am more than ready to listen."

Gerry looked at Francesca. She hesitated. It was not a story she wanted to share, but Mrs. Royce seemed to have some influence over her brother and that might be useful at this point. "It's a simple matter," she said. "I have been dealing with a blackmailer. Tonight I was to give him a sum of money in exchange for a letter of some importance to me. Gerry met the man in Strand Lane—a shabby, ill-lit street off the river— while I waited for him a short distance away. As he came out of the lane he was set upon by thugs. He was badly beaten and he was robbed. The letter, of course, is gone. I found Gerry in the street an hour later, barely conscious and his head streaming blood. I believe he took some other blows, though he insists they were nothing."

"There were only three of them, Francie. Nothing to make a fuss about. If I hadn't been taken by surprise, I would have decked them all handily."

"No doubt," his sister said drily. She had already ascertained that her brother had sustained no serious hurt. "But the real question is the letter, isn't it? Was it taken by accident or by design?"

Livia had gone to the heart of the matter. Francesca looked at her with respect. "Exactly. It was most likely a coincidence, robbery's not unknown in that part of town. In which case the letter would have been discarded. They have Gerry's money and watch. Unless one of them is clever enough to make the connection . . ."

"Better tell her, Francie." Francesca nodded and Gerry continued the story. "It's Nicholas Warwick; the letter bears his name and they might go to him and then there'd be hell to pay. Francesca was trying to keep it quiet. Fortunately, Grimson knew enough to come to her first."

"But Grimson—that's your blackmailer?—might have set it up in the first place. That's what you're thinking, isn't it? And Gerry wants to confront him and have it out before Grimson sends one of the thugs with a new blackmail offer?"

"There's a possibility you haven't mentioned," Francesca said. "He may want to sell it to someone else."

This was a new idea for Gerry. He rose. "That settles it. I'll find that bastard tomorrow and throttle him, if I must, but I'll have the letter off him or your money back. No, both." He sat down suddenly. "As soon as my head stays in one place."

"That would be an idiotish thing to do, Gerry," Livia said. "If you ask him, he'll laugh in your face and say he delivered the letter fair and square. If you offer him violence, he'll call for help and have you in charge before you half get your fingers round his throat. Either way you gain nothing."

"Then what's to be done? We can't do nothing at all."

"I suppose you might keep an eye on him, though I'm not certain what help that would be. Do you know where he's to be found?" Gerry shook his head. "Good. Then looking for him should keep you out of mischief for a day or two."

Gerry looked at Livia with loathing, but Francesca came to her defense. "Your sister's right, Gerry. There's little we can do but wait. Nicholas may be approached at home, but I'll see that Parkhurst refers any suspicious callers to me. If I'm approached directly, we'll know Grimson's behind it and can plan our tactics accordingly."

"And if he has another market in mind?"

"That's why you're to dog his steps. Discreetly, of course."

Francesca asked for her carriage. Livia rang for Sandringham who came with suspicious promptitude. While they waited, Francesca said with some hesitation, "Mrs. Royce, Livia—"

"It's only among the three of us," Livia assured her. She did not mention Sandringham.

She also did not mention the other eavesdroppers for she did not know about them. Gwendolen and Eddy had been roused by Gerry's noisy arrival and had crept as far down the stairs as they dared. They gathered that Gerry had been hurt and Aunt Francesca upset and that something important had been lost. Hidden in darkness, they strained to hear more, but could make little sense of it till Livia and Gerry came out of the drawing room and moved to the stairs. The children scuttled up ahead of them.

"How much did she pay?" Livia asked out of curiosity.

"Two thousand pounds. In small bills."

Livia was aghast. To her it was a fortune.

"Her father's a wealthy man. But yes, it's a great deal of money, even for her."

"Was it so important then?"

"The letter? Oh, yes. Francesca said it could ruin Nicholas Warwick."

Back in bed the children lay with open eyes, staring into the dark. "Eddy, we have to Do Something."

"Yes. But what?"

"I don't know yet. I need time to think."

Obviously they had to find the letter. But to do that they would need more information than they at present possessed.

"Gerry and Aunt Francesca and Livia know about the letter," Gwendolen said the next morning. "Gerry and Aunt Francesca are the ones that seem to have lost it, so they're the ones we'll have to go to."

"You mean ask them?"

"Don't be knuckle-headed, they'd never tell us. We have to

do it with Guile and Stealth."

"Who are they?"

"Not who. What. Guile means playing a trick, that's what Aunt Letty said Miss Bernam did when she got Mr. Fanshawe to make her an offer. And Stealth is being quiet and secret about things, like when you got the gooseberry tarts when we ran away."

"Oh, I see." Eddy thought for a bit. "But how will it help to play a trick on Gerry and Aunt Francesca even if we're quiet about it?"

"We aren't going to play a trick," Gwendolen said patiently.

"But you just said—"

"Not that kind of trick. I mean we have to find out about the letter without their knowing that's what we're finding out about."

"Gerry might tell us if we asked. He's a good sort, and it would be easier."

Gwendolen considered this. She always took Eddy's suggestions seriously, even if they were on the face of it preposterous. "Yes," she said finally, "it would. But if he says it's none of our affair, then we've lost everything because he'll be On His Guard. So I think it's better if we do it the other way."

"You mean with Gerry? Or Aunt Francesca?"

"I think Gerry's best. He's more likely to talk to us. Besides, he's here. I asked Sarah this morning and she said he was still in bed and had a fierce head and didn't know if he'd ever get up again. I like Sarah. She answers your questions without asking first why you're asking them."

Eddy nodded. It was a quality he had found missing in most adults. "I'll go see Gerry," he volunteered. "I'm so small he won't think as much about talking if it's just me in the room, and if his head hurts he won't mind much what he's saying."

Gwendolen watched in approval as Eddy gathered a dozen or so of his lead soldiers to take with him. "Tell him you thought he'd like a little male company instead of all those fussing

183

women. He'll appreciate that. I'm going to talk to Sandringham."

"With Guile and Stealth?"

"I don't need to. We saw him listening at the door."

She found him in the butler's pantry polishing the silver and reciting a soliloquy from *Richard III*, a role he had not yet been given the chance to play. Gwendolen was loath to interrupt him, for she loved listening to the roll of his sonorous voice which made the shelved glassware tremble with sound. But this was an emergency.

"Sandringham," she said, "Gerry's still in bed. Something happened to him last night."

He broke off in mid-iamb and looked at her. "I shouldn't be alarmed, miss. Colonel Scott may have had a drop too much brandy, but he'll soon mend."

"You know there's more to it than that."

He put down the creamer and picked up a heavy silver tray. "You aren't doubting my word, Miss Gwendolen?"

"Sandringham, I'm talking about Overhearing Private Conversations."

He did not deign to reply.

"It's not that I want to cause any trouble," she explained, "but it's very important that I know what you heard. There's a letter and if it isn't found something terrible will happen to my father."

Sandringham had debated the wisdom of listening to Gwendolen or denying her accusation outright—after all, it would be his word against the child's—but this last decided him. The girl was not simply making mischief. He put down the tray and they pooled their information. Gwendolen told him of the money paid by Lady Francesca and the talk of ruin to her father if the letter were not found. Sandringham provided details of the attack and robbery.

"Perhaps I should offer my services to Colonel Scott," he suggested. "I am familiar with the neighbourhood where he met with his unfortunate accident. Some judicious inquiries—not in these clothes, of course," he added, looking at his formal attire, "but suitably garbed. I could pass, say, as a merchant from Leeds, not above some sharp dealing. Or a gentleman down on his luck, ruined by women and gin. Or—"

"An actor."

"I am always an actor. The question is, which part is right for the scene?"

"Whatever you think best. But I don't think you should ask Gerry. He likes to be up and doing things and he'd probably tell you to leave everything to him. I think you should talk to Mrs. Royce. If you're worried, you can tell her I was the one listening at the door."

"You were listening at the door. At the staircase, rather."

"I mean, you can tell her I was the only one."

"It's a magnanimous offer, but I could not possibly accept it. Besides, she already knows. I will leave your name out of it. My concern for the safety and honour of the family leads me to offer my assistance."

They shook hands solemnly, and Gwendolen went to the drawing room where she curled up in a window seat to watch for her father's arrival. He often stopped in at Charles Street about eleven, and she hoped he would have some time to spend with her. Her plan of promoting his acquaintance with Claudia was well underway, but it did not seem to be going any forwarder. The trouble was that though he and Claudia saw each other frequently—in the halls, at the breakfast table, even driving in the park—there were always other people about. She herself was in the way, but since her father ostensibly came to see his daughter, Gwendolen found it difficult to remove herself from the picture. This morning she was going to propose a walk. That always allowed time for dawdling or running ahead, thus giving the adults opportunity to enjoy one another's company. She would take Eddy to make sure she could wander off from her father without comment.

Nicholas came and agreed that, yes, it was too fine a day to be indoors. Gwendolen ran upstairs to fetch her bonnet and her friend, but Eddy refused to leave his post in Gerry's bedchamber. He had a hasty colloquy with Gwendolen in the linen closet. "He forgot I was in the room and I heard him telling Sandringham to order a carriage. He's going out and I'm going with him."

"He won't take you."

"Yes he will. He won't know I'm in it."

Gwendolen applauded his resolution. When she returned downstairs she found that Livia had been added to the party. She looked for signs of impatience on her father's face, but found none. He was clearly not displeased by the arrangement and that was not a good sign. Here was Claudia wearing a morning gown of a pale apricot that warmed her skin and a smile that warmed everyone who looked at her. How could Daddy not see where his interest lay? She would have to appropriate Livia for herself.

This proved more difficult than she expected. Nicholas had given an arm to each of the sisters and was dividing his attentions impartially between them. There was a good deal of laughter which floated back to Gwendolen who had stopped to remove a stone from her shoe. The laughter was hopeful—her father did not laugh nearly enough—but it would be better if he laughed only with Claudia. Gwendolen ran up and took Livia by the hand, forcibly detaching her from the trio. "I need to talk to you," she announced.

When it came to it, Gwendolen was not sure how to begin. She walked awhile in silence, scuffling her feet to slow them down and allow the others more privacy. She looked up finally and saw Livia's face, amusement blending with concern. Gwendolen decided to be direct. "I heard you last night. Why will the letter hurt my father?"

Livia stopped, her expression now serious. "I don't know. I don't know what's in the letter. Nor does my brother. I think perhaps you should talk to your Aunt Francesca."

"She won't tell me."

"Are you sure?"

Gwendolen shrugged. They resumed their walk. "It couldn't be about anything that Daddy did. He wouldn't do anything that would have to be hidden."

"I believe that to be true, but not all men are honourable. Someone could have told lies about him."

"But people wouldn't believe them. Not if they knew him."

"Not everyone knows him, Genny. And there must be men he's opposed, men he worked with even, who would be glad to believe bad things about him. Politics is not always a gentleman's game."

Gwendolen nodded. The small circle that was her world could be trusted, of course, but she had had vague glimmerings of a world outside that was quite different. "But if that's so, why shouldn't Daddy know about it so he can defend himself? Why should Gerry and Aunt Francesca want to keep it from him?"

"I don't know," Livia said, with something less than honesty. Nicholas Warwick, she had reason to know, was quick of temper. She could imagine his treatment of a would-be blackmailer, and it might not be to Warwick's advantage. "Can you think of any reason?"

Gwendolen swallowed. Tears pricked her eyes, but she would not let them fall. If the letter were about her mother, it would explain the need for secrecy. She had never told anyone, though she thought Aunt Isabel might know something about it. She had once been on the verge of asking her aunt, but a sense of loyalty had kept her silent. Now, perhaps, she should share her secret with Livia if it would help her father. She dropped Livia's hand and drew a little apart, as though the distance meant she was not sharing quite so much. "It might be something about my mother."

Livia was careful not to look at her. "Yes?" she said in a neutral voice.

"I was seven when she died. It was very sudden, in a carriage accident. One night she left and the next day they told me. I didn't get to see her until they laid her out and she looked calm

187

and peaceful. She was very beautiful, you know. Her name was Lillie and people used to say she was like a flower. She had the softest hair."

"Yes, Mrs. Amesbury told me she was very lovely."

"She came to see me that night. The night before she went off in the carriage. I was in bed, and she must have thought I was asleep because she didn't speak to me. She just stood at the door, and then she came over to the bed and kissed me on the forehead." Gwendolen looked up at Livia. "I knew she was saying goodbye."

Livia turned to her in surprise. "You knew?"

She nodded. "I didn't say anything. Daddy wasn't there, and I didn't want to tell anyone else. I'm not sure I would have told even him. It was her secret. But I always wondered, if I had told someone and she hadn't gone out that night, if she would have died."

Livia longed to put her arms around the girl. To have carried this load of guilt these past years was unconscionable. She was appalled and angry. Her father should—well, she wasn't sure what he should have done. But the child should not be left so much alone.

"You mustn't feel sorry for me," Gwendolen went on in a matter-of-fact voice. "I said I knew, but of course I never really knew anything for a fact, and I was only seven so it wasn't really my fault. My mother wasn't a bad woman, she was kind to me, and sometimes gay and sometimes sad, and I loved to be with her when she had time, but she didn't have much time. I knew she was unhappy, and I knew she liked to flirt with men, and I knew there was one special man. But no one would ever talk to me about it, and after she died they acted like none of it had ever happened, so of course I couldn't ask them. Especially Daddy. He wouldn't talk about her at all. So if it's something to do with my mother, then maybe that's why Aunt Francesca thinks he shouldn't know about it."

Livia felt her way carefully. She was not at all sure how to handle this young realist. "I'm honoured that you've told me, Genny."

"Oh, but I had to. You know about the letter and maybe this will help to find it. You can tell Gerry if you like. Or Aunt Francesca. The important thing is to not let anything bad happen to Daddy."

Till this moment Livia had not realized the extent to which she was committed to saving Nicholas Warwick. "We'll do everything we can, Genny. And we'll tell you right away what we find out. You'll be one of us."

"That's good. Eddy's one of us, too. He's hiding in a carriage with Gerry."

Livia tried to hide her dismay, but Gwendolen recognized it without difficulty. "Maybe it's better if we don't do any more hiding?"

"Much better." Livia looked up and saw her sister and Nicholas waiting for them. "Shall I tell Claudia?"

Gwendolen knew Claudia would be sympathetic, but if Claudia was to be her second mother she should not be burdened with memories of the first. "No, I don't think we should bother her with this. Then she won't have to be devious with Daddy. I don't know if she's very good at being devious."

"No, she's not." Livia paused. "Aren't you worried about me?"

Gwendolen regarded her for a moment before taking her hand and drawing her on to meet the others. "No, I'm not worried about you at all."

Chapter 12

Gerry returned home in a foul temper. He propelled Eddy through the door and pointed a finger at the stairs. "March!" Eddy walked with head down, his hand dragging on the banister. Livia came out of the drawing room, took in the scene at a glance, and decided not to interfere. Gerry's foray had obviously been unsuccessful. He would need time to recover.

It proved more than disappointment or chagrin, however. Gerry's head had begun to ache abominably, or so he informed Sandringham when he rang for brandy. Livia intercepted the butler at the door of Gerry's room and told him to leave the tray on the hall table. She then entered the room and closed the door firmly behind her.

"I am come to minister to you. Whether you like it or not."

Gerry groaned and turned his head away.

"And then we are going to talk." She felt his forehead, decided he seemed feverish, and rang the bell. Sandringham came without delay. Perfecting his understanding of human nature again, Livia decided, and ordered cold compresses.

"I appreciate what you are trying to do, Gerry," she said after the butler left the room. "And I have no doubt that were it simply a matter of honour between gentlemen, I could leave you safely to it. Were it even a matter of using your fives, I would have no qualms whatsoever." She removed his cravat and opened his shirt. He was perspiring freely. "But we're moving in the dark. We don't know where to begin to look for your blackmailer, and we don't know what to do with him once we have him in hand. We have to think this through and we have to plan what to do next."

"Sister mine, you plan entirely too much."

"It's my widowed state. I've learned to be cautious."

Sandringham returned. Livia laid a cold cloth on her brother's forehead and told him to lie still. Sandringham adjusted the curtains to darken the room and showed a disposition to remain. Livia dismissed him.

Gerry removed the compress and began to sit up, then abruptly lay down again. "I'm sorry, Livy, but I've got to get up. I can't leave you and Francesca to deal with this alone. Grimson's a plausible rogue, but he's ugly underneath. I don't want you to have anything to do with him."

"We have Sandringham."

"A butler?"

"No, an actor."

"My God! That explains a lot. I knew there was something rum about him."

"He's devoted to us. And he wants to help."

"You told him?"

"Don't be absurd. He has an unfortunate tendency to listen at doors."

Gerry snorted. "You're too easy by half. I won't hear of it, Livy. You tell your butler to tend to his butling."

"He could be helpful, Gerry. He knows all sorts of people, that is, the sort of people who might know where someone like Grimson is to be found. You're in no condition at all to prowl the streets, at least for a day or two. He could be your legs."

"Who'll answer the door?"

"Eddy."

"Scamp. Do you know what he did?"

"I have an idea. And I'm not sure I want to know more."

Gerry ignored her. "I didn't take him knowingly. Don't

191

know how he managed to follow me without my seeing him, but he did. Then when I'd got the carriage he hung on behind, and when the driver discovered him we were too far gone to turn back."

"Oh, Gerry, he might have been hurt."

"Serve him right."

Livia removed the compress and felt his forehead. "I can always tell when you're not quite the thing, you lose your natural sweetness of disposition. I'll send Sandringham in to remove your boots. You can talk to him or not, as you please. But for now you'll have to stay in bed. Now try to sleep, Gerry, do. I'll look in later."

Livia left the room, frowning. The problem, she realized, was that there was actually not much they could do. London was a large city and Grimson could have gone to earth anywhere. He could even—a daunting thought—have left England altogether.

She went in search of Sandringham and told him to attend to Colonel Scott. "On no account is he to get up," she said. "If he tries to leave the house, let me know at once. And Sandringham, I think it best if you say nothing to him. The idea must be Gerry's, but if he cares to employ you, I'll see that you are relieved of some of your duties."

She went to the library and sat down to think. Without more information, there was little likelihood that Grimson could be found. What was it they actually knew? That he had recently arrived in London. Why? What brought him here, and how did he come to have such recent possession of the letter? And who besides the Warwicks would pay to have it?

Livia was not prone to waste time in fruitless speculation. She sat down and addressed a note to Lady Francesca, asking her to call the next afternoon at an hour when she knew Claudia was engaged.

Livia realized she had never been alone with the Warwick widow. Claudia professed to like Lady Francesca, but then she liked most people. Livia thought Lady Francesca clever and enjoyed her company, but was not sure she would trust her friendship. She seemed all surface and was evidently easily bored. For the moment the Nevilles amused her, but she could drop them as quickly as she had taken them up.

Except, possibly, that they were Gerry's sisters. Though Francesca treated Gerry with the same cool detachment she showed toward other people, she had turned to him when she needed help with Grimson, and she had been genuinely concerned when Gerry was hurt. Gerry's past friendship with Justin Warwick must be important to her. Livia suspected that her brother might have more interest in his friend's widow than was warranted by that friendship. Or was she imagining it? She hoped so. Lady Francesca would set her sights higher than a penniless officer. Livia did not want her brother hurt.

When Lady Francesca called the next afternoon, Livia pushed these speculations aside and apologized for her interference in the Warwick affairs, pleading her concern for Gwendolen.

"There's no need for apology," Francesca assured her. "We might not have come to you by choice, but you're clearly in the game now. To tell the truth, I'm glad to have you with us. You're an intelligent creature, and you seem to have some control over Gerry. Heaven knows I don't. And I don't want him endangering himself. It's none of his problem."

"But it is now. Your husband's friendship was important to Gerry. This is a debt he owes to that friendship, and you must allow him to pay it."

Francesca smiled wryly. "Whatever. At any rate there is no way of stopping him now. I only want him to be careful."

"I can't promise that. But perhaps if we could channel his energy? It seems to me the search could be narrowed if we knew something more about Grimson. Do you know why he came back to England? whom he might have seen?"

Francesca stared at her. "Of course. I've been muddle-brained about this, I should have thought of it immediately. The solicitor." She told Livia what she knew of Grimson's inheritance and his discovery of the incriminating letter.

Livia knew she was not hearing the whole, but no matter. She had no wish to pry into the secrets of the Warwick family. "Then if we could trace the solicitor, we would know where Grimson is to be found. Or at least where he was when he first arrived. Grimson would have had to give the man his direction. Could you trust Gerry with it? That is, when he's recovered."

Francesca considered. "No. This is something I can do, and with more discretion. And I long to be doing something. Don't say anything to Gerry yet. It may all come to nothing."

Livia agreed, then raised a question that had been troubling her. "I can understand why you might not want to confide in Mr. Warwick, he has a wicked temper."

Francesca smiled appreciatively.

"But Lord Melbrooke is devoted to Mr. Warwick's interests and can certainly be trusted to do nothing rash. Have you thought of asking him for help?"

"Yes, and almost did. But the matter is political and he has his own career to think of. If Nicholas does run aground over this, Edward will be more helpful if he hasn't been involved."

"And Lady Crawford?"

"There too. She has a son-in-law who plans to stand at a by-election in Northhampton. Though I confess the real reason I haven't talked to Aunt Isabel is that she will take the problem away from me. It's mine, and I intend to solve it myself."

"And what about me? Will I get in your way?"

With one of the impulsive gestures which were part of her charm, Francesca place her hand over Livia's. "No. I don't know why, but I don't mind your being in this at all. It baffles me, but there it is."

Two days later Gerry was out of bed and from then on Livia saw little of him. He no longer accompanied her and Claudia to social engagements and he seldom had time for the children, though to Livia's relief Eddy was once more in his good graces.

Gerry made no further opposition to Sandringham's help.

Livia insisted that Sandringham remain in Charles Street during the times when they were likely to have callers, but gave him the early mornings and the hours after they went out in the evening. What he did during those hours was as mysterious as the manner in which Gerry was now occupying himself. Livia did not enjoy being kept in ignorance. Talking to her brother was sure to be useless, so she approached Sandringham. She was, after all, his employer.

To her surprise, Sandringham was not at all reluctant to discuss his activities. He had that morning, he informed her, played the role of a grieving father and haunted the wharves searching for his son who was being lured overseas by promises of fortunes to be made in the Indies. The wretch who was robbing him of his son answered to Grimson's description, down to the mustaches and the many-caped box coat. Unfortunately the wretch had not been seen.

Livia agreed that it was unfortunate. "You think Grimson might go abroad?"

"It's possible. He has a large sum of money, and if he is in truth responsible for the attack on Colonel Scott, he has good reason to make himself scarce in these parts. Colonel Scott has been questioning all the establishments where there are carriages for hire, and the offices of the stage and mail coaches as well. He also rides by the Serpentine each morning—if Grimson is in town and plans to sell the letter again, he may well choose the same location—and in the evenings he visits the gambling clubs. They seem a likely haunt for a man just come into money."

"And you? What do you do in the evenings, Sandringham?"

"The taverns, Mrs. Royce. And certain other establishments I shan't enumerate. You take my meaning."

Livia nodded absently. She had had another idea. "The men who attacked Gerry, they wouldn't have been Grimson's friends, Gerry said Grimson hadn't been in London long. So he must have hired them. Where does one go, Sandringham? That kind of thing must be known."

"Colonel Scott's thought as well. He didn't have much view of them, though he remembers the largest had black hair and a broken nose. I've made inquiries of—well, of some persons of my acquaintance. Something may develop, but the thing takes time."

She looked up. His expression was properly deferential, but she sensed an undercurrent of excitement. "Sandringham, you're enjoying this, aren't you?"

"I enjoy playing new roles, ma'am. And if I may say so, Mrs. Royce, my position in this household has greatly enlarged my repertoire. I am most grateful."

And we are most grateful to you, Livia thought. Still, it wouldn't quite do to say so. Respectable widows kept their distance from their servants.

When Francesca called later that day, Livia told her of Sandringham's activities and, of necessity, who he was and how he came to be employed by the Nevilles. Livia had some anxiety about confiding the story of Sandringham's profession, but Francesca thought it a great lark. It was not surprising, she said, Harry was mad about the theatre.

Francesca was less confident about Sandringham's involvement in the search for Grimson. "Perhaps it was wrong of me," Livia admitted, "but he had overheard or guessed much of the matter, and I thought he might serve as a brake on Gerry. He seems to have contacts in parts of London I would as soon my brother did not enter."

"I am sure there is little Gerry does not know."

"Yes, but that is not quite what I meant. It is one thing for a gentleman to frequent low places, it is another for him to seek information there. In the first instance he may lose his purse—well, he has already done that—but in the second he risks far more. I don't fancy having my brother come more or less whole from the wars only to be knifed in a mean alley. Gerry is impetuous, but Sandringham is not a foolish man."

Francesca did not look convinced and Livia continued. "Besides, he is in Gwendolen's confidence."

196

"What has that to say to it? She doesn't know—did your butler tell her?"

"He would never do such a thing! The children heard Gerry when he came home after his meeting with Grimson. Then I'm afraid they heard us talking after you'd left. They put together a great deal and decided they had to do something to save Mr. Warwick. Fortunately Gwendolen talked to me before they'd put a scheme in motion. I hope I've convinced her to let us handle it. Sandringham keeps her informed and that keeps her out of mischief, and Eddy follows her lead."

Francesca laughed helplessly. "I see I have much to thank you for."

"Not at all. I care for my brother, and I'm very fond of Genny. She's been most upset about it and I'd like to help her." Livia hesitated a moment, then decided to risk the disclosure. "Gwendolen is convinced her father could have done nothing wrong, but she fears the letter may have something to do with her mother. She knows—well, I am not sure exactly what it is she knows, but it is more than a ten-year-old should be asked to bear alone. Someone should talk to her, if not her father, then you perhaps? or Lady Crawford? She seems to feel guilty about her mother's death."

Francesca looked at Livia in astonishment. "She was barely seven."

"Even so."

Francesca was silent for a moment. "Yes, someone should talk to her. I can't, I don't have her confidence and I haven't the knack. Heaven knows, Nicholas should, but I don't know if he could. Aunt Isabel might, but let me think on it for a bit. It's all tied in with the letter, you see." Francesca got up abruptly and moved to the window, then turned and faced Livia. "No, of course you don't see, you didn't know Lillie. Genny's mother. She was a lovely woman, but she was impulsive and frantic for admiration and Nicholas' concerns were quite beyond her. It might have been all right if she had taken to motherhood, some women do, but Lillie hated being tied down. In her way I think

197

she loved Genny, but she had to be surrounded by people, she couldn't bear to be alone."

Francesca turned back to the window. "I didn't see this at the time. I was fearfully jealous at first, and then I felt rather sorry for her. But we were never close." She returned to her chair and looked at Livia. "It was an unfortunate marriage—not worse than most, but unfortunate in its consequences. They were both absurdly young. Nicholas had just left Oxford and Lillie was only seventeen. She flirted, of course, and she had many admirers, but I don't think she took any of them seriously. Until she met Peter. He was a few years younger than Lillie and ethereally handsome and he was wax in her hands. She was wildly in love, probably for the first time, and more so as she couldn't bear the thought that she was past her first youth. I think it was her idea, the elopement. I didn't know, of course, but I guessed that was what had happened. She talked him into running away with her, then she pawned all her jewels and hired a carriage to take her to his estate in Essex and a wheel came off and the carriage overturned. She was killed instantly."

Livia made an inarticulate sound of pity. From what Gwendolen had told her, it was much as she had supposed, but hearing the tale firsthand brought it home more forcibly. "Did Mr. Warwick know?"

"I'm sure he did. That's how he came to write the letter. It was to Peter Yardley. I think Nicholas knew that Yardley had beggared himself buying jewels for Lillie and that the elopement must have been chiefly her doing. Nicholas couldn't return the jewels so he sent Yardley money instead. I suspect Nicholas has always felt somehow responsible, as though he should have known and been able to prevent it." Francesca shrugged. "We didn't talk about it at the time. We don't talk about it at all."

"And there was a letter with the money and Grimson got hold of it? Was he related to Yardley?"

"His cousin, and his heir."

"I can see," Livia said at last, "that Mr. Warwick might want to keep his wife's . . . behaviour from public view, particularly for his daughter's sake. But surely he is not the first man to be so afflicted. He would be more likely to elicit sympathy than ridicule if the story were known. It is hardly a matter of social ruin for him or for Gwendolen."

"Is that what Gerry told you, that Nicholas would be ruined? He doesn't know the whole. It's a political matter. Yardley was in the House and shortly after he received the letter he supported—most unexpectedly—a bill Nicholas had introduced. You see what could be made of that."

Livia nodded. "I have read of such things, but the letter surely would not support such a charge. At the worst, it might give cause for conjecture. That is hardly enough to ruin him."

"Perhaps not. But Nicholas has a reputation as a man of integrity. If he turns out to be like all the others, he would never be fully trusted again. It would kill him."

"I don't believe it. He seems made of tougher fibre."

"All right then. But it would hurt him deeply. I would spare him that."

"He stands high in your esteem."

"You mean, not many do? Yes, he's always been kind to me and I would like to see him happy."

Livia was silent. There seemed to be many sides to Nicholas Warwick. And to his sister-in-law.

After this, Livia did not see Francesca for several days. Then they met at a breakfast given by the Countess of Pettington. A strange name for the entertainment, Livia thought, for it did not begin until two and was sure to last well into the evening.

Claudia had been dancing half the afternoon, first on the gravel walks in front of the terrace and later in the drawing room as the sky clouded and the dancers moved indoors. Livia made the round of their acquaintances, then escaped into the gardens.

Francesca found her there a quarter of an hour later. "I have discovered him," she said. "The solicitor. At least I have good reason to think this is the man. He is quite respectable, but I would rather not approach him myself, he may feel obliged to inform his client about any inquiries that are made. Do you think that Sandringham—" She stopped and looked at Livia.

"He'll revel in a new role. Give me the particulars and I'll send him off tomorrow."

Two days later they met again, this time by prearrangement. "It's done," Livia told her, "and rather more than we bargained for. I'm afraid it's my fault, I gave him the entire day and he decided to go after Grimson himself. No, wait, he's done nothing to compromise your interests. He got Grimson's direction, apparently without difficulty. He posed as a distant cousin—on the maternal side—from Aberdeen who was most anxious to see his dear Jasper again. Sandringham assures me his accent is beyond reproach and that he aroused no suspicion. Then he left the solicitor's office and went to Grimson's lodgings. Grimson was out, but he told the same tale to the landlord who let him into Grimson's rooms—I gather some money also changed hands. Sandringham turned them inside out, though he was careful to leave no trace of the search. He says it is a skill he acquired when playing Iachimo in *Cymbeline*. He almost got caught for his pains and had to leave by a window, but he swears the letter is not in the room. If Grimson has it—and Gerry insists nothing will persuade him that the theft was not Grimson's doing—he carries it on his person." A thought struck her. "Unless he placed it somewhere for safekeeping? Perhaps with his solicitor?"

Francesca shook her head. "No, he would want to have it immediately available if he found another buyer. Unless he has already passed it on. In which case I have been outbid."

It was Livia's idea that they hold a council-of-war with Gerry. Once he learned that Grimson had been located, he was very likely to approach him on his own and they were anxious to prevent a confrontation.

To their surprise, it was Gerry who suggested they make use of Sandringham again, this time to pose as a prospective buyer of the letter. The scheme, which involved Gerry in an attack upon Grimson at the moment of the feigned purchase—a reversal of roles which he contemplated with the greatest satisfaction—was approved by all four conspirators and put in practice the next day. But when Sandringham, suitably disguised, went once more to Grimson's lodgings, he found that their quarry had left and given his landlord no indication of where he was going.

Livia was devastated and Sandringham in little better state. Had Grimson found evidence of the search and become suspicious? Had the landlord, breaking his purchased silence, told him of the "cousin" who had called? Or had Grimson simply found his buyer and melted away? They were back where they had begun.

Francesca refused to accept apologies. "It's not your fault," she told Livia, "nor is it Sandringham's. You must assure him of that."

Gerry was not convinced, but at a glance from Francesca decided to hold his tongue.

"Perhaps we've been going at this the wrong way round," Livia suggested. "We can't seem to find Grimson. It might be easier to find the buyer."

Gerry looked up, then turned to Francesca. "Who?"

Francesca laughed. "There are any number of people who would be glad to see Nicholas put down, even in his own party."

"Yes, but think," Livia went on. "It would have to be someone with a strong grudge, and someone with the money to indulge it. Or perhaps someone not vindictive at all, just a man ambitious for advancement and not overly scrupulous about how he makes his way."

"Barstow-Greene," Francesca said, "to the life, though he's a Whig and not even in England. Clutch-fisted besides. Leveredge possibly. Or maybe Gifford. But I can't honestly see

201

any of them paying the money Grimson would demand."

Gerry stood up. "I'm not giving up, Francesca. But I think we'll add Whitehall to our round of inquiry. Sandringham will like the change."

Francesca smiled and rose to leave, but as the three of them were standing by the door, she said seriously, "You were a capital friend to Justin, Gerry. The best he had. You don't owe him anything more."

Gerry looked at her for a moment, then grinned. "I do, you know. Five pounds. My watch was in hock when I left Lisbon and Justin redeemed it and sent it after me. Don't be an idiot, Francie. You never would listen when Justin and I tried to get you to stay out of things."

"Yes," Francesca was forced to agree. "And as I recall, I was usually right." She left it at that and went out to her waiting phaeton. Livia turned to Gerry. Gerry ignored her and went off whistling to find Sandringham. Livia looked after him. She wasn't just imagining things. Now what was she going to do about Gerry?

Chapter 13

The search for the letter was not Livia's only concern. June was now more than half gone and Claudia had not received a single offer—if you did not count Warkworth, who hadn't a penny of his own. Claudia was in as much demand as ever, but when it came to a lifetime commitment, beauty and charm seemed to be outweighed by lack of fortune and the absence of relatives who might advance a husband's career. And the Italian connection. Nothing had been said to Livia's face, but she suspected that their mother's origins and their parents' unconventional marriage were causing more than a little gossip.

Then there were the children. With a trust that seemed unwarranted, given the results so far, they had turned the problem of saving Gwendolen's father over to Livia and her brother. Gwendolen made no special demands—she did not once allude to the disclosures she had made—but Livia felt that the girl's happiness had been carefully laid in her own none too steady hands.

Miss Calisher continued to mend and the Nevilles were told that she would soon be fit to resume her duties. But not until after Lady Crawford's ball which was taking the energies of nearly all the occupants of Warwick House.

At Claudia's request, Lady Crawford had put forward the

date so that Harry and Jack might attend, and they arrived with only two days to spare. They put in token appearances at their respective homes but declined to dine with their families. They went to the Little Theatre in the Haymarket and spent the rest of the evening over a late supper at a coffee-house where they found some university friends and got a trifle bosky. Thus it was noon of the second day before they presented themselves in Charles Street, armed with bouquets of white roses for Claudia.

Miss Neville, Sandringham informed them, was out. She had been called for early by Lady Myerson and her daughters. He believed they were going shopping and would be gone most of the day. Colonel Scott was also out, as was Miss Diana, but then she was seldom at home. Lord Melbrooke had taken his son and Miss Gwendolen to the park. Mrs. Royce might be in, if they wanted him to inquire.

"Oh, dash it all, Jonathon, don't be so formal." Harry had not yet recovered from his first evening at home and his spirits were dampened by the news that he was not to see Claudia. "Here, you'd better put these in water for Miss Neville."

"Thank you, sir. I have always prided myself on not stepping out of character."

"You do superbly, Sandringham, though you give rather more information than is strictly necessary." Livia came down the stairs and held out her hands. "I'm so glad you're back, we've missed you. Was it dreadful?"

"Yes," Jack said and with great presence of mind presented her with his bouquet.

"The outside of enough," Harry added, his good humour now restored. "Can you talk to us? Aunt Isabel's turned the house upside down and no one has time to tell us anything."

"Of course." She looked at them with affection, diagnosed their condition with accuracy, and handed Sandringham the second bouquet. "We'll be in the breakfast parlour. Would you ask Mrs. Fraser to send up food—something that can be prepared quickly and in large quantities—and a pot of coffee as soon as it can be made."

Mrs. Fraser, who had few enough challenges in this house, sent up the remains of a Yorkshire ham heated with her own mustard sauce, an omelet with morels and fine herbs, hot biscuits, muffins studded with raisins and citron, fresh strawberries with custard sauce, and a hot gooseberry pie that had been intended for dinner. An hour later, Harry threw down his napkin and leaned back contentedly. "Now tell us about Claudia. Is Jeremy still hanging about? Or Dunstable? What about Waterford?"

"Has she developed a *tendre* for anyone?" Jack attacked his third piece of pie. His appetite was enormous and had no effect whatsoever on his lean, narrow-shouldered frame.

"A *tendre?*" Livia considered. "I don't think so. I'm not even sure I would know if she had. She shows no partiality and seems as happy with poor little Skeffington as with the duke and her earls."

"Who else is in the running?" Harry asked. "Aunt Isabel wrote that Claudia was a splendid success, but she scanted on details."

"If having three or four engagements an evening and never being without a dance partner is a splendid success, then Claudia certainly is one. To say nothing of invitations to drive and walk and attend concerts and the latest exhibitions. Huntley has cried off, but Lord Seaton is still around, much to your aunt's dismay. There's Mr. Rumford, he plays the viola d'amore and has a passion for ancient stringed instruments. He wears his hair long and tied back—quite outmoded—and affects black coats, but despite his posing he's rather charming and very kind, though a little old for a marriage partner."

"Fifty if he's a day," Jack muttered, "but rich as Croesus. Very good family. Never knew him to dangle after a female before."

"We met him at the Capehart musicale and he's been dancing attendance ever since. Then there's the Marquis of Dinsdale, very fashionable and always superbly mounted.

Races his own stable, Gerry says—you don't know our brother yet, do you? you'll meet him soon—and a capital fellow, but a trifle weak in the upper story for Claudia, Gerry thinks he'd bore her. Not that I've ever know Claudia to be bored."

"She has the disposition of an angel," Harry breathed.

"Perhaps. She says the secret is listening just enough to not make a fool of oneself and living with one's own thoughts the rest of the time. Then, let me see, there's the Viscount Erlin—I think we must take him seriously, he's a man of some intelligence and passably good looking, and with only a touch of the dandy which perhaps he'll outgrow. I don't think he's more than twenty-four or five. And Mr. Paston and his great friend Eversley and their great friend Simonton who's the Earl of Deavers. They do everything in threes, and this past month or so they've been hanging about like leeches."

"Good family, Paston, goes back for years," Jack said. "Better than Eversley, though his estate's not as large. Leiscestershire. Good hunting country. Deavers the best of the lot, even if he is an earl. Good-tempered, good manners, got a tartar of a mother, but they all do that."

"Thank you. We'll put that down in our Book of Matrimonial Prospects."

"Livia, you don't!" Harry was appalled.

"No, but I suppose we should. How many is that now, counting Jeremy and Dunstable and Waterford?"

"Nine or ten, I should think," Harry said.

"Eleven," said Jack who could do figures in his head.

"I'm sure we've left some out, there always seem to be a dozen or so underfoot. Of course, there are Gerry's friends, officers he's known on the continent and most of them with pockets to let. Though there is a Colonel Ralston who's a real pet and seems genuinely fond of Claudia. I like him too."

"Glad there's one, at least," Jack said. "Isn't much time, is there? Season over soon. Guess you won't be coming back."

"Jack, you ass!"

"No, Jack's quite right, Harry. We've been talking as though it's a bit of a game, and I suppose it is, but it's a serious one. Claudia has absolutely no money at all and no one has made her a serious offer—one can't call Jeremy serious. I don't want her to be unhappy, but she means to marry and she'll accept the first man who asks for her hand, whether he's suitable or not."

"She needn't marry anyone she doesn't want to. We'll take care of her." Harry's statement did more credit to his sentiments than to his sense.

Jack was more of a realist. "We'll see which way the wind's blowing. Keep our ears open. Who's serious, who's not. Then nudge whoever she wants into making a declaration."

Harry nodded. They were back in town and could take things in hand. His chest expanded as he thought of an enterprise worthy of his skill.

Livia recounted the conversation to Claudia when her sister returned to Charles Street in the late afternoon. "You'll have to make time for them tomorrow, without fail. Harry is longing to see you—longing to be seen with you would be more accurate. They've been working very hard and say they deserve a reward. And they claim they won't be able to talk to you at all at the ball, they'll never get you alone."

Claudia made a pretense of calculation. "I can give them an hour, say between two and three—I can put off Miss Ainsley, her mother's a dreadful gossip and her brother can't keep his hands to himself. Oh, of course I'll have time for them, Livy. The truth is, I've been rather homesick and it will be good to be cozy with friends again."

Livia looked at her sister in surprise. "Homesick? I thought you were enjoying the Season. I thought you liked being an Incomparable."

"Oh, I am. I do. I've been having a wonderful time and I don't mean to complain. You're the one who has cause, it must be inexpressibly dreary to be always in black. You've been so good, Livy, and I do appreciate it. I won't let you down."

Livia looked at her sister in dismay. "I haven't complained. Have I?"

"No." Claudia reached for her hand. "But there have been—"

"Touches of envy hiding just around the corner? Perhaps. But they're nothing serious."

"You've been making all kinds of excuses to avoid coming out with me."

"Not you, love. It's the company you keep. I can't abide the Myerson girls."

"They're silly, I'll admit, and not a thought in their heads, but they're good-humoured and without a trace of malice. If you didn't have to play the respectable widow and could be yourself, you might even enjoy them."

Livia smiled. Her mother's wedding ring was on her left hand, and she twisted it absently. "Claudia . . . out of all your beaux, is there anyone special? Anyone for whom you feel some partiality?"

Claudia shook her head. "They're a most agreeable and engaging lot."

"You despicable woman, you're having me on! You can't like them all."

"I like them in different ways. Colonel Ralston makes me laugh. I have wonderful conversations with Lord Erlin. Jeremy makes me feel motherly, and in a funny way Mr. Rumford does too, though he's old enough to be my father. Waterford makes me feel a very great lady indeed, and he's rather sweet under all that starch. I could make do with most any of them, I think, but despite all the white roses and the filled dance cards, no one seems about to make me an offer. Lady Crawford says there's always a raft of engagements at the end of the Season and that I'm not to worry, but I do, sometimes. But even if nothing comes of all this, we've made some good friends. The Warwicks have been so agreeable, and no one could be kinder than Lord Melbrooke."

Livia nodded, struck by a sudden thought. Claudia's last

words made her realize that—for all her concern about her sister's future—she had never once thought of the two men who were now almost daily visitors, who took obvious pleasure in Claudia's company. Lord Melbrooke was by far the most amiable man of their acquaintance. Was he a possible suitor? No, Livia decided reluctantly. Though he could certainly be accounted their friend, he had never given a hint of more particular feelings. According to popular rumour—seconded by Lady Crawford and Francesca—he was still grieving for Eddy's mother who had been dead less than two years. Besides, thought Livia, kindly diffident Melbrooke would never let his attentions fall where—

Where he felt his friend had a prior claim. How strange that it had never occurred to her before. She had thought of Nicholas Warwick as Lady Crawford's nephew, Gwendolen's father, her own opponent—but never as Claudia's suitor. And yet when she thought of it, there was more than friendship in Nicholas' manner toward Claudia. And whatever his feelings for his dead wife, he did not appear to be grieving for her. Not that it was likely to come to anything. More than most men, an ambitious politician had to exercise great care in choosing a wife.

"You're not to worry, Claudia," Livia said, more stoutly than she felt. "And you're not to accept a man unless you are truly attached to him."

"You are an incurable romantic, Livy. I don't expect to make a love match. I want a home and a family and a husband I can respect. The rest is a matter of luck, and with that affection will come in time. We haven't the luxury of being particular."

"But you won't—"

"Marry a man like your John?" Claudia laughed. "No, I'll have Gerry make him pass muster. At least I don't have to worry about fortune hunters. What a horror that must be for a woman, not knowing if a man truly cares for her or not."

"If a woman has that much money, she can afford not to

marry at all."

"And when I marry—if I marry—" Claudia continued, resolutely ignoring these words, "you can put off your weeds and we'll find you as romantic a match as you like."

"I don't think that will be necessary. Unlike you, I find fault with almost everyone I meet. As a husband, that is. I'd rather stay a widow and be a doting aunt to all your children."

"You've never doted in your life." An invitation card had fallen from the gilt-framed mirror above the mantel. Claudia picked it up and took rather a long time fitting it back into place. "Do you like Mr. Merriman?"

"Mr. Merriman?"

Claudia finished with the card and turned to her sister. "Yes, puss, Mr. Merriman, and you can spare me the blushes. I can tell he admires you. Do you admire him? Or has he faults too?"

"You mustn't tease me because I'm hard to please. I don't expect to marry, but if I did, I would require nothing more than a man of intelligence who could converse sensibly and not bore me. And with a passable appearance, though I'm not overly nice in that regard. Now, do I like Mr. Merriman? Yes, I do. He has a lively mind and he's clever and he has the most devastating eyebrows. He's ambitious and possibly arrogant, but as far as faults go, I doubt that he has more than I do myself. If you persist in this inquisition, I daresay I could think of one or two other gentlemen I might consider." Her voice grew serious. "I only wish you were harder to please yourself."

"I promise not to marry a man who will beat me."

"If he dares, Gerry will call him out!"

Claudia laughed and went to dress for dinner. Livia lingered in the drawing room. The conversation had done little to allay her concern for her sister. She picked up a book at random, then put it down unopened. She was about to follow Claudia when she heard a scratching at the door. It was Gwendolen and Eddy, and they seemed unusually solemn.

Eddy looked at Gwendolen. "You tell her," he whispered.

"No, you were the one who saw them."

"But it was your idea to tell her."

"Aren't you sure any more?"

"Yes, I'm sure, but—"

"Eddy has something to tell you," Gwendolen announced in a full voice. She gave him a small push.

Eddy squared his shoulders. "It's the man that comes here sometimes," he announced. "The one with the eyebrows."

Livia smiled. "Mr. Merriman?"

"Yes, I think that's his name."

"What about him?"

"We saw him. I mean I saw him, then I told Genny."

"I see." Eddy clearly thought the sighting worthy of note. "Where did you see him? In the park?"

"Yes, by the Grosvenor Gate."

Livia nodded encouragement. "And?"

"He was talking to a man. It was the man we'd seen before, at Astley's, talking to Aunt Francesca. Genny didn't see them, she was talking to Papa, but Hotspur was chasing my ball and I went back for him and there they were. I ran after Genny to tell her, but by then they'd gone away. Genny thought you ought to know about it. She said it might be important."

Livia rose and went to the children, trying to hide her shock and dismay. "I see. Thank you, Eddy. Thank you very much. I'm not sure what it means, but yes, it might be important."

"What are you going to do?" Gwendolen asked.

"I don't know yet. I'll talk to Gerry and Francesca."

Gwendolen nodded and moved toward the door, then turned back with a final question. "Do you think he has the letter?"

"I don't know." But I hope not, Livia said to herself. Oh, I do hope not.

Chapter 14

Lady Crawford surveyed the entrance hall of Warwick House with satisfaction. Outwardly calm, she was rapidly making a dozen decisions and giving a dozen directions on the placement of plants and the movement of furniture. The ball was her annual entertainment and Nicholas, though he provided the champagne and stood with her at the head of the stairs, left its planning and disposition in her hands. "I will be extravagant," she told him when she began to make his house her London home, "but it will be my own money. Indulge me, please."

Lady Crawford's balls could not compare with those given at Waterford House. Smaller and less sumptuous, they were also less formal and, her guests agreed, infinitely more amusing. Isabel Crawford had a wide acquaintance that extended well beyond the *haut ton* and her invitation list was sure to include writers and artists and at least one or two persons whose reputation just bordered on the respectable. Her guests enjoyed themselves and invitations were eagerly sought.

She had given considerable thought to the decorations. Because the ball was, in a sense, for Claudia, Francesca suggested white roses. "Much too obvious," her aunt had replied, "and the ball is not to be seen as for Claudia, though of course it is. But white, yes. White and blue, and perhaps a touch of lavender. I have an exquisite length of blue silk I am having made up. The Baron de Gillat obtained it for me in Turkey, of all places. I gave him the commission months ago and had almost given it up. Claudia will wear white, though, I shall insist upon it."

"But no roses?"

"No roses. Ostentatious flowers. Pretty enough with one or two, but vulgar when they're massed. Pity it's too late for apple blossoms. I want a feeling of lightness, and just a touch of disorder. My guests are not to take themselves too seriously."

Now, the preparations complete and the ball itself only hours away, Lady Crawford moved into the supper rooms where above two score of tables rented for the occasion had been laid with spotless white napery and napkins of a pale blue—an expensive conceit, for she had had to have them specially made for the occasion. Lord Gambier's head gardener, Mr. Tomson, had provided the plants that nestled in the moss-filled baskets set on each table, tricolour violas— Lady Crawford preferred the old name of heartsease—in shades of blue and lavender.

Mrs. Amesbury, whose role on these occasions was limited to overseeing the cleaning of the house and the silver and giving vague orders which Lady Crawford was forced to contradict, came in and stood beside her. "So pretty, Isabel, so pretty," she said, and for once it did not remind her of anything. She scurried on, intent on procuring some broth for Miss Calisher who was well out of danger but still a bit weak, though not above helping Mrs. Amesbury with an arrangement of lace on the gown she planned to wear that evening.

Lady Crawford debated following her sister-in-law into the kitchen, but decided against it. She had had a fearful row with the Warwick cook who expected, as a matter of course, to prepare lobster patties for the ball supper. "Everyone," Lady Crawford told him, "has lobster patties. It has become *de rigeur*. I refuse to be a slave to fashionable whim." They had compromised on something with baked oysters and a delicate mousse of Scottish salmon. He had, in the end, become enthusiastic about the menu, but she dared not risk distracting him. She went instead to count the chairs in the ballroom.

Livia went to her room in a thoughtful mood to prepare for the ball. She would have to tell Gerry and Francesca about Merriman tonight—she did not want to tell Gerry without Francesca's restraining influence. She would have to ask Merriman, somehow, about his meeting with Grimson. And she would have to keep close watch on Claudia and Claudia's purported suitors. Her mood near despair, Livia stripped off her dress. At any rate, she was determined to enjoy Lady Crawford's ball.

She stood before the cheval glass in her white shift, took down her hair and began to brush it in long rhythmic strokes. It tumbled about her face in luxuriant waves, the evening sun picking up strands of a coppery hue. "You," she said aloud to her reflection, pointing the brush for emphasis, "don't look at all like a widow." She laughed and moved to the dressing table to pin her hair into its customary severe style. I cannot, she thought, and with sudden resolution picked up the scissors and cut short a lock of her front hair. Freed from its weight, it sprang into a soft curl. The cut portion lay limp in her hand. She had a moment of sudden desolation, then it passed and she raised the scissors again. When she was through, a mass of soft curls framed her face. She twisted her back hair into a loose knot and surveyed the effect. She was pleased and felt reckless. She picked up the scissors and went to the bed where her dress for the evening was laid out. The first cut was longer than she had intended. "Oh, well," she said, talking aloud once more, "in for a penny." For the next hour she cut and stitched. It was only the neckline, but it made all the difference. When she walked into Claudia's room, Diana, who was helping her elder sister with her hair, let out a whoop and ran to embrace Livia. Claudia followed with exclamations of approval. They made so much noise that Gerry came in, his cravat still untied. He looked bemused, then said he was glad to have his sister restored to him.

The approval of her family cheered Livia and she turned her attention to Claudia. Lady Crawford had presented her with a dress and for once neither Claudia nor Livia had demurred. The underdress was of fine white silk, cut wide and low to reveal Claudia's flawless shoulders and bosom, and unadorned save for a band of cording around the hem. The overdress was of white spider gauze, gathered to give fullness at the back. At the point of the décolletage the dressmaker had placed a cluster of white silk flowers. Claudia had removed these and put them in her hair. In their place was a single rose of dark velvety red.

"You are feeling bold tonight, aren't you?" Livia said.

"Mr. Warwick sent it."

It meant nothing, Livia told herself. After all, the ball was intended for Claudia.

"Isn't it a great joke?" Claudia continued. "I swear I will wear no other flowers. You don't suppose Lady Crawford will disapprove, do you? I don't want to spoil her colour scheme."

"No," Livia assured her, "she's always the first to appreciate the unexpected touch."

"Then she'll appreciate you too," Diana said, looking at Livia's altered black dress. "I'd almost be willing to go—almost, I said—just to see their faces."

These words returned to haunt Livia as Gerry led his two sisters up the steps of Warwick House. They had been asked to dine with the Warwicks *en famille* and expected as a matter of course to find both Lord Melbrooke and Jack in the company. Claudia was in high spirits but Livia, who had left Charles Street with an air of bravado, had become suddenly quiet. Gerry looked at her and grinned. Odious man, he could always read her thoughts. She forced herself to smile back.

Nicholas met them in the drawing room, his eyes full of admiration for Claudia, then turned to greet Livia. She saw him hesitate, a look of surprise on his face, but the moment was

215

gone as he handed her courteously into the room. Was there a hint of disapproval in his eyes? After all, he supposed her to be just past her first year of widowhood. But as she drew near the others, her fears subsided. Francesca smiled in frank approval, and Lady Crawford did the same. Mrs. Amesbury liked the way she had done her hair and said that it put her in mind of Amabel Laughton who had worn it in much the same manner, though her hair was not nearly so thick and she had to wear a hair piece and was greatly embarrassed when it began to slip during one of the country dances at the Rendell's engagement party for their son and she had run into the retiring room and refused to come out for the rest of the evening, saying her life was ruined and she would have to go into a convent, which was nonsense because they weren't R.C., though she was so emotional she might as well have been. Mrs. Amesbury's story was interrupted by the announcement of dinner. Jack slipped to Livia's side and whispered that she was looking dashed well, more up to the rig, like she used to. Melbrooke, who took her into dinner, was frankly admiring. Livia's unease vanished and she prepared to enjoy the evening.

Ten o'clock found Lady Crawford and Nicholas at the head of the stairs, waiting to receive the guests. Francesca, who was happy to relinquish her responsibilities as hostess, had disappeared. Mrs. Amesbury was hovering just inside the ballroom, uncertain how to conduct herself now that everything had been done and there was no one in sight to talk to. Livia took pity on her and suggested they tour the room so they could admire its transformation.

Lady Crawford had banished vases and pedestals—she said they got in the way of the dancing—and massed the flowers in hanging baskets filled with moss and ferns. There were sweet-scented gillyflowers—Livia identified the white Rousseau and the white and blue striped William Pitt—spiky blue larkspur, fragrant white jasmine, and violet-blue bellflowers. At the far end of the room was a raised gallery in which the musicians had taken their places. They were dressed in white satin trimmed with dark blue velvet and their hair was powdered. As Livia and Mrs. Amesbury completed their turn about the room, the musicians finished tuning their instruments and began to play an air by Rameau.

It was a perfect setting for Lady Crawford. Mrs. Amesbury's comfortable dowdiness and Livia's scarcely more fashionable black—no matter how low-cut—were out of place. Claudia was not. Livia saw her sister across the room talking with Melbrooke and felt a surge of pleasure. Nothing would spoil this evening.

The room was filling rapidly. Mrs. Amesbury left to greet some friends and Livia went in search of Gerry. As she hoped, he was with Francesca. At Livia's request, Francesca led them to a small room at the back of the house and shut the door. "We can be private here," she said, "but I mustn't stay long. You have news?"

Livia nodded and repeated Eddy's story. "Would he really recognize Grimson?" she asked her brother. "Or is he simply embroidering because he knows you've been searching for him?"

"No, I'd trust the boy," Gerry said. "He's very observant. Damn!' he added in frustration. "Pardon me, but it is damnable. We may be just too late. Did Eddy see any paper or money change hands?"

"Nothing, he had only a glimpse. We can't be sure, Gerry. Grimson may have approached Mr. Merriman, but that doesn't make him guilty. I won't believe it, not until I've spoken with him."

"And what will you say? Pardon me, but have you had any dealings with a blackmailer lately? Could you for my sweet sake turn over that letter you've just bought so dearly? Don't be so muddleheaded, Livy!"

"Wait, Gerry," Francesca laid a restraining hand on his arm. "Merriman may have been approached by Grimson, but I doubt that he purchased the letter. Not that he might not be capable of using information that came his way, particularly if

217

he believed it to be true. And he may be ready to believe ill of Nicholas. But though Merriman's not a poor man, I doubt he has the kind of ready money that would be needed to satisfy a man like Grimson." Indeed, it was the reason Francesca had not earlier numbered Merriman among the possible buyers of the letter. That and the fact that she'd thought rather better of him, for all his differences with Nicholas. And perhaps because of his attentions to Livia. Francesca realized that Livia might have as much reason to be on Merriman's side as on the Warwicks', but she dismissed the idea. Livia was not a woman to change loyalties.

Gerry groaned. "Then where does all this leave us?"

"With support for our suppositions," Francesca said. "Grimson is still in London and must have the letter—he'd not approach a man like Merriman otherwise."

"But if Merriman wouldn't buy—"

"He'll try someone else. Unless . . ." Francesca hesitated. "There's Barstow-Greene."

"You said he was out of the country."

"He could return. He's only in Paris. It wouldn't take long for a letter to reach him. And Merriman's by way of being his protégé." Francesca moved to the door. "There's nothing more to be done now, Gerry. You might as well enjoy yourself for the evening. And I must get back, I'm promised to Edouard de Lisles for the first dance." She smiled brilliantly at brother and sister and left the room, her dress rustling softly.

"She's very lovely." To her surprise, Livia was wholly without envy. "Do you know, she quite frightened me when I first met her. She was so elegant, so clever—even, I thought, a touch malicious. But she's not, really, not as you know her."

"She's all of that," Gerry said moodily. "And a managing female into the bargain. Always one to get her own way. Was she warning me off? Or has she tired of the game?"

"Neither, I think. But she's a realist, Gerry. She won't waste time on what can't be helped. Come, don't be blue-devilled. Take me back to the ballroom and we'll watch Harry being very grand. He's opening the ball with Claudia."

"Harry? Isn't that Warwick's prerogative?"

"I suppose it is. But Jack told me in private that Harry went about with such a hangdog look that his brother took pity on him. Something about rising to a man's responsibilities. Harry's devoted to her. Jack is too, but he's settled for a country dance. Like Francesca, he's a realist."

The quadrille was just beginning as they entered the room. Gerry settled his sister, then went off, he said, to find some fresh air. Balked of his hero role, Livia thought. She wondered if Merriman had come and was searching the room for him when a slight disturbance at the door drew her attention. The Waterford party had arrived. The Dowager Duchess led a stately progress down the room, giving Livia the briefest of nods in passing. Marianne failed to notice her, but Waterford paused and said a few words of greeting. He was perfectly correct, but his eyes told Livia that he found her in exceptionally good looks. A small triumph, but she enjoyed it.

Colonel Ralston claimed her attention and she lost track of the dancing until Jack came to sit by her. "Imposing woman," he said, "but not at all clever."

"Who?"

"The duchess. Aunt Isabel's great friend. Tit for tat as it were."

Livia was usually adept at following Jack's train of thought, but this took her a little time. She finally got it. "Marianne."

"Yes. Dressed her wrong. Colour hard for any girl to wear, makes muddy."

He was right. Marianne was dressed in a yellow deep enough to border on gold. It overpowered her fair hair and did nothing for her pink-and-white complexion. "Can see what she was about," Jack went on. "Aunt Isabel told her what she planned. Told her about Claudia's dress, too."

"She should have stayed with pink, it suits her."

"Couldn't. Everyone's seen her in pink. Blue. Lavender."

"She does draw the eye."

"Yes, that's the trouble."

Livia had to agree. A bright sun in a summer garden was the effect desired, she judged, but Marianne only looked out of place. She glanced at Jack to see if he shared her amusement, but his face was serious. His aesthetic sense was offended.

She looked up to find Oliver Merriman standing before her. Jack tactfully withdrew and Merriman slipped into his seat. "Thoughtful young sprig. I was hoping to have you to myself." His eyes rested on her for a moment. "Is it just the effect of this delightful room, or is there some lightening in the severity of your mourning?"

"I think perhaps June overcame me."

"I'm glad. You belong to summer. No, forgive me," he went on, "I did not mean to make light of your grief."

"In all honesty," she said, wishing that she could indeed be honest, "my grief was spent long ago. But I am not yet sure how to go on living."

"By degrees. The knack will return to you. I would help you if I could."

Before Livia could respond, their conversation was interrupted by Lady Wellerby and a stout gentleman she presented to Livia as her brother-in-law, lately returned from India. The pair passed on, but the moment with Merriman was gone. Livia was not sure whether to be glad or sorry. She would have to press him for information and she was reluctant to do so. He is undeniably attractive, she thought, and he finds me attractive too. And he has never given more than passing attention to Claudia. It was heady knowledge.

"I haven't thanked you for tonight's invitation," he said. "I am persuaded it was your doing. I am not a frequent guest at Warwick House."

"I assure you that was not the case. Lady Crawford's parties are entirely her own. She certainly did not consult me on her guest list." Livia felt her face grow warm. While it was true that she had not been consulted, Lady Crawford was observant enough to note Merriman's interest and try to foster it. "I am not certain why that should be so," she went on, referring to his last statement. "The political differences between you cannot be that great. You are both ambitious, I daresay, but I know for a fact that you share some concern for reform, and I have seen you meet without rancour at a score of houses."

"I assure you I was greeted with the utmost cordiality tonight. But you have to understand that my views on the direction our party should take are paramount to me, as Warwick's views must be to him. And despite what you may think, it is not solely a question of ambition." He was, she saw, utterly serious.

"So you would not make common cause, even when you do agree?"

He smiled. "I am not above expedience. But I believe strongly that the fortunes of my party depend upon a measured approach to change and a firm adherence to the principles on which our party is based."

"Then we disagree. For I believe that principles, no matter how admirable, must be reinterpreted in light of present conditions. And when the need for change is great, surely it should not be measured." She smiled. "If I may be allowed an opinion."

"But of course. I find it charming."

This remark left Livia feeling absurdly cross. It was easier now to raise the question of his encounter with Grimson. "You have made quite an impression on my young friend Eddy. Lord Melbrooke's little boy, you must have seen him at our house."

"Of course. Looking over the stair rail to watch the visitors. And how did I impress him?"

"I am not quite sure, but he refers to you as 'the man with the eyebrows.' He says he saw you today when his father took him walking in the park."

"Yes, I was there, but I don't recall seeing either Lord Melbrooke or his son."

"That's hardly surprising, it's crowded at that hour and they were on their way back to Charles Street. Besides, you were probably engaged."

"No doubt, I must have spoken to above a dozen people. But I'm honoured that he found me worth his notice."

"To tell the truth, he's most attached to Claudia—my sister—and pays close attention to all the men who call on her."

"Surely I do not belong in that category?"

"True, but he is hardly to know that. He has conceived a firm dislike of Lord Deavers because he saw him being far too attentive to Miss Claremont only last week."

"You terrify me! Should I expect a challenge?"

"No, you are safe for the moment. Eddy says he saw you talking to a large man with mustaches and a coat with many capes. Diana—my youngest sister—says Eddy has a splendid eye for detail."

Merriman laughed. "Of course. William Alderly. An old friend of my father's, unfortunately fallen on hard times. He manages a chance meeting with me every now and then—generally to borrow money. I wish young Eddy had thought to interrupt us."

Livia smiled, successfully concealing both her triumph and her shock. Did she mind? Yes. How much? She wasn't yet sure. She would think about it later. It was stupid of Merriman to have lied. Did he suspect her? She thought not—he had no reason to do so. He was talking easily now, relating an amusing piece of gossip. In all likelihood he simply did not want word of his meeting with Grimson to spread.

They parted not long after and Livia was claimed by Lady Langdon who wanted her opinion on her plans to re-do her drawing room. From there she moved to old Mrs. Middleton who wanted to talk about her granddaughter's latest confinement, then to Major Travis-Lord who was unexpectedly attentive, and then to the Ladies Pembroke and Swinnerton who were engaged in unabashed and glorious gossip.

Livia was relieved when Gerry appeared at her side, saying curtly that he needed to speak with her. Scarcely waiting for her to reply, he strode out of the ballroom at a rapid pace, his shoulders set and a stern expression on his face. Had he found out more about Merriman? Should she tell him what she had learned or would it only make matters worse?

Gerry pulled Livia into the room where they had met with Francesca. Livia saw that his mouth was twisted in a wry smile. "Sorry for the dustup," he told her, "but I don't know what to make of this and I'm not sure what I should do. Or whether I should do anything at all. In fact, it's a matter for congratulation, or it should be. It's certainly wonderful for the family, but it doesn't seem like us at all."

"Gerry, stop dithering, what are you talking about?"

"Claudia. Waterford's going to make her an offer."

"Waterford? You're bamming me." Livia stared at him, all thoughts of Merriman forgotten.

"No, it's true. He told me. That is, he asked me, man to man, did I approve. Seeing that I stood *in loco parentis.*"

"That's absurd. What did you tell him?"

"What could I tell him?" He smiled ruefully. "She's of age, I can't control her. I said if that's what Claudia wanted, I'd be perfectly prepared to welcome him as a member of the family."

"Gerry, you didn't! He would think you were patronizing him."

"He's insufferably patronizing himself. I can't say that I much fancy him for a brother-in-law, but I didn't think it was my place to raise objections. At any rate, my tacit agreement seemed enough, he'd satisfied the forms."

"Yes, I think his grace is rather high on the forms. Not that he isn't perfectly pleasant about them. *Noblesse oblige.* It's rather daunting."

They were silent for a few moments. It should have been no surprise, Livia thought, Waterford had been paying court to Claudia since the night of his mother's ball. Small wonder, since Claudia was surely the loveliest eligible of the Season. But that Waterford would, when it came to the sticking point, actually offer for a penniless girl without connections seemed the outside of enough. "Gerry," Livia said with a sudden pang, "he doesn't think there's any money?"

"Money? No, I made that clear enough, though it was an awkward business. I must give him credit, he handled it very well, told me politely not to be an ass, all he wanted was a biddable girl of gentle birth. Not in those words, of course," he added hastily. "I did say that as her brother I'd found Claudia had a mind of her own, but he assured me he found her behaviour beyond reproach. As it damn well is. He's luckier than he knows if she'll accept him."

"Of course she'll accept him," Livia said with doleful certainty. "That's why we came to London. It will be her first serious offer and there isn't much time left." Now that it had come, Livia felt neither elation nor relief. Of course it was what Claudia wanted, what Livia had wanted for her. It was the justification of all their scrimping and scheming. Claudia deserved to make a good marriage and she would make a splendid marriage. Waterford would treat her with consideration, she would be beautifully cared for, and her children would have an enviable start in life. "Gerry," Livia said, "we have to stop it."

"Now wait a bit. This is Claudia's decision, not ours. She won't do anything she won't like."

"Oh, but she will, Gerry. She'll persuade herself that it's just what she would like. She won't admit it, but she'll think she owes it to us. It's not as if she's in love with him."

"What has love to do with it? Marriage is a lot of things and it ought to be agreeable, but I'm not sure Claudia's the type to have a grand passion. More in your line."

"Gerry!" She was outraged.

"True. You're the romatic among the Nevilles, for all your bookish ways. Don't deny it. Claudia wants a home and a family and if Waterford can give them to her and she doesn't take him in aversion, why shouldn't she have a chance? It's not you that will be living her life."

Livia was conscious of a momentary bitterness. "I'll tell you why, Gerry. If a man marries wealth, he finds it very agreeable indeed. His life is enlarged and he does very much as he pleases. If Claudia marries wealth, she'll tailor her life to her husband's measure. And in Waterford's case, that means his mother's as well. She'll have the friends he approves of and wear the clothes and jewels he thinks befit her position. She'll entertain constantly and see next to nothing of her family. She'll have no one to laugh with and no one to cosset or comfort."

"She'll have her children."

"She'll never see them. There'll be wet nurses and nursery nurses and governesses and tutors. The children will be brought to her every evening before she goes out and she won't be allowed to hug them for fear of spoiling her dress. Her husband will treat her with exquisite courtesy and won't give her one simple warm human feeling. Do you want a life like that for your sister?"

"Here, here, my girl. You're not giving Claudia much credit. Surely she could manage him better than that."

"Some women could. Claudia won't. She's honest and direct and she'll stick to her bargain."

Livia had Gerry's full attention and, she knew, his agreement. He would put the weight of his wits and his authority behind the effort to stop the match. She did not hear the door open, and it was a moment before she was aware of another presence.

"I beg your pardon." Nicholas stood in the doorway. "I didn't know there was anyone here." He paused a moment, then shut the door and came into the room. "Forgive me, but are you all right? Is there anything I can do?"

"We're quite all right, thank you, Warwick." Gerry looked at his host speculatively. "You might say that we've had a surprise, but it's not exactly an unpleasant one. The Duke of Waterford has asked my permission to pay his addresses to my sister. He's going to make her an offer tomorrow."

There was a moment of silence. "I see. But that's hardly a surprise is it, Scott?" Nicholas turned to Livia. His face was impassive and he made her a slight bow. "I must congratulate you, madam." He turned quickly and left the room.

At the same time, a similar conversation was taking place on the floor above in Harry's bedchamber. "Heard them, I tell you!" Jack insisted. "Waterford and Colonel Scott. Didn't know I was there. Couldn't very well leave once they'd started."

"Even so, she wouldn't," Harry insisted. "She'd never sell herself for a coronet."

"Done all the time. What the Marriage Mart is all about."

"But Claudia is different."

"Not really. Less silly, goes without saying, but knows what she's about. Why do you think she came to London?"

"It's a great chance, of course." Now that the initial shock had worn off, Harry was reflective. He had never really thought of Claudia as married, but of course she would be, one way or another, before many more months had passed. What would be his relationship with a married Claudia? One of those family friends, an escort always available, a confidant when she needed it? His spirits began to brighten. Better a fashionable marriage with a London house than buried in the country with dozens of children and not enough servants.

"Thing is," Jack was saying, "how are we going to stop it?"

"Stop it? Why should we?" Harry was getting used to the idea and did not understand his cousin.

"Not right for her. Rich as Golden Ball, of course, all the clothes and carriages she could want, but not her thing."

"Doesn't she like Waterford? They look well together. He's a stiff one, but he'd treat her all right. Thinks too well of himself to do anything else. And she'd have a good deal of freedom. She could have all the friends she'd want"—Harry counted himself chief among these—"and I daresay her sisters could live with them. Livia could make a good marrige, and so could Diana if she put her mind to it."

"That's not the problem." Jack took a turn or two around the room, struggling to express what seemed to him to be the obvious. "Needs someone kind, really kind. Warm-hearted. Shouldn't waste it all on her children."

"But she'd make a splendid duchess!" In his heart, Harry knew his friend was right, but he took a perverse pleasure in clinging to an image of himself as the cicisbeo of the most beautiful duchess in England.

"Lady Francesca would be better."

"Well . . . I see what you mean. But I don't see what we can do about it. It's Claudia's decision."

"We could warn her. Give her time to think. Shouldn't spring these things on a girl."

"I daresay she'll ask for time if she thinks she needs it. Still, it would be hard to turn down a duke, especially when he's been the greatest catch on the Marriage Mart these past six or seven years. I can't say I much like the idea of talking to her, though. It was a private conversation, makes us look like sneaks."

"No time for personal feelings, old boy. Got to do something tonight. Claudia is much too good for a prig like Waterford. Money's not everything. She don't care for position."

"I know, I know." Harry was pacing the room. He had a brief vision of himself as Claudia's knight, joined in battle to save her from a hated marriage, but the urgency of the moment brought him back to reality. "I tell you," he said, "we'd better go talk to Nicholas. He'll know what to do."

Chapter 15

It was almost four before the last of Lady Crawford's guests left Warwick House. It had been, they agreed, one of the most diverting parties of the Season, a tonic to those surfeited with entertainments which grew indistinguishable in memory. The laughter of a departing group floated up South Audley Street, and near the corner two fashionably dressed gentlemen supported a third, his legs having turned waxen beneath him.

The Warwick family was gathered in the library along with Melbrooke, Jack, and the Nevilles, none of whom counted as guests in the ordinary sense of the word. A tea tray had been laid and there was an array of bottles. We are all, Livia thought, a trifle foxed, but whether from champagne, fatigue or triumph I'm sure I can't tell. She sipped her tea gratefully and relaxed in a corner of the sofa.

Livia had wanted to leave earlier, for she was anxious to speak to Claudia, but her elder sister had convinced her that Lady Crawford would see this as a defection. "The best part of a ball is talking it all over afterwards, and as we have been in on its birth, we should help lay it decently to rest." Claudia was still in high spirits. She had danced every dance, her colour was high, and she was laughing a good deal. Livia suspected that she had been imbibing more wine than was her wont.

"Isabel, my dear, that was the gayest party you've ever

228

given." Mrs. Amesbury was also in high feather. "Mrs. Bedford said the same, and Colonel Stanton said he was utterly charmed. He's a dreadful old curmudgeon, absolutely unbearable to his wife and daughters, and I would never have expected it of him. He was carrying on shamelessly with little Miss Peabody, and she's such a goose she didn't know how to get away, though I could tell she was longing to escape his attentions. He has a way of clutching the girls so when he dances, and his waltzing is positively indecent, it reminds me of the dancing master Lady Britten had to discharge, and her eldest girl was sent to the country for the longest time and looked dreadfully pale when she returned, poor thing, but she made a splendid marriage all the same, which only shows that girls can't be too careful, and if they can't they need clever mothers."

"Aunt Letty," Harry interrupted with a flourish, presenting her with a handful of jasmine he had plucked from a hanging basket on his way to the library. They were fading but still fragrant and Mrs. Amesbury buried her nose in them, allowing a more general turn to the conversation.

"What was the row just after supper?" Gerry asked. "I happened on it when I was going back to the card room. Handsome woman in green, must have been wearing a fortune in gems."

"Georgina Nelliston. She had a dreadful fight with Lord Berresford and gave him his *congé.*" Lady Crawford had been everywhere and had missed nothing of the evening's events. "He had the temerity to take her own stepdaughter into supper, a fetching little thing, fresh from the country and in her first Season. It's been hard on Georgina, taking the girl about, for she's scarcely out of her twenties herself and is certainly not an antidote. Berresford has been her particular property these two years"—she did not add that the affair had been a small scandal when it was first begun—"and she's bound to resent any withdrawal of his attentions."

"Beg to differ, Aunt Isabel." Jack was diffident, but sure of his ground. "She made it public, you see. Clever woman, makes her look the injured party. Thing is, grown tired of him, eyes elsewhere."

"And I think I know where," added Francesca, who had also missed nothing. "You would, too, Aunt Isabel, if you'd seen her just after the last quadrille. He's an attaché at the Austrian embassy and blond and heroic in a Teutonic way. They looked splendid together."

"There were so many handsome couples on the floor." Mrs. Amesbury raised her head from the flowers. "Miss Beasley and Lieutenant Corneley, and the Irish couple—isn't their name Morland?—imagine, dancing together though they've been married a twelvemonth, and Lord Dinsdale and Marianne—though I didn't think Marianne was in her usual good looks, perhaps she was bilious."

"Dress didn't suit her," Jack said.

Mrs. Amesbury looked at him blankly. "I thought it very pretty. I told her mother so, but she gave me the most peculiar look and passed on without a word. I know it's uncharitable, but I cannot like that woman. I may not have a title, but the Amesburys are as old a family as the Howlands and she had no call to cut me."

"She was in a towering rage, Aunt Letty," Harry explained. "Wanted her Marianne to be the sun around which everything revolved and Claudia put her to shame."

"Harry, please," Claudia objected.

"Well, whatever got into her maggoty brain," Mrs. Amesbury said with unaccustomed sharpness, "she put a little unpleasantness into what should have been a perfect evening."

"Then let me make up for that, for I have some news I trust you will all find very pleasant." Nicholas had been quiet until now, and they turned to him with surprise and anticipation. He was standing in front of the fireplace, the ghost of a smile on his face. "Miss Neville—Claudia—has done me the honour of consenting to be my wife." He coloured slightly under the intensity of their combined gaze, then turned to Claudia who was standing near him and lifted her hand to his lips. "And may I make her as happy as she will make me."

The betrothed pair stood engulfed in silence. Livia heard a sharp intake of breath, a smothered exclamation. She glanced quickly at the others. Lady Crawford was wearing a bemused smile, Gerry looked astonished, Melbrooke impassive. Mrs. Amesbury clutched her bosom in a parody of joy. Francesca's face was unreadable. Harry was staring at his brother in outrage and was about to give vent to his feelings when Jack moved purposefully to Nicholas and put out his hand. "Congratulations, sir. All the best."

He was followed by Lady Crawford who embraced them both. "What a splendid finish to my entertainment! I don't know when I've been so pleased."

Francesca put her arms around Claudia and kissed her while Mrs. Amesbury clasped Nicholas in a wide embrace. "My boy, my boy, I'm so happy," she sniffed, for sentimental occasions always brought on her tears.

Livia watched a confused flurry of handshakes and embraces as Gerry, Melbrooke, and even Harry joined the throng around the couple. She could not move. She was conscious only of a great hollow inside until Claudia broke away from the others, sat down beside her and flung her arms about her neck. Livia returned the embrace, looked up to meet Nicholas' eyes, and managed to smile.

"When is it to be?" someone said. "Do you go abroad?" "Will it be a large wedding?" and more questions in this vein until Claudia was moved to protest. "Please, please, we know nothing, we've planned nothing, it's only just been decided. It's almost daybreak and my head is reeling and I haven't had time to think. Have you?" she added, turning to Nicholas. He smiled and shook his head.

"But we must give a betrothal party, just as soon as the decorations are down and we can issue invitations." Mrs. Amesbury fumbled in her reticule for a pencil. "What day would suit?"

"No." Livia rose. Her voice was firm though she had not yet sorted out her feelings. "This time we shall give a party. I know we have not entertained, but this is something we want to do. Gerry?" He moved toward her and put his arm around her shoulders. "It will be very informal," Livia explained, "just the families, and early because the children should be there. Early next week, Claudia?" Claudia nodded. Livia forced herself to look at Nicholas and he also assented.

"As soon as possible," Gerry said, "for I may be recalled at any time."

There was a murmur of surprise, but Livia—who had known of the possibility—ignored it. "Tuesday then. And after that, dear Mrs. Amesbury, you may entertain a properly betrothed couple as much as you please."

The group broke up. It was nearly five. The servants had long since been sent to bed, but Parkhurst remained to see Lord Melbrooke and the Nevilles and young Jack Newfield out and to lock the heavy front door. Nicholas, who could not sleep, returned to the library, but the others ascended to their bedrooms in silence. Even Mrs. Amesbury had run out of conversation about wedding clothes and wedding journeys and what a mercy it was that that child would now have a mother to keep her out of mischief.

Lady Crawford said little, but she entered her room in perfect charity with her sister-in-law, her nephew, the Nevilles, and herself. It could not have worked out better. Claudia would be the perfect wife for Nicholas, warm and loving and sensible and not at all like Lillie. It would be the making of Gwendolen, it was obvious the girl adored her. She removed her sapphire eardrops. A happy stone, not her best jewels, but they had been a gift from her husband. She wondered if Nicholas would be happy, if he would let himself be happy—there was no doubt he was pleased, but that was not quite the same thing—and then she wondered what had brought him up to the mark tonight. Claudia had looked very lovely, but then she was always lovely. They would suit, Lady Crawford decided, unfastening her gown with difficulty—she had insisted that her maid not wait up—and she could at last stop worrying about her eldest nephew and his daughter.

Francesca was not so sanguine. She opened the curtains, leaned her forehead against the cool glass and stared unseeing into the street below. She was not concerned for Nicholas—indeed, she was genuinely happy for her brother-in-law. She was also happy for Claudia, though she had to confess to the tiniest bit of envy when she remembered Claudia's glowing face. She forgot that she had thoroughly enjoyed the ball and wondered why the evening now seemed to have been so insipid.

She would have to leave Warwick House. Not that Nicholas would expect her to, nor in justice would his future wife. But Francesca had been lady of the manor in all but name and it would be unfair to Claudia not to step aside. Perhaps Waterford could now be brought up to scratch. Or perhaps she could join her father. Lord Lyndale was in the process of discarding a tiresome mistress and might welcome his daughter's return. Still, she could scarcely do anything until the matter of the letter was resolved. It was tiresome of Gerry to be leaving before this had been sorted out, though obviously he could not help it. Still, he might have warned her. He was going out of her life as abruptly as he had returned to it. She moved away from the window, closed the curtains with a vicious tug, and prepared herself for bed.

Down the hall Harry was brooding. Jack had offered to stay and talk, but Harry had turned his friend off abruptly, saying he preferred to get foxed by himself. Then Nicholas had gone back to the library and Harry's plan to abstract the brandy bottle was thwarted. Damn Nicholas! It was his own fault, too.

If he had said nothing, Nicholas would surely not have spoken. Claudia would have accepted Waterford and made a brilliant marriage of convenience, but her heart would have been untouched and Harry would have been her faithful admirer, always ready to do her service. As Nicholas' wife she would be one of the family and that was wonderful, of course, because she would always be around, but then there would be the nights when she would be behind the closed door of Nicholas' bedroom down the hall. This did not bear thinking on, so Harry put it resolutely out of his mind.

He was glad Nicholas was taking a wife—Nicholas must have felt he owed it to Gwendolen—but surprised that he had done so. His brother had been so occupied with the disastrous fortunes of the Whigs that he had had little time for dallying after women. It was probably because Claudia had been put so much in his way. That, and her taking Gwendolen into her home. It wasn't as though Nicholas would be changing his way of life, in fact he might be busier than ever because now there would be someone at home to look after his daughter. His wife would be left much on her own resources.

Claudia would manage beautifully, of course, and she would never admit to being lonely, but she would undoubtedly be glad to have a fellow about to keep her company when the House was sitting. There'd be lots of evenings like that, and even though he had to go back up to Oxford, there were the vacs, and if need be he could drop out for a term or two. A sister. It was better, really, than a friend and wouldn't cause any comment—not that he cared for himself, but it might have made Claudia uncomfortable. Yes, he liked the idea of being Claudia's brother. In fact, and taken all around, it was a damned good idea. Harry sat down and removed his shoes. Damned good.

Meanwhile the rest of the party were slowly walking home. They had been giddy and garrulous as they left Warwick

House, but had now fallen silent. Gerry had an arm around each sister. Melbrooke and Jack walked behind. The sky was lightening and the stars had begun to fade, but the streets were still quiet.

We are all suddenly serious, Melbrooke thought. A marriage changes everything—brothers, sisters, friends. He was conscious of a profound sadness. He looked at Claudia. Her white figure seemed insubstantial and unreal in the dim light. If things had been different, he thought, I might have had such a wife. He had admired her so much when they first met, but then Nicholas had admired her as well, and Melbrooke had not let his thoughts follow their natural bent. Now he found himself frankly jealous. He had an image of Claudia as he had seen her a few days ago, seated with Eddy in what had become the Nevilles' nursery, the two faces bent seriously over a book. Eddy needed a mother too, and Eddy's father needed a wife. Well, it was up to him really. Perhaps in a few months time, when Mrs. Royce threw off her mourning, he would see. She was a sympathetic woman, though there was an occasional glitter in her eye that he found daunting and she lacked the sweetness of her younger sister. Of course Mrs. Royce's life had been harder, and there was no denying her rare quality. He looked up from his musings and found they had reached the corner of John Street. He raised his hat in farewell and bade them all a good morning.

Jack went a block further with the Nevilles before he too parted from them. He was worried about Harry and wondered if he should have stayed, but then shrugged the problem aside. He had seen Harry take these queer starts before and knew they were short-lived. Foxed too, he'd have the devil of a head. Better leave it till morning. The larger matter still puzzled him, however. Far better that Claudia marry Warwick than Waterford, but it seemed an odd match. Still, he'd seen some rum pairings in his life and knew better than to second guess the caprices of the human heart. Nicholas was a sound fellow, though inclined to be starchy, and Claudia was determined to be happy. They would suit.

Livia slept little that night. The hollow feeling had returned. It was the loss of Claudia, of course. Though the past three months had been devoted to just this end, she had never fully realized that she and Claudia would part. For part they would. Not for the world would she engage to live in Warwick House. If it had been Waterford, the situation would have been different. Livia would have stayed as her sister's companion, a buffer between Claudia and her mother-in-law, a support through the inevitable difficulties of Claudia's new role. As Nicholas' wife, Claudia would have no need of companionship. In truth, Livia would be in her way. Gwendolen should have one mother, not two, and Nicholas should have—but that was absurd, what would she be to Nicholas? What could she be? For that matter, what did she want to be?

Livia got out of bed and threw open the curtains. It was full morning. The day was grey, but there was a promise of sun to come. She took a deep breath and forced herself to say it. I don't want to be his sister. I want to be his wife. I want to marry Nicholas Warwick.

For a moment she could simply wonder at it, with amazement and a curious and dangerous elation. The thing she had been so sure would never happen had happened. How unfair, how cruelly unfair that it should be able to sneak up on you like this, that you should be totally unaware until it was much too late to escape. And much too late, she told herself firmly, to do anything else. Nicholas had chosen Claudia. Claudia appeared happy with the match. Besides, said her better sense, you're simply jealous of Claudia's good fortune. But the side of her that remembered the day at Richmond was not satisfied with that explanation. She returned to bed, but it was a long time before she slept. And when she woke, the pillow was damp.

*   *   *

The house was beginning to stir. Diana ran down to the breakfast parlour—since her brother's arrival a full breakfast was always laid—and found Gerry there before her. He had learned the trick of waking on command in the field, and he was shaved, brushed, and alert. "I didn't expect to find you," Diana said, joining him at the sideboard. "I thought you'd sleep the day away."

"I have an important engagement, puss." He gave her a quick kiss on the forehead. "Got to save a man from making an ass of himself."

"That sounds noble, though I wouldn't have thought it was quite in your line. Do you care about him so much?"

Sandringham entered with coffee and Gerry waited until it had been poured and they were alone again. "It's a matter of my own self-respect. I'm more or less responsible for getting him into a pickle."

"Who is it?"

"His very gracious grace, the Duke of Waterford."

"Gerry, you're bamming me!"

"No, 'pon my honour. Or what remains of it. You see, I more or less gave him my blessing to address your eldest sister."

"He's going to offer for Claudia? But that's monstrous! Well, it's incredible, really. Can you imagine Claudia spending her life pouring out tea?"

"What do you think she does at home?"

"That's different." Diana reached for the marmalade and spread it lavishly on a piece of toast. "But you've seen the light, is that it? You're going to tell him you can't consent and he can cast his lures elsewhere? Good man, I knew you could be counted on, even if you are a trifle slow."

"No, or to be more precise, not exactly no." Gerry was enjoying himself. "It's not up to me, really, is it? I mean, it's Claudia's life and Claudia's decision. Maybe she'd like to be a duchess."

"Fustian."

"Possibly. But it's an academic point. She's managed to get

237

someone else to come up to scratch and you're about to have a brother-in-law."

Diana shrieked, jumped out of her chair, and launched herself on her brother, both fists flailing. "You beast! You toad! You satanic worm! How dare you treat me like an infant?"

Gerry grasped her wrists and twisted them behind her back. "Hold, child, or I'll paddle you, I swear I will!"

She wriggled out of his grasp and onto the floor, seized his legs, upended him and his chair, then straddled his chest and gave his hair a yank which failed of its vicious intent because they were both weak from laughter. Sandringham opened the door to see what was amiss. Livia came in behind him, pushed under his arm, and dragged Diana off her brother. "Shame on the pair of you! Get up, Gerry. If you've broken Lady Hartlebury's chair there'll be the devil to pay."

"It's Gerry's fault," Diana said, putting her dress to rights while Sandringham mopped up the coffee that was staining the table linen a dark sienna. "Claudia's to be married and he won't tell me to who."

"Whom. It's Nicholas Warwick, infant." Gerry's voice was penitent, but his eyes gleamed with mischief. "You might as well wake Claudia, though I doubt she's slept through this."

"May I offer my congratulations to the family, sir." Sandringham was smiling broadly, for he had taken on the Neville cause along with his position. Gerry wrung his hand and asked for fresh coffee. Livia put her head in her hands. Diana paused in the doorway. "So you feel obliged to tip off the duke? I can't see why, it might do him good to be wounded right in the middle of his *amour-propre.*"

"It's a matter of honour among men. We have to stick together. Damned house of women, there's no peace to be found anywhere."

Diana reached in her pocket but could find only a piece of chalk. It landed directly in his egg cup.

*   *   *

The house was in turmoil all day. Livia told Sandringham to put off all callers, save of course Lord Melbrooke or Jack or members of the Warwick family. Nicholas was expected later in the day. He and Claudia had planned to tell Gwendolen together, but the children of course heard everything long before he arrived. The news spread from kitchen to attic within ten minutes of Gerry's announcement.

Gwendolen and Eddy shouted in jubilation and ran noisily about, but when Claudia came to the nursery, Gwendolen was quiet and rather shy. Eddy congratulated Claudia with a painfully correct little speech, then disappeared. Diana found him later putting his soldiers through a furious battle. She took him for a walk.

Gerry returned at one and informed Claudia that Waterford sent his congratulations. "I think his actual words were, 'Pray tell your sister that I can only wish her happy and send her my most sincere felicitations.' He also said he wouldn't call today since you no doubt had many private concerns, but he would see you in a few days and express his sentiments in person. Would you have liked to be a duchess, Claudia? If you'd held out, you might have done the trick."

"No, Gerry, I think I have the better man. And I can guess why you saw Waterford today. Nicholas told me."

"Told you?"

"That he had heard on the best authority—you, you idiot—that the duke was going to make me an offer and that he did not want to pressure me into an immediate decision. Not in those words precisely, but the meaning was clear."

"That was an honourable thing to do. Why were you so hasty?"

"Poor Gerry, you wanted me to be a duchess. I know I could have been useful to you, but it's much better for your character for you to rise on your own merits."

"I never thought you lacked all semblance of sisterly feeling. I think I'll go write some letters."

"What a paltry excuse. You never write letters."

"Then I'll visit my bootmaker. Do I have a bootmaker? I

239

should. Don't want to bring shame on your new family." He made an elaborate show of going to the door.

"Gerry!" Claudia called after him, her expression suddenly serious. "You'll be here, won't you? For my wedding? I want you to give me away."

Gerry crossed the room and sat beside her. "Scared, little sister?"

Claudia didn't meet his gaze. "It seems strange, that's all. I can't quite imagine being married."

"Practical Claudia, taking care of us all." He took her hand and kissed it. "I have to go back, you know. But it's only to Paris, and if you give me any notice at all, I'll call in every favour owed me to be here."

Nicholas arrived an hour later bringing Melbrooke with him. Diana, who saw them from an upstairs window, wondered at this unloverlike behavior. "You'd think he's afraid to be alone with her. It's not at all what I expected." Diana's views of Nicholas were much coloured by their first encounter.

"It's not that," Livia said. "He knows that Eddy will need his father." She went downstairs to meet them and tactfully took Lord Melbrooke off to the nursery to visit his son. Eddy, she feared, was having a bad day. Melbrooke was the gentlest of fathers, but he had a distressing tendency to avoid dealing with problems head-on. "Eddy," Livia said firmly, "I know that Gwendolen will be returning to her own home, but you don't have to leave here. Not unless your father wants you to, of course." Melbrooke was about to protest, but she went on. "We're going to be here another month at least, and if you like you can stay with us until it's time for your summer holiday."

Eddy looked at her with a solemn expression, then turned to his father. Melbrooke gave a slight nod. Eddy's face brightened and he drew his father down to the floor to judge his strategic arrangements. Livia, who liked chess but not battles, went downstairs where she was waylaid by Diana who pulled her into her bedroom.

As usual, Diana went straight to the point. "What happens to us?"

"You mean, where do we go?"

"Exactly. Do we live with Claudia? Do we go back to Oxford? Do we stay in London? Though I don't suppose there will be any money for that."

"No, I'm afraid there will be very little money. But Claudia, of course, will be well settled. We haven't talked about it yet," Livia said, reverting to her sister's earlier question, "but I intend to go back to Oxford. I imagine Claudia would be happy to have you with her if you'd like to stay."

"Why don't you want to live with them? You'd feel in the way, is that it?"

"Yes, I suppose I would. But that's my business, puss. You may do as you like."

Diana gave her a shrewd look, but made no comment. "I'd like to stay in London," she said after a moment, "but I think I'd better go with you. Not that Claudia wouldn't be perfectly splendid about everything, but Mr. Warwick"—Diana was sure she would never be able to call him Nicholas—"has a look about him that makes me feel he'd want to set me straight. Whatever that is. I don't think I'd like it."

Livia guessed what the decision to leave London cost her sister. "We can visit them, you know. It's not as if we'll be marooned on an island, all cut off from the world. You'll still spend time in London."

Diana smiled bravely. "Exactly. The best of two worlds. Unless—you don't suppose Cousin Sophronia would have me, do you?"

"I'm not sure you'd want to be had. But I'm inviting her to the betrothal dinner. You can ask her yourself."

When Claudia learned of this conversation, she had a dreadful row with Livia. It had never occurred to her that her sisters would not remain as part of her new family. Livia was adamant. "I'm sure Mr. Warwick will be a very caring and

241

thoughtful husband, but it's too much to ask him to take on your two unmarried sisters."

"One unmarried. You're still a widow."

"And how I long to leave London so I can stop being one!" Livia saw Claudia's expression and ran to embrace her sister. "Not you, love, never you. But you must have time to get used to one another. Then when you're an old married couple and grown just the slightest bit tired of each other's company, we can talk again. It will work out, you'll see."

In private, Livia was not so confident. It was clear that Claudia's marriage would permanently alter the shape of their lives. However, there was much to do and she put such thoughts from her mind. Rumours of the betrothal had spread, though an announcement had not yet appeared in the *Morning Post*, and there were innumerable callers. There were also engagements that could not be set aside, the dinner to plan, the children to spend time with—it had been agreed that Gwendolen as well as Eddy would remain in Charles Street—and wedding clothes to be thought of. Lady Crawford was a frequent visitor, as were Harry and Jack, and Nicholas came once or twice a day, usually accompanied by Melbrooke.

They saw little of Francesca and Gerry was moved to make a caustic comment about her apparent preference for the delights of the *beau monde*. Her absence was also noted in the Warwick household. Nicholas, of course, was oblivious to the matter, as was Harry, but Mrs. Amesbury said she had never known Francesca to be so much away from home. Lady Crawford came close to understanding Francesca's feelings, but was wise enough to know there was little anyone could do to relieve them.

It was to Lady Crawford that Francesca broke the news, four days after her aunt's ball. She was standing in the doorway of Lady Crawford's dressing room, carefully fastening a bracelet—they were both engaged at the Kingston soirée that evening. "I've accepted Waterford," Francesca announced calmly.

Lady Crawford gave her niece a long look. "You're sure that's what you want?"

Francesca laughed, but the sound was harsh. "No illusions, Aunt Isabel. It's a life that will suit me, and I'll enjoy the precedence."

"George won't be"— Lady Crawford searched for the right words—"a very amusing husband."

"No," Francesca agreed gravely. "He won't be amusing. But he's quite malleable, and he'll give me my head. As long as I observe the forms, and you know I've always observed the forms."

"Always?" Lady Crawford raised delicate eyebrows.

"Ever since I was old enough to care about the good opinion of others. It's a mistake not to care about opinion."

"I've never said the contrary."

"I know. You're a very wise woman. You watch." This time Francesca's smile was genuine. "I will do great things yet."

"Yes," Lady Crawford said after a moment. "Yes, I think you will."

Chapter 16

I should not be on edge, Livia told herself. It's a simple family dinner and we're all friends. Well, almost all. Claudia had decided that the Newfields should be invited. They were Jack's parents and Almeria Newfield was Lady Crawford's sister-in-law. Livia had met them several times during the past few months, though they had never exchanged more than polite words. Then Diana had asked that Henry Ashton be included. "For you can't deny that he was of great help to us," Diana said, "and besides he's Paul's best friend and you're asking Paul." So Henry was invited. Cousin Sophronia had been asked and, to everyone's surprise, had agreed to come.

"Of course, she knows Mr. Warwick," Livia told her elder sister. She could not bring herself to use his given name. "Perhaps she thinks he might be useful. She'd scarcely come for something as frivolous as a betrothal."

"For shame, Livy. I know she hasn't seen much of us, but family is family."

Livia apologized. She was pleased that Sophronia was coming. It was only the combination of Sophronia and his grace of Waterford that made her uneasy. Claudia had met Francesca and the duke in St. James' Park the day before and impulsively invited him to join their party. The just manageable number of guests had now swelled to nearly twenty which would strain the resources of Lady Hartlebury's handsome, but smallish dining room. Sandringham assured her they would contrive. Fortunately there was service for twenty-four.

Mrs. Fraser had risen to the occasion—indeed, she had been much in her element with the increased company of the past few days—and firmly begged Mrs. Royce to stay out of the kitchen and leave the meal to her. Livia had to pass the time doing the flowers, an occupation which did not show her at her best. She was trying for an unstudied effect, but Lady Hartlebury's blue iris were stiff and unyielding.

"I think you're putting too many in the vase." Gwendolen had come unnoticed into the drawing room. "Aunt Francesca says they look better if there are just a few."

Livia removed three of the blooms and replaced them with some plumes of meadowsweet which had unaccountably appeared in Lady Hartlebury's formal garden. "You're right. It's much improved. Would you like to try your hand? There's another vase."

They worked in silence for a while. Gwendolen stepped back to survey her effort. "Aunt Francesca's going, you know."

"Yes, I heard. Are you pleased about her engagement?"

"I guess so. We always expected her to get married again. Aunt Letty says it's a perfect match, but I'm not so sure. I mean, Aunt Francesca liked it when we went to Astley's and somehow I don't think the duke would."

Once, Livia would have been in complete agreement with Mrs. Amesbury, but the more she knew Francesca, the more she inclined toward Gwendolen's point of view. She had an odd feeling that Lady Crawford might agree with her, though Lady Crawford had never mentioned the matter. Harry hadn't either, except to remark in passing that it would be dashed queer to think of Waterford as one of the family. Livia wondered what Nicholas thought—he knew Francesca as well as any of them did—but she could scarcely ask for his opinion. He might have said something to Claudia, but Livia hesitated to discuss the matter with her sister. Claudia had been sincerely pleased about the engagement—it cleared her conscience of refusing Waterford and of ousting Francesca as mistress of Warwick House. Gerry, on the other hand, had said nothing at all and had made an excuse to avoid visiting the Warwicks the previous day.

"Of course," Gwendolen was saying, "Aunt Francesca will be a duchess instead of a lady, and she'll be very rich. Though I don't think she cares about money."

"You don't when you've always had it," Livia said, relegating the problem of Gerry until after the dinner party.

"But I don't think you and Claudia care about money, and you don't have much, do you? That's what Aunt Letty said. 'She hasn't a penny, but it won't matter a bit to Nicholas.' Funny, isn't it. 'Not a penny.' Because you do have some money, don't you? Otherwise you wouldn't be living here. Even I know it costs a lot to live in Charles Street."

Livia bundled up the cuttings. She had done her best with the iris and with Gwendolen's help the effect was almost right. "Yes, we have a little money."

"Anyway it doesn't matter now, because Daddy has enough for all of us."

Livia was startled. The "us" had an ominous ring.

But Gwendolen was on another tack. "You could have Aunt Francesca's room when she gets married. You'll like it. She has her own boudoir, all in green and white. Of course, you might want to change it, but I've always thought Aunt Francesca had good taste. There's a smaller room across the hall that Diana might like, it gets the sun. It was supposed to be a sitting room, but Mummy—none of us uses it much."

Livia wondered if Nicholas had said anything to his daughter. Unlikely, Livia had already told Claudia of her plans. She looked at Gwendolen, unwilling to deny her outright. "I'm very glad there will be room for us when we descend on you. But I think we'll give Claudia time to settle in with all of you before we come for a visit."

"A visit? But you're to live with us! I made sure of that. That was part of the reason—" Gwendolen looked unhappy and confused. "I mean, I thought I'd be seeing you all the time as well as Claudia—and Diana, too, of course—and you have to leave here anyway because Lady Hartlebury will want the house back. You will stay in London, won't you?"

"No, we're returning to Oxford. We have a house there, you know." Livia knelt to retrieve some fragments of greenery and allow Gwendolen time to wipe away the tears that were threatenng to overflow.

"You could come to the country with us." Gwendolen's voice was more subdued. "Everybody goes away to the country for the summer."

"But we aren't everybody, Genny." Livia rose. "We've always spent our summers in Oxford. And our autumns and our winters—"

"And your springs. Aunt Letty's right, isn't she? You don't have much money."

"No, we don't. But we've led quite happy lives without it." Livia could hear an undertone of regret in her voice and hoped it was not apparent to Gwendolen.

"Well, I'm going to make Daddy do something about it."

"Gwendolen, don't you dare! It's none of your concern. Claudia will be your mother. I'll only be your aunt, but aunts have rights, including not being embarrassed by their nieces."

"But Aunt Francesca lives with us. Aunt Letty lives with us. Even Aunt Isabel lives with us some of the time. I don't see why you should be embarrassed to live with us. It's stupid."

"Stupid or not, it's my own choice, and I choose to live in my own house. Besides, I won't be your real aunt, not by blood ties." She was aware as she said it that she had both weakened her argument and raised a divisive note. She hastened to make amends. "But you'll always be like my real niece to me, Genny. So please, not a word, all right?"

Gwendolen was sullen, but she nodded. "All right."

Neither of the children was in evidence the rest of the

afternoon. Livia was relieved, for she found herself unexpectedly busy. A large serving platter had been broken which was vexatious because it was expensive and would have to be replaced. Jeanie had been scalded by her carelessness with a pot of steaming broth and her right hand was bandaged so they were shorthanded in the kitchen and Mary Beth had to be pressed into service. Claudia returned from a shopping expedition with Lady Crawford and Livia's comments and advice about her purchases were earnestly solicited. Cousin Sophronia arrived, saying she had been in the neighbourhood and was sure they would not mind if she simply remained in Charles Street rather than returning home and coming back again for dinner. "As for my dressing for dinner, I assure you no one could tell the difference, for all my gowns look alike and I know you do not stand on ceremony." She was very kind to Claudia and showed genuine interest in her wedding plans. When tea was over she went off to the nursery with Gwendolen. A sensible child. Sophronia expected a good deal from her. What else she did Livia was not to know, for she did not appear again until the other guests began to arrive.

The Newfields also arrived early, a regrettable habit of which Jack had never been able to cure them. But by that time the Nevilles, Gerry, Gwendolen and Eddy were all dressed and ready to receive them. Conversation was polite and predictable and if the Newfields were surprised to find children in the drawing room, they were too well bred to say so. Claudia disarmed them by alluding to it directly. "This is such a special occasion and only for our families. I am so happy you are able to be with us." Livia noted a perceptible relaxation and made an interesting discovery. Under her dignified exterior, Mrs. Newfield was shy. She resolved to try to know her better, but Cousin Sophronia had pinned her into a corner and was talking, Livia feared, about the plight of homeless girls.

The Warwicks arrived together along with Melbrooke and for a time the conversation became general. The mood was festive and Livia began to enjoy herself. I rather like playing hostess, she thought. Only the children were unaccustomedly stiff, but since they had been warned to be on their very best behaviour this was probably all to the good. Diana was wearing a new dress of pale green that set off her glowing hair which was tied back neatly with a ribbon of the same colour. She looked fresh and innocent and, since she was taking the trouble, her manners were very good. The flowers looked far better than expected, the table was laid, and the last progress report from the kitchen favourable. For once, Nicholas Warwick was going to see Livia playing a responsible role and playing it superbly.

"Livia." Gwendolen had been avoiding her ever since their conversation earlier that afternoon, so Livia was surprised to find her touching her arm and indicating that she needed to speak to her in private. They moved a little apart from the others.

"It's the Duke of Waterford," Gwendolen said. "I saw him through the window. He's just getting out of his carriage."

"Yes, of course, he's been invited."

"I know that, Claudia told me. But did you invite the women he has with him?"

"Women?" Livia thought wildly of the arcane habits of the aristocracy. Waterford would have a coachman and perhaps an extra footman or two to let down the steps, but she didn't think she'd ever heard of female attendants. A terrible thought occurred to her. She looked across the room at Claudia. It had been a hasty and impulsive invitation. Could it have been open to misinterpretation?

The doors were flung open. Sandringham gave a cough—too discreet for Drury Lane, but loud enough to alert his mistress—and said, hoping he got the order right, "The Duke of Waterford, the Dowager Duchess, and Lady Marianne Howland."

The group in Lady Hartlebury's drawing room opened to receive the newcomers, then closed around them, but it was permanently altered. Its warmth noticeably decreased, though thanks to Francesca, Claudia and Lady Crawford, there was no diminution in its surface amiability. Only Sophronia seemed immune to the new influence. As Livia slipped out of the drawing room to confer with Sandringham, she saw her cousin approach Waterford, tap him on the arm, and say she would be glad of a word with him in the course of the evening.

Sandringham was waiting for Livia in the adjoining sitting room. She kept her voice low. "It is most provoking, but it cannot be helped. Can you contrive?"

"It will be crowded, the table does not seat above twenty with ease. Shall we give Miss Gwendolen and Master Edward dinner in the nursery?" He did not say that the duchess would not take kindly to dining with children.

"On no account. I know it's irregular, but we have promised. They are part of Miss Neville's new family—well, Gwendolen is at least. And I would not for the world isolate Eddy for the sake of the table. We said it was to be informal and if her grace chooses to join us, she must just put up with us. Let us be crowded—and please convey my apologies to Mrs. Fraser."

Sandringham smiled and inclined his head, then turned to go belowstairs. Livia re-entered the drawing room through the sitting room door just as Paul and Henry came in from the hall. They must have let themselves in. Livia decided not to worry about the duchess' response to her butler's dereliction of duty. Eddy, who had been a bit overawed by the arrival of the ducal party, looked up happily. He hadn't seen Henry since the occasion of their running away and he liked him very much. Perhaps he'd finished his story by now and would tell it to them. "Cousin Paul!" he said, when Livia had finished greeting and introducing the new arrivals. "Henry!"

"Hullo, Mr. Ashton." Gwendolen jabbed Eddy in the ribs. "You *are* Mr. Ashton, aren't you? We've heard so much about you." Out of the corner of her eye, Gwendolen saw light dawn on her father's face.

Livia saw it too. Well, they hadn't given themselves entirely away. Melbrooke hadn't seemed to notice and it was Melbrooke who had the power to punish Paul. Perhaps Nicholas wouldn't say anything to him, though—remembering Nicholas' face and words on the day the children had run away—she doubted it. She moved forward to draw Paul and Henry into the circle and noticed that the hall doors were opening again. Dear God, who else? Surely Sandringham wouldn't announce Paul and Henry belatedly.

He wouldn't. The doors, left ajar by Henry, were being pushed open by someone much smaller than Sandringham. Having opened them far enough to see into the room, Hotspur gave a delighted bark and launched himself at Paul.

The duchess dropped her fan. Gerry picked it up and returned it to her. Paul calmly pushed Hotspur down. Hotspur—as if he hadn't made things clear enough— transferred his attentions to Henry. Nicholas addressed Henry and Paul.

"I hate to disillusion the two of you, but I'm afraid he does this with everyone, friend or stranger. Probably with burglars as well, though that hasn't been tried yet. Down, Hotspur."

Rather to everyone's surprise, Hotspur obeyed this command. He began to trot toward Nicholas, but he was distracted along the way by the sight of a new face. Or more precisely, a new lap. The duchess'. Hotspur laid his head in it and looked up at her beseechingly.

Livia stifled a strong desire to laugh and moved quickly to rescue the duchess from the dog's attentions. "Hotspur! I beg your pardon, your grace. He must have escaped from belowstairs. I'm afraid in all the confusion he hasn't been given his dinner."

He had been fed a whole lamb chop by the besotted Mrs. Fraser and rather more by the rather more besotted Eddy. Eddy started to deny that he would be so negligent in the care of his pet, but was silenced by a look from Gwendolen. Gerry, judging that Livia had done more than her share, took Hotspur by the collar and pulled him, protesting, from the room. Francesca sat down beside her future mother-in-law and professed an interest in one of the Howland cousins who had recently married but was as insipid as ever. Nicholas talked horses with Waterford. Sophronia found something to say to the children which turned Eddy's attention away from Hotspur's banishment. Melbrooke turned a one-sided conversation between Mrs. Newfield and Mrs. Amesbury into a nearly three-sided conversation. Ralph Newfield, who had an eye for pretty girls, was delighted to find himself next to Claudia. Lady Crawford, noting that everything was under control and that Francesca was handling the duchess far better than she could herself, began to talk to Harry and Jack.

In Gerry's absence, Marianne singled out Paul and Henry as the only two interesting and unattached men present. A little young, perhaps, but better than the Warwick and Newfield cubs. She managed to ascertain that Paul—who had an attractive, if not precisely a handsome face—was a painter and asked his opinion of Benjamin West.

It was unfavourable and Paul had no hesitation in giving it.

"I think you are being unfair." Diana, who had been sitting quietly beside Francesca, suddenly spoke up in a voice that was not in the least girlish or submissive. "His composition is good and his conception—"

"Is well beyond his modest talents."

"I know he's not an inspired artist," Diana admitted. "But you have to grant that he's able to learn and keep developing."

"He has no understanding of the human form. His poses are strained and he distorts heads and limbs. Look," Paul said, fumbling in his pocket and producing a handkerchief—a clean one, Henry had seen to that—and a pencil stub. He dropped to the floor and began to sketch rapidly. Diana stood up, excused herself politely to Francesca and the duchess, and squatted down beside him.

"They're hopeless." Henry smiled at Marianne, hoping she had a sense of humour. As Francesca could have told him, she hadn't.

Livia saw them and wondered what to do just as Gerry came

back into the room.

"Sandringham's under oath to keep Hotspur shut up until after dinner," he said quietly beside her. "But Mrs. Fraser wants to see you. Something about the soup."

At times like these, one learned to be grateful for small things. Such as the ability to keep one's head high and one's face composed. And the fact that the difficulty with the soup, while a difficulty, had been solved by the time one reached the kitchen. And the fact that things couldn't possibly—could they?—get any worse.

They could. Coming back upstairs, Livia saw Nicholas standing in the hall, apparently waiting for her. Since the night of the Warwick House ball, any meeting with him had been something of a trial and those when they were alone together far worse. And, whatever he had to say to her, past experience argued it was unlikely to be positive. Just when she'd been feeling charitable for his handling of Hotspur. What was wrong now? Was it Diana and Paul? Or Gwendolen and Eddy?

"Not," said Nicholas, coming to meet her, "that I don't believe you equal to the situation, because you are handling it superbly, but I wondered if there was anything I could do to help?"

She looked at him blankly, recovered herself, and said, "No. Thank you. Unless—things haven't gotten any worse in there?"

"No, no," Nicholas assured her. "Not worse."

He looked at her. Livia looked back at him. They both erupted into helpless laughter, only checked—with an effort—when they realised Lady Hartlebury's walls might not be as thick as one would wish.

"I think," said Nicholas, his eyes belying the gravity of his expression, "that it is time we called a truce. Livia?"

His use of her given name shocked her out of laughter and into more dangerous thoughts. But of course it could mean nothing. Other than that he was going to be her brother-in-law. She managed a smile and accepted his hand.

"Truce," she agreed.

As Nicholas had said, things had not gotten worse. Livia briefly reassured Gerry about the soup, ran an eye over the others and stopped to speak to Sophronia and the children, still happily occupied with one another. "Livia," Sophronia said in the voice that enabled her to dominate a meeting or quell a disturbance. "I had the most interesting conversation with your butler. Gwendolen tells me he was once an actor."

Across the room, Gerry choked. Diana covered her face with her handkerchief. Claudia looked at Livia. Harry and Jack looked at the floor. Mrs. Amebury started to speak. Sandringham threw open the doors.

"Dinner is served, madam."

The Dowager Duchess of Waterford—Lavinia Shaftesbury that was—surveyed the table. She had long been accustomed to getting her own way and was not above stooping to subterfuge. She was quite aware that she had forced herself on the party and quite aware that Lady Crawford—Isabel Warwick that was—knew it, but she wanted a closer look at the Neville family. She was grateful that George had escaped the Neville girl's clutches, but he would still be allied with the family through Lady Francesca. This was the duchess' first opportunity to view the family at close quarters, and she was going to make the most of it.

She had had no fault to find with her reception, though the presence of children in the drawing room had surprised her. Still, it was an intimate family gathering, she had not been expected, and allowances must be made. As for the arrival of the dog—words failed even Lavinia Howland.

However, she had been taken into dinner, as was most proper, by the head of the family, Colonel Scott, and was now seated appropriately on his right. On her own right sat Ralph Newfield, a man of no particular interest but of respectable birth and comfortable fortune. Lord Melbrooke would have been more to her taste, but he had been alloted to her daughter at the other end of the table.

The duchess was not a stupid woman, and she knew how to make herself agreeable. She conversed easily with her dinner partners, but long experience had taught her to do so while attending to conversations elsewhere along the table. Still, it was a few minutes before she was aware that the children had not been quietly gathered up by a governess or other respectable female and whisked out of sight. Her shock caused her to miss a query from Colonel Scott and she answered at random. Never since she left the schoolroom had Lavinia Howland sat down to table with anyone under the age of seventeen.

Almost to her disappointment, the dinner was excellent and she reminded herself to compliment Mrs. Royce on her chef. There had been a light soup of pureed asparagus, then a cold salmon with a sauce of great delicacy. The wines were undistinguished, but acceptable. Across the table, the butler was refilling Isabel's glass. The duchess never noticed servants, but she gave this one some attention. Just before they left the drawing room, she had heard the Neville cousin remark that he had been an actor. The man looked perfectly correct, but she could credit the report. Odder things had happened. What was more difficult to accept was the fact that Sophronia Neville had found this out by conversing with the man. A strange woman and likely to prove something of an embarrassment to Nicholas Warwick, though heaven knew every family had its eccentric.

This reminded her of a story she had heard about the Nevilles. About their mother. Italian, it was said—though the children hardly seemed Catholic, thank goodness—and something odd about the marriage. The duchess addressed Colonel Scott. "Lady Francesca tells me your given name is Germanicus. I don't think I've heard it before. Is it a family name?"

"No, your grace—that is, not precisely. Germanicus was the

elder brother of the Emperor Claudius. My father—my step-father—specialized in the Julio-Claudian emperors."

The duchess went directly to the one pertinent piece of information. "Your stepfather?"

"Yes." Colonel Scott did not appear a bit disconcerted. "I never knew my own father. By the time I was born, my mother was married to Thomas Neville. My stepfather named me. My father had been a soldier and Germanicus was a great general."

The salmon was followed by a saddle of lamb and the arrival of the new course cut short the duchess' inquiries into the Neville genealogy. She decided to let the matter rest. She already knew quite enough.

On Colonel Scott's other side, Isabel was talking with Melbrooke's young nephew who was eating little and drinking probably a great deal more than was good for him. He seemed strangely elated and once the duchess saw him exchange an odd sort of smile, down the length of the table, with the little Neville girl, the one with the red hair. Melbrooke was engaged with her, leaving Marianne to content herself with Jack Newfield, a very silly young man. She was pouting. The duchess had warned her about that, it spoiled the line of her chin. However, her son, seated further up the table next to his fiancée, appeared quite contented. Across from him Sophronia Neville was waving her hands like disoriented birds. Thin and unadorned, they were a constant accompaniment to her rapid conversation. The duchess could not see her partner, but as the hands grew quiet a higher voice made it clear that she had been talking to Warwick's daughter. Children had no business at table, and no business talking in the unlikely event that they found themselves there. Sophronia Neville should not be encouraging the chit.

Sophronia was finding the chit a more agreeable companion than the gentleman on her other side. As far as she could ascertain, Ralph Newfield had no interests beyond gossip, wine, and the peerage. Gwendolen, however, had just posed, in simple language, a complex moral dilemma: does the end justify the means?

"In principle, no," Sophronia said. "But I have often found it necessary to take a roundabout road if I am to get anything done, and I do not scruple to appeal to the baser instincts if in doing so I can gain a desirable end."

"But suppose you reach that end and it turns out it isn't quite what you expected it to be?"

"Things are never quite what we expect them to be. That doesn't mean you don't continue to work for what you think is good."

"But suppose you decide you want a different end than the one you thought you wanted?"

"Then I would strongly advise you to be very sure of what you want before you do anything to bring it about."

"Oh, but I was very sure. I mean, people usually are, aren't they? Livia—Mrs. Royce—was telling me about the other Livia, the one who was married to Augustus, and how she wanted her son Tiberius on the throne after her husband died and so she made her son marry Augustus' daughter Julia. But Julia didn't want him, and he didn't want her because he already had a wife that he loved very much, and his mother made him give her up, so he was very unhappy and he wasn't very nice to Julia or to anyone else either and it was all because he was so unhappy, but I don't think Livia—the other Livia— ever expected things to turn out that way." Gwendolen was involved in her tale and her voice had risen. Three seats down, the duchess eyed her with disapproval. Nicholas, seated on her other side, paused in his conversation with Claudia, a wry smile on his face. "So you see," Gwendolen went on, "the problem is that it's people who don't turn out the way you expect."

Gwendolen's dilemma was a genuine one. She held herself responsible for her father's engagement. Hadn't she taken every opportunity to point out to him that Claudia would make a wonderful wife and—with a wistful expression—mother? Hadn't she schemed to see that they were alone together whenever her father came to visit? Hadn't she run away in the first place so that she could bring all this about?

The trouble was that her father was not behaving as she had expected. He did not seem happy. Gwendolen had not thought he would act like a loopy schoolboy in the throes of first passion like Uncle Harry, but something was missing. He was kind and gentle and polite to Claudia, and Claudia was kind and gentle and polite to him. That wasn't right. Gwendolen could still remember the raised voices, suddenly hushed arguments, and sullen silences from her childhood. She didn't want that, of course, but she had expected something more between them.

It was strange that she hadn't seen this until today. It had been her talk with Livia that had opened her eyes. And that was funny, because they hadn't talked about Daddy at all. She looked down the table and saw Livia, her head bent to say something to Eddy, and felt a stab of jealousy.

She had to be honest with herself. It wasn't her father, it was Livia. She loved Claudia, but it was Livia she didn't want to lose.

Beside her, old Miss Neville was speaking. "I beg your pardon," Gwendolen said, feeling her cheeks grow warm. "I didn't hear you."

"I said," Sophronia Neville repeated, "If things don't turn out the way I expect, then I do something to set them right."

Chapter 17

It was several days later that Diana mentioned in passing that Paul had a painting hanging in the European Museum and they might want to see it at some time or other. "It's near Pall Mall on Charles Street, the one off St. James' Square. It's not a museum really, it's run by a man named John Wilson and he takes pictures to sell on commission. It's a respectable place," she added, referring to the quality of the work, not the nature of its clientele. "He's got some quite good things and then the usual collection of rubbish."

"But of course we'll go," Claudia said. "I long to see some of Mr. Redmond's work."

"It will cost you a shilling."

Claudia suppressed a smile. "Oh, dear. Livia, do you think we can possibly—"

Livia pursed her lips and looked at Diana. "If you're sure we'll get value for our money?"

Diana threw a pillow at her. "A lot more than the Summer Exhibition, and you didn't complain about that."

"I don't recall that it cost us anything at all."

"That's because you were escorted. Ladies are supposed to be above money."

"I'm not." Livia threw the pillow back. "Here, put that where it belongs. But you've given me an idea. We'll find some

259

gentlemen to go with us and then we needn't worry about shillings at all. Has Lord Melbrooke seen it?"

"I don't know. Paul didn't say."

"He's told him, hasn't he?" Claudia asked. "He really ought, I know Lord Melbrooke is very proud of his nephew."

Diana shrugged.

"We'll ask him," Livia said. "Gerry can't be relied on to be available, but maybe Mr. Warwick will come. He thinks Paul is very talented. You can come with us, too, puss, and tell us what's worth spending time on and what we can pass by."

Diana gave an evasive consent, but when Nicholas and Melbrooke called a few days later to take the Nevilles to view the collection she declined to join them, saying she had already seen it and in any case she preferred looking at pictures by herself. She refused to describe the painting, saying they should come to it without preconceptions, but it was unquestionably one of the finest works in the gallery, though it was abominably hung.

Livia was relieved, for there had been a hint of amusement in Nicholas' eyes and she did not want Diana to be patronized. Diana had an easy-going tolerance for the foibles of others, but she was passionate and committed about art.

Livia was also relieved because Diana would have been an intrusive presence. Since the night of the dinner there had been an easy camaraderie among the four of them—Claudia and Nicholas, Melbrooke and herself. The absurdities of that evening—for there was no other way to describe the mixture of children, dog, Mrs. Amesbury's reminiscences, Cousin Sophronia's canvassing for support for her young women and climbing boys, and the Waterford hauteur—were not lost on any of them. Nicholas had taken none of it in dislike, and indeed had seemed to relish the experience. He and Claudia appeared on easier terms, though they avoided being alone together and Livia was as likely to find herself paired with Nicholas as with his friend. Nothing more had been said about her own future plans, and Livia did not know how to bring the matter up. Perhaps there was no need to. When Claudia returned from her wedding journey, she and Diana would be back in Oxford.

Nicholas brought the barouche. The day was fine and Claudia opened a frivolous white parasol to shade them. Livia had borrowed one of her sister's dresses, a pale lavender muslin. It fit her poorly and it was not her best colour, but she felt singularly liberated. Melbrooke said with some delicacy that he was happy to see her able to throw off the gloom of mourning.

They turned into Piccadilly, then down St. James' Street. It was mid-afternoon, the streets were filled with carriages, and progress was slow. Claudia always attracted attention and they stopped several times to speak to acquaintances and admirers. The distance could not have been above a mile, but it took them a full half-hour.

Livia had been to the Somerset House exhibition where she was buffeted and elbowed from one room to another, scarce able to see the pictures which were hung floor to ceiling with little regard for compatibility of style or subject matter. It was, Diana told her when she complained about it, a question of who you were. Paul might have exhibited—it was his own fault really, he had been dissatisfied and had worked his painting over a score of times—but his work was sure to have been allotted the darkest corner of the darkest room.

The European Museum was not the Academy. It was smaller, of course, and though there were still a great many pictures to look at, they were hung with greater regard for their effective display. But there were a surprising number of people and progress was slow. Livia had found Paul's name in the catalogue—Paul Redmond, *Artemis at Dawn*—but had yet to glimpse anything remotely suggesting the goddess.

"I see classical subjects are still in style." Nicholas had also found the entry. "You should be pleased."

"Oh, I am. It means pictures of people and I confess I much prefer them to landscapes or animal studies."

"The immutable variety of the human face?" His tone was mocking, but his eyes were kind.

"Yes. I know it's fashionable to admire landscapes, and while I can find them exciting, particularly if they're stormy, I prefer them at first hand. But people are endlessly interesting."

Claudia pointed to a portrait of a heavy, taciturn man in an impeccable frock coat, his scowl barely concealed by his effort to preserve his sense of self-importance. "I would hate to live with that. He seems to have permanent dyspepsia. I would take a placid landscape any day."

"But I see your sister's point." Nicholas looked judiciously at the portrait in question. "An unhappy face, wouldn't you say? I wonder why? I wonder how he lived his life to make him see the world in just that jaundiced way."

"However he came to it, he must have made life miserable for his wife and children."

They moved on, at least as much as the surging crowds would allow, and Livia found herself with Melbrooke. He drew her into an alcove where they could have some momentary privacy, but seemed reluctant to speak. Then he said abruptly, "Is she happy?"

The unexpectedness of the question disconcerted Livia. She temporized. "Claudia has always had a cheerful disposition."

"You know that is not what I mean."

"You are fond of her."

"I am fond of all the Nevilles." He smiled, then turned grave. "I admire your sister greatly. I would not want to see her . . . to see her discontented."

"But why on earth should she be? I cannot think Mr. Warwick will be anything but kind."

"Oh, please—I did not mean to imply—Nicholas is the finest of men and the best of friends. He is very intense and he drives himself hard, though he does not give that impression when he is in company. I do not doubt he loves her deeply— she must never be unsure of that. It is just that she may feel he

262

has not made sufficient room for her in his life, and that would be a dreadful mistake. He has been hurt in the past, and he is hard to know."

Livia was not sure how to respond to this extraordinary declaration. Finally she said, "Claudia is not a young girl, expecting constant devotion. I am sure she knows that her husband will have a life apart from hers." It was a kind of answer, but she had not really responded to Melbrooke's concern. Would Nicholas give her sister the warmth, the emotional give and take, on which she thrived? Or was this too much to expect from any husband? Would she find it then in her children? Claudia had always been firm about having lots of children. For the first time Livia understood what they might mean to her.

They were interrupted by the Misses Tiverton and Kimball-Smythe who complained bitterly about the crush—Miss Tiverton had had her flounce torn. They were in alt, however, over a rendering of Cupid and Psyche and had found much to admire in a genre piece of a young woman distilling herbs, watched over by an old crone who was either a witch or a very nasty grandmother. Livia and Melbrooke exchanged pleasantries and moved on.

By this time Claudia and Nicholas were out of sight. They caught up with them in the next room. Paul's picture must be here, but Livia could not at first locate it. In the corner perhaps, obscured by a knot of people—if so it was certainly ill-placed, for it was hung low. As they edged into the crowd, Livia heard scattered comments—"Yes, I know he's an R.A., but all those acid greens . . . I told him to his face that if he ever so insulted me again I would . . . No, I've never heard of him and I wouldn't give above a hundred guineas for the bitch . . . What glorious hair!"

This last at least referred to Paul's Artemis, though she did not fit Livia's image of the huntress. Early morning sun, brilliantly captured as it filtered through the leaves of trees just coming into leaf, a few scattered flowers not yet open to the sun, a young girl standing joyous on the bank of a stream. The symbolism was a bit heavy, Livia thought, but the effect was charming. The girl stood poised on a rock. She was about to bathe and her short diaphanous garment, which failed to conceal the soft curves of her body, had slipped down to expose one perfectly formed breast. The sun struck her hair, giving golden tints to the fiery aureole surrounding her face. The face itself was fresh, innocent, not yet awakened to the ripening body. It was perfectly conceived and executed with a boldness which even Livia, with her scant experience of the art, could recognize as that of a real painter.

It was Diana, of course, but Livia was so entranced that it took her a few moments to realize the implications of what she was seeing. She caught a coarse comment or two, moved to Claudia's side and pressed her sister's hand in warning. "The wretch," she said under her breath, "not to prepare us." She makes a splendid model, she thought, but she's likely to land us in a fearful coil. She was afraid to look at Nicholas and did not know what to say to Melbrooke. A glance passed between the sisters, compounded of amusement and exasperation. Claudia turned to Melbrooke. "My eye is untutored, but I think it is quite splendid. The rendering of light is positively luminous. You should be very proud."

A tall, aesthetic young man turned to look at them. "Redmond. He's related to you, ain't he, Melbrooke? Demmed fine work. Oh, your pardon, Miss Neville." He bowed as far as the crowd about him would permit.

Claudia smiled at him. She had danced once with Mr. Wigley and thought him rather sweet. There was a little eddy around them as the connection between Melbrooke and Paul became known. Melbrooke murmured his thanks as he and Nicholas maneuvered the ladies to an alcove in the adjoining room. Claudia dropped her gloves as they escaped and Nicholas went to retrieve them. He returned to find his friend in earnest apology.

"I will never forgive the scoundrel. To have compromised

your sister in this way is unforgiveable."

"Please," Claudia said, "you make too much of it. I am not overset, I assure you."

Nicholas returned the gloves, now sadly soiled, to his betrothed. "You are too charitable. He had no business to expose your sister in this way." He frowned, apparently regretting his choice of words.

Livia was overcome with mischief. "Didn't you find it a good likeness?"

"That is hardly the question, Mrs. Royce."

"But of course not, how stupid I am. A portrait should bring out the inner person, not the outward form. And I am persuaded he has done it to perfection. Though it is, of course, not a portrait at all, but an evocation of a period in time, not necessarily classical time, but a time in our own lives which we forget at our peril."

"We're not speaking of art, we're speaking of a very young girl's reputation. Did you know of this? Did you approve?"

"Of his using her likeness? No, I did not. Not that I would necessarily have objected to having her sit for him."

"Sit is hardly the word in this case."

She had made him angry. Melbrooke looked miserable. Claudia's mouth was twitching. Livia burst into laughter. "Oh, but you do not mean—you did not think—" She could not go on.

Nicholas nodded at some passing acquaintances, then turned back to Livia. "We would be advised to keep our voices low. I find your levity surprising, Mrs. Royce. You should have better care of your charge."

Claudia laid a hand on his arm in protest, but it was Livia who spoke. "Diana did not pose, at least not for the entire picture. She is not lost to all sense of propriety," Livia was not certain of this last, but thought it wise to keep her doubts to herself.

"Are you sure? I would be much relieved to think better of my nephew." Melbrooke removed his hat and wiped his

265

forehead with his handkerchief. Though they were away from the crowd, the room was warm.

"I too would be relieved." Nicholas was not yet won over. "But how can you be certain? Particularly," he added grimly, "since you do not always keep informed of the whereabouts of your youngest sister."

Livia glanced at Claudia but saw that her sister could not trust herself to speak. Oh dear, Livia thought, he knows we are laughing at him. She lowered her eyes, seeking for a way to phrase it with delicacy. "It's just that—well, my sister does not—she is not—not made in just that way."

It took them a moment, but only a moment. The tension was broken. Nicholas actually laughed. "It was unwise of him," Melbrooke said. "No, it was worse than that, using her likeness without permission. Fortunately she is still very young and doesn't go into society. She won't be recognized."

"And when she is older," Nicholas added, "she can simply deny it. Aunt Isabel claims that one can deny anything and be believed if one does it with enough authority. And from what I know of the child, authority is one thing she'll never lack."

Restored to good humour, Nicholas prepared to escort the ladies out of the gallery. As they moved down the room a shrill voice which they recognized as that of the Dowager Duchess of Waterford rose above the noise in the adjoining room. "Good God! It's the Neville chit!"

The duchess was not normally an intemperate woman. Her disapprobation was expressed in a raised eyebrow or an imperious sneer, perfected by long practice over nearly thirty years. Her outburst had been deliberate, a gleeful taking advantage of a rare opportunity to discredit the entire Neville family and her old friend, their sponsor. Because it was out of character, it commanded immediate attention. Rumour swept the room. Those who had seen enough were moved to turn back and look again. Those just entering were drawn into the maelstrom. Someone remembered seeing Colonel Scott with a little red-headed girl. Another claimed to trace a resemblance to the beautiful Miss Neville. Still a third said the resemblance was entirely to her elder sister. No, said a fourth, Mrs. Royce's figure was too slight, Artemis took after the divine Claudia. Though appealed to, the duchess said no more. It was all inexpressibly embarrassing for her son.

Francesca was amused. She found the picture charming, betraying Paul's youth but also his energy and his not inconsiderable technique. She had, of course, recognized Diana at once, but as an acute observer of her fellows, knew that Paul had used at least two models. Still, to have posed at all was unexpected. The girl was more interesting than she had thought.

However, she could not let these attacks on Diana's virtue go unopposed. "But that's nonsense!" Francesca's high clear voice rang out above the general muddle. George was urging her away, but she held her ground. "I've seen the girl, and the face is something like—he may have sketched her at one time—but she was certainly not the model for Artemis."

This stopped some of the more vociferous comments, but the damage had been done. Francesca allowed George to lead her into the adjoining room where the duchess, having withdrawn from the fray, was awaiting them. "I found that most distasteful," Waterford said as they made their way out of the gallery. "There was no call for you to get involved, and I had much rather you had not."

"You would have let the rabble have their way? For shame, Waterford, I am sure the explanation is innocent enough."

Francesca's future mother-in-law gave an eloquent sniff. "Appearance is everything, my dear. You would be advised to be careful. That so-called rabble is the *ton*, and they can do immeasurable damage. You know it well enough. That ramshackle family either does not or does not care. George, see to the carriage. Looking at pictures always fatigues me, though I confess this view has been more interesting than most."

George bowed and left them standing just inside the entrance to await the crested barouche. The two women stood in silence. The duchess had been much relieved when Miss Neville was taken out of the running for the post of her daughter-in-law. Lady Francesca—by birth, beauty, and the possession of a private fortune—was unexceptionable, but she was not entirely without fault. An outspoken young woman—that came from having been married before—and somewhat lacking in the requisite amount of deference to her future husband and his mother. Still, she would have to do. The duchess had long urged her son to marry and set up his nursery. His infatuation with Miss Neville had seriously alarmed her—she was certain he was thinking of making the girl an offer—and she was wise enough to settle for George's next choice.

When the carriage arrived, the duchess directed it to an address on Clarges Street, then turned again to Francesca, picking up her conversation as though there had been no lapse in time. "I know you cannot completely avoid the connection, Francesca, but you would oblige me by seeing as little of them as is decently possible."

This was not the tone to take with Lady Francesca. "I am much attached to my present brother-in-law," she said sweetly, "and I am excessively fond of his future wife. I count her as one of my closest friends. As I do Mrs. Royce."

"That is nonsense, Francesca. You haven't known them above three months. I count such friendships as nothing, and by the winter you will be of the same mind."

"I assure you, I know my own mind perfectly well."

The duke hated contention and he hastened to intervene. "No one doubts that Miss Neville is an estimable young woman, but I've been much disappointed in her elder sister. I had thought her quite sensible, but of late she has shown an unbecoming lightness of mind. I cannot think her a good influence, and her failure to keep her youngest sister in hand is proof enough."

"George, you're being prosy."

"Call it what you like, Francesca, you can't deny the family isn't quite the thing. One sister is on her way to being an eccentric, the second is too agreeable to stand up to her, and the third appears totally out of control. I won't comment on the brother."

"And what is wrong with the brother?" Francesca's voice was dangerously even.

"A good enough fellow, I suppose, and an agreeable rattle, but hardly fit to be head of the family. Not that he seems to see himself in that light. Mrs. Royce appears to lead them all by the nose."

Francesca was furious. George was being insufferably stuffy, but she had always known him to be so. She should be able to manage him better.

They pulled up in Clarges Street while the duchess made a brief call. Francesca and Waterford waited in the carriage and Francesca made another effort to mend matters between herself and her betrothed. "George, I'm sorry we disagree, but it is not to be expected that a couple will like all the same people equally well. I assure you I will never raise an objection to any of your friends."

Waterford appeared to be collecting his thoughts. "I appreciate that, but I don't think you have quite grasped my point. I owe something to my family and what it stands for. I expect no less from you."

"You would tell me whom I may or may not see?"

"I would ask you for the utmost discretion."

"I will not deny Nicholas. He has been very good to me."

"I would hardly ask that of you, my dear. Nor do I ask you to cut his future wife. As for the rest of the family, I see no need for any further intimacy."

Francesca seethed. She had not expected this much opposition. "George, please let us understand each other. I am not a young girl out of the schoolroom, to be molded as you like. Surely you realized this when you offered for me. We have some shared tastes, and I am convinced we will deal very comfortably together. I would not for the world bring disgrace upon you, and I will not inflict on you any persons whom you may find disagreeable. But you must know I am fond of society. I like to be amused and I like people who are amusing, and I will not be dictated to in my choice of entertainment."

"You find such entertainment as that provided by the Nevilles on Tuesday last to your taste?"

"Yes," Francesca said with decision. "Yes, I do."

"You surprise me," he said drily.

Francesca made one more attempt. "Come, George. I know they do not live in just your style, nor in the Warwick style either. They do not have a great deal of money, but that is surely no disgrace. You can hardly judge people by the number of footmen they keep."

Waterford nodded. He had been surprised by the absence of any footmen at all.

"You were uncomfortable," Francesca continued, "because your mother and Marianne were there. It was clear the Nevilles had not expected them—yes, yes, I know, it was shockingly careless to not be more precise in the invitation—but they were as kind as possible under the circumstances. Had just the two of us gone, you might have enjoyed yourself."

"I doubt that I would have done so, Francesca." He looked bleak.

Her voice softened. "You are so hedged about by your position. I am only trying to help you escape now and then from the constraints under which you must live."

Now he was clearly offended. "You mistake me, madam. I am quite satisfied with my position, constraints and all."

"Then I am truly sorry." She would have said more, but the duchess returned and made inconsequential small talk until they delivered Francesca to Warwick House. Francesca pleaded a headache and said that she would not join them at Lady Burney's rout that evening, then hastened indoors.

Lady Crawford was out and Mrs. Amesbury was above stairs,

but she found Claudia, Livia, and Melbrooke in the drawing room with Nicholas. He offered her tea. "From your expression, you could do with a cup."

"I certainly could. That woman is insupportable. I would much rather not discuss it, but you'll have to know."

"I rather think we know already," Nicholas said, correctly assuming that only the duchess could have provoked such an outburst. "We didn't see you there, but we heard her grace's voice as we were leaving. Did it cause much comment?"

Francesca described the scene to them, including her own efforts to undo the damage. "Though I doubt I did much good. It was deliberate, I am sure of it, or she would never have spoken so in public. I shall never forgive her."

Nicholas, whose feelings had taken yet another turn since hearing the duchess' outburst, laid a hand on her shoulder. "I advise you to do so, Francesca, or you will have a very uncomfortable life. The damage is done. The story will be all over London before nightfall. I am thinking of sending Diana down to Waverley until it blows over."

Livia looked up, startled. Nicholas' high-handed assumption of a guardian role enraged her. Her eyes grew stormy. "You wouldn't dare."

"Indeed I would. And don't tell me I have no right to interfere. Your sister has given me that right, and I am certain she is in full agreement with me."

Livia turned to Claudia. Surely her sister would not allow herself to be browbeaten by Nicholas. She wouldn't. Claudia met Livia's gaze and said, clearly voicing her own opinion, "Yes, Livia, I think it an excellent idea."

Livia stared at her sister. Of course. Though she was perfectly tolerant of her family, Claudia had always been more conventional than the rest of them. And people changed to fit new roles. Claudia was already becoming Mrs. Nicholas Warwick.

Nicholas took advantage of Livia's silence to press home his point. "I am aware that you have given your youngest sister a measure of freedom far greater than what is usual, and I have tried to respect your choice, but it is clear to me that she is now wholly beyond your control."

"You will answer to my brother, Mr. Warwick." Livia tried to keep her voice light. For Claudia's sake, she did not want a quarrel.

"By all means. I am sure he too will agree with me."

This might be true. Rage as she might at the unfairness of it, Diana had placed them all in a most difficult position. Their hope that no one would recognize her—reasonable, considering that few of their acquaintance had ever seen her—had been dashed by a vindictive woman. But Livia was not about to hand her sister over to the keeping of Nicholas Warwick, who, she was convinced, quite failed to understand Diana. She would take Diana away herself. No, she could not leave Claudia at a time like this. She would send Diana back to Mrs. Henderson in Oxford and she would do it at once, before Nicholas could put his odious plan into effect.

Livia caught Francesca's eye. Francesca said nothing, but Livia could read her face. Never mind, was the message, he is a bear, but he can be made to dance. Livia lowered her eyes. Let him take her silence for assent. Nicholas Warwick would never get the better of her.

Chapter 18

Unlike Francesca, Livia and Claudia attended Lady Burney's rout on the evening of the day they had all viewed the painting. Lady Crawford insisted. "The worst thing you can possibly do," she told them, "is appear to be out of countenance. Hold your heads up and deny everything. The story is absurd and you have no idea how it could have been put about. That way you place it all on Lavinia, and she deserves it."

They left Warwick House and went home to dress for the evening. There was some constraint between the sisters, the inevitable result of their disagreement over Diana. Livia longed to talk to Gerry, but he of course was out. They had seen little of him these past few weeks. Since the announcement of Francesca's engagement to Waterford, he had been away more than ever.

Instead, Livia had to face the inevitable, inconclusive scene with Diana who failed to see anything wrong with either the painting or her role in it. "I can understand your not wanting me to walk in Mount Street," she said, "but this is ridiculous. Paul is a serious painter and he's very respectable and he's our friend. It hasn't hurt anyone."

"No one," Livia agreed in a voice made cold by Nicholas' threat to take charge of Diana. "No one, other than yourself and your family. You, of course, don't mind. You might argue

273

that Gerry and I don't mind either, but you have perhaps forgotten that Claudia has recently become engaged and that her fiancé is a man who takes his responsibilities seriously. He proposes to send you into Sussex for safekeeping.''

At that, Diana became silent. Before the distressed Claudia could intervene, she said in a quite different voice that she was extremely sorry and marched off to her room. Livia let her stay there.

Both Livia and Claudia were relieved to leave the house for the predictable gaiety of Lady Burney's small but exquisitely furnished house in Jermyn Street. They were escorted by Nicholas and Lord Melbrooke. The sight of the divine Claudia with her fiancé—the announcement of their betrothal had appeared only the day before—proved of far more interest than rumours about the identity of Redmond's model.

Livia accepted congratulations on Claudia's behalf and ignored one or two whispered conversations and a speculative look from Lord Dinsdale. Instead she prepared to enjoy herself. Oliver Merriman was there. He said just the right things about Nicholas' good fortune and appeared to have no interest in art whatsoever. Livia found it hard to believe that he had designs on Nicholas' reputation. She set herself to be charming and was rewarded by an invitation to drive the following afternoon. She accepted without any devious intent.

It was only as they took a turn around the room that she noticed he was walking with a slight limp. She taxed him with it and he smiled ruefully. ''Not the sort of story one wishes to get about. I was set upon and robbed on my way home from my club two nights ago. Fortunately I wasn't carrying a great deal of money.''

Livia's surprise was genuine. She had left the matter of dealing with Merriman to Gerry and Sandringham, saying she preferred to know as little as possible. She decided she had been quite right. She considered mentioning that her brother had been the victim of a similar incident, then resolutely held her tongue.

274

The Nevilles left the rout early, and it was not much past one when Nicholas and Melbrooke brought them home. Nicholas said he had a meeting in the morning which might run late, but he would call to discuss Diana's future as soon as he could get away. He pressed Claudia's hand and nodded almost brusquely to Livia. Melbrooke told Livia in lowered tones that he would see Paul in the morning and they were not to worry. Livia, who had hitherto considered Lord Melbrooke a man of sense, wondered if she should revise her opinion. Nicholas at least had not made any such foolish suggestion.

Gerry was still out when they returned and Livia went straight to bed, too tired to wait up for him. Much better to face him with the problem in the morning. But when she entered the breakfast parlour shortly after nine, Sandringham told her that Colonel Scott had already gone out and had taken Miss Diana with him.

Dear God. What maggoty notion had her brother and sister taken into their heads? Livia sat down, allowed Sandringham to pour coffee and drank over half a cup before she became aware of the folded sheet of paper by her place, addressed in Diana's beautiful hand. She finished the coffee, requested another cup, then dismissed Sandringham and opened the note. Diana was very sorry for the trouble she had caused. She had persuaded Gerry to take her to Cousin Sophronia's. She planned to stay there two or three days—she was sure their cousin would oblige her—and when she returned she would try to discuss the matter sensibly. She wouldn't hurt Claudia for the world, and her absence at this point would make it easier for everyone.

Little beast, Livia thought, and smiled. It was actually a very good decision, though she would not have dared approach Sophronia herself. Still, this would give her time to plan how to deal with Nicholas Warwick.

Claudia came down an hour later, looking beautiful and faintly troubled. Livia told her they were not to be divided by any difference of opinion about Diana. In any case Diana was

275

staying with their cousin for a few days and they would sort it all out when she returned. The rift mended, Claudia prepared for a shopping expedition with Lady Crawford. Livia saw them off with relief, made sure the children were suitably occupied, told Sandringham she was not at home, and shut herself up in the library. She had a great deal of thinking to do and she would do it best unhampered by members of her well-meaning household. Within the next few weeks, perhaps only a matter of days, she had to rescue Claudia and Claudia's future husband—as she determinedly referred to Nicholas—from social ruin, thanks to Diana and Paul, and from political ruin, thanks to Oliver Merriman. In addition, she had to extricate herself and Diana from Nicholas' high-handed control.

She could count on Nicholas, Melbrooke and Lady Crawford to help her with the first, and on Gerry and Francesca to help her with the second. She could count on no one, including perhaps Claudia, to help her with the third.

She had made little progress on any of the three when, half an hour later, Sandringham tapped at the library door and informed her that she had a caller.

"Didn't I say I wasn't at home?" A caller, in particular one who had visited the European Museum, was the last thing she was prepared to face.

"Yes, ma'am. But I thought perhaps you might wish to see this particular caller. It is Mr. Merriman."

Lord Melbrooke rarely lost his temper. He had, for instance, never beaten his son and seldom even raised his voice. Few people had ever seen him angry. His nephew was privileged to witness this rare event the morning after Melbrooke had seen *Artemis at Dawn*.

"How could you, Paul—an innocent young girl—practically a child—she probably didn't have the least idea what she was doing."

Paul had arrived at his uncle's lodgings shortly after nine

276

o'clock in response to an urgent message delivered the previous evening but unread until a very late return from a night's drinking. Paul's head ached. He was sitting on a chair in his uncle's study, not saying anything for the simple reason that he couldn't think of anything he needed or wanted to say.

"It didn't," Melbrooke continued, "occur to you that her reputation would be in danger? You didn't think that to paint a gently bred girl in such a garment, such a—"

"I didn't," Paul said, hearing a point he needed to make, "paint Diana Neville. I painted Artemis. Diana Neville just provided the taking off point."

Lord Melbrooke—unacquainted with the thought processes of artists—sighed, more exasperated than ever. "Paul, have you considered what this means to her family, how they must feel? Yes, I know you don't care, you needn't say it, but Diana is going to have to care. It isn't easy for girls to defy convention."

Paul considered this. He had never really thought of it before, but now that he did . . . "It's unfair, sir, it's damnably unfair."

"Unfair? Paul Redmond, I have done my utmost to be reasonable and considerate—"

"Oh, not you, Uncle Edward. It's unfair that Diana has less freedom than I do."

"We aren't discussing the proper way to bring up young girls."

"No, we aren't. Sorry. What are you going to do, sir?"

Melbrooke sighed. "You're your own master. I shall do my best to repair any damage that may have been done to Diana's reputation. You can probably help most by staying out of the way."

"Of course, sir." He paused. "My allowance?"

"Your allowance? Is that all that concerns you?"

"No, sir, but I'd like to know. If it stops, I'll have to do something that will sell."

Melbrooke considered his nephew with disfavour. "I won't

stop your allowance, Paul," he said at last. "Go back to your lodgings and do Diana a favour by staying away from her."

"Goodbye, Uncle Edward." Paul started for the door, but paused, his hand on the latch, a faint line between his brows. "Uncle Edward?"

"Yes?" Melbrooke asked wearily.

"Do you really think Diana is going to be hurt?"

Melbrooke stared at him in astonishment. From the day he had been confronted with an abstracted fatherless twelve-year old to this moment, it was the first word of personal concern he had ever heard his nephew express over anyone.

In Paul's absence, there was a fierce discussion underway in his rooms. "It's out of the question," Henry Ashton said for at least the tenth time that morning. "Even if we had enough room, you couldn't stay here. You're not that kind of girl."

Diana glared at him from her perch among the paint boxes on the sopha. "I'm not any kind of girl. I'm me. I need a place to live and I don't see why you won't help me."

"I won't help you because you have no business living alone. It's not safe. It's not—" Henry searched for an acceptable word, then gave it up. "It's not respectable."

Diana snorted. "Cousin Sophronia lives alone."

"She has a companion."

"Then I'll get Jeanie to come live with me."

"It's not the same. Can't you stay with your cousin?"

"For a day or two, maybe. But it wouldn't be fair to entangle her in this. And if I don't set up on my own, I'll ruin things for Claudia and Livia—and very likely the Warwicks as well. Besides," she added practically, "if I don't leave home, Mr. Warwick will send me off to Sussex and Claudia will back him up and I don't think even Livia will be able to help me."

"Then go home to Oxford."

"And leave London? Never!"

Henry ran a distracted hand through his hair. "Diana," he

278

said, speaking very slowly, "if you do this you'll never be accepted in society again."

"I don't think I'm accepted now. And I don't care. I can support myself—I don't need to find a husband to do it for me. That's what respectability is all about, isn't it?"

Henry could not find an answering argument. Fortunately, at this juncture Paul walked in.

"Paul, I'm leaving home and I need some help finding a place to live," Diana said by way of greeting.

Henry at once appealed to his friend for assistance, but Paul merely said, "Yes, I've thought about that. I'm going to Paris. You'd better come with me."

Henry gaped at him. Even Diana was surprised. "Now see here," Henry said, "you can't just run off at a moment's notice."

"It isn't a moment's notice. I've been thinking about it for some time. David's been exiled to Brussels, but there are other people I'd like to study with. Besides, I'm no earthly good to the family as it is."

"Confound it, Paul, you can't take Diana. She's underage and you know what they'll make of that."

Paul wasn't paying attention. "There's every reason to go and no logical reason not to go. But I can't go off and leave Diana in this mess I got her into."

Henry groaned at his misplaced chivalry.

"You didn't get me into it," Diana pointed out. "I can take care of myself. I was just telling Henry."

"I still don't want to go without you. Don't you want to come? You can study there and you can take life classes. They're not stiff-necked about it like they are in England."

Diana's eyes were shining. She nodded.

"Now wait a minute," interrupted the much tried Mr. Ashton. "You'd better think about this."

"What's there to think about?" Diana demanded. She turned to Paul. "I'm staying with Cousin Sophronia for two or three days. I have a bag there."

"Right. We'll pick it up and go straight to the coast."

"But your sisters!" Henry protested. "Lord Melbrooke! You'll have to let them know."

"If we do," Diana said, "they'll come tearing after us and things will be worse than before. They won't miss me for a day or two. We'll write from Dover. Or maybe from Calais. It will be much better in the long run."

"How?" demanded the practical Henry. "How will you get to Dover, let alone Calais? You can't go all the way to the coast in a hackney."

Paul considered this. "No, I suppose not. We'll hire a carriage and horses. Henry, could you—"

"Oh, no," Mr. Ashton said firmly. "I'm not having anything to do with this harebrained scheme."

"All right, I'll go. It shouldn't take long." He shifted some of the paintboxes on the sopha. "Diana, would you pack my paints while I'm gone? I won't take much."

"What about clothes?" Henry demanded to deaf ears. "What about food? What about money?"

The only subject of debate seemed to be how many of Paul's canvases they could take. This last being settled satisfactorily, Paul said, "I'm off, then. There's bread in the cupboard if you're hungry. I'll be back within the hour."

"Oh, never mind," Henry said wearily. "I'll go. If you insist on this corkbrained plan, the least I can do is see you do it properly. No, no,"—he waved aside Paul's proffered purse and Diana's small reticule. "Think of it as a going away present." He went out, leaving Paul and Diana to pack up vital necessities such as paints, drawing pencils and canvas.

Oliver Merriman was standing by the drawing room fireplace, his head bent, but he looked up at Livia's entrance with the smile she had once found so attractive. No, to be honest she still found it attractive.

"Mr. Merriman," Livia said. "I did not expect you at this hour."

He took her hand, then seated himself opposite her. "I am afraid I cannot stay long. I had so looked forward to our drive this afternoon, but I must cry off. Please forgive me."

Her hand, settling her skirt, did not pause in its motion. "I'm sorry. I trust it is nothing serious?"

"No, no. A matter of business. I would much prefer to spend the afternoon with you, but it cannot be put off. I know you will understand."

Livia nodded, unreasonably disappointed. She had wanted time to herself and Merriman was, in a matter of speaking, the enemy, but she enjoyed his company and had never, in her three months in London, been taken driving on her own account. She got through the rest of the interview with reasonable social grace and saw him off with his promise to call in a day or two. She watched his curricle drive off from the drawing room window, then returned to the hall where she was met by Sandringham.

"I hope I was not out of order, Mrs. Royce, but I had a word with Mr. Merriman's groom. Apparently Mr. Merriman is going into Kent, though his groom is to be left behind. He is bound for an inn a mile or two beyond Dartford, somewhere near Jack-in-the-Hole. It's called the Bell and Candle. I thought you might be interested."

For a moment Livia's incisive dark brown eyes met Sandringham's expressive blue ones. Dartford. Lord Barstow-Greene had a house near Dartford, Francesca had told her, not far from the old Roman road. He must have returned to England.

"Yes," she said, "thank you, Sandringham. I might be. Of course I am, very interested." Her mind worked furiously. Merriman must be headed off before he could meet the older man. "I find I am called out of town," she told Sandringham. "I will need a carriage as soon as possible, then I will have some letters to deliver."

She returned to the library and scribbled two hasty notes, went upstairs and said a quick goodbye to Gwendolen and Eddy, then put on her bonnet and pelisse and made some other preparations for the journey. When she returned the carriage had arrived. She gave Sandringham one of the notes. "This is to be delivered personally to Lady Francesca. Find her if necessary, but do not leave it with anyone else." She handed him the second. "Give this one to Colonel Scott as soon as he returns."

Sandringham received his instructions with equanimity and held open the front door.

"I don't know how long I shall be," Livia added as she went down the steps. "Tell Miss Neville she is not to worry."

Which, Livia thought as her hired carriage pulled out of Charles Street, meant that perhaps Lord Melbrooke was a man of sense after all.

Francesca was with her fiancé when Livia's note reached her. Waterford had called just before eleven, surprisingly early, though to be fair he was not one of those who invariably slept till noon. And he had not been out late the evening before. He had only stayed at Lady Burney's as long as politeness required. He had not enjoyed himself. He was most anxious that things should be put right between himself and Francesca. He was certain that after an evening's reflection they would both see things more clearly.

What he really meant—though he would never dream of saying it—was that he was certain Francesca would see things more clearly. His own vision had been crystal clear from the beginning.

Francesca was tired and cross. She had not slept well the night before. She was worried about the Nevilles and worried about Merriman, she hadn't seen Gerry in two days, and she was in no mood to humour George. Later, when the other problems were settled, she would contrive a better strategy for dealing with George and his mother. At the moment she simply wanted to be left alone. She was in the process of persuading Waterford to leave when Parkhurst came in with Livia's note.

282

Francesca looked at the handwriting, apologized to Waterford, and tore the note open. She read it through once and stood up. "George, you'll have to excuse me. I've been called out of town."

"Called out of town?" Waterford was on his feet as well. "My dear Francesca, what has happened?"

"It's a family matter," she said briefly, for she was desperately anxious to leave. She started for the door. "I may not return to town tonight, but I expect I shall see you tomorrow."

His lordship was disturbed. "Have you forgotten the Langdons' ball this evening?"

Francesca continued across the room. "I daresay it will go on very well without me."

"And that we are engaged to dine with my mother beforehand?"

That brought her up short. Damn the woman, did she have to interfere in everything? Francesca drew a breath. "I'm sorry, George. You'll have to make my excuses to your mother. You know I would not disappoint her if the cause were not urgent."

"Mother has invited some of her oldest friends to meet you—"

Francesca started for the door again. "George, don't be ridiculous, how many friends can your mother have whom I haven't known since I was a child?"

"To present you as my future wife," Waterford continued stiffly. It was unforgivable of Francesca to put him through this twice in twenty-four hours. He would not have expected it from a woman of her breeding. Of course her first husband was known to have been reckless and her father's reputation . . . "If you insist on running off like this, Francesca, I think you must give me an explanation."

Francesca turned back to face him. She couldn't. Even were she not in such a hurry, she couldn't possibly tell him of her predicament. How could she ever have contemplated spending the rest of her life with him?

"I told you, George. It's a family matter. A private one."

"Your family will soon become mine. A wife can have no secrets from her husband."

"I'm sorry, George." Now that she was no longer going to be his wife, she was conscious of a momentary pity. "Someone should have told you. I don't take an ultimatum from anyone. I expect you are feeling shockingly abused, but you ought to be grateful for your escape." She took off the ring, a Waterford heirloom, which he had given her only three days before. "I should make an abominable duchess."

She opened the door because there was no more to be said and she had lost enough time as it was. Waterford followed her into the hall, but any answer he might have made was forestalled by Mrs. Amesbury who was coming down the stairs.

"Aunt Letty," Francesca said, managing to speak before Mrs. Amesbury could comment on the scene. "I have some unexpected business to take care of and am in a dreadful hurry. Waterford is just leaving. Could you ring for Parkhurst?"

She started up the stairs without waiting for an answer. "I can't imagine what business you could have that couldn't wait for a few hours," Mrs. Amesbury said plaintively. She rang for the butler. Waterford bowed and took his leave.

Francesca went to her room, pulled a pelisse over her morning dress and hurried back down the stairs, buttoning her gloves. Mrs. Amesbury had lingered in the hall. "If it's financial troubles, Francesca, you really should wait until Nicholas comes home, why remember poor Lady Merrington, she lost an entire fortune in just two years for want of advice, and it was not even her own money, her husband had left it in trust for their eldest son—or was it her grandmother?—and then the bailiff came and spoiled a perfectly splendid dinner party and she had to go and live in a dreary German spa, though I must say it did wonders for her complexion. She brought back a tonic which does me no end of good when I get nervous and it might help you too, so do come upstairs and rest until Nicholas returns."

Francesca kissed Mrs. Amesbury's cheek, said she wasn't sure when she'd be back and not to worry and walked briskly to the stables where she informed Giles, Nicholas' groom, that she was taking the curricle. Giles looked at her, gulped, and asked which horses he should put to the carriage.

Francesca raised her brows in the look her father used to damp the pretensions of under-secretaries and minor royalty alike. "The bays. Naturally."

Naturally. Well, Mr. Warwick did let her drive them sometimes and Giles knew she was a good whip—better than Mr. Justin had been—but . . . "Mr. Warwick didn't say anything about it," he ventured.

"Mr. Warwick," Francesca said with truth, "has a great deal on his mind. And I am in a great hurry."

She softened her manner when Giles brought the curricle round ten minutes later. Giving him an enchanting smile, she took up the reins and set off to find Gerry.

Gwendolen and Eddy were alone in the upstairs of the Charles Street house but they had, thanks to some judicious hanging about the stair railings, a very good idea of the whereabouts of at least one member of the family.

"It's that letter thing, isn't it?" Eddy said. "The one Gerry and Aunt Francesca lost."

Gwendolen nodded absently.

"Isn't it Mr. Merriman that Papa and Uncle Nicholas don't like?" Eddy persisted.

"They don't always agree with him," Gwendolen corrected carefully.

"It's the same thing," Eddy said, scorning diplomacy.

Gwendolen was frowning intently. "It's going to be awful if Livia can't get the letter back from Mr. Merriman."

"Awful," Eddy repeated, relishing the word.

"We have to help somehow," Gwendolen continued.

"How are we going to do that?" Eddy demanded, sure that she would have an answer.

"By following Livia, of course."

Eddy had no fault to find with this suggestion, but it did not seem to tally with Gwendolen's earlier strategy. He felt bound to point this out. "You said we had to behave with Guile and Stealth."

"That was before things got Desperate. There's a time for Guile and Stealth and a time for Action."

Eddy nodded, impressed by the gravity of the situation. "How are we going to follow Livia?" he asked, again sure that Gwendolen would find a way. Gwendolen was not as sanguine, but before she could be put to the test, she heard two familiar voices in the hall below.

"Oughtn't to enter unannounced. Not at all the thing."

"Oh, stuff! That don't matter here. Dashed queer, though. Wonder where Sandringham can have gotten to."

"Uncle Harry!" Gwendolen ran down the stairs, Eddy at her heels. "Jack!"

"Genny!" Harry exclaimed. "What are you—"

"Never mind. Come in the library. Quickly!"

Whatever her faults, Gwendolen did not enact dramas without cause. Without further hesitation, Harry followed her into the library, Jack and Eddy behind him.

Jack looked around. "You all alone?"

"Never mind about that," Harry said, echoing his niece. "Is something wrong with Claudia? Or Livia?"

"No—that is, not directly. We're the ones who need help."

"Oh." Harry drew back a little.

"Do whatever we can of course," Jack said more tactfully, "but nurseries not quite in our line."

"We aren't in the nursery," Eddy objected. "I go to school."

"Not a real school," Jack pointed out. "Not Eton or

anything. Still in the nursery till you go to Eton, aren't you, Harry?"

"I daresay."

"Listen to me!" Gwendolen said in the voice her father used to get the floor in the heat of debate.

"All right." Harry was resigned. "What is it?"

Gwendolen drew a deep breath. "It's—it's a letter I think."

"About what?" said Jack.

"Who wrote it?" asked Harry.

"Daddy wrote it." With a careful lack of sentiment, Gwendolen added, "I think it's about Mummy." Jack, only dimly aware of the circumstances of Lillie Warwick's death and conscious that these were not to be spoken of—especially in the presence of children—frowned.

Harry rose, crossed to Gwendolen's chair and dropped down beside her, laying a hand over hers. "All right, brat," he said, "I think you'd better tell me about it. From the beginning."

The worst over, Gwendolen hastily explained the facts they'd managed to uncover. "And if Mr. Merriman isn't stopped," she concluded, her customary manner returning, "Daddy will be ruined! We just have to do something!"

Harry and Jack exchanged glances. Their chivalrous instincts had been instantly aroused, even if the damsel in distress was only ten.

"Besides," Gwendolen went on, "Livia may be in danger." Actually, she believed that Livia was fully capable of coping with Mr. Merriman, but she judged rightly that this argument would firmly tip the scales in her favour.

"Have to do something," Jack said. "Family matter."

"Then you'll take us?" Eddy asked from the sidelines.

"Not the sort of thing for children," Jack cautioned.

"We're going," Gwendolen told them, "whether you take us or not."

"How?" Harry asked. "How will you get there?"

"We'll manage," Gwendolen said with determination. "But we'd be a lot safer with you."

Having lived in the same house with Gwendolen for the past ten years, Harry was sure that this at least was true. "All right," he said, not wasting time on expostulation. "Though God knows how we'll get there. I suppose I could take Nicholas' curricle—"

"No," Gwendolen and Jack said in one breath, not quite drowning Eddy's exclamation of pleasure at the prospect of riding behind Nicholas' bays.

"Can't take your brother's carriage," Jack protested. "Imagine the kickup."

"Oh, I can. I suppose we'll have to hire one. Lucky I just got my allowance. I should be able to stand the nonsense. No, Jack, I'll take care of it. Like as not you'd hire a pony cart or some such thing."

"My dear fellow!"

"All right, I didn't mean that. Here, you leave a note for Claudia, and mind you don't say anything that will put her in a pucker." He ran quickly out of the room. Jack settled down to write the note and Gwendolen looked unbelievably smug.

Henry Ashton's doubts as to the success of Paul and Diana's venture only increased as he saw the couple off. No sooner had their carriage rattled down Little Russell Street than he hailed a hackney and set off for Lord Melbrooke's rooms. He caught his lordship just returning home, his mind warring among Claudia, his nephew, and reaction to the new Corn Law. He was in the act of firmly pushing Miss Neville out in favour of the political problem when Henry accosted him.

"My lord."

"Henry. Is something the matter?" Henry's hair was more than usually disarranged.

"Yes. No. Not with me. Might I have a word with you, sir?"

"Did Paul send you?" Melbrooke asked when he had let Henry into the study.

"Not precisely. He—your words made a great impression

on him, sir."

"I should hope they did," Paul's uncle said grimly.

"Yes. Well, I don't think they had quite the effect you intended."

That did push Claudia Neville from his lordship's mind. "What's he done?" Melbrooke demanded in a level tone.

"He's—well, he's gone off."

"Gone off?"

"Gone off with Diana Neville."

Melbrooke stood up. His voice trembled. "Do you mean that not content with ruining that child's reputation, Paul's dragged her off to Gretna Green?"

"No, no," Henry hastened to assure him. "You're wrong, sir. Wrong on three counts. Diana's not a child, she's almost seventeen. Paul didn't drag her. And they haven't gone to Scotland."

"You mean they aren't getting married?"

"Oh, I'm sure they'll get married," Henry said with more confidence than he felt. "But probably not in Dover."

"Dover?" Lord Melbrooke was bewildered.

"Yes. Most likely in Paris."

"In Paris?" Melbrooke's hand went to his head. "Good God. And you let them go?"

"Well, sir, you know Paul. He's—well, he's not exactly the easiest person to talk out of things. Neither is Diana. Everyone was upset about the picture and they were only trying to help."

"I daresay." Wasting no further time, Melbrooke stood up. "I'm much obliged to you, Henry."

"I'm sorry, it was my fault in a way. Is there anything I can do?"

"No, I think I'd better handle things from here. But I shouldn't bargain on having your rooms to yourself for long. Paul will be back this evening."

Nicholas had been right to conjecture that his meeting

would run late. It was past one when he arrived in Charles Street, only to be informed by Sandringham that none of the family was at home.

"None of them?"

"That's right, sir. Mr. Harry and Mr. Jack called and took Miss Gwendolen and Master Edward driving, Miss Neville is out with Lady Crawford, and Mrs. Royce was suddenly called out of town."

"Out of town?" Nicholas interrupted before Sandringham could mention Gerry or Diana, which was perhaps just as well. "Is something the matter?"

Sandringham's face was wooden. "As to that, I couldn't say, sir. She didn't inform me of the particulars."

"Who went with her?" Nicholas asked, his voice suddenly sharp. "Did she take Miss Diana?" Confound the woman, she should know by now that he didn't mean all he said when he was in a temper. He thought she'd been overly quiet when he made his threats about Diana the day before. It would be just like her to have taken Diana and returned to Oxford or God knows what other obscure place—

"No, sir," Sandringham was saying. "Miss Diana did not accompany her."

Which, on reflection, was even more odd and perhaps more alarming. "Who went with her then? Did Scott—no, don't tell me." A glint of amusement crept into Nicholas' eyes. "She went alone, she didn't inform anyone of her destination, and she said not to worry."

"Yes, sir. Except that as it happens I do know her destination." Nicholas looked at him sharply. "She went to an inn near Jack-in-the-Hole, just beyond Dartford. It's called the Bell and Candle." Sandringham's voice suddenly did not sound as if it belonged to a butler. "If you'll forgive me, sir, I think it might be a good idea if someone went after her."

But Nicholas was already halfway down the front stairs and off in the direction of Warwick House at a brisk pace that might almost have been called a run.

Chapter 19

The Bell and Candle was not known for its elegance or the excellence of its accommodations. It was not a posting house and, though it made hopeful provision for the occasional traveler, its position just off the Dover road meant that its custom was largely local. So the arrival on foot of a slight young man, carelessly but expensively dressed, and a very young lady swathed, despite the heat, in a black wool traveling cloak was enough to cause the landlord to don his coat and his wife to shed her apron.

The young gentleman, who said his name was Mr. Endymion, explained courteously if a trifle vaguely that he and his sister were traveling to Dover and had suffered a minor but debilitating accident to their carriage. Their driver had found a wheelwright who had engaged to undertake repairs, and it was the wheelwright who had directed them to the Bell and Candle. They required refreshment and possibly accomodations for the night. Mr. Muggs offered them a private parlour, pleased at having guests sure to order a handsome meal. His wife had her reservations. Mr. Endymion and his sister didn't resemble each other in the slightest, and the hood of the young lady's traveling cloak had slipped back to display a blaze of coppery hair. Mrs. Muggs doubted that anyone with hair of that colour could be entirely respectable.

But guests were guests and she was glad enough to have them, so she went to the kitchen to see to the fowl roasting on the spit while her husband conducted the young couple into the larger of the two private parlours.

Mrs. Muggs gave a disapproving sniff when she brought in a tray half an hour later, but on closer observation she decided her suspicions were unfounded. No lover would treat his lady in the offhand manner Mr. Endymion used with his companion.

Indeed, it was hard to imagine two people less like a pair of runaway lovers. Mrs. Muggs was so pleased to have her doubts quenched that she failed entirely to notice the couple's odd topic of conversation. They grew silent while the covers were removed, but Mrs. Muggs attributed this to fatigue and a natural and quite becoming shyness attendant on traveling for the first time. She smiled benevolently and went out, leaving her becomingly shy guests to continue debating the merits of Constable.

Francesca drummed her fingernails against the seat and wound the reins absently through her hands. The sight of a beautiful young woman driving an elegant curricle drawn by a spectacular pair of matched bays had elicited more than a few surprised stares at the Bull, but Francesca's mind was not on appearances. She anxiously scanned the inn doorway and was relieved when Gerry appeared. He grinned cheerfully, sprang back into the curricle and said, "The Bell and Candle's another mile or so down the road. They can't imagine why we want to go there. The kitchen boy saw a carriage that could be Merriman's drive by less than an hour ago."

Francesca set the horses in motion and pulled out of the inn yard. "Don't be so cheerful, Gerry. You're in a towering rage."

"I am?"

"Livia said so in her letter. I'm to restrain you."

"Just try."

"We follow her lead, Gerry, it's much safer. She may even have retrieved the letter by the time we get there. In which case it will only be necessary to retrieve her reputation."

Gerry dismissed this last as a paltry consideration. "If she hasn't succeeded," he said seriously, "I'll challenge Merriman to a duel. That should distract him long enough for you and Livia to look for the letter."

Francesca pulled up the horses abruptly. "Gerry!" she said, her equilibrium completely shattered.

"Mind the horses," Gerry advised. "I probably won't have to challenge him, but if we accuse him of making off with your property he's bound to challenge me."

"Do you imagine," Francesca inquired with asperity as she set the horses in motion, "that resorting to pistols is going to improve matters?"

"I am a tolerable shot, you know."

She knew very well, but that was not the point. "I've never heard a riskier or more dangerous idea."

"I could take a poke at him. Or bash him over the head. You didn't think to bring a blunt object, did you?"

Francesca looked at him in disgust. "At least your sense of humour is unchanged."

"It's my one undeniable asset. Here, you've been driving since we left. Unless you'd rather not trust me with Warwick's cattle?"

"There's never been anything wrong with your driving." Francesca handed him the reins.

It was Gerry who broke the ensuing silence. "I was beginning to think you'd lost yours."

"Lost my what?"

"Sense of humour."

"What on earth makes you think so?" Francesca asked, torn between curiosity and exasperation.

"Our meeting at the de Lisles' for one. You didn't see its humourous side at all."

"There wasn't a humourous side," Francesca said frostily.

There was a brief silence. Gerry studied her profile out of the corner of his eye. Her lips twitched ever so slightly.

"We did have fun," he ventured.

"Yes, we did." Francesca smoothed a wrinkle in one of her kid gloves.

"Then," Gerry said, his voice suddenly serious, "what makes things so different now?"

"People grow up, Gerry," she said quietly.

"Yes."

This time it was Francesca who stole a look at Gerry's profile and noticed it was suddenly grim. "Your fiancé won't approve of this expedition, will he?" Gerry said. "What are you going to tell him?"

"If you mean Waterford," Francesca said, "he doesn't. But as he is no longer my fiancé, his opinion is no longer of any consequence." Was it her imagination or did his expression really lighten?

"You never fail to surprise me," Gerry said after a moment. "What happened?"

"I found I prized a sense of humour more than I realized. Justin at least had a sense of humour." Her voice was cool, but she began to toy with one of the pearl buttons on her gloves.

"Why didn't you write?" Gerry asked, voicing the question that had been troubling him for years.

"Justin wrote."

"But you didn't. After I left Lisbon I heard nothing from you."

The pearl button was released abruptly. That was the last straw. "*I* heard nothing from *you!*"

"I wrote."

"'Give my regards to Francesca'—not even Francie—scrawled at the end of your letters to Justin."

"You were married," Gerry pointed out. "And it saved paper."

"It wouldn't have been so bad," Francesca persisted, the attempt at humour quite lost on her, "if you hadn't gone off in the first place without even saying a proper goodbye."

Gerry turned his eyes briefly from the road to stare at her. "I didn't—don't tell me that's been bothering you all these years."

Francesca gave something suspiciously like a sniff. "Bothering me? Of course it's been bothering me. Wouldn't it have bothered you?"

"Well, yes," Gerry conceded," but I suppose I didn't think you'd care."

Francesca regarded him with exasperation. "Oh, no, of course not. After having you practically one of the family for more than a year, it meant nothing at all that you were going off to get yourself killed."

"Francie," Gerry's eyes were fixed on the road ahead, "it was pretty obvious what Justin's intentions were."

Francesca wrinkled her nose. "I don't see what Justin's intentions have to do with—oh!"

"He was my best friend," Gerry continued doggedly, "but I wasn't going to stand around and watch—"

He broke off. Francesca was staring at him. "Germanicus Scott, do you mean to say that you—"

"Damn it, Francesca, you know every officer at the embassy was head over ears in love with you."

"They didn't all insist on returning to the front because Justin wanted to marry me."

"They weren't all Justin's best friend."

"I had to marry someone," Francesca said. "I was growing up and Father didn't know what to do with me and you were goodness knows where being shot at—"

"But—could you repeat that last?"

It was her turn to look away. "I was only a child," she excused herself, a slight tremor in her voice.

"Earls' daughters don't marry penniless officers." Gerry's voice was bitter. "And penniless officers with a shred of decency don't offer for young women of fortune."

"Lyndales," Francesca said, "do as they please."

"You've always done so."

"Exactly."

It took perhaps another five seconds for her meaning to penetrate. "I'm not quite penniless now, Francesca, but near enough. We don't run in the same race."

"I don't want to marry you for your money, Colonel Scott. I don't imagine you want to marry me for mine."

"Marry you? I can't marry you!"

"I'm very conventional, Gerry. I shall insist upon marriage."

Gerry looked at her in growing wonder. Lady Francesca maintained a dignified silence. Undaunted, Colonel Scott pulled her into his arms. Francesca made no protest and was only returned to reality several seconds later when the curricle veered dangerously toward the verge of the road.

She pulled away from him abruptly. "It's my head Nicholas will have if anything happens to his horses. Now will you give me the reins before we land in a ditch?"

Her guests having gone for a walk, Mrs. Muggs finished clearing away the remains of their meal. A smart curricle pulled into the inn yard. Observing the elegantly dressed gentleman who alighted from it, Mrs. Muggs was instantly sorry that they had given the better parlour to the young couple. However, the gentleman—though perfectly polite—seemed a trifle abstracted, so perhaps it would have been wasted on him. Regrettably he did not require food, but he did order a bottle of claret and volunteer the information that he was expecting a visitor.

Mrs. Muggs' suspicions, aroused again, were confirmed a short while later with the arrival of a third carriage whose only occupant was an unescorted young woman—dressed in black of all things—who asked after a Mr. Merriman.

Mrs. Muggs replied austerely that Mr. Merriman was at present in one of the private parlours.

"Would you be so good as to take me to him?" the young woman said with a warm smile, apparently unaware of Mrs. Muggs's unspoken reproof.

She did not look the sort of woman to be involved in a clandestine rendezvous. But why else would she and Mr. Merriman be meeting at what Mrs. Muggs was forced to admit was an out-of-the-way establishment? With a good deal of curiosity, Mrs. Muggs conducted the new visitor to the second parlour and tapped at the door.

"Your friend is here, Mr. Merriman," she said.

If Mr. Merriman was surprised at the identity of his friend, even the watchful Mrs. Muggs could not have seen it.

"Mrs. Royce," he said, "how pleasant."

Mrs. Royce entered the room and gave Mr. Merriman her hand, and Mr. Merriman gave Mrs. Muggs a polite but firm look of dismissal. She left the room reluctantly, regretting that she would miss the best part of the scene. She was right, though not perhaps in quite the way she imagined.

As the door closed behind Mrs. Muggs, Livia's grip on Merriman's hand tightened. "Thank God!" she said. "I am not too late!"

Oliver Merriman was rarely disconcerted, but at this his magnificent eyebrows rose. "Too late?" he asked. "My dear Mrs. Royce, what is the matter?"

Livia retained her grip on his hand. "Has my brother been here?"

"Colonel Scott? No, isn't he in London? Has he been recalled to the continent?"

Livia shook her head, struggled visibly to compose herself and released Merriman's hand. "No, but he is traveling in this direction. I'm afraid he is following you, Mr. Merriman."

There was a slight pause, during which Livia noted with pleasure that Oliver Merriman could appear shaken. Perhaps Nicholas Warwick could as well. Merriman recovered and drew a chair forward. "I see. Or rather, I don't see at all. I take it Colonel Scott has his reasons for following me?"

"Yes, he—" She broke off, looked confused, and sough refuge in the proffered chair. "It would be ludicrous if weren't so serious. I don't understand it in the least. It seem that my brother is dreadfully angry with you and I don't know why. He learned that you were headed for Dartford and set of in the most towering rage. Do you have any idea what it coul be about?"

"No, none at all. I scarcely know Colonel Scott." It was th bald truth. Merriman sought frantically for a logical explana tion. The last thing he wanted was the presence of a impetuous young officer at his forthcoming meeting. Surel Scott couldn't be angered over his attentions to Mrs. Royce No, it was absurd. Scott appeared to be a fond brother, bu scarcely an overprotective one. And Merriman had never gon beyond light flirtation. But other than Mrs. Royce, he had n link with Scott whatsoever. He tried to recall the last time h had seen the colonel—probably the ball at Warwick House Merriman had an image of Colonel Scott waltzing with Francesca Warwick. It was followed by other images—Scott in Hyde Park being driven in Lady Francesca's elegant phaeton Scott seated beside Lady Francesca in the Nevilles' drawing room, Scott coming down the second floor stairs of the Nevill house with young Melbrooke on his shoulders . . .

Of course. It was too much to hope that Scott's following him at just this point was mere coincidence. Lady Francesc had learned of his plans—never mind how for the moment— and had understandably not wanted to go to Warwick. Wh better to turn to than her late husband's best friend, the ma who was about to become Warwick's brother-in-law?

It fit. Damnably well. He looked at Mrs. Royce. How much did she know? Surely she was not in her brother's confidence or she would scarcely have come to warn him. Besides, he ha reason to know that she was far from enamoured of Nichola Warwick.

"No," he said again, "I'm afraid I have no idea. It must be misunderstanding. I daresay it can all be cleared up whe

Colonel Scott arrives. But I thank you for the warning—" He broke off and stared at her. "Did you come alone?"

"Except for the coachman. There was no time to summon anyone else."

"Mrs. Royce, did you undertake a journey of near twenty miles simply to warn me of your brother's pursuit?"

She coloured slightly. "It seemed a small price to pay. I should never forgive myself if any harm befell either of you."

Merriman's brows rose again. In a voice that mingled amusement and surprise, he said, "No, indeed, but even were your brother's anger not rooted in misunderstanding—as I must believe it to be—it would scarcely come to that. We are both grown men."

Livia smiled. "You are. I am not certain my brother deserves the title. You have never seen him in a temper. I have, and there is little that can be done to calm him. And I fear he has grown coarse—understandably so—since his experiences on the Peninsula." Some of the former urgency returned to her voice. "But however immature he is in some ways, he is a capital shot. I thought my presence might serve as a buffer between you. You see my concern."

He did to a degree. At least better than he had. He smiled again. "Whatever the cause, I am delighted to have your company, though I am afraid you will have to leave soon if you mean to return to London at a respectable hour. May I offer you some claret before you go? I'm afraid I can't vouch for its quality."

Livia said she wasn't particular and sat quietly while Merriman poured the wine. He handed her a glass and she drank gratefully—she was badly in need of fortification—but Merriman had not yet touched his glass when there was a knock at the door. Barstow-Greene, no doubt. Merriman had hoped to be rid of Mrs. Royce before he arrived, but there was really no harm in their meeting.

"More friends of yours, Mr. Merriman," Mrs. Muggs called and opened the door to admit Lady Francesca and

Colonel Scott.

Merriman's back was to Livia so she missed his expression. She didn't wait to hear his voice. "Gerry!" Livia sprang to her feet. "Pray control yourself! There is no need to be in such taking! Everything will be all right if you will only refrain from doing anything silly."

Gerry assimilated these messages as best he could and contented himself with a baleful look in Merriman's direction. "Oh?" he said grimly. "Will it?"

"Certainly," Merriman answered easily, hoping against hope that the colonel could be diverted. "I'm glad you're here Scott. I am sure Mrs. Royce would be glad of your escort back to town. Lady Francesca, as always I am delighted to see you. Please sit down." He turned to draw a chair forward for Francesca. Gerry looked at Livia in desperate inquiry. Livia gave a warning shake of her head. Colonel Scott decided his anger had suddenly abated.

Francesca sat down and smiled her thanks at Merriman. He nodded, quite as if the little party was of his making, and wondered exactly what Scott and Lady Francesca intended to do and which of them he should be most worried about. He offered them refreshment. Francesca declined, but Gerry— feeling as much in need of fortification as his sister—accepted. Merriman handed him his untouched glass. Livia sent her brother a frantic look, which Merriman mercifully failed to see. Unfortunately so did Gerry, but Francesca had been looking directly at Livia. A moment later the glass was broken and its contents scattered over the floor and Francesca's skirt.

"Gerry, how clumsy!" Francesca jumped to her feet. "You've ruined my favorite pelisse and wasted poor Mr. Merriman's claret. Mrs. Royce, do you have a handkerchief?"

Silently Livia handed her handkerchief to Francesca. Gerry, feeling as if he had discovered in the middle of a game that some one had neglected to inform him of the rules, looked at his sister again.

"Oh, dear," Livia said. "This is all so awkward. We sha

have to start all over."

"No problem at all," Merriman said, wondering at Scott's reticence. He poured another glass of wine. "Except for the damage to Lady Francesca's pelisse, everything is turning out most pleasantly."

Gerry and Livia exchanged glances. They could try getting Merriman out of the room. No, it would only rouse his suspicions. Besides, the thing was likely to be on his person. Better try the blunt approach. Gerry stood up. "See here, Merriman, there's no sense in pretending. We know all about the letter."

"Letter?"

"The letter which Lady Francesca purchased from Jasper Grimson. The letter which was subsequently stolen from her and which is now in your possession."

Merriman did not need to feign astonishment. "My dear Scott, I haven't the least idea what you are talking about. I hope you don't mean to imply that I am in any way responsible for a theft from Lady Francesca."

"I don't imply anything. I'm asking you to return the letter. If you do so, the matter will end here."

"The matter will most certainly end here. There is nothing more to be said. I am unable to return the letter. I have never had it in my possession."

"In that case you won't object to a search of this room?"

"Gerry!" Livia decided she was still on Merriman's side. "That's outrageous!"

Gerry sent her a withering look. "Stay out of this, Livia, it's none of your affair."

"You go too far, sir," Merriman said. "If you don't take care—"

"I have very little to take care of, Merriman. Are you prepared to return the letter or shall I take it from you?"

"Once more, sir, I have no letter."

"You lie, sir."

Merriman's face went white. "You will answer to me

301

for that."

"Certainly," said Colonel Scott.

"Gerry!" Livia said, this time in real alarm.

"Gerry!" Francesca echoed, half-rising from her chair.

"This is absurd," Livia said, collecting herself.

"That," Merriman said grimly, "cannot be helped. It was not I who offered the insult."

"It was not I," said Gerry, "who offered the challenge."

Francesca crossed to Gerry's side and laid a hand on his arm. Neither man paid any heed.

"Lady Francesca, Mrs. Royce." Merriman made a formal bow. "I apologize for any inconvenience this may cause you. Well, Scott, are you ready?"

"Perfectly," Gerry returned, disengaging himself from Francesca and avoiding his sister's eyes.

"And where," Livia inquired in a scathing tone that covered her sense that the world was totally out of control, "do you expect to get weapons?"

The gentlemen exchanged glances. The problem had not occurred to them. But the ladies' relief was short lived, for Merriman stalked to the door and called for Mr. Muggs.

The landlord came hurriedly down the hall. Was anything amiss? What did they require? Pistols, his elegant guest told him. Or swords. Though pistols would be preferred. Greatly alarmed, Muggs looked from his guest to the newly arrived officer. Well yes, he admitted, as it happened there was an old pair, left at the inn some time ago, but—

"Splendid," Merriman said curtly. "If you'll be so kind as to let us borrow them for a short time."

Muggs hesitated. He didn't at all like the idea of a duel taking place near his inn. On the other hand, he didn't want to offend these rare wealthy customers. Besides, Merriman was looking at him in a way that really left him with no choice. Muttering to himself, Muggs retreated while the combatants removed their coats and urged the ladies to return at once to London. The ladies refused.

302

Mr. Muggs returned with a battered case and hovered about anxiously while the would-be duelists inspected and loaded the pistols. Livia and Francesca looked at each other. The men were beyond reason and beyond distraction.

Any hope that the pistols would prove inadequate to their purpose was extinguished when Gerry and Merriman nodded politely to Mr. Muggs. Merriman held the door open for the ladies. Clearly he was not so lost in anger as to allow any opportunity to search his belongings. The duel was proving truly pointless.

Mr. Muggs directed them to the south meadow. A flustered Mrs. Muggs appeared and protested feebly. "But that's where Mr. and Miss Endymion went walking."

"Who?" Livia asked, turning back.

"Mr. Endymion and his young sister. They're in the other parlour. Do you know them?"

"No," said Livia. *At least I hope to God I don't.* She hurried after the others.

The men came to a halt in the middle of the meadow and inspected their weapons one last time.

"What was in the wine?" Francesca asked Livia.

"Laudanum."

"I wish I'd let Gerry drink it."

Livia debated the merits of throwing herself between the two men. Reading her intent, Francesca put a restraining hand on her arm. "No," she said, "it's a matter of honour now. They won't shoot to kill. They may even delope." Livia subsided.

Apparently the weapons were in suitable order. Livia, unacquainted with duelling etiquette, did not know what would happen next and was destined to remain uninformed. As Gerry and Merriman turned, a cry from the edge of the meadow disrupted everyone's attention.

"Gerry!" shrieked Diana Neville.

Francesca looked at Livia. "Endymion," Livia muttered, "I might have known." She looked at Gerry, hoping he could explain Diana's presence. Gerry shrugged. Merriman, who only vaguely recognized the youngest Miss Neville, demanded to be told what was going on. Paul appeared, sketchbook in hand, and asked Lady Francesca what the row was about. A letter, she said shortly. Merriman complicated matters by suggesting that Gerry make Paul his second. Paul declined. He objected, he said, to the sight of unnecessary blood.

"Gerry," Diana repeated. "Livia, he can't—"

But before Diana could launch into a tirade against dueling, Gerry seized the initiative and demanded to know what she was doing here.

"I'm going to Paris with Paul," Diana said calmly, "to save the family from disgrace."

"Oh, good God," said Livia.

"You can't do that," Gerry told Diana.

"You can't fight a duel."

Her statement had the undesired effect of reminding Colonel Scott of the reason for his presence in the meadow. "Livia," he said, "will you take Diana out to the carriage and wait until—"

"No."

"I'm not leaving," Diana said firmly.

"Then Francie, will you—"

"No,'" said Francesca, even more firmly.

"Very well." Gerry turned away. "Merriman."

"This is a ridiculous way to settle an argument," Diana protested. "Besides, it's dangerous. Paul, do something!"

But Mr. Redmond, who had been staring meditatively at a clump of wildflowers, did not seem to be taking an interest. "It isn't any of our affair, Diana," he said with a slight shrug. "Best leave well enough alone."

"Paul! If we don't do something, someone is going to be killed!"

"They won't let it go that far."

"Don't you care?"

"I said it wasn't any of my business. After all, I scarcely know your brother. I'm going to see if there's any word about our carriage." He sauntered back toward the inn while Diana stared after him in outrage. It was one thing to be self-absorbed, a fault she freely admitted. It was quite another to be completely heartless. She turned to Livia. Livia shook her head. "Nothing," she said, "is going to stop them now."

A moment later she was to bitterly amend her words. Gerry and Merriman had cocked their pistols and begun to pace off. As the duelists neared the turn, they were brought up short by the sound of approaching hoofbeats, frantic barking, and high pitched screams. A handsome bay, clearly out of control, galloped between the combatants and circled the meadow in apparent frenzy. Livia wondered if she could be going mad. For there, clinging to the horse's back, were the two children she had left, looking suspiciously angelic, in Charles Street.

Chapter 20

Harry ran out of the inn yard and down the lane leading to the south meadow. "Gwendolen!" Harry called in alarm. "Gwendolen, stop!"

"Told you they shouldn't be left alone." Jack, who could be fleet of foot when the occasion called for it, was by his side.

Harry spared him a withering look and kept running, intent on the rearing horse and the crazed dog which was circling it, impeding the efforts of two men in shirt-sleeves to bring the horse under control.

"Right," Jack said, veering in that direction, "head it off."

Harry swerved, but the bay broke free and galloped toward a line of willows that bordered the stream marking the boundary of the meadow. The dog, barking wildly, followed. The shirt-sleeved men raced after, separating to get the horse between them. Harry and Jack sprinted down the middle to close the gap. They failed to notice the two women who were also making for the trees. The children continued to scream.

Near the willows the horse pulled up abruptly, reared once more, then turned sharply to the left, the dog yapping at its heels. One of the men ran toward it, shouting and waving his arms. The horse slowed, hesitated, then plunged down the bank and into the stream. The dog stopped at the stream edge, sat down, and barked louder than ever. The horse stopped in the middle of the stream, but something—perhaps the sight of six gesticulating figures converging upon it—caused it to rear suddenly and make for the opposite bank. There was a different kind of scream, a splash, and only one rider.

The two coatless men plunged into the stream, heedless of their highly polished boots. One made for the opposite bank where he seized the horse's mane and forced the animal, trembling with exertion, back across the stream. The other waded after the fallen rider, preceded by the dog who had paddled out into the stream and was thrashing about.

Eddy surfaced on his own. He grabbed Hotspur round the neck, lost his footing, and went down again. His rescuer stretched out an arm and found the dog's teeth round his wrist. One of the women—the one in black—reached them and pulled the dog off. The man seized the spluttering boy and swung him onto his shoulders. Livia, her fingers wrapped firmly around Hotspur's collar, looked up into Oliver Merriman's grey eyes. She could not speak. Let him have the letter.

On the bank, Francesca, Harry and Jack waited for the rest of the group to return. Gerry reached them first. He turned the bay over to Francesca, lifted Gwendolen off its back, and went to help Livia up the bank. They were all strangely quiet. Merriman put the boy down. Eddy ran to Gwendolen who stripped off most of his clothes, took his hand, and said she thought she would take him back to the inn to get dry. She avoided everyone's eyes. Harry and Jack, equally subdued, said they would take the horse to the stable. Livia removed her shoes and stockings and, taking Francesca's arm, walked barefoot into the meadow. The men walked beside them. As they reached the centre, they stopped. Gerry and Merriman looked at each other, nodded, and of one accord continued on to the inn.

Livia and Francesca followed more slowly. Francesca smiled. "At least she put a stop to it. I confess I would never have thought of it."

Livia looked at her in astonishment. "You mean they planned it? Those wretches! They might have been killed!"

"Hardly that. Gwendolen has been riding bareback since she could walk and Eddy nearly as long. I'm sorry you were distressed. They were in very little danger, at least at first. Gwendolen has ridden the bays before, and I daresay she was urging him on deliberately. If it hadn't been for that disreputable dog, Eddy might have walked out of the stream by himself."

Livia stopped. Hotspur. She looked around for Eddy's friend. He was at the far end of the meadow. She called and the dog, who had found something of interest down by the willows, raised his head and ran toward her.

The women turned back to the inn and saw a familiar figure striding toward them. Hotspur saw him at the same time and ran past Livia to greet the newcomer. The dog shook himself free of stream water and then—his tail wagging—jumped up to place muddy forepaws on the now drenched Nicholas Warwick.

Nicholas had had a bad two hours on the road. He had been informed by a stricken Giles that Lady Francesca had seen fit to take not only his curricle but his bays, the fastest horses in his stable. She had been, Giles said, in a fearful hurry. Nicholas reflected bitterly that he seemed fated to be linked to strong-willed women and ordered Giles to harness Francesca's phaeton. Her horses, a showy, cream-coloured pair, were fortunately sound and driving took only a part of Nicholas' attention.

What could Livia be up to? Visions of danger to the exasperating Mrs. Royce kept intruding on his speculations about the reasons for her flight. This, he reminded himself sternly, was ridiculous. There was no woman of his acquaintance—barring his sister-in-law and Aunt Isabel—better able to take care of herself. In any event, why should he care? But he did care, and care desperately. The knowledge shook him.

He drove through Bexley Heath and set himself the task of considering only likely alternatives. Whatever her faults, Livia—Mrs. Royce—was devoted to her family. Would she have driven off in pursuit of her brother? Unlikely. Colonel Scott was well able to take care of himself. Claudia? Claudia could hardly be in any kind of difficulty, and he knew his betrothed was spending the day with Aunt Isabel. She had told him only yesterday—of course. Yesterday he had informed Mrs. Royce of his plans to take charge of her youngest sister. It must be Diana. The chit had run away and Livia was going to bring her back. That at least showed some sense. Nicholas was more determined than ever to send Diana to Waverley. In fact, he would welcome a few weeks in Sussex himself. He tried to picture Claudia at Waverley, but her hair seemed to have unaccountable touches of red. Odd, that.

He was so preoccupied that he had driven through Jack-in-the-Hole and past Horn's Cross before he realized that the Bell and Candle must be off the main road. He stopped to make inquiries, but could find only a toothless old man sunning himself on a stile. The gaffer did not seem to understand his question. Nicholas repeated it with several variations. The man was forced to acknowledge that he had heard somewhat of the Bell and Candle, it was in John's Hole. Nicholas said it was the same thing. The man shrugged. Nicholas persisted. He was finally directed to a lane a short distance back, running south from the main road. Nicholas tossed the man a coin, turned the phaeton, and whipped Francesca's horses into greater speed. He overshot the lane and had to turn the phaeton once more.

He pulled up at last in the inn yard with mounting anxiety and a growing temper. He jumped down and handed the reins to the stable boy, a half-grown lad with a thatch of white-blond hair. Had a young woman—a lady—arrived in the last hour or so? The boy scratched his head and said slowly that he thought several young ladies had arrived that afternoon. That was manifestly impossible—no ladies would come willingly to the Bell and Candle. He would have to seek information from the landlord. Nicholas gave the boy directions for the disposition of Francesca's horses and, as the boy opened the stable doors, saw two curricles and a horse that looked suspiciously like Castor. Francesca. He might have known.

Nicholas strode out of the yard and made for the open door of the inn. He wanted answers and he wanted them now. He was met instead with further questions. Eddy—barefoot, shirtless, his trousers wet—was running toward him, crying out that he had fallen in the stream and Hotspur had jumped in to save him and Livia had too, then Mr. Merriman had pulled him out. Nicholas told himself that he must have misheard the last part of this story, though he had no trouble at all believing the rest. Livia must have brought the children with her—what was she about?

He looked up to see his daughter walking slowly toward him carrying Eddy's wet clothes. She did not seem particularly pleased to see him. He gave her a hard look and she turned and pointed toward the stable, then wordlessly took Eddy's hand and led him to the inn.

Nicholas rounded the stable and made for the meadow beyond. He was brought up short by the sight of his younger brother leading a bay horse. Pollux. "Is it too much to ask you, Harry, what you are doing with my horse?"

Harry was feeling ill-used. He had been gulled into bringing his niece on a harebrained expedition to rescue a woman who did not appear to have been in any danger at all. Genny had thanked him by stealing her father's horse and subjecting both herself and Eddy to danger and, what was worse, risking injury to the horse. Harry had been involved in an undignified scramble involving people who had no business being here. He was hot and thirsty, his cravat was askew, and he had soiled his new trousers. His brother was the last person in the world he wanted to see.

"Not his fault, sir," Jack assured Nicholas. "She took the

horse. No harm, no harm at all."

"Mrs. Royce took the horse?"

"Livia?" Harry looked full at his brother and gave a harsh laugh. "She had nothing to do with it. It was your daughter, and when I get my hands on that hell-born brat—" He broke off, then added defiantly, "Well, she is. I told them distinctly to stay by the stables while we scouted round. It wasn't my fault she decided to go riding."

Pollux broke free, walked toward Nicholas and nuzzled his shoulder. Nicholas absently stroked the horse's nose. "Then she didn't bring the children?"

"No," Harry admitted. "We did."

"I daresay you had your reasons?"

"Well of course, do you think we'd do anything so rattlepated without cause?"

Nicholas was silent.

"You see," Harry went on, "Jack and I called on the Nevilles this morning."

"Nothing wrong with that," Jack interpolated helpfully. "Very proper thing to do."

Harry gave him a scathing look.

"And Miss Neville and Mrs. Royce were out," Nicholas said, "but you found Gwendolen and young Edward and calmly set off for an obscure inn in Kent."

"Of course not, we weren't in the least calm," Harry protested. "But dash it, Nicholas, we couldn't let them go off alone!"

"And why were they proposing to go anywhere at all, let alone to Jack-in-the-Hole?"

Harry began to speak, then realized that the confused story Gwendolen had told him was not meant for her father's ear. "It was something about Livia," he mumbled. "Genny thought she was in danger."

"All right, sir," Jack said quickly, seeing the look on Nicholas' face. "She'll be coming along just behind us. Lady Francesca with her."

311

"Take Pollux to the stable," Nicholas told his brother, "and see that he's rubbed down properly. Better yet, do it yourself. We'll talk later."

Nicholas set off for the meadow. He could see two women walking toward him in the distance. In his eagerness to reach them he failed to properly note the two men who passed him with looks of surprise. At this point he was set upon by Hotspur.

Nicholas carefully disentangled himself from the dog and looked at the approaching women. They might have been out for a country stroll, save that Livia's face was more than usually pale, her skirt was wet, and she was carrying equally wet shoes and stockings.

"Wading again, I see," he said pleasantly. "I trust the water wasn't cold."

Livia was too startled to speak. Francesca said, equally pleasantly, that it was very nice to see her brother-in-law and she would be glad of his arm, for her shoes were not meant for walking.

Nicholas suggested she might like to remove them as Mrs. Royce had done. Francesca said he was unkind, Livia had only been trying to help. Livia said tartly that it was none of his affair how she chose to behave in the country and she was returning to the inn. She walked on, leaving Nicholas and Francesca behind. Hotspur followed her.

"There are a number of things I fail to understand, Francesca," Nicholas said calmly as they walked after. Now that Livia was clearly in no immediate danger, he felt his mood lighten. He was almost tempted to laugh until he recalled the condition of his horse. "Perhaps, when there is time, you would care to explain them to me. Including your reasons for commandeering my curricle and giving my horses unaccustomed exercise."

Francesca chose not to reply.

"You drove them yourself?"

"I took the greatest care," Francesca assured him. "So did

Colonel Scott," she added, then wished she had omitted this particular piece of information.

"Scott? Is he here too?" Nicholas had a dim recollection of the men he had passed. That must have been Gerry, and the other—could Eddy have been right?

"Nicholas," Francesca said suddenly. He would have to be given a story and the one they had already used would serve. "I'm so sorry you've been embroiled in this. It's about Gerry, you see. He had a quarrel with Mr. Merriman, heaven knows why, and they were going to come to blows. Livia came after to stop them."

"And you came too? Driving Colonel Scott to his rendezvous? How very helpful of you, Francesca."

"You know it was not that way at all. I was trying to make Gerry see reason, and I did not want Livia to be alone." Nicholas was working out the probable time sequence of these actions when Francesca continued. "I suppose you know that Gwendolen and Eddy are here as well. We don't know why, though I daresay they got wind of the quarrel somehow and decided to intervene. I'm sure Harry and Jack were only trying to keep them under control." There. That should account for everyone and stop further speculation.

But Nicholas was not yet convinced. "Then this has nothing to do with Diana Neville?"

Oh, lord. Diana.

Mr. Muggs stood in the doorway of the Bell and Candle, a bemused look on his face. He was not unused to the ways of the quality, but he found he preferred the rough farmers, traveling tinkers, and the like—even the carriage drivers now drinking in the tap room—to the custom with which his inn was presently blessed. With farmers a man knew where he stood. With the queer crew that had descended upon him one by one and two by two—not to mention the strangely mixed party of four—things were at sixes and sevens. Still, the day would be profitable and perhaps some of them would spend the night and make him richer still. He called to Jem, the tow-headed stable boy, and discussed accommodation of horses and carriages. Under control, Jem informed him, though he didn't know what they would do if another showed up.

Muggs wondered idly whether the duel had come off. There had been distant shouts and the commotion with the horse—which he had told Jem to ignore and leave well enough alone—but he had not heard any shots. That was all to the good.

The sound of voices made him aware that his guests were returning. The first to appear were the children. The boy had apparently been swimming, but the day was warm and he would come to no harm from that. The girl spread his wet clothes on the bench beside the door and they sat down in silence. They looked tired, Muggs thought, but satisfied.

They were probably waiting for the young men who had brought them, a foppish, useless pair who were now leading the horse into the stable. At least they'd had the sense to bring it back. The prime piece of horseflesh seemed no worse for the experience. The dog was nowhere in sight.

The duelists came shortly after. At the sight of the grey-eyed gentleman who had been so insistent in the matter of the pistols, Muggs judged it wise to disappear for a bit. The men looked tired too, but he did not trust their current amity.

"Hullo brats," Gerry said conversationally. Merriman continued on into the inn.

The children looked at Gerry briefly. He did not seem angry, but it was best to be certain. "Thank you for saving me," Gwendolen said in a small voice.

"Thank you for saving me." Gerry was equally polite. He sat down beside her. "That was the idea, wasn't it?" She smiled at him but did not answer. They sat a few minutes in companionable silence, closing their eyes against the sun, then were startled out of their reverie by a rush of wet fur. Hotspur launched himself on Eddy, stepping on Gerry's boots and muddying Gwendolen's dress in the process.

"Your dog has atrocious manners, Eddy," Livia informed him as she came up. "He's already soiled Mr. Warwick's breeches. Do you suppose I could leave my shoes and stockings here to dry, they're a nuisance to carry." She grinned impartially at children, brother and dog. Gerry offered her his seat. She accepted gratefully, spread her skirt to catch the heat of the sun, and idly moved her toes in the warm dirt. Her feet were filthy. Eddy could not stop staring at them. He had never seen a lady outdoors with bare feet.

Nicholas and Francesca joined them. Though he was a gentleman and did not stare, Nicholas could hardly refrain from a glance himself. She looked ridiculously young. A matter of association, he thought, for Claudia's elder sister was surely well past her first youth. He pushed down Hotspur, who had abandoned Eddy for his other friend, and began to frame the first of the many questions he had to put to her.

He was forestalled by Diana who stalked out of the inn carrying a black cloak and a large parcel tied up in a shawl. "Livia," she announced, "I'm not going to Paris."

"Paris!" Nicholas exploded.

"Thank God," breathed Germanicus Scott.

"I say," Jack said in an undertone—he and Harry had just joined the group—"what's she doing here?"

Nicholas turned to Livia. He spoke with icy calm. "Did you feel obliged to send this child so far away, madam, to keep her from my very necessary supervision?"

"It's not so far," Diana said. "And it has nothing to do with Livia. I'm going with Paul. I *was* going with Paul," she amended bitterly. "And if Gerry hadn't insisted on fighting a duel, I might never have found out and I would have made the most terrible mistake of my life."

Nicholas' attention was deflected. "Duel?"

Francesca intervened quickly. "I told you there'd been some unpleasantness and tempers were a trifle hot, but it need not

315

concern you. The matter seems to have cooled."

"Yes," Livia agreed gravely. "I've often found that cold water has a salubrious effect."

Nicholas looked at her with aversion.

Eddy got up and tugged at Gerry's sleeve. "Where's Mr. Merriman?"

The three conspirators looked at each other. The letter. Had he left the inn and taken the letter with him? How could they stop him if he had? How could they stop him if he had not? How above all were they to rid themselves of Nicholas Warwick?

The preoccupied group standing at the entrance to the inn failed to notice the arrival of another carriage. Eddy was the first to become aware of it. "Papa!" he cried happily.

Not knowing his quarry's destination, Lord Melbrooke had had a long and frustrating journey from town. After a great many stops and a great many questions, he had found his nephew leaning on a farmyard fence, making a life study of a dirty white sow and nine piglets. Paul objected to the interruption, saying he was not yet finished. Melbrooke ordered him into the carriage, said he thanked God for the accident that had delayed Paul's flight and the good fortune that had allowed him to discover it, and prayed that Diana had not come to any harm. Paul looked hurt. He would never, he said, harm Diana. Melbrooke told his nephew he was an idiot who had no notion whatever of what was owing to gently bred young girls. Paul could go to Paris if he liked, or he could go to the devil—it was all the same to him—but Diana Neville was returning to her family at once. They must be frantic with worry. Paul doubted this, but thought it best to say nothing. He directed his uncle to the Bell and Candle and said no more until they reached the inn and joined the group assembled outside the door. Diana refused to look at him.

For the next few minutes Lord Melbrooke was occupied with his son and with Hotspur who was equally glad to see him. Diana, who was a fair-minded person, went to Melbrooke and said quietly, "It's not Paul's fault, sir. I wanted to go. But I don't want to go any more, so you don't need to worry. I'm sorry you've come all this way for nothing."

Before the bewildered Melbrooke could respond, Oliver Merriman came out of the inn. His boots were damp, but he was wearing a superbly cut coat and he carried a traveling bag. "You'll forgive me if I don't stay," he said to the group at large. "I've been expecting a friend, but I think it best to head him off—the inn has grown a trifle crowded. My room is at your disposal." He put down his bag, removed his hat, and went to Francesca. "Madam," he said, taking her hand, "my most profound compliments. I would very much like to know how you did it."

Francesca regarded him blankly. He dropped her hand. "I see." He turned to Livia, admiration in his eyes. "Then it is you I must compliment. I can only tell you how much I wish I could count you among my allies."

Livia began to protest, caught his meaning, and said instead, "I'm sorry about your boots. Do you mind very much?"

"No, it's been worth it." He smiled at her with rueful affection. "And I don't mind. I rather think I don't mind anything at all."

He kissed her hand, replaced his hat, and picked up his bag. "Warwick," he said as he made for the stable, "you're marrying into a very talented family."

There was a long silence. "What," Melbrooke asked after Merriman had moved out of earshot, "did that mean?"

"It means," said Livia, "that no one has to kill anyone after all. Explanations by all means, but hadn't we better go inside? It's likely to take a rather long time."

This much everyone could agree to. There was a general move toward the inn. Livia explained to the flustered Mrs.

Muggs that they would not be staying the night but would appreciate the use of the parlour Mr. Merriman had just vacated. Mrs. Muggs's cousin's daughter, who helped in the kitchen, hurried in with an apron full of eggs. In a loud whisper that would have made Sandringham wince she informed Mrs. Muggs that another carriage had just arrived. Mrs. Muggs sat down abruptly.

Livia and Gwendolen exchanged glances. "It must be Claudia," Gwendolen said. "She's the only one left."

Chapter 21

Claudia and Lady Crawford returned to Charles Street in the early afternoon to find that Livia was out, did not know when she would return, and her sister was not to worry. Puzzled, Claudia requested tea and they went into the drawing room. On the mantel was a note addressed to Claudia in Jack's precise hand. She read it, gave a sharp exclamation, and rang for Sandringham. As was his custom, he came promptly.

"Sandringham," Claudia said with forced calm, "what exactly is Jack-in-the-Hole?"

"A small village on the Dover Road, Miss Neville, about two hours out of London. I believe it is more often found on the maps as John's Hole."

This information only increased Claudia's agitation. She turned to Lady Crawford. "Two hours! The wretches. To take them all that distance and without a by-your-leave!"

"Claudia, my dear. What on earth is in that letter?"

Claudia glanced down at the letter which she had unconsciously crumpled in one hand. She felt in no condition to cope with the situation on her own and relinquished the letter willingly. It was brief.

> Obliged to go off to Jack-in-the-Hole. Not to worry
> about the children. With us. Take good care of them.
> Yours, etc . . . Jack

Sandringham gave a discreet cough. "If you'll forgive me, your ladyship, Miss Neville, I believe I may have some information that is pertinent."

"Yes?" said Claudia hopefully.

"I suspect young Mr. Warwick and Mr. Newfield and the children may have gone after Mrs. Royce."

"After Livia?" Claudia was bewildered. Even Lady Crawford looked surprised.

"Yes, miss. Mrs. Royce left shortly before noon for an inn on the outskirts of Jack-in-the-Hole. I believe it's called the Bell and Candle."

"I fail," Lady Crawford said, "to understand the attraction of Jack-in-the-Hole. You wouldn't happen to know what she was planning to do there?"

Sandringham returned her look blandly. "She was following Mr. Merriman."

"Following Mr. Merriman?" Claudia repeated.

"I don't fully understand her reasons," Sandringham went on, not quite truthfully, "but they are not—er—what they might at first appear to be."

"Of course not," Lady Crawford said with decision. "Did she go alone?"

"Yes, my lady. But I thought—I took the liberty of informing Mr. Warwick—the elder Mr. Warwick, that is—of her destination when he called. I believe he has gone after her."

Claudia sat down suddenly. In the three months they had spent in London, she had been the pivot around which their lives revolved. Excessive self-regard was not one of Claudia's faults and she was uncomfortable in this role, but she had accepted her central importance to her family's future. She had even grown accustomed to it. Now it appeared she was no longer central. She was a bystander in events she could not begin to comprehend.

Lady Crawford looked unusually thoughtful. "I think," she said, "that we should go after them. I confess I do not fully

320

understand what is afoot, but one of my nephews is sometimes too stubborn to be sensible and the other two are frequently not sensible at all. Fortunately they have Gwendolen with them, but one should not rely too much on a ten-year-old."

Claudia looked at her gratefully and they made preparations for departure. As they moved toward the door, Sandringham asked, with some diffidence, if they would like him to accompany them. Lady Crawford considered the matter seriously. No, she thought they could rely upon her coachman. However, she would appreciate his taking a message to Mrs. Amesbury—it appeared that most of the family would not be home for dinner. Then he had best return to Charles Street. There should be someone trustworthy in the house to receive messages and to ensure that any of the household who returned home stayed there. She specifically mentioned Colonel Scott, of whose whereabouts the three of them were ignorant, and then, as an afterthought, Lady Francesca.

The ladies passed the early part of their journey in silence. Both were preoccupied, though their thoughts had little to do with the whereabouts of Eddy and Gwendolen.

Claudia knew she had no real cause for worry. But while giving some final household instructions to Mary Beth, she had received a graphic description of Nicholas Warwick's face when he left the house earlier in the afternoon. It was clear that his feelings had been strongly engaged and on her sister's behalf.

Claudia set herself to think of Nicholas and Livia. There was an undercurrent of friction in their relationship that had often distressed her. On the other hand, there were also moments of genuine accord, of shared laughter and shared sympathies. Claudia knew that her future husband liked her and that he enjoyed being in her company, just as she enjoyed being in his. But there was nothing between them, she realized, to match those moments of rapport between Nicholas and her sister.

"I think," Claudia said, "that I have made a dreadful mistake, ma'am."

"Yes," Lady Crawford agreed without surprise, "though I do not think the mistake is yours." It is mine, she thought, I have been incredibly blind. I have not paid enough attention to Livia and I have paid none at all to Nicholas. She met Claudia's gaze, her blue eyes thoughtful. "Do you mind?"

Claudia was frowning. "No," she said, as if that was the last thing on her mind. "That is, I mind because I didn't see it earlier, but I'm exceedingly glad that I saw it before it was too late. There is still time to set things right."

"It will be difficult," her friend warned her. "They are both very sure of where their duty lies."

Claudia smiled. "I can manage my relation, ma'am. I trust you can manage yours."

The group at the Bell and Candle had moved into the parlour taken by Paul and Diana, this being the larger of the two. Paul had disappeared, but their number had been augmented by Claudia and Lady Crawford. Nicholas had ordered a fire, and Livia and Eddy were standing barefoot in front of it. Their wet clothes and Gerry's boots had been taken to the kitchen for attention. Mrs. Muggs and her cousin, their curiosity dangerously inflamed, were laying out a cold repast.

"Still don't understand what Merriman was doing here," Jack muttered.

"Political affairs, I daresay," Nicholas said in a tone that was meant to end the matter, at least until the Muggs family had departed.

But Jack was determined to get at the truth. "No, dash it, Nicholas, that ain't right." Harry glared at him. Jack recalled Gwendolen's story and rephrased the question. "That is, know why he was here. Political affairs. Sort of. That still don't explain why anyone had to get killed."

"Politics is a dangerous matter," Gwendolen said sententiously. She was feeling quite cheerful. They had stopped the duel. Livia had handled Mr. Merriman as Gwendolen had known she would, and Gwendolen had only to detach her father from Claudia.

"But that's just it. Isn't really. Dangerous. Not like the army," Jack insisted and was further confused by the silence his last statement engendered.

"A singularly tactless remark, Jack," Lady Crawford said as Nicholas, looking rather grim, ushered out the Muggs women and shut the parlour door.

"Wait a minute," Harry jumped to his friend's defense, "that's a bit much. No need to start on Jack. Besides, tactless is one thing he ain't. Nothing wrong with talking about the army—"

Jack, more attuned to the social nuances, interrupted with a cough. "Brother," he muttered. "Widow present. Unpleasant association. Apologies, Lady Francesca."

"Oh, for heaven's sake," Francesca said impatiently. "I'm all right. Do let's sit down."

Harry looked from Francesca to Nicholas to Lady Crawford to the quiet Melbrooke. "You aren't thinking of Livia, are you?" he demanded. The idea was so funny that he had to laugh.

"Harry!" Nicholas said sharply. The younger Mr. Warwick sobered himself with an effort.

Livia looked at Nicholas, then at the rest of the group and made a decision. She couldn't go on lying to them forever. "I have a confession to make," she said with obvious reluctance. "I—we—count you all as our friends, and I owe it to you." Her voice grew firmer. "I must tell you that it was all my own doing and had nothing to do with Claudia, so you must not blame her in any way. It's about Captain Royce." She had their full attention. "You see, we weren't married."

The silence produced by Jack's reference to the British army was nothing compared to that now produced by Livia. Lady Crawford, that model of composure, sank down onto the nearest chair. Francesca looked at Gerry. Melbrooke looked at Livia, then turned to Claudia. Nicholas stared straight ahead, not focusing on anyone. Eddy didn't quite understand. Gwendolen did and decided very quickly that she didn't mind.

Those who knew the truth observed these reactions with bewilderment. It was Livia who understood first. "I'm sorry," she said, stifling a laugh. "I've given you the wrong impression."

"Yes," Claudia said quickly before her sister could explain further, "and of course it was dreadful of us to take advantage of you in this way—for I assure you I acquiesced in the deception and am quite as much to blame." She turned to Nicholas and with an expressive gesture removed her ring and held it out to him. "I cannot marry you, Nicholas. I must not. You would never be able to trust me again."

Livia was appalled. Claudia was throwing away everything they had worked for and doing it—despite her pretense at nobility—with every appearance of cheerfulness.

Nicholas refused the ring. Claudia took his hand and placed the ring in his palm. "You must take it, Nicholas. I know what you are going to say and I honour you for it. I hope I may not entirely forfeit your regard, but I have to release you from our engagement."

This was something Eddy did understand. "Oh, good!" he exclaimed involuntarily. "Now you can marry Papa!"

Everyone looked at Eddy. He looked back—confused, defiant, and finally uncertain.

Nicholas looked at Melbrooke as if struck by a sudden thought, then turned to Claudia whose colour was unaccountably high. Gwendolen observed this byplay with a good deal of satisfaction. Melbrooke, however, failed miserably to take advantage of it and stared at the floor as if it was the only tactful place to look. Gwendolen was disappointed. Someone should Do Something. Daddy was likely to insist on marrying Claudia out of pure chivalry. "I think," she said, "that Uncle Edward and Claudia should discuss this in private."

At that Melbrooke looked up and met Nicholas' eyes. With a rare show of assertion, Lord Melbrooke crossed the room and took Claudia by the hand. She looked at him with a radiance her sisters and brother hadn't seen in all their time in London and allowed him to lead her to the door. "No," Melbrooke said firmly to Eddy, "you stay right where you are."

Realizing that things needed to be said that would not be said in their presence, Gwendolen took Eddy's hand. "Come on, we'll go to the kitchen and see if your clothes are dry."

"But I'm not cold," Eddy objected.

"Yes, you are," Gwendolen said and propelled him from the room by sheer force of will and superior height. Hotspur, who had been dozing on the hearth, padded after them.

"Bravo, Claudia," Lady Crawford said softly.

Nicholas gave his aunt a hard look. "Am I to thank you, ma'am, for depriving me of the comfort of a most estimable wife?"

"She did it herself, Nicholas. And you know she'll be far happier with Edward. Didn't you see her face?"

"Yes, Aunt Isabel," he said gently. "It was a sobering sight. But Edward—why in God's name didn't he tell me?"

"He's a diffident man, Nicholas."

"He's a fool." He stared into the fire, a smile playing about his lips.

Livia looked happily from Gerry to Diane. "Well," she said with relief, "all's well that ends well."

"Mrs. Royce!" said Nicholas, turning to her in outrage.

Livia grinned at him. "I'm afraid even I can be trite upon occasion."

The eloquent Nicholas Warwick was momentarily bereft of speech.

Another silence filled the room. Francesca said she wished Claudia and Edward every happiness, but they still needed to address Livia's problem.

"But it isn't a problem," Harry said. "I mean, not in the way you think. I mean, they really weren't married."

"That," said Nicholas, speech returning, "is evident."

"No, no," Harry said. "You don't understand."

"All our fault," Jack offered by way of vindicating the Nevilles. "Oughtn't to have let Livia do it."

"Do what?" exclaimed Nicholas. "Do you mean to say that you abetted, you encouraged—"

"No," Harry said. "I mean, it wasn't our fault. I mean it was, but not in the way you think. I mean, you're thinking all the wrong things, so—"

"Royce a scoundrel," Jack said, trying to clarify matters. "Should have said so in the beginning. Gerry knew all along," he added handsomely.

"Gerry!" said Francesca. "You didn't—"

"Of course not," Colonel Scott said hastily.

"He didn't have anything to do with it," Harry explained. "It was Livia's idea."

Livia nodded and tried to speak, but was overcome by laughter.

Nicholas turned back to her. "Mrs. Royce—Miss Neville—I fail to—that is, we need to decide what to do about—"

"Tell the truth," Jack said. "Only thing to do now, Livia."

Nicholas, Francesca, and Lady Crawford (who had sensibly dropped out of the conversation) turned appalled eyes on him. "Certainly not," Nicholas said. "Of all the—"

"But you don't know the truth," said Harry with exasperation. "If you'd just let us—"

He broke off at the sound of a commotion in the hall.

"Good God," said Gerry, "what now?"

Then Paul's voice could be heard saying, "They ought to be in here, sir," and Mr. Muggs was mumbling something and a voice strangely familiar to at least some of those present demanded, "What's going on here?" The parlour door was flung open. Even before the elegant figure standing there could be revealed, Francesca had sprung to her feet.

"Father!"

Lord Lyndale disengaged his elegant superfine coat from

326

Francesca's grip and surveyed the company with cool green eyes very like his daughter's. A quarter century in the diplomatic service had given him a distinguished manner only enhanced by the grey streaks in his dark hair. He was noted for his remarkable composure and his ability to deal with any situation. Even the appearance of Colonel Scott, whom he had last seen in Lisbon, did not seem to surprise him. On the contrary. "Gerry!" said Lyndale warmly, "I'm glad you're here. Nicholas, it's good to see you. Harry, Jack—I won't say you've grown, I expect it's the last thing you want to hear. Isabel,"—he crossed to Lady Crawford and lifted her hand to his lips—"you are looking positively enchanting."

Paul closed the door on the interested Mrs. Muggs and retired to a corner with his sketchbook. Francesca recollected that she was a dignified widow of twenty-four and introduced her father to Livia and Diana. "Charmed," his lordship murmured with a slight bow. He turned back to his daughter. "Would it be too much to inquire what you are all doing here?"

"Well, yes," Francesca said frankly, "I'm afraid it would. At least, it would be excessively complicated. But never mind about that. Why didn't you tell me you were coming home?"

"That," said Lord Lyndale, "would be at least as complicated as your story, my dear. I didn't tell you because I didn't know myself until the last minute. I had meant to surprise you in London."

"What brings you to the Bell and Candle?" Francesca persisted.

"You, my dear. I doubt if anyone else could."

"You knew I was here?"

"Yes. I ran into Barstow-Greene on the boat. Disagreeable man, but I felt obliged to offer him a seat in my carriage. He has a house near here, you know. We were on our way there when we ran into Oliver Merriman. He had some business with Barstow-Greene and mentioned that you were at the inn. I must say I fail to understand the attraction of Jack-in-the-Hole, but I daresay that is part of what would be excessively complicated."

"Yes," Francesca said, "but I'm very glad you're back because, you see, Gerry and I—"

"Gerry! Good lord, my memory's going. I've a splendid surprise for you. I was going to search you out as soon as we got to London."

"We?" Francesca asked. Perhaps he hadn't discarded the mistress after all.

"Yes, I'm rising in the world. I've been given a military escort. He says he's a friend of yours, Gerry. John Royce."

Chapter 22

Reactions to his lordship's statement were varied. The Nevilles and Gerry looked as though their world had been shattered beyond any hope of repair. Harry and Jack were tongue-tied. Even Lady Crawford was momentarily bereft of her usual *savoir-faire*. Nicholas felt a sudden unaccountable and acute depression.

The others took the news more calmly. Francesca looked from Gerry to Livia, puzzled by their reaction. Paul was interested but detached. It was Lady Crawford who recovered first. Rising with a rustle of skirts, she put a firm hand on Livia's shoulder. "My dear, I know this is a great shock."

Lord Lyndale cocked an inquiring eyebrow at his daughter. Francesca looked back helplessly. Livia tried to rise to the occasion and failed. She murmured something inarticulate. At this point Nicholas decided to be noble. "Perhaps," he said, misreading her distress, "you would prefer to have your reunion with Captain Royce alone. I'm sure everyone will understand."

"No!" said Livia and Gerry in one breath. Before the mystified Nicholas could inquire further, the door swung open to admit a tall, broad-shouldered man in brilliant regimental dress. His carriage was erect, his hair dark and curling, his eyes a deep blue. Altogether he was a very fine figure of a man.

329

"Told you he'd look like a hero," Jack said to Harry.

"Excuse me, sir," the newcomer said to Lyndale, "but—oh!" He stopped short at the sight of the rest of the company

"Come in, John," Lyndale said smoothly. "It appears you have several acquaintances here."

"Gerry!" Royce exclaimed in delight.

"Hullo, John." Gerry rose to shake hands with his friend "Wonderful to see you again. I didn't—this is a grea surprise."

"I know," Royce said cheerfully. "Lyndale tells me you'd al given me up for dead. I always said headquarters was i confusion. I was badly wounded and in no condition to do much of anything for a few months. A farm family took me in And I—er—had my reasons for lying low for a bit."

Gerry, surmising that these reasons took the form of money owed, grinned in spite of himself. "Listen, John, I need to tall to you."

But Jack, prompted by some misguided guardian angel decided to express his delight. "Wonderful you're back Royce. Marvelous news. Best in weeks. Months actually. She' been waiting for you."

"Waiting?" Royce turned a blank face from Gerry to Jack

Nicholas, who had been lost in his own thoughts, was rouse by this. "Now see here, Royce, do you mean to cut this woman after she's been faithful to you for so long?"

The bewildered captain transferred his gaze from Jack t Nicholas. "I'm sorry," he began, "I don't think I know—"

"My name is Warwick, sir, and I believe you have a grea deal to answer for."

"Nicholas!" Harry said in sudden alarm. "He doesn't! Tha is—"

Lady Crawford cast a quelling glance in Harry's direction "Nicholas, there's no need to get upset. We can all discuss thi in a civilized manner."

"That's right," Jack piped up. "Civilized, that's the ticket No more nonsense about duels. Bad *ton*."

Livia decided it was time she took a hand in the situation which was, after all, of her own making. She came forward, prepared to speak.

"Why, it's Miss Neville," Royce said, wondering briefly why her feet were bare. He took her hand. "I'm sorry to see you in mourning. Is it Dr. Neville?"

She nodded. "Yes, last summer." She drew a deep breath. "Captain Royce, I owe you an apology."

"No!" said Harry and Jack in one breath.

"Can't," Jack amended. "Not now. Ruin everything, Livia."

While he subsided under a crossfire of looks from Nicholas and Lady Crawford, Francesca spoke up. "This really is a private affair. I'm sure the Nevilles and Captain Royce would feel more comfortable if the rest of us withdrew."

"Not at all," said Royce, baffled but friendly. "I've nothing to hide."

Nicholas glared at him.

"Oh, no," Harry said hastily, "we wouldn't dream of running out just because things are rough. We aren't cowards."

"Help a lady in distress," Jack added. "Our fault too."

While Francesca attempted to sort out the meaning of this exchange, Nicholas rose and took the captain aside. "See here, Royce," he said quietly, "you've got to marry her, you know. The sooner the better."

By this time Captain Royce was sure he had stumbled into a nest of lunatics. He looked around for Gerry, but Colonel Scott had sunk down on the window seat, his head in his hands.

"That's it!" exclaimed Jack. "Marriage. Get married at once. Make everything all right."

"It will not make everything all right," Livia said, then broke off—not for want of something to say—because a high feminine voice could be heard directly outside the door.

"Cheri! Où es-tu?"

The voice did not wait for an answer. Before anyone could reply, the door was opened to reveal an enchantingly pretty girl of no more than eighteen.

Oh no, Francesca thought, a French one.

"Whew!" Harry, who had risen to remonstrate with his brother, sat down again. The girl glanced inquiringly about the room with wide, china blue eyes. She wore a pale pink pelisse and a chip straw hat tied with cherry coloured ribbons covered her fair curls. Her pretty mouth was drawn into an expression of annoyance. Her face cleared as she caught sight of Royce and she ran to him impulsively.

Royce put a protective arm around her. "It seems we can clear up a misunderstanding." He looked around the room. "I'm sorry if there's been some mistake," he said politely but firmly, "but I'm afraid I can't possibly marry anyone. This is my wife."

In the stunned silence that met his words, Diana decided it was time she did something. Sandringham had given her a strong sense of the theatrical. She swallowed the last of her bread and cheese—she was the only one who had touched the food—rose, gave a strangled exclamation and fell to the floor in a graceful faint, just managing to miss sundry pieces of furniture. Really, she thought with detachment, Mrs. Siddons couldn't have done it a bit better.

One look sufficed to tell Paul that Diana was creating a diversion. He returned to his sketchbook. Diana's brother and sister were equally aware of her intent, but for want of a better course of action decided to follow her lead. Gerry stroked Diana's forehead and talked to her in a soothing voice. Livia hunted in her reticule for smelling salts—she never carried them—and found only an empty bottle of laudanum. Francesca abandoned any attempt to explain the situation to her father and supplied the vinaigrette she kept for Mrs. Amesbury. Seeing that Diana was well taken care of, Nicholas strode purposefully to Captain Royce who was looking to Lord Lyndale for succour. Lyndale watched the scene with, Francesca considered, positively heartless amusement.

"I don't know the exact state of your relationship with Mr

Royce," Nicholas said with determination, "but I do know that you've got to do something to make things right for her, and you've got to do it quickly."

Rather to Nicholas' surprise, Royce showed no sign of annoyance. He nodded seriously. "Yes, I know it's hard for Ninette, being so young and a foreigner in a strange country, not able to speak a word of English, but—"

"You misunderstand me, sir. I mean the first Mrs. Royce— Miss Neville."

"Miss Neville?" Royce looked at Livia who was waving the vinaigrette under Diana's nose. "I'm afraid I don't follow you, sir. Miss Neville was very kind to me when I saw her in Oxford last year, but I hardly think I owe her anything."

"Sir!" Nicholas said in outrage.

Diana decided it was time to recover. She pushed the vinaigrette away, opened her eyes and murmured in a voice that carried surprisingly well, "I'm sorry I was so silly. It was seeing John again. I've always been dreadfully afraid of him."

"Nothing to be afraid of now," Gerry reassured her in a fatherly tone that held an undercurrent of warning.

Diana ignored her brother. "John's always had a horrid effect on me, even though I was quite small when—when it happened. I suppose," she added in a tremulous voice, "it was because Papa never approved of him."

"Yes, Diana," Livia said, "you've said quite enough. Just lie down and try to rest."

"I still remember Papa saying he wasn't trustworthy."

"What!" Royce had spent a total of fifteen minutes in Dr. Neville's company, and Dr. Neville had seemed too preoccupied to have formed any opinion of Royce whatsoever.

"*Qu'est-ce qu'elle dit?*" asked Ninette.

"That's it," Jack said. "Not trustworthy. Not trustworthy at all. Rakehell. Bad business. Knew so all along."

"Why didn't you say anything?" Francesca demanded.

"Couldn't," Jack decided.

"We didn't want to," Harry amended hastily. "because we

333

didn't want to hurt Livia." He had a sudden inspiration. "You see, she *thought* she was married."

"Why you—" Words failed Nicholas Warwick.

"Cad," Jack supplied. "Very nasty customer. Not at all the thing. Did things that were unmentionable."

"Cheated at cards," muttered Diana.

"Now wait a minute," Gerry said, "this man is my friend!"

It was at this point that Livia, still kneeling beside the recumbent Diana, was struck by the complete impossibility of the situation. She opened her mouth to speak, decided it was useless and collapsed back on her heels, laughing helplessly.

The sound of her laughter effectively stopped Nicholas from doing Royce some violence. He walked quickly to her side and said in lowered tones, "Mrs. Royce—Livia—please,—I assure you the situation is not hopeless. I—we will think of something."

But his reassurances had no perceivable effect on Livia. She shook her head, still laughing. "You don't understand! It's all so ridiculous!"

"I couldn't agree with you more," said Captain Royce fervently.

"*Qu'est-ce qu'elle dit?*" inquired Ninette, tightening her grip on her husband's arm.

Francesca was growing alarmed by Livia's laughter. She tugged at Gerry's sleeve. "Can't you do something?"

"I'm thinking."

Lady Crawford decided it was time someone took charge. In her clear, lovely voice she called the group to order. "Jack, Harry—stop whispering. Diana—sit up. Livia—control yourself, please."

To the rest of the party's surprise, these commands were instantly obeyed. Captain Royce, grateful for a sane voice, sat down with Ninette beside him and prepared to listen to any remotely reasonable explanation. Harry and Jack realized that the time of reckoning had come and held their tongues. Diana sat up, pushed her hair out of her eyes and looked expectantly

334

at Lady Crawford. Livia ceased her wild laughter, moved from the floor to a chair, twitched her skirt into place and demonstrated her gift for looking composed in any crisis. Nicholas, seeing she was all right and deciding he no longer understood anything, sat down beside her. Gerry ignored a bewildered look from Francesca, stood up and drew her back to the window seat, muttering that it would all make sense in a few minutes—he hoped. Paul and Lord Lyndale watched with interest.

When she was sure her audience was quiet and ready to listen, Lady Crawford turned to Livia. "I think I begin to understand. The problem is that you and Captain Royce were *really* never married?"

Livia nodded. "Yes. I—we—wanted to give Claudia a Season in London. We needed a chaperone and didn't have any female relatives who could possibly serve, so I decided to become a widow."

It took a few moments for these words to sink in. Nicholas looked at Livia with surprise, annoyance, and relief. Livia, by this time beyond shame, returned the look helplessly.

"The rest," she said, "is quite simple. We thought it safer to give my late husband a real identity and I'm afraid we hit on Captain Royce. We knew he had no family."

"It was my idea," Diana put in.

"It was quite unforgivable of us," Livia said to Royce. "We had no notion how far it would go. You see we thought—"

"That I was dead. Yes, I quite see that, but—"

"*Qu-est qu'elle dit?*" asked Ninette, seeing her husband's confusion.

"I might have known you wouldn't be in need of rescue," Nicholas said under his breath.

"Unfortunately," Livia continued, not acknowledging this comment, "Harry and Jack embroidered the captain's history and he was talked about a good deal."

"Stands to reason," Jack said. "Livia shouldn't have had an ordinary husband. Deserves more than that."

"Yes," said Livia with a quelling glance worthy of Lady Crawford. "This went on until Gerry returned to London. Not knowing of our plan, he told some rather different stories."

"Did you, Gerry?" Royce said appreciatively. "Which ones?"

"That," said Lady Crawford, "we can leave for another time. The point is—"

"The point," said Livia, "is that we have used Captain Royce abominably and we have no one but ourselves to thank for the scandal that is sure to ensue. I am going to return to Oxford and will make the truth known before I leave London. No one could possibly blame you for what I have done."

"You can't," Harry blurted out.

"Bad *ton*," muttered Jack.

"Do something, Gerry," whispered Francesca.

Royce shook his head. "There must be another way out. I wouldn't feel comfortable knowing that—"

"But it isn't your fault, Captain Royce," Livia said quietly. "It has nothing to do with you. I'm quite prepared to pay the price for my own actions."

"Admirable," said Lady Crawford. "But don't forget you have sisters—"

"That's all right," Diana interjected, "I don't care."

"I am well aware that you do not. But you have another sister. And a prospective brother-in-law by this time I shouldn't wonder."

A prospective brother-in-law with an active political career. Livia had temporarily forgotten Claudia and Melbrooke. It would be the cruelest of ironies if she had saved Nicholas from Merriman—she still wasn't sure precisely how—only to ruin Lord Melbrooke through her own stupid blundering.

"Yes," she said thinking rapidly, "I quite see we shall have to come up with something more acceptable than the truth." By 'we' she referred to her immediate family, but she saw that everyone—even Lord Lyndale—had taken the problem on. She decided this was no time for pride. She needed all the help she could get.

The company sat in silence for some time. At length Jack looked up and said, "Marriage."

"What?" asked several voices at once.

"Marriage. Really get married. Make everything all right."

"Certainly not," said Livia.

Jack was not so easily deterred. "Only answer. Don't see why you object, Livia. Respectable family. Good match."

"But dash it, Jack," Harry protested, "Royce is already married."

"Get a divorce," Jack decided.

"No!" said the captain forcefully.

"Don't be a sapskull, Jack," Harry advised.

"Get a divorce," Jack persisted "Marry Livia. Get another divorce. Remarry first wife. Most secret. No one know the difference."

"Now wait a minute," Royce said, "I'm willing to help, but when it comes to marriages and divorces and—"

"No one," said Livia, "is going to marry or divorce anyone. A divorce would cause as much scandal as the truth."

Jack was forced to agree. He lapsed into silence.

"I say," Diana said suddenly. "What if the man Livia married wasn't Captain Royce? I mean, what if he was a distant cousin or someone with the same name? There must be hundreds of John Royces."

"Won't do, I'm afraid," Gerry said regretfully. "Those stories I told are defintely about John."

"Maybe Royce could be someone else then," Harry suggested.

"That's it," Jack agreed. "New identity. Easiest thing in the world. Got a cousin in the Foreign Office."

"What does that have to say to anything?" Harry demanded.

"Things to take care of," Jack said vaguely. "Papers and whatnot."

Captain Royce was looking more and more alarmed. "I'm

337

afraid that would be quite impossible," Lord Lyndale said. "We have met far too many people on our journey."

Silence reigned once again. This time it was Francesca who broke it. "I don't suppose it could have been a marriage of convenience?"

"What good would that do?" Gerry asked.

"If it had been, divorce would be more acceptable."

"Won't do. If anyone wanted to meddle they could prove it was all a sham and then where would we be?"

"Annulment," said Jack suddenly.

"What?" Harry asked.

"Annulment. No scandal with an annulment. Whole affair wiped out completely."

"What about records?"

"Really get one then," Jack decided.

"But they aren't married."

"Doesn't matter. No one knows." Jack was immensely pleased with himself. "Get an annulment. Everyone know about it. Get married again. No scandal."

"But dash it, Jack, you can't just get an annulment. You have to go to the Archbishop of Canterbury or something."

"Could try," Jack persisted.

"Anyone," said Lady Crawford, "who was going to grant an annulment would check into the matter first most carefully and that is exactly what we are trying to prevent. We have to think of Claudia and Edward."

"Miss Neville," Francesca explained to her father, "that is, I suppose she's really Miss Claudia Neville—"

"No," Livia said absently. "She's Miss Neville. I became the eldest as well as a widow. Not that it signifies."

"Good God!" Nicholas exclaimed. "How—no, never mind."

"I'm twenty," Livia said calmly.

Nicholas stared at her. He had judged her to be twenty-five at least. Why, she was little more than a girl. Then abruptly his expression changed. "In that case," he said, sounding like the masterful Nicholas Warwick for the first time in the past hour, "you were underage when you married—when you allegedly married—Captain Royce."

"I suppose so. I mean, of course, I still am. It doesn't really change anything."

"Doesn't it?" Nicholas smiled and sat back in his chair as if he had just scored a point in debate. "We have Diana's word for it that your father considered Royce untrustworthy. He would certainly have forbidden the merest mention of marriage between him and his young and defenseless—well, at any rate his young daughter. Wouldn't he, Diana?"

"Absolutely." Diana grinned. "It would have sent him into a rage. In fact, now that I think about it, it did. Remember, Gerry?"

Gerry nodded solemnly.

"The marriage, of course," said Lady Crawford, by this time smiling as well, "was never consummated. They slipped off and got married just before Captain Royce had to return to the continent. Livia's father learned about it and arranged an annulment."

"But by the time it came through, Papa had died," Livia added. "He neglected to tell me he was having my marriage annulled?"

"He was waiting for the papers," Nicholas decided.

"Yes, all right. He wrote to Gerry, I expect."

"He did?" said Colonel Scott.

"Well, one of us had to know. Why didn't Gerry tell me?"

"He was afraid you would undergo a nervous collapse," Nicholas said. "You see, by this time you had received news of Royce's death and your brother thought it best to allow you to think yourself a widow."

"I say, Nicholas," Harry said, "I never knew you had such an imagination."

"What about records?" Gerry asked.

"We were married in Iffley," Livia suggested.

"How does that help?"

"One of the Iffley churches burned down last January."

"And the annulment papers?"

"If it's that long ago," Lady Crawford said, "no one is likely to raise any questions. And if anyone does, I can always pull a few strings."

"Will it work?" Francesca asked.

"It will work," said Lord Lyndale, his voice composed, "because Isabel and I will earnestly assure people of its truth." He turned to Royce. "I think it might be best if you and your wife stayed away from town for a bit. Lyndale Court is set in a remarkably secluded part of Devon and is generally accounted to be lovely about this time of year. I'm sure you and your charming wife would enjoy a short honeymoon there."

"Thank you, sir, most decent of you."

"You'd probably better get married again," Gerry said thoughtfully. "Just to be on the safe side."

Ninette, seeing his words were directed at her, looked inquiringly at her husband.

"*Qu'est-ce qu-il dit?*" she inquired.

Royce told her. Sparks of anger flew from Ninette's eyes. She stamped her foot and unleashed a flood of rapid French that needed no translation. She was only stopped by Nicholas who gently asked her in her own language where she had been married.

In the registry office, Ninette was forced to admit, clearly not best pleased with this aspect of her otherwise happy nuptials.

"Then," Nicholas said, "I am sure you would like a proper wedding in a church with bridesmaids and a white gown, wouldn't you?"

Ninette fervently assured him that she would.

"Well, if you go to Lyndale Court and remain there for a fortnight, when you come up to London I shall see that you have a proper wedding."

Ninette needed no more persuading. Livia said she could not let Nicholas go to such trouble and expense, but he cut her off. "My dear Miss Neville, you are scarcely in a position to argue the matter." Seeing the wisdom of this, Livia held her tongue—at least for the moment.

Since things were more or less settled, Captain Royce and Ninette wanted to resume their journey. There was a flurry of handshakings and apologies and farewells and the young couple departed in Lord Lyndale's carriage, Lyndale saying he would return to town with his daughter.

"Now," Lady Crawford said, "there can be no more nonsense about going back to Oxford, Livia. In any event, you and Diana will want to be in London for Claudia's wedding."

"Yes," said Diana, "I'm not going to Paris with Paul."

"Now, dash it," Harry exclaimed, "if that isn't the outside of enough, Redmond. To get Diana into a scrape with that cursed rum picture and then go off and not face the consequences."

"He's not!" Diana hastened to defend Paul. "I'm the one who doesn't want to go anywhere with him."

Jack did not think going to Paris advisable, whatever Diana's sentiments. Couldn't trust foreigners. He said so.

"I didn't say Diana should go to Paris," Harry protested. "All I said was that Redmond shouldn't walk off and abandon her."

"Don't see why not," Jack said. "I mean," he corrected, seeing the look on Harry's face, "can't be called abandoning. Why should Redmond hang round Diana? Nothing but trouble. Not as if they was engaged or anything."

"Exactly," said Diana.

Paul looked up, but was diverted before he could speak.

The more immediate problems solved, Francesca remembered why they had come to the Bell and Candle in the first place. "Livia," she said, "what have you done with the letter?"

Chapter 23

"Nothing," Livia said, making the transition from one crisis to another with ease. "I didn't take it. Not for want of trying."

"No need to worry," said Gerry, "Merriman certainly doesn't have it."

"Yes, but where is it? We can't risk someone else finding it." Francesca turned to Nicholas and Lady Crawford. "I'm sorry," she said, "it's part of what's excessively complicated."

Paul rose and moved across the room. "Excuse me, Lady Francesca, I think perhaps this might be of interest to you." He opened his sketchbook and handed it to her. There, between the pages, was a letter written in Nicholas' bold hand. Livia looked over Francesca's shoulder, then turned to her sister.

"Diana," she said, "I think you owe Paul an apology."

"Why?" asked Diana indignantly. Then comprehension dawned. "How did you do it?" she demanded.

"A back window."

"Oh, Paul, how splendid of you to think of that!" The youngest Miss Neville flung her arms around Mr. Redmond's neck.

Jack tactfully lowered his gaze to the floor. "Have to marry her now," he muttered. "No other alternative."

"Of course." Paul disengaged himself from Diana without haste or embarrassment.

Livia and Gerry looked at each other, started to speak, looked at Diana and remained silent.

"Oh?" Diana sounded mildly interested.

"I was planning on it sooner or later," Paul said. "Weren't you?"

Diana considered. "Yes," she decided. "In a year or two?"

"That sounds about right."

"Wait a minute," Jack said, noting a violation of the rules. "Brother hasn't given his consent."

Diana turned to Livia and Gerry. "You won't fuss, will you?"

"Not in a year or two," Livia said. Gerry nodded his agreement. "Speaking of consent," he added, turning to Lord Lyndale, "I suppose I ought to ask yours. Francesca and I are going to be married."

"Are you?" inquired the unflappable earl. "When was this decided?"

"Two or three hours ago," Francesca said happily. "Do you approve?"

"My dear, I'm delighted. Naturally. I must say I rather suspected something of the sort."

Livia hugged Francesca enthusiastically. "Have you told Waterford?"

"I dealt with him first. I like to keep my affairs tidy."

Nicholas shook Gerry's hand and said he couldn't be more pleased. Diana was surprised but had no fault to find with this development. Harry was nonplussed—when he had left the house this morning, Francesca had been engaged to Waterford—but Jack offered his congratulations as punctiliously as he had several days before . . . Lady Crawford smiled serenely. So far, things were working out very well indeed.

At this point Claudia and Melbrooke returned looking blissfully happy. There was a fresh round of good wishes. While Claudia was being introduced to Lord Lyndale, Melbrooke managed to draw Nicholas to one side.

"Are you sure you don't mind?"

343

"About Francesca and Scott? On the contrary. By the way, Edward, next time you fall in love drop a word in my ear before I offer for the lady."

Melbrooke smiled, but was not entirely convinced. "I know there's bound to be talk—" he began.

"Yes," Nicholas agreed, "I daresay there will be. Tiresome. But you can stand up with me at my wedding and I'll stand up with you at yours. That ought to quiet things down."

"Of course I'll stand up with you. And I—there's someone else?"

Nicholas' eyes drifted briefly to the other side of the room where Claudia had drawn Livia into a corner. Melbrooke followed the direction of his friend's gaze. "Well," he said, his face relaxing into a grin, "that's all right then. Best of luck."

"Thanks," Nicholas' eyes were still on Livia, "I have a feeling I'm going to need it."

"Livia," Claudia was saying anxiously at about the same time, "was John Royce really here? He's alive?"

"He's very much alive. There were one or two complications—he has a charming young wife—and it was very awkward for a time, but he was very nice about it and I think everything's been taken care of. I'll tell you the whole story, but not now, unless you fancy staying here for the rest of the night."

Claudia did not and Livia's last comment reminded her that it was growing late and they should get the children back to town. She hugged her sister and made her way across the room to her betrothed. Melbrooke was relieved that the Paris venture had been stopped, but was unwilling to let Paul and Diana return to London on their own. He proposed taking them in his own carriage along with Claudia and Eddy. And Hotspur. Paul and Diana had no objections. "Our carriage isn't ready, Uncle Edward," Paul told him, "and we'd be glad of a ride. But wouldn't you and Miss Neville rather be alone? We'd be glad to take Eddy with us."

Melbrooke looked at Claudia and very nearly agreed. "No,"

he said firmly.

Nicholas informed Francesca that if it was all the same to her, he was driving his curricle back to London himself. She and Gerry could take the phaeton. Lady Crawford offered a seat in her barouche to Lord Lyndale and suggested that her nephews sent their hired carriage back and return with her as well.

As they waited in the inn yard while the various equipages were made ready, Eddy held tight to Claudia's hand. He was as happy as his father and prospective stepmother, but one small doubt remained and must in good conscience be cleared up before they departed. He disengaged his hand from Claudia's and walked resolutely over to Gwendolen.

"Are you angry?"

Gwendolen appeared to have been thinking of something else. She looked at Eddy in surprise. "No, not at all."

"Well, are you upset?" Eddy persisted. "It's all right to be upset. I was," he confided, "when I thought Uncle Nicholas was going to marry Claudia."

"I'm not upset," said Gwendolen, finally giving him her full attention. "Or angry or hurt or anything. Honestly."

She sounded sincere. On the other hand, Gwendolen—as Eddy had cause to know—was an excellent dissembler. "You can visit us," he offered. "Lots. Maybe we can all have vacations at Melbrooke instead of Waverley. Claudia won't make any difference between us. And by the time you're old enough to make your come out and everything, I expect I shall be too old to need a mother. Well, not much anyway."

"Eddy." Claudia had moved close enough to get their attention but not close enough to eavesdrop. "The carriage is ready."

She looked at Gwendolen with just the slightest doubt. She knew the child had been delighted by her betrothal to Nicholas. On the other hand, she patently adored Livia. Claudia moved closer and bent to kiss Gwendolen's cheek. "Your father is going to bring you back to Charles Street," she said. "I'll see you soon."

Gwendolen smiled and looked once more at Eddy. Eddy looked back at her and then, with a sudden grin, held out his hand. Gwendolen shook it solemnly and watched as Melbrooke handed his son and fiancée into the carriage. Hotspur jumped up after them. They looked like a family already.

Gerry and Francesca were the next to leave. Gerry had his arm around Francesca and Francesca looked happier than Gwendolen had ever seen her. Gwendolen was pleased. It would keep both of them in the family. They drove off after a brief argument about who would take the reins which, Gwendolen noted with approval, Francesca won.

By this time Lady Crawford's carriage was ready for departure as well. As Lord Lyndale offered her his arm, Harry said suddenly, "Where's Livia?"

"She's gone to the kitchen to fetch her shoes and stockings," Lady Crawford told him. "I don't know why she left them there."

"But how will she get to town?"

Lady Crawford turned and looked at Nicholas. Nicholas looked pointedly away. "She has her own carriage," Lady Crawford said. "Come along, Harry. Livia will be quite all right."

"Yes, but—"

"Harry, this is no time for questions."

"Said enough already," Jack added. Harry looked puzzled, but climbed into the carriage without further protest.

Gwendolen grinned happily. "Well?" she asked her father when Lady Crawford's carriage had pulled out of the inn yard.

Nicholas looked down at his daughter. "Well?"

"I think," said Gwendolen, "that it would be unfair to ask Aunt Isabel to bring me out as well."

"I'm not sure Aunt Isabel would agree with you," said Nicholas, "but I rather think that I do."

"Good."

As Livia, now properly shod, came out of the inn, both Warwicks quickly exercised the family talent for dissembling. Livia looked from father to daughter. "Where is everyone?"

"I'm afraid," said Nicholas, "that Claudia assumed you would return to town with Aunt Isabel and Aunt Isabel assumed you would return to town with Claudia. And unaccountably, your own carriage was sent off as well. It will be crowded in my curricle, but we've managed before. Would you mind coming inside for a moment before we leave?"

"I think I forgot my gloves in the kitchen," said Gwendolen, who despised gloves and certainly had not been wearing them. She was off before Livia could ask questions.

"Miss Neville?"

Mystified, Livia went back into the inn. "We have some unfinished business," Nicholas told Mrs. Muggs and opened the door to the parlour they had just vacated.

"And what business do we have," Livia said as she entered, "that we couldn't have taken care of on the way back to town?"

Nicholas closed the door. "As advanced as are my views on the education of the young, I stop short of proposing in front of them."

Fortunately, there was a chair beside her. She did not sit down, but she laid a hand on it for support. "Mr. Warwick, shouldn't you choose your words with better care? Your meaning is liable to be misinterpreted."

"I choose my words with the greatest care, Miss Neville. And I believe my meaning is clear enough."

She almost sat down then. She did draw a deep breath. "I'm not in the least upset about Captain Royce," she said truthfully. "And I believe the story will answer admirably. There's no need to worry about me."

"Worry about you? Do you seriously imagine I would make you an offer because I was worried about you?"

"Wouldn't you?" Livia smiled. "You think it's your responsibility to take care of everyone, don't you? I

347

understand better than you think. I feel the same way myself. But it's a poor foundation for marriage."

"It certainly is. You should credit me with enough sense to realize that. Livia—" He took a step toward her, but checked at her expression.

"Are you very upset about Claudia?" she asked quietly.

"Am I—? No, certainly not. She and Edward were made for each other. I should have seen that from the first."

"But she was your ideal wife, wasn't she?" Livia persisted. "A womanly woman."

"Yes," Nicholas admitted, "she was so—so different from Lillie." It was the first time Livia had ever heard him mention his wife. After a moment Nicholas continued. "It wasn't love, not with either of them, though I thought it was with Lillie. I was arrogantly adult at the time, but it was a schoolboy infatuation. I didn't make her very happy. I don't know that I would do any better with you, but I would like to try."

"I'm not a particularly womanly woman," Livia warned him.

Nicholas smiled. "I had noticed. I said Claudia *was* my ideal wife. I thought our life together would be calm and tranquil. I thought that was what I wanted. I was obviously mistaken because I want to marry you very much and I don't imagine our life will be in the least tranquil or calm."

The expression in Nicholas' eyes was not conducive to clear thinking. Livia looked away. This was no time for romantic fancies. "In that case," she said, "why the devil do you—"

"Why the devil do I want to marry you? Because I love you," Nicholas said.

Livia sat down.

"What is it?" he said quickly.

"I believe you." She sounded dazed.

As Gwendolen had told Eddy, there is a time for Guile and Stealth and a time for Action. Nicholas crossed the room purposefully, took Livia by the shoulders and pulled her out of the chair and into his arms. It was some time before Livia could

348

speak—or to be quite honest, had any desire to do so. But she did feel bound in all fairness to remind Nicholas of one or two things. "I'm not at all the sort of wife for a politician," she cautioned.

The ambitious young hope of the Whig party grinned at her. "The other Livia didn't do Augustus' career any harm," he pointed out.

"No," Livia agreed. "But she wasn't a very good step-mother."

"They had an empire to tangle things up. I haven't even a title. Gwendolen doesn't have any doubts."

What doubts Livia had were fast fading. But there was one more thing. "I like to have my own way," she admitted.

"Yes," said Nicholas, tightening his arms around her, "so do I."

Gwendolen climbed happily onto Livia's lap, as she had on the ride home from Cousin Sophronia's, and slid an arm round her neck, which she had not done before. Daddy and Livia looked exactly the way people who were going to be married ought to look. This time she had been perfectly, one hundred percent right.

Nicholas was about to spring up beside them when he felt something hard beneath the cushion. "What the devil—?" He reached underneath and withdrew two ancient but serviceable dueling pistols. He looked at Livia. "Are these yours?"

"Certainly not. They belong to Mr. Muggs. I have no idea how they got here. Do you, Gwendolen?"

"Yes, but I didn't hide them." Gwendolen sounded regretful. "Diana did it while Eddy and I were on the horse. She told me about it afterwards. Wasn't it clever of her?"

"Very clever," Livia said, "but I think the pistols should be returned to Mr. Muggs."

"So do I," Nicholas agreed. "Gwendolen, keep an eye on her."

He returned five minutes later, climbed into the curricle and cocked an inquiring eyebrow at his fiancée.

"It's rather a long story," Livia said.

Nicholas took up the reins and gave the bays their office. "That's all right," he said comfortably, "we have plenty of time."